Morgan Kavanagh

Origin of language and myths

Vol. 1

Morgan Kavanagh

Origin of language and myths
Vol. 1

ISBN/EAN: 9783337198183

Printed in Europe, USA, Canada, Australia, Japan

Cover: Foto ©Andreas Hilbeck / pixelio.de

More available books at **www.hansebooks.com**

ORIGIN

OF

LANGUAGE AND MYTHS.

ORIGIN OF LANGUAGE

AND MYTHS.

By MORGAN KAVANAGH.

Vol I.

SAMPSON LOW, SON, AND MARSTON,
CROWN BUILDINGS, 188, FLEET STREET.
1871.

INTRODUCTION.

Some fourteen years ago I published a work entitled *Myths traced to their Primary Source through Language;* and though I was then, as it were, only feeling my way, I was not the less convinced that the discovery to which I laid claim was real; and, however strange it may now appear, I cannot help still entertaining the same opinion. In that work I showed, as well as I could, how man must have first acquired the use of speech; and by the knowledge thence derived I was enabled to account for the ancient belief in the Divine origin of language, to trace letters to their birth, to discover the primary forms and meanings—hitherto unknown—of many words; and finally, to prove that the fables of the heathen mythology, as well as those of religion and ancient history, were first suggested by the several meanings that a name had at different times obtained.

And I may here, perhaps, without stating too much in advance, give the reader some idea of this latter proof of the truth of my discovery. At the time the sun became a great object of worship over all the world, if one of the countless appellations by which it was then known happened also to designate some celebrated character of the past, the latter was at once revered as a divinity, even as the sun itself. And if his name, besides signifying the *sun,* did also happen to signify other ideas, such as *merchandize*, *traveller*, *thief*, &c., then was this celebrated character of the past revered as the god of merchants, travellers, thieves, &c.; that is to say, it was his name, with its several meanings, first suggested this strange belief. Now, how did I find out that a name took different forms, and consequently different meanings? By having first discovered the origin of speech, letters and words; for the knowledge thence derived allowed me to perceive that the same word was susceptible of different forms, and consequently of different meanings. Hence came my discovery of the origin of myths; and from its having thus grown out of the discovery of the origin of language, it affords proof the most undoubted of the truth of the latter. These two discoveries must therefore stand or fall together. To admit the reality of either and not of both were too absurd.

But of the first part of this twofold discovery, namely, the origin of language, I have now another very convincing proof to offer, which did not occur to me in 1856. And this is the proof: a body of the most enlightened men in the world could not make a language; and yet a handful of the most ignorant of the human race have, while living wholly apart from the rest of mankind, been known to do so very easily, and even very well, and philosophically, as the most competent judges in such matters have, to their great astonishment, been often obliged to admit. This appears wonderful, very wonderful, and yet it is not wonderful, but very simple, as the reader will see in the proper place. The effort required for the creation of language—if effort it may be called—is so uncommonly easy that this *apparently* great achievement must have been performed unawares, and that too by some nations so low in the scale of humanity as not to possess sufficient intelligence for enabling them to count beyond two.

But from language having been thus acquired so very easily, it may be regarded by many persons as a natural gift, and yet—as we shall see presently—it is no such thing. Language was *made,* but with so much ease that man, while teaching himself for the first time the use of articulate sounds, can have had no idea of the eventful labour—of one so full of wonders for the future—he was then engaged upon. And when we shall see how all this can be very easily accounted for by a knowledge of the origin of language, this circumstance will, it must be allowed, afford very powerful proof of the reality of this first part of the twofold discovery to which I lay claim.

With these several proofs that my pretensions are by no means visionary, why, the intelligent reader may ask, have they not been at once received as real? Because whatever lies beyond the reach of common understandings cannot be easily understood, or, if understood, be easily admitted. The narrow mind recoils within itself from every thing of the kind, and takes only to what its limited means can afford it the power of conceiving. Hence respectable mediocrity, or even that which is far from being respectable, has many more chances of immediate acknowledgment and success than an important discovery. But so has it ever been, and so is it ever likely to remain. Man has been fashioned so, and he cannot now change his nature.

The discoverer should be endued with a much larger stock of patience than any one else; and that he might live till the reality of his pretensions was admitted, his existence should be lengthened to at least a century or two beyond the period usually assigned to all other human beings.

Now, having this belief, why, it may reasonably be asked, do I again come forward with my pretensions after the very short space of some fourteen years? why not wait some eighty or ninety years longer, so as to make up at least one century, when perhaps some one of superior intelligence may, by drawing attention to my views, be the means of having at last my discovery acknowledged as real.

The cause of my being so very precipitate is this: I have been for years out of England, and without knowing, or much caring to know, what was going on there in the literary world, until about some two or three years ago, on passing a Paris bookseller's shop, my attention was accidentally drawn to a book in the window, entitled, "La Science du Langage, Cours professé à l'Institution Royale de la Grande Bretagne, par M. Max Müller, Professeur à l'Université d'Oxford, Correspondant de l'Institut de France, &c., &c. Ouvrage qui a obtenu de l'Académie des Inscriptions et Belles-Lettres le prix Volney en 1862. Traduit de l'Anglais, sur la quatrième édition, avec l'autorisation de l'auteur, par M. Georges Harris, Professeur au Lycée Impérial d'Orleans, et M. Georges Perrot, Ancien Membre de l'École d'Athènes, Professeur au Lycée Impérial Louis-le-Grand."

I purchased this book, and learned from the introduction to the translation that it was creating a great sensation not only in England, Germany, and France, but even in Italy, where a translation of it was then about to appear. From this introduction I further learned that M. Max Müller's great work gave rise to a world of excitement and discussion among the leading reviews of England, and that in Paris two highly distinguished literary characters, M. Barthélemy Saint-Hilaire and M. M. F. Baudry, had given very able notices of it; the former in a series of learned articles in the *Journal des Savants*, and the latter in the *Revue Archéologique*.

These eulogiums induced me to send at once to England for the work itself. It soon arrived in two fine large volumes, fifth edition; and each edition three thousand copies, at least so we are told in the title-page.

Now, if I had ever entertained a doubt of the reality of my old discovery, it would have been driven from my mind the moment I had finished the reading of M. Max Müller's two volumes. And why so? Because the principles of this old discovery of mine at once enabled me to detect the numerous mistakes with which these two volumes abound. But to what should we ascribe those mistakes? Not to M. Max Müller's want of capability or want of learning, but to his total want of knowing how man first acquired the use of speech; and that he has not this knowledge he himself thus admits: "We cannot tell as yet what language is." This happens to be a mistake, for M. Max Müller knows very well, and so does every body else, that language is the expression of our thoughts by articulate sounds; but what he meant to say is this, that we cannot tell as yet how man first *acquired* the use of language. That this is what he really did mean to say appears evident by his continuing thus, while still referring to language: "If it be a work of human art, *it would seem to lift the human artist almost to the level of a Divine Creator* [1]."

[1] Lect., vol. i. p. 3.

This statement I am not prepared to contradict, for the simple reason that I said the same thing myself as far back as the year 1856, that is to say, five long years before M. Max Müller said it, since, according to the title of his work, he did not begin his lectures until 1861. These are my words : " We cannot for an instant suppose that speech was ever invented—that man ever said to himself, Let me find out a means of communicating thought by sounds instead of signs [man's first language]. *This would be to place a human being almost on a level with God Himself;* to raise his wisdom to an eminence immensely beyond his reach ; and the more so as there was nothing either in nature or the ways of the world, while yet in its infancy, to suggest an idea at once so very original and extraordinary[2]."

The words in Italics in those two passages show how very close the resemblance between M. Max Müller's sentiment and mine.

But does M. Max Müller, I may be asked, acknowledge my sentiment in any way whatever? He does not; nor could he do so without allowing his readers to perceive that of the science of language he knows absolutely nothing. Were he to give a single etymology by the application of the principles that have grown out of the discovery to which I lay claim, he would be, as it were, committing suicide—be, as a philologist, no longer in existence. He alludes to almost all philologists, both living and dead, but he carefully avoids all allusion to the author of the "Origin of Myths." As we should, however, return good for evil, I do not mean to slight M. Max Müller, but to draw attention to his great

[2] Myths, vol. i. p. 12.

work, at least a few times perhaps many times: we shall see.

Now, if M. Max Müller knows nothing of the science of language, as I shall have occasion to show, it is difficult to suppose that the scientific bodies over all parts of the world with which he claims connexion, can, in this respect, be any wiser than he is himself. Here are the names of all these learned bodies; I give them along with the title page of M. Max Müller's work:—

"Lectures on the Science of Language, delivered at the Royal Institution of Great Britain, in April, May, and June, 1861, by Max Müller, M.A., Foreign Associate of the Royal Sardinian Academy; Honorary Member of the American Academy of Arts and Sciences, of the Royal Asiatic Society, of the Asiatic Society of Bengal, of the Royal Society of Literature, of the Anthropological Society of London, of the Ethnological Society of London, of the Ethnographic Society of France, of the Archæological Society of Moscow, of the Literary Society of Leyden, of the German Institute of Frankfort; and of the American Philological Society; Foreign Member of the Royal Bavarian Academy; Corresponding Member of the French Institute, of the Royal Society of Gottingen, of the Royal Irish Academy, of the American Philosophical Society, of the Royal Academy of Berlin, and of the American Oriental Society; Member of the Asiatic Society of Paris; and of the German Oriental Society: Taylorian Professor of the University of Oxford; Fellow of All Souls' College," &c., &c., &c.

What a grand display is this of M. Max Müller's scientific connexions! Surely there never was before, nor, in all probability, will there ever be again, so glorious a title-page. Why it were enough to make the fortune of any book. Is there, in the whole world, a philological society of any note whatever to which M. Max Müller may not be said to belong? How well he must know all that is known of both the past and present state of the science of language! And if of this science he knows, however, so very little as not to have it in his power to discover the etymology of the most common-place words, are we justified in supposing that there can be even one of those scientific bodies, with which M. Max Müller seems to be so closely connected, a shade more enlightened in the science of language than he is himself? Certainly not. And as this great work of his has been often reviewed— not only throughout Great Britain, but over the Continent, and probably in America also—and as its faulty etymologies are allowed to remain uncorrected, even in the fifth edition, which has, we are assured, been "carefully revised;" does not this go to prove that the public press of those countries happens to know no more about the science of language than any of the learned bodies set down in M. Max Müller's title-page? Hence the necessity—if what is here stated be found true—for our discovery of the origin of language, and the principles that have grown out of it; and hence, too, we may add, the proof that this discovery is no idle dream, but a very serious reality. And of this I am still further convinced on looking through M. Littré's fine dictionary of the French language, now in course of publication, for its enlightened author appears to be as far out as M. Max Müller whenever he tries to trace a word to its original source. And the cause is still the same, his knowing nothing of the origin of human speech.

But M. Max Müller appears to be thoroughly impressed with the belief that, to use his own words, " the principles that must guide the student of the science of language are *now firmly established* [3]."

It is much to be regretted that M. Max Müller does not give us, either in his " Lectures on the Science of Language," or in his " Chips from a German Workshop," a list of those *firmly established principles.* It is also to be regretted that he did not think of applying them to his own etymologies, in order to avoid the many serious mistakes he has made in his endeavours to account for the origin of some of the most common-place words and ideas. But why does he keep them concealed from his friend M. Littré, who, of all the literary characters now living, is perhaps the one who needs them the most, seeing that his great dictionary, so valuable in other respects, is in etymology extremely defective ; and it is all for the want of those firmly established principles which M. Max Müller, though not using them himself, will not allow any one else to use. This conduct is, to say the least of it, very unkind, nay selfish. It reminds one of the fable called the Dog in the Manger, who though he did not eat the hay himself, would not allow the horse to touch it.

---

[3] " Chips from a German Workshop," preface, p. 19.

MONSIEUR LITTRÉ, MEMBRE DE L'INSTITUT DE FRANCE.

On having run through M. Max Müller's great work on the science of language, I next endeavoured to find out who was at the time allowed to be the greatest of all French philologists. Every one's answer was, "Why it is M. Littré to be sure, whose noble dictionary of the French language is now in course of publication, and is likely so to continue for years to come. Seven thousand copies of it are thrown off at every issue, and they are all bought up the moment they appear. No work can be more highly and justly valued." This is how Frenchmen talk of M. Littré's fine dictionary; and as far as a foreigner may presume to offer his humble opinion on the merits of so great a work, it seems to me that M. Littré's countrymen do not praise it too highly. His definitions are precise and clear, and the examples given under each word are perhaps more in number than can be found in the dictionary of any other language. And these examples date from all times, from the most ancient known records down to the present day.

But how does M. Littré trace words to their primary meanings? As well as M. Max Müller or any other philologist, but no better. And why so? Because standing in need of what M. Max Müller would fain make us believe must exist; namely, those *firmly established principles* that are for the future to serve as infallible guides to the student of the science of language. If M. Littré had such principles—and he could not fail having them if his correspondent and friend M. Max Müller himself knew any thing of them—his dictionary would, of course, be greatly superior to what it is at present. M. Littré, in his endeavours to trace words and ideas to their birth, is like a man trying to build a great house without stone, wood, mortar, or any of the requisite tools. All he can do in his etymologies is to submit to his numerous readers the various forms a word has taken in several languages and their dialects.

He tries sometimes, it is true, to discover the primary meaning of a word ; but then his efforts are, though highly commendable, mostly always failures; indeed I might say they appear never otherwise, except when there is no difficulty in the way; but when there is the least difficulty to be overcome, all he can do is to give up, or, from his having no certain rules to be guided by, to hazard a bold guess. And some of his guesses appear rather strange. Only witness his derivation of words so well known as *galetas* and *boucher;* the first of which he traces to the great tower Galata at Constantinople, and the second to a word signifying a *buck goat.* And for both these etymologies M. Littré gives what he conceives to be very sound reasons; but when the reader comes to the real origin of each of these words, he will be obliged to admit that M. Littré's reasons are very weak indeed.

But this acute observer does not yet perceive half the difficult questions suggested by any of the etymologies which he may regard as perfect. Thus, supposing he says that *main* is *manus* in Latin, this is no etymology, for it does not tell us the primary signification of either *main* or *manus,* and this is what the philosophy of language requires. *Main* and *manus* are but two different forms of the same

a

word, and if M. Littré gave us fifty other different forms of the word *main* or *manus* in as many languages and their dialects, his etymology would be equally worthless, unless he could name to us the idea after which *main* or *manus* was first called. And suppose that M. Littré did name a certain idea—and the true one—after which *main* or *manus* was first called, the etymology would be still incomplete, unless he could show after what that certain idea itself was called, and so continue, until he reached the source beyond which no word can be traced, but up to which every word should be traced to make an etymology perfect.

Here the inquisitive reader may wish to know after what idea the final source now referred to was called. It is as if he were to ask me what round comes after the topmost round of a ladder. That word which is itself the primary source of all other words cannot possibly have an original, any more than a ladder can have another round above its topmost one. We shall see in the proper place the primary source of all words.

And ought not this single circumstance to convince every one of the reality of my discovery? And it will, too, convince every man who has sufficient respect for his own mind as to dare to think for himself. But your great philologist cannot think for himself; he is always thinking just as others thought before him. There are, however, some exceptions to this general rule. Thus when M. Littré derives the very common French word *galetas* (a garret), just mentioned, from *Galata*, the superb tower at Constantinople, his thought is, I must admit, original, very much so, for no one ever thought of the like before; but it is a blunder, nay, a very gross blunder, there being no more relationship between *galetas* and the tower at

Constantinople than there is, as we shall see, between *galetas* and the tower of Babel.

And when M. Max Müller, in his etymology of our word *soul,* traces it to a Gothic word meaning the *sea,* and says, "We see that it was originally conceived by the Teutonic nations as a sea within, heaving up and down with every breath, and reflecting heaven and earth on the mirror of the deep," his thought is also original, very much so, but it is not the less a gross blunder, a very gross blunder. That idea, however, of the soul "heaving up and down, and reflecting heaven and earth on the bosom of the deep," looks very grand, very much so. Oh, how I should like to know what it means! No doubt M. Max Müller does. Happy man!

And when the same high authority derives the Latin *mare* (the sea) from the Sanskrit word *mar*, which·means *death,*—that is to say, a word expressive of boisterous commotion, from one implying silence and immobility,—the thought is very original, upon my soul it is, very much so, such a derivation having never, I am sure, entered into any man's mind before. But it is nevertheless a blunder, a very gross blunder, as we shall see.

Let it not now be said that philologists never think for themselves, and that they do but repeat what was often said before; for judging from the little we have just seen, and from the great deal we shall have yet to see before we reach the end of this work, it must be admitted that they do think sometimes—not very often—for themselves, and that then their thoughts are, for the most part, wonderfully original. But I prefer such wild guesses to no guess at all. M. Littré in his etymology of *eau* gives more than twenty different forms of this word, but he does not tell us after what it was man first named *eau.*

He sets down as many more different forms in his etymology of *loup*, but says nothing to guide us to its original meaning; that is to say, we are not told why this animal was named *loup*, λύκος, or *lupus*, not to mention any of the many other names assigned to it by M. Littré. And his dictionary is full of such etymologies, if so they may be called. But it could not be otherwise; M. Littré needed the means, he needed the "firmly established principles of the science of language," and he has had no principles of any kind, either good or bad; not even that principle which ought to be the leading one of all the others—I mean the primary form of the first letter of the alphabet. If he had only this knowledge, a man of his great ability could in a minute or two find the etymology of so common a word as *garçon*, which he is compelled to give up in despair, with the admission that the original of this word remains to be found. Diez, a learned German, who is continually quoted by M. Littré, traces *garçon* from a word for *thistle* to some other word meaning the *heart of a cabbage;* and then to one meaning a *bud.* And though M. Littré admires this etymology as *fort ingenieuse!* he thinks, however, that it does not bring home complete conviction, *que cette dérivation ne porte pas dans l'esprit une conviction complète!* and his conclusion is that the "*étymologie de garçon reste en suspens.*" What egregious nonsense! only imagine a very learned man tracing a word meaning *boy*, to a *thistle*, the *heart of a cabbage*, and finally to a *bud;* and only imagine another very learned man regarding such a derivation as very ingenious! and in the face of such rubbish as this, we are told there are *now* firmly established principles that must guide the student of the science of language—a statement sincerely but unwittingly made, for one more destitute of truth has never perhaps appeared in print. Long, long before I shall have to notice *garçon* somewhere in the body of this work, every reader will be sufficiently acquainted with my principles to enable him to discover its real original, and in which he will find no allusion to *thistles, the hearts of cabbages,* or *buds.* The primary form of the word *garçon* lies on the surface. And every one will, I am sure, admit the reality of such an etymology; every one, except your genuine philologist. But why should not he admit it? Because it would upset all his previous notions of his favourite science, and oblige him to unlearn all he has ever learned of philology, which would be for him a most painful labour.

Many persons suppose that opposition of this kind to new discoveries should be ascribed to envy. But this seems to be a mistake. When Harvey discovered the circulation of the blood, was there one great medical man in the world who believed in the reality of his discovery? There was not; and he who was then, perhaps, the most distinguished of them all—the leading physician of Paris— published two works against the circulation, with his name attached to each. This man must have been therefore sincere in his belief, or he would not have thus openly acknowledged himself the author of two such productions. Harvey answered the first attack, but he would not condescend to notice the second. It may be then supposed that the exposition of this discovery was not at first sufficiently clear; but according to Hume, "Harvey had the happiness of establishing at once his theory on the most solid and convincing proofs; and posterity has added little to the arguments suggested by his industry and ingenuity[4]." And a late very eminent physician says that Harvey "displayed his discovery so clearly to others, that to doubt it in the present day would be considered insanity[5]."

Hume further states, "It was remarked, that no physician in Europe, who had reached forty years of age, ever to the end of his life adopted Harvey's doctrine of the circulation of the blood; and that his practice in London diminished extremely, from the reproach drawn on him by that great and signal discovery: so slow is the progress of truth in every science, even when not opposed by factious or superstitious prejudices."

And if Harvey were now living, and if he were to come before the world with his grand discovery, what more chance would he have of succeeding in our enlightened days than he had met with some two hundred years ago? In all probability he would have none whatever; for human nature is still the same, is still as much afraid of truth as it ever has been. Moral courage is wanting, no one dares to think otherwise than as others have thought before him. And it is remarkable that they who are regarded as the most competent judges in any science are, respecting the appearance of an original discovery, the last to give a decisive opinion. But why should this be? Because a favourable opinion from such men is equal to their admitting that they have themselves been long in error; and this is what few men, except those of very superior minds, are willing to admit. When Fulton's first steamboat was tried with success on the Seine, a committee of men the most competent were ordered by

---

[4] Hume, Hist. of England, Charles II.
[5] See the Harveian Oration by John Elliotson, M.D., &c., p. 49.

Napoleon to examine it carefully, and let him know what they thought of it; but their opinion was very unfavourable, and they unanimously declared that Fulton's views were visionary, and that they could never be realized; upon which Napoleon is reported to have said, that the man should be sent to Charenton, which is the Bedlam of France.

And how was he who proposed to light all London with gas received? As a madman, and his abettors as idiots. "Even the liberal mind of Sir Humphry Davy," says a respectable authority, "failed to take in the idea that gas was applicable to purposes of street or house lighting[6]." This great chemist was, however, looked up to as the most competent judge then living of all such matters.

And so it always is with discoverers; even when their discoveries cannot be contradicted, the best judges are afraid to receive them as real. I sent last year to the French Institute, as a competitor for the prix Volney, a large fragment of the present work. But as it contained many of the false etymologies to be found in M. Littré's learned dictionary, with not a few taken from the works of their correspondent, M. Max Müller, my pretensions were not, it would seem, received with favour. But the committee was composed of M. Littré and his friends (six in number), and this circumstance of my having corrected their colleague's many mistakes may, *unknown to themselves*, have influenced their judgment. It were not fair to insinuate that gentlemen who stand so high in public opinion did not each decide to the best of his belief and as his conscience dictated.

Though the members of the Institute never publish

[6] See Diprose's Account of the Parish of St. Clement Danes.

their opinions respecting the works of which they do not
approve, I happened to obtain through mere chance from
one of those gentlemen the following statement respecting
my *brochure*: "Il s'agit de la solution d'une question très-
ardue, que j'ai bien pu exposer consciencieusement et
fidèlement comme rapporteur, mais sur la question je ne
me sens en mesure ni de vous approuver, *ni de vous
contredire.*"

This was written by M. Patin, a very learned man, the
highest judge in philology, and the eldest, I believe, of
all his colleagues, having been born in 1793. I am
astonished at his admitting that *he cannot contradict me*,
this being equal to his granting that my pretensions must,
according to his conscientious belief, be real; for if he did
not find them so, he would never make such an admission.
It is not difficult to account for his not granting me his
approval; it would be too much for him to conceive that
the discovery of the origin of human speech, even of the
first word that man ever spoke, could have remained until
now unknown. And this is how almost every one will
reason with himself respecting my pretensions, and no one
will be more inclined to do so than he who will have never
seen my book.

The prize was adjudged to a work entitled *Glossaire des
mots Espagnols et Portugais dérivés de l'Arabe;* its author
being, like M. Max Müller, a correspondent of the
Institute, and consequently a gentleman of some literary
merit. Now we all know, on looking into the glossaries
explaining the old words of such writers as Chaucer,
Spenser and Rabelais, that compilations of this kind, if not
very original, are at least found to be sometimes very
useful; and no one should, for this reason, object to their

authors obtaining gold medals. But between such a production and one which puts not only almost every Frenchman in the way of discovering the original meanings, hitherto unknown, of the most common-place words in his language, but which does also enable his learned academicians and members of the Institute to correct the thousand and one etymological mistakes to be met with in by far their very best dictionary, there is, I dare assert, in point of utility—putting aside originality—some little difference.

I might also assert that there must be some little difference between a mere compilation and a work to which the highest authority of the Institute cannot deny the claim put forward by its author, that of having discovered the origin of language and myths. There is in such an admission, when we consider the pure and enlightened source from which it emanates, something rather startling. Nine persons out of ten will, I am sure, feel inclined to think that if I have not made the discovery in question, I must have gone very near it ; have done it at least in part, if not completely. But there can be no doubt about it. Facts, proofs in abundance, have been obtained, not through blind chance, not through ingenuity, but through the application of the principles of my discovery. But M. Patin could not go farther than he has gone. He is *le doyen de la faculté des lettres,* and, from the duty of his high station being to examine the learned youth of France, who, on having finished their studies, aspire to high places in the state or to academic honours, he cannot sanction opinions contrary to the Established Church of his country; and this alone were sufficient to induce him to withhold his *complete* conviction that I have made the discovery of the origin of language, since I do not ascribe its beginning to its having been first spoken by Adam in Paradise.

But how, it may be asked, did I obtain M. Patin's opinion respecting my work, since it is not usual to grant such favours? It happened in this way: the Institute never returns works sent in for the prix Volney, though their authors have the right of making extracts from them. But when I went to the Institute for this purpose my manuscript could not be found; and as it was last seen with M. Patin, his address was given me with the permission of writing to him about it; and from his letter in answer to mine, I have taken the liberty of copying the passage already submitted to the reader.

With regard to my theory of the origin of language, I am well aware I may be often blamed for being opposed to the belief of its having originated with Adam in Paradise.

But some men when they meddle with religion are more favoured than others. M. Max Müller says: "The author of the Mosaic records, though rightly stripped, before the tribunal of physical science, of his claims as an inspired writer, may at least claim the modest title of a quiet observer [7]."

No scientific man in the world, except one made blind through fear or prejudice, can find fault with what M. Max Müller has here stated, for it is a statement supporting what is strictly true. But it is not the less, according to the opinions of some persons, very gross blasphemy; for it not only denies to Moses the gift of divine inspiration, but it also makes light of Christ's teaching, in which Moses is referred to as a true prophet. And this is not only shown by Luke xvi. 31, but also by the following: "Do

[7] Lectures on the Science of Language, vol. i. p. 377.

not think that I will accuse you to the Father: there is *one* that accuseth you, *even* Moses, in whom ye trust.

"For had ye believed Moses, ye would have believed me: for he wrote of me.

"But if ye believe not his writings, how shall ye believe my words [8]?"

According to those words of Christ, every sincere Christian must believe in Moses as a true prophet, and accuse every one of gross blasphemy who happens to think otherwise; for such an opinion is condemnatory, not only of the Old but of the New Testament also. M. Max Müller has been, therefore, highly favoured for his not having been called to account for making such a statement as the one just quoted from the fifth edition of his book. He may say that he has truth on his side; but, in religious controversy, truth is not always a safe protector. Has not many a good and excellent man, as all the world knows, been burned alive before now for having dared to speak the truth? But M. Max Müller does not seem to be aware that in making the statement above quoted, he was saying any thing likely to shock the religious feelings of a certain class of true believers in the Christian faith; for on the next page preceding the one from which the above extract is made, he states as follows: "I defy my adversaries to point out one single passage where I have mixed up scientific with theological arguments [9]."

According to this passage it is nothing at all to deny to Moses divine inspiration in opposition to the words of Christ. But as every man should be allowed to state what he believes to be true, I am glad to perceive that this liberty has not been denied to M. Max Müller. But this

[8] John v. 45—47. [9] Lect., vol. i. p. 376.

should teach M. Max Müller to be equally indulgent to
others. In one of his two volumes on the science of
language, he alludes to a German philologist, from whose
work he would quote a passage, but declines doing so,
because he believes it to contain blasphemy. The passage
should, however, be given, and the reader be allowed to
judge for himself. What does this German philologist
dare to assert? Does he do more than deny to Moses
divine inspiration, by which a disbelief in Christ is also
implied? M. Max Müller himself does as much, yet no
one accuses him of blasphemy; and he should not, for
this reason, be so severe upon others, nor take upon
himself the liberty of thinking for his readers, but allow
every one to think for himself. It is by acting thus freely
and liberally that error has been hitherto often discovered,
and truth made evident.

I cannot now call to mind either the name of the
German philologist censured for his blasphemy by M.
Max Müller, or in which of the two volumes on the science
of language it may be found; but unless I mistake, it
it is on a left-hand-side page, nearer to the top than the
bottom, and that the objectionable passage, which M.
Max Müller dares not to quote, is replaced by asterisks.
I have turned over many pages of both volumes, but I
cannot find it.

But the unusual favour shown to M. Max Müller must
not lead me—because I am no German—to expect from
Englishmen an equal amount of indulgence and fair
play.

In the account given in my former work of the origin of
myths, I should, I am told, have considered those parts of
the heathen mythology which bear a rather startling

resemblance to the Christian faith, as only so many ancient types of the truth not yet made known; such being the interpretation they have received from eminent divines of the Church of England, as well as from other learned and pious individuals. But as I do not *now* offer any argument opposed to this belief, it follows that when, in the course of this work, the reader happens to meet with any of those resemblances which are received as symbols, I should not be accused by such Christians as have no faith in the doctrine of types, of introducing matter contrary to revelation. On all those occasions I only state facts in the development of the science I am endeavouring to expound, and so do allow, by the results obtained, every one to think and judge for himself.

But as there are many denominations of Christians, and as on some points they differ widely from one another in their opinions, it may be that all of them cannot be brought to believe in the doctrine of types, though some very learned and good Christians do. And this being the case, my discovery and its principles may be censured or slighted by many who might otherwise receive them with favour. But all who look coldly on scientific results, because revealing truths contrary to the belief in which they have been brought up, can be no great honour either to their God or to their religion. Had all men, in the past, views so confined, the world would be now in so very backward a state that we should be still denying the diurnal motion of the earth, and be accusing every one of blasphemy who took part with Galileo.

But for innovations and discoveries of all kinds, man entertains, we are allowed to understand, a natural antipathy. Thus M. Max Müller observes: "New ideas do not gain ground at once, and there is a tendency in our mind to resist new convictions as long as we can[1]." Yes, when our views are very limited, and our share of ideality is rather scanty. But to the capacious mind new ideas are ever welcome, for in such a storehouse they mostly always find room in abundance. Indeed the mind rich in imagination is too often, from its very greediness for every thing original, the dupe of its own superior powers. But as such minds are comparatively few, hence the belief that man is by nature opposed to new ideas, which, though true on many occasions, is not always so.

Words, it will be argued, fall within the reach of every intelligence. They require, in order to be examined even very closely, no previous scientific knowledge, such as astronomy or anatomy requires, without an acquaintance with the former of which Galileo could have never known how the earth moves, nor could Harvey, if ignorant of the latter, have discovered how the blood circulates. The authors of grammars, dictionaries, glossaries, as well as of works of logic and philosophy, are all of them constantly referring to words and commenting on them, and they have done so from the earliest times down to the present hour. Hence the conclusion must naturally be, that if such a discovery as the origin of language were possible, it would have been made long ago. And this argument, though very fallacious, is, it must be allowed, very plausible, and so effective, that it will, in all probability, prevent most persons from approving, in my work, of many things which their reason assures them must be true, the want of respect to their own minds not allowing them to declare their belief.

Hence such a discovery as mine has been long since

----

[1] "Chips from a German Workshop," vol. ii. p. 46.

regarded as impossible; some one has even asked if I do myself believe in its reality. But I have, I dare hope, hit upon a means of removing for the future all doubt respecting the sincerity of my belief in this respect. Thus I have, as a competitor for le prix Volney to be next awarded, offered to wager one thousand francs (1000 frs.) against one hundred (100 frs.) that I have made the discovery of the origin of language; and in order to give to such a challenge its due weight and importance, I object to its being accepted by any one except a distinguished philologist; and I do therefore propose M. Littré. I ask this gentleman if he will accept it; and I answer that I think he will not, for the reason that he is too clever a man not to perceive, on reading with attention my *brochure* presented to the Institute last year, and which takes up so many of his own blunders as well as of M. Max Müller's, that he would not have so much as the mere shadow of a chance to win my thousand francs. And to prove to him that I am, on this occasion, very serious, and that I do really own so large a sum as a thousand francs (*mirabile dictu!*), I have named to him the stockbroker in Paris where the money is lodged. And if he should object to take my thousand francs, I tell him that, in this case, he may have them added to the next gold medal to be adjudged to the successful competitor for the *prix Volney.*

But who is, I have been asked, to decide between M. Littré and me in the event of his taking up my glove? And to this question I have answered, that I accept twelve of his own colleagues to be chosen by lot, but their opinions to be given in writing. Than this nothing can be fairer. Let it not, therefore, be any longer asserted that I must doubt in the reality of my own discovery.

But I am no way surprised at its having been asked if I do myself believe in what I am pleased to call the discovery of the origin of language; for the Committee of the Institute advise all competitors for the prix Volney to confine their views rather to comparative than general philology, which advice they would never give if they could believe in the possibility of the origin of language being one day discovered. But my system embraces all—it is both general and comparative. The following is, in their words, the advice given by the Committee of the Institute: " Mais la commission ne peut trop recommander aux concurrents d'envisager sous le point de vue *comparatif et historique* les idiomes qu'ils auront choisis, et de ne pas se borner à l'analyse logique, ou à ce qu'on appelle la *grammaire générale.*"

But this learned body would never so advise had they known that all the languages ever spoken sprung from the same single source, and that for this simple reason nations which had never so much as heard of one another, have often ideas expressed by the same words, which circumstance has sometimes led learned men to find a relationship between the inhabitants of certain parts of the world where none had ever existed. Godfrey Higgins says, " If I had an English and Hebrew dictionary as full as Parkhurst's Hebrew and English Lexicon, I think I could make out of the two languages a language in which conversation might very well be carried on by a Hebrew and an Englishman respecting all the common concerns of life[2]."

M. Max Müller, however, says that " Hebrew and English are not at all related[3]." And this may very well be,

---

[2] Analysis, vol. i. p. 796.
[3] Lecture on Science of Language, vol. ii. p. 284.

though the two languages have, to a certainty, many words in common, and of which we may have now shown the cause.

Though the discovery of the origin of language be thus regarded by the French Institute as impossible, I can quote two very high authorities who entertain a different opinion, namely, Jacob Grimm and M. Ernest Renan, the latter celebrated linguist being a member of the Institute. Jacob Grimm's argument favouring the possibility of such a discovery is to this effect: that if language be a Divine gift we have neither the right nor the means of discovering its origin; but if it be a human contrivance, it were not impossible, he believes, to trace it to its very cradle; by which he understands, to the earliest state of its existence, even to its birth.

M. Renan, alluding to the objections which the title of his own work ("De l'Origine du Langage") is likely to suggest, quotes at the same time Jacob Grimm's opinion, and of which we have just seen the substance. M. Renan's words are: "Le titre soulèvera peut-être les objections des personnes accoutumées à prendre la science par le côté positif, et qui ne voient jamais sans appréhension les études de fondation récente chercher à résoudre les problèmes légués par l' ancienne philosophie. Je suis bien aise de m'abriter à cet égard derrière l'autorité d'un des fondateurs de la philologie comparée, M. Jacob Grimm. Dans un mémoire publié en 1852, sur le même sujet et sous le même titre que le mien[4], l'illustre linguiste s'est attaché à établir la possibilité de résoudre un tel problème d'une manière scientifique. Ainsi qu'il le fait remarquer,

---

[4] Ueber den Ursprung der Sprache, Berlin, Dummler, 1852 (tiré des Mémoires de l'Academie de Berlin pour 1851), pp. 10 et suiv. et pp. 54, 55.

sile langage avait été conféré à l'homme comme un don céleste créé sans lui et hors de lui, la science n'aurait ni le droit ni le moyen d'en rechercher l'origine; mais si le langage est l'œuvre de la nature humaine, s'il présente une marche et un développement réguliers, il est possible d'arriver par de légitimes inductions jusqu'à son *berceau*[5]."

But M. Renan is, as we shall see, very far from tracing the origin of language to its *berceau*. He is not, in this respect, more advanced than Jacob Grimm or any other philologist. His work, which is beautifully written, contains no etymologies, either good or bad, in support of his opinion.

Let us now see if I have made the very important discovery of the origin of language—a discovery which, according to the two high authorities just quoted, is conceived not to be impossible. But my own most sincere conviction is that I have made it; for how can I else account for the many happy results obtained through its means? Am I to ascribe these results to blind chance? Impossible. Am I to ascribe the whole of them to ingenuity or address? Equally impossible, for this would be granting to myself a hundred times more merit than I do really deserve, or than any other mortal ever deserved for his ingenuity. Thus it may have been rather difficult to have made the discovery to which I lay claim; but to have obtained, unassisted by its principles, the startling results—and they are not few in number—that have grown out of it would, however ingenious I might be, appear infinitely more difficult; in short, so much so, as not to be conceived possible by any unprejudiced mind, however limited its share of common intelligence. But if, notwith-

---

[5] De l'Origine du Langage, préface, p. 4, 5.

standing all the pains I have taken to bring this discovery home to every understanding, it should be still found not sufficiently evident, and its reality be consequently denied; such blindness, whether real or affected, may suggest to the philologist of future times an observation similar to the one made by Dr. Elliotson respecting the circulation of the blood; namely, that from its being so clearly displayed to others, "to doubt it would, in his day, be considered insanity."

And how has this discovery of mine been made so very evident? By its owning certain fixed principles which can be very easily applied. It therefore follows that with the necessary means any one else might have obtained as much as I have myself: there are, no doubt, many persons who, from their being possessed of superior discernment, might in my place have obtained a great deal more. When I do, therefore, by the applying of those principles, trace back a word of which the meaning has been lost to the whole world for many an age, to its primitive source; let not this be ascribed to ingenuity, but to its real cause, that is, to the discovery of the first word ever spoken by man; for there it is, and there alone, that all the merit lies.

CONTENTS.

ORIGIN

OF

LANGUAGE AND MYTHS.

CHAPTER I.

PROOF THAT SPEECH NEVER COMES NATURALLY TO MAN.

THIS is made evident by the fact, that, of the several human beings who were lost or abandoned during their infancy in woods or other solitary places, none were ever found, when long after discovered and captured, to have the power of expressing their thoughts by articulate sounds. All such persons ought, however, if speech were a natural gift, to have had a language of some kind or other; but they had none.

Another plain proof that speech cannot have come naturally to man, is this, that persons born deaf without the least defect in their vocal organs, never speak. The mere want of hearing ought not, however, if speech were a natural gift, to prevent them from learning to express their ideas by articulate sounds.

B

CHAPTER II.

HOW MEN MUST HAVE FIRST SIGNIFIED THEIR WANTS AND
DESIRES.

BUT if men had not from the beginning the use of words,
how must they, when totally dumb, have expressed their
thoughts to one another? Just as we see any two of them
do at the present hour when neither understands the language of the other. That is to say, men must, previously
to their having yet acquired any knowledge of words,
have made use of signs.

Signs must have therefore been man's first language,
and consequently his only natural one; and I can quote
three very high authorities who were of the same
opinion—Condillac, and the two celebrated Scotch philosophers, Reid and Dugald Stewart. Thus Condillac, in
the opening of his fine Philosophical Grammar, says,
" Les jestes, les mouvements du visage, voilà les pre-
miers moyens que les hommes ont eus pour communiquer
leurs pensées." Reid expresses himself to the same effect.
"If mankind had not," he says, "a natural language, they
could have never invented an artificial one." The writer
means by " a natural language," the language of signs,
and by " an artificial one," the language of articulate
sounds. He continues thus : " It appears evident from
what has been said on language, that there are natural
signs as well as artificial; and particularly that the
thoughts, purposes, and dispositions of the mind have
their natural signs in the features of the face, the modu-
lation of the voice, and the motion and attitude of the
body; that without a natural knowledge of the connexion
between these signs and the things signified by them,

language could have never been invented and established among men." . . . " Is it not a pity that the refinements of a civilized life, instead of supplying the defects of natural language, should root it out, and plant in its stead dull and lifeless articulations of unmeaning sounds or the scrawling of insignificant characters? The perfection of language is commonly thought to be, to express human thoughts and sentiments distinctly by these dull signs; but if this be the perfection of artificial language, it is certainly the corruption of the natural [1]."

Dugald Stewart argues to the same effect in favour of natural language, by which he also means the language of signs [2].

But M. Ernest Renan, who has also written on the origin of language, makes light of all such opinions as those expressed by Condillac, Reid, and Dugald Stewart. The whole of his arguments amounts to this, and no more:—As soon as men began to think and reason, they began to speak. But if it were so, how does it happen that the man who has no defect in his vocal organs, but who has been merely born deaf, never speaks? yet he thinks as much and as well as any other man.

But M. Renan agrees with all sensible men in denying that speech can have been either a gift or an invention; and taking advantage of these two just opinions, and also of the argument of the three high authorities above cited,—namely, that speech cannot have come naturally to man,—he concludes that there can be no other means of accounting for its origin than the one he suggests—that the combined powers of the mind, acting spontaneously, must have called it forth when man wanted

[1] Reid's Works, vol. ii. pp. 226, &c.
[2] See his Outlines of Moral Philosophy, part i. page 33.

to give expression to his thoughts [3].   Such reasoning as
this does certainly appear very conclusive; for if language be neither a gift nor an invention, and if it has
not come naturally to man, there can, surely, it may be
argued, be no other means left of accounting for its origin
than by ascribing it, as M. Renan does, to the faculties
of the mind, acting when needed of their own accord.
There is, however, another means, and one of which
M. Renan had no suspicion, as I am now going to show.

CHAPTER III.

SHOWING THAT SPEECH MUST HAVE BEEN EASILY ACQUIRED.

IT is well known that no people can be found unprovided
with a language well adapted for its own use.   Hence
the late Mr. Crawford, F.R.S., makes the following important statement, in a paper read at the British Asso-
ciation in September, 1867.

"Man, when he first appeared on earth, was without
articulate speech, and, like the lower animals, must have
expressed himself by what was little more than mere
interjection.   He had, therefore, to frame a language—
a *seemingly* difficult achievement, yet one which every
savage tribe had been able to achieve, and that not in
one place only, but in *several thousand separate and
independent localities."* . . . . "The languages of a
people so low in the scale of humanity as the Australians,
incapable of reckoning beyond duality, were found to be
not only skilfully, but even completely constructed."

[3] See page 89, and almost every other page of his beautifully written
work entitled "De l'Origine du Langage."

This very respectable authority has here justly observed that the framing of a language was a *seemingly* difficult achievement; for it was in truth, and as we shall see presently, a difficulty *only in appearance.* Were it otherwise, a people scarcely above the class of idiots, such as those incapable of counting as far as three, could have never formed a language of any kind whatever, and much less could they compose one which was both skilfully and completely formed. Connected with the passages already quoted from Reid, there is one which to some persons may appear an exaggeration; it happens, however, to be very far from it. This is the observation he makes, " Had language, in general, been a human invention as much as writing or printing, we should find whole nations as mute as the brutes." Reid should rather say, that in such a case we should not find, on the face of the earth, a single individual gifted with the faculty of speech, nor having so much as a remote idea of what it is. Nothing can have been, however, more easily acquired than the use of language, though no body of learned men could invent it. But why so? Because of its wonderful simplicity—their learning would prove the greatest obstacle. And what infinite wisdom we have here shown us! While the human mind must have been yet in an infant state, with intelligence scarcely above that of the brute creation, a means inconceivably easy was given to man for enabling him to acquire that faculty of which he has ever since had the most reason to be proud. Let us now confirm the truth of this statement by submitting to the reader—

CHAPTER IV.

OUR DISCOVERY OF MAN'S FIRST WORD.

FROM knowing, as we now do, that the several individuals found living singly in a wild state, had not the use of articulate sounds; and also that persons without any defect in their vocal organs, but who are merely born deaf, are equally unprovided with speech of any kind; it is self-evident that this faculty never comes naturally to man, and that words must be heard and learned in order to be acquired. Now, this being granted, what follows? That men must, as already stated, have first expressed their ideas by signs, just as any two of them do at present when speaking no language in common. And as they must have often, while so engaged, uttered an inarticulate sound for the sole purpose of drawing attention to what they were endeavouring to represent, it is easy to conceive that their first word must have grown out of a sign made by the mouth. And when the sun was in this way referred to, such a sound as the O (then a hieroglyph) obtains in the alphabet, must have been invariably heard. And this is so true that the learned orthoepist Walker, referring to this character, observes, " It requires the mouth to be formed in some degree like the letter, in order to pronounce it."

Man could not have heard this peculiar sound a great many times without remarking that it referred always to the sun; so that he must have soon begun to use it for indicating this object instead of the sign out of which it grew, and but for which it could have never been known.

But why should the name of the sun more than that

of any other object have been man's first word, and consequently the beginning of human speech? Because, signs
having been the means by which man began to express
his thoughts, it is reasonable to suppose that it must
have been through a sign the use of speech was obtained; and granting this, it is easy to conceive that
such a sign must have been made by the mouth. Now
the mouth can represent nothing in nature except what
is circular. Thus, however we may make it gesticulate,
we cannot force it into the shape of an animal, a bird, a
tree, a mountain, a river, or any thing of the kind; and
if it even had this power as well as that of representing
a circle, the sun would be still preferred to every thing
else, for the reason that of all other natural wonders it
appears by far the greatest and most attractive, and, on
account of the benefits it confers, the one that must in
the beginning have appeared the most deserving of man's
attention and gratitude.

And if we now bestow a serious thought on the infinite wisdom of God by His thus affording to man the
most simple means imaginable for enabling him to acquire that faculty of which, as we have already said, he
has ever had most reason to be proud, ought we not to
be filled with astonishment and admiration? At the
birth of language, human intelligence can have been
scarcely above that of the brute creation. Man could
not therefore acquire the use of speech by the force of
reason, and hence the necessity of his being so formed as
to need no mental effort whatever for the framing of a
language. Then how did our wise Creator make up for
this evident deficiency of mind in man at the very early
period to which we refer? By a means of all others the
most simple—by having so formed him as to give to his

mouth the power of representing a circle. No more than
this was needed; speech then came of itself; no effort
was required. So that he who first used the sound of the
O as a name of the sun instead of the sign out of which
it grew, and but for which, as we have said, it could
never have been heard, little thought that he was then
in the act of erecting a mighty edifice, a monument so
wonderful in all its parts, that the wisest men of the world
would through all time be led to believe that its foundation-stone must have been first laid by the hands of an
all-powerful God. Hence Dugald Stewart, referring to
language, makes the following very just observation :—
" When we first begin to philosophize on it, and consider
what a vast and complicated fabric language is, it is
difficult for us to persuade ourselves that the unassisted
faculties of the human mind were equal to the invention[4]."

We have now seen how the use of speech was first
acquired. It was not a gift, nor an invention, nor did
it come naturally to man; nor, as M. Renan asserts,
was it called forth by the powers of the mind acting
spontaneously all together. But it came unsought for,
unawares, even unknown to him who first used it; and
at a time when man can be scarcely said to have had a
mind did it come, he being then in so crude, imbecile,
and undeveloped a state as to be, in point of intelligence,
barely above the animal of the field. Nor should this
opinion be regarded as an exaggeration, seeing that after
so many ages since men first spoke, whole nations are
even still incapable of counting beyond duality.

What then must man have been when, unknown to
himself, he uttered his first word ! When he used the
sound of the O as meaning the sun, instead of the sign

[4] Vol. iv. p. 22.

out of which it grew! This single and very natural sound was, however, the origin of human speech. But had not man received from his wise Creator the facility of giving to his lips a circular form, he must have remained for ever dumb, having only the power of uttering inarticulate sounds, and which would be chiefly used, by the noise so produced, for drawing attention to his signs.

CHAPTER V.

THE NATURALNESS OF THE FOREGOING ACCOUNT OF THE ORIGIN OF LANGUAGE.

HAVING thus clearly accounted for the origin of man's first word, and consequently for that of language in general, I might stop here, and declare my discovery already fully made. And how reasonable such a conclusion must appear when closely examined! Thus, how natural it is to suppose that men must have first signified their thoughts to one another by signs, it being made evident by the arguments above stated, that the use of speech has never yet been acquired without its having been first learned from others! When we are therefore compelled to admit that man's first language must have been that of signs, how reasonable it is to suppose that his first significant word must have come to him through a sign made by his mouth; no other part of his body, such as his eyes, hands, or feet, by which he made signs, having the power to utter a sound or make any kind of noise that can be supposed likely to give birth to a word!

And when we now admit, as we must do, that the mouth can represent nothing in nature except what is circular in form, what can be more reasonable than to suppose it was while signifying the sun by the rounding of his lips, man first obtained its name, he having at the same instant uttered a sound for the sole purpose of drawing attention, by the noise so produced, to the object he was then representing? Hence let any one try to show with his mouth the shape of the sun, and allow, while so doing, his voice to be heard, and he will invariably, even in spite of himself, produce exactly the name given by every child to the O when calling over the letters of the alphabet.

And on this peculiar sound having been heard many times, and always on the same occasion, how easy it is to conceive that it must, instead of the sign out of which it grew, have been used for signifiying the sun; and that the O was therefore the first word, first name, and first root—all three combined in the same single sign, itself a hieroglyph!

But the fact that it is impossible to find in any language on the face of the earth an idea to which the name of the sun can be traced, ought to be considered as another startling proof, from its thus having no original, that it must be, as above shown, the primary source of human speech.   The notion hitherto entertained by philologists—but by philologists only—that the sun has been called after the idea signified by such a word as light or heat, is too absurd to deserve being discussed seriously; for must not every one know, except a philologist, that such an idea as light or heat must be finally traced to the sun, and not the sun to either light or heat? Poor Moses has been rather too severely called to account for his having committed a similar mistake—that of having made the sun come several days after the light.

But do our learned philologists, with all their additional knowledge obtained through the present greatly advanced state of science, prove themselves any wiser than the famous lawgiver of old, when science, such as we have it now, was yet unborn?

But if an idea could be found after which the sun was called, then indeed would my lofty pretensions be brought low; for the very foundation-stone of the edifice upon which they have been raised to so high a pitch, would be not merely shaken, but be completely swept from under them—and away. But why so? Because this finding would prove the name of the sun to be only a derivative, and not what it really is, the original word out of which human speech has grown over all the world.

Now, is such a name of the sun ever likely to be found? In order not to appear over sanguine, which is always offensive to certain very sensitive minds, I will say that it is likely; though, to be candid, I cannot believe it to be half so much so as the discovery of the quadrature of the circle or that of perpetual motion. And if we may believe the scientific world, neither of these discoveries will ever be made; at least not for some thousands of years to come. He who would therefore find the original idea after which the sun was called, should be endowed with no slight stock of patience, as he may, before his discovery can be made, have some little time to wait.

Here, as already stated, might I stop; for the origin of human speech, even of the first significant word ever uttered by man, has been made known. Then why proceed any farther? It is but for confirming by numerous instances the reality of so important a discovery, and also for showing the rare advantage of the knowledge thence derived. Hence, what is now to follow will, I dare hope, be found to contain a considerable amount of philological information hitherto unknown. But were it also found to contain in the application of the principles which have grown out of the analyzing of words, some mistakes—even many mistakes—this would not afford the least proof deserving of serious notice, that the discovery itself to which I lay claim—that of the origin of language—is not real and as complete as it needs be.

CHAPTER VI.

HOW LANGUAGE HAPPENED TO FALL INTO THREE DIVISIONS WITH ALL PEOPLE, EVEN UNKNOWN TO THOSE WHO FIRST MADE WORDS.

IT is now well known that the sun was the first object of divine worship over all the earth; which belief arose from this great luminary appearing to animate all nature. Its name became therefore another word for Maker or Creator[5]; and on being modified for the sake of distinction, the same word must have been made to signify such ideas as the great object it designated suggested, namely, *light, heat, day, life, goodness,* &c. And however scantily gifted with intelligence men in their earliest state may have been, they could have easily expressed all similar ideas after this manner; they could not even help doing otherwise, this means being so very easy, natural, and simple.

[5] The learned admit, as we shall see farther on, that *maker,* or artificer, was an epithet belonging to the sun.

So much for the creation of this first portion of human speech. We see that it required no effort of the mind; nothing like ingenuity, nothing deserving the name of invention.

But other words were needed. How did man obtain those that were necessary for expressing such ideas as we now signify by the verbs to *carry, bear, hold, have, take, seize, strike, keep, give, do, form,* and the like? All these actions must have been expressed by the name of the instrument—still variously modified for the sake of distinction—by which they were accomplished; that is to say, they were called after the HAND, and they can be traced directly or indirectly to this source, as we shall see.

But after what must the *hand* itself have been named? After the idea which is expressed by the word *maker,* one of the epithets belonging to the sun, from the belief that once prevailed of his having been—as already stated—the maker of all nature.

Nor can this second portion of human speech have required of the mind the least share of ingenuity or invention. It is reasonable to suppose that man would call after the *hand* whatever was done through its means. This must, in the beginning, have been as natural to him as to call the child after its parent, or the stranger after the land of his birth, which is just as man does at present, and as he ever has done, and as he ever will do.

Only one more portion of human speech was necessary for enabling man to express himself to the full. By words traceable to the name of the sun he could, as stated above, express such ideas as *good, high, noble,* &c., but he wanted those of opposite meanings. How did he obtain them? Very easily; and still no ingenuity, no mental effort being required. Thus, after the moon, of which the name and that of the sun were radically the same, he called *night*, and after *night* he called *darkness*, from which source came words expressing negative qualities, such as *noxious, badness, vice, lowness, death,* &c.

So much for the origin of speech. Man had, in the beginning, the above three simple divisions of it; and he has them still, but no more, because no more is needed. And thus has it been with all the nations of the earth; every one of them whose language is not the dialect of another, has made, after the manner just stated, a language of its own—the sun, out of whose name human speech has grown, being common to them all. This will account for what has often astonished the philologist, namely, that nations between whom there has never been the least connexion have languages that are, when radically considered, so much alike as to leave no doubt of their having emanated from the same unknown source, whatever that might be.

CHAPTER VII.

HOW IT HAPPENS THAT OPPOSITE IDEAS ARE SOMETIMES EXPRESSED ALIKE.

But from those three divisions of language making, as it were, only one, since every word, to whatever division it may belong, can be finally traced to the first name ever given to the sun; does it not follow, I may be asked, that words of opposite, or at least very different meanings, must be sometimes alike in form? It is even so; and this, too, has often astonished philologists. Hence the word which in one language means high may in some other language mean low. It may even happen in the same language, witness *altus* in Latin, which has these two opposite meanings. The same may be said of the French words *sus* and *sous*, and *dessus* and *dessous*, for it is only conventionally that every two such words differ from each other, as we shall see farther on. The same may be said of the Gaelic words *nasal* and *iosal*, of which the former means *high* and the latter *low*. In a work which I have but very lately met with, entitled "Les Eléments primitifs des Langues découverts," par M. Bergier, Docteur en Théologie, this circumstance, of the opposite ideas *high* and *low* being expressed by the same word, is thus accounted for (p. 35): "אל (al) *altus*, exprime haut et profond, parce que la hauteur et la profondeur sont également la distance des deux extrémités considérées en ligne perpendiculaire."

This is very plausible, but that is all: it is not true. For such an explanation cannot account for the identity of many other words having no such meaning as high and low. Thus the English word *bleach* cannot differ from *blach*, nor *blach* from *black*; yet to *bleach* means to *whiten*, which is the opposite of *black*. In French also *blanc* does not differ from *blac*, which is the same as *black*; for, as, according to one of my rules, every vowel may or may not have a nasal sound,—that is, take an *n* or an *m* when it has not one, or lose one if it should have it,—there can be therefore, no difference between *blanc* and *blac*, that is, *black*. And this is so true that in Saxon these two opposite ideas (black and

white) are expressed by the same word: the only difference is this, that one of them has for the sake of
distinction an accent over its *a*, thus, *blác*, which means
white, and the other (*blac*) has none.

Webster, though unable to account for this apparent
anomaly, has not failed to notice the identity of *bleach*
and *black*, and to which he justly adds *bleak*. He observes as follows: " It is *remarkable* that *black, bleak,*
and *bleach* are all radically one word."

We now know why two ideas so opposite as *high*
and *low* or *white* and *black* may be sometimes expressed
alike. We see that it arises from *night, darkness, lowness*, and *blackness* being traceable to the moon as their
parent source, and the moon to the sun, to which must
be traced the names of such ideas as are expressed by
the words *day, light, height*, and *white*. These two
divisions of human speech (the first and the third) are
therefore as one and the same, though signifying opposite ideas. And the second division may be joined with
them ; for the *hand* (its primary source) means the *maker*,
and the Maker or Creator was a well-known name of the
sun. The three divisions of human speech do thus
blend and fall into one another, and become, as it were,
only one. Nor could it be otherwise, since all words
have grown out of a single sign, the hieroglyphic O,
first name of the sun.

Another plain instance of the same word expressing
two opposite ideas, is afforded by the Hebrew word אור
aŭr, of which the usual meaning is *light;* but it is also
sometimes used to mean *night*. Thus I find in Sander
and Trenel's *Dictionnaire Hébreu-Français* the following (p. 14): " Dans le Talmud אור *aur* signifie quelquefois *nuit*."

CHAPTER VIII.

MAN'S FIRST LANGUAGE OF ARTICULATE SOUNDS.

AND this O was not only man's first word, but even his first language, for a single word may, by various modulations of the voice, express many different ideas. Thus in Annamitic, according to M. Max Müller, the word *ba* "when pronounced with the grave accent, means a lady, an ancestor; pronounced with the sharp accent, it means the favourite of a prince; pronounced with the semi-grave accent, it means what has been thrown away; pronounced with the grave circumflex, it means what has been left of a fruit after it has been squeezed out; pronounced with no accent, it means three; pronounced with the ascending or interrogative accent, it means a box on the ear. Thus—

Ba, bà, bâ, bá

is said to mean, if properly pronounced, Three ladies gave a box on the ear to the favourite of the prince[6]."

I learn from the same authority, that in Cochin-China, where all words are monosyllabic, "people distinguish their significations only by means of different accents in pronouncing them;" and that, according to Léon de Rosny, "the same syllable—for instance *dai*—signifies twenty-three entirely different things, according to the difference of accent[7]."

It must have been in this way, and while language

---

[6] Lectures on the Science of Language, 2nd Series, p. 30.
[7] Ibid. p. 29.

c

was yet in its most infant state, and man stood in need of very few words, that the O served, by being differently pronounced, as his only language; but when his vocabularly increased, and he began to express the different meanings of his O not only vocally but graphically, he must have soon made for himself an alphabet, and hence a comparatively copious language.

CHAPTER IX.

PROOFS FROM THE ADMISSIONS OF THE LEARNED, THAT ALL WORDS MUST HAVE EMANATED FROM THE NAME FIRST GIVEN TO THE SUN, THEN WORSHIPPED AS GOD, HENCE THE BELIEF IN VERY ANCIENT TIMES THAT LANGUAGE HAD A DIVINE ORIGIN—THE WORD.

THE reader is doubtless aware that all the names of the heathen deities were in the beginning appellatives, or, as they are also called, common names, just as the now proper names, Mr. Taylor, Mr. Carpenter, and Mr. Mason must have previously been. Now as this cannot be doubted, nor is it denied by any one, it follows from the admissions of the learned (unwittingly made), that, as the names of all the gods and goddesses of antiquity served at one time or other to designate the sun, even without regard to sex, so must all other words have done, as it cannot be conceived that such multitudes of words could have ever had this single meaning without all other words having had it also—that is, when primarily considered.

Here is what Sir William Jones—a man profoundly acquainted with as many as twenty languages, and beyond all doubt the most learned Oriental scholar England has to boast of—says on this subject: " We must not be surprised at finding, on a close examination, that the characters of *all* the pagan deities, male and female, melt into each other, and at last into one or two ; for it seems a well-founded opinion that the whole crowd of gods and goddesses, in ancient Rome and modern Váránes, mean only the powers of nature, and principally those of the *sun*, expressed in a variety of ways and by a multitude of fanciful names[8]."

I beg to refer the reader to the work from which the above extract is taken, for other opinions to the same effect, confirmed by those of the learned of ancient times. Thus, it is shown that Jupiter was both male and female, not only the father but also the mother of the gods. And " Apulcius makes the mother of the gods of the masculine gender, and represents her describing herself as called Minerva at Athens, Venus at Cyprus, Diana at Crete, Proserpine in Sicily, Ceres at Eleusis : in other places, Juno, Bellona, Hecate, Isis, &c.; and if any doubt could remain, the philosopher Porphyry, than whom probably no one was better skilled in these matters, removes it by acknowledging that Vesta, Thea, Ceres, Themis, Priapus, Proserpine, Bacchus, Attis, Adonis, Silenus, and the satyrs were all the same[9]."

And according to Hesychius Servius (upon Virgil's Æncid, l. ii. 632), in Cyprus Venus is represented with a beard, and called Aphrodite !

[8] Dissertation on the Gods of Greece and India, quoted in the Anacalypsis, vol. i. p. 50.
[9] Ibid. p. 49.

And, according to Bryant, Metis is said to be, like the others, of two genders, and to be also the sun [1]!

In the Anacalypsis (vol. i. p. 44) I find also the following : "After a life of the most painful and laborious research, Mr. Bryant's opinion is, that all the various religions terminated in the worship of the sun. He commences his work by showing, from a great variety of etymological proofs, that all the names of the deities were derived or compounded from some word which originally meant the sun. Notwithstanding the ridicule which has been thrown upon etymological inquiries, in consequence of the want of fixed rules, or of the absurd length to which some persons have carried them, yet I am quite certain it must, in a great measure, be from etymology at last that we must recover the lost learning of antiquity."

" Macrobius [2] says that in Thrace they worship the sun or Solis Liber, calling him Sebadius; and from the Orphic poetry we learn that all the gods were one :—

εἰς Ζεύς, εἰς 'Αΐδης, εἰς "Ηλιος, εἰς Διόνυσος,
εἰς Θεός, ἐν πάντεσσι [3].

Nonnus also states, that all the different gods, whatever might be their names, Hercules, Ammon, Apollo, or Mithra, centred in the sun.

Mr. Selden says, " Whether they be called Osiris, or Orphis, or Nilus, or Siris, or by any other name, they all centre in the sun, the most ancient deity of the nations."

While language was yet in a very infant state, no word being composed of more than one syllable, just as it is at present in China, it could not be difficult to

---

[1] Bryant, vol. i. p. 204. Ed. 4to.   [2] Sat. l. i. 18.
[3] Orphic Fragm. IV. p. 36. Gesner. Ed.

perceive that all names, when traced up to their original source, did not differ from that of the sun, whence the belief that he (then adored as the universal god) and all the other divinities were but one and the same character.

This too accounts for the origin of myths, for the worship not only of human beings as gods, but even of animals and inanimate things. But when a name was first given to a person, or an object, it could not then lead to a belief so erroneous as to induce men to pay divine honours to either the one or the other; for the real signification of such a name must have then been well known, as it was of course ever given on account of some quality found peculiar to the person or object it served to designate. But when with time such a name underwent so considerable a change that no one could tell what it first meant, and that it was perceived to be, however, one of the countless names of the sun, or to be easily traced to this source; then must superstition have begun respecting whatever such a name designated, whether man, animal, or object. Hence the vast number of divinities with some people, as with the Egyptians for instance, who are reported to have had many thousands of them, perhaps nearly as many as they had words in their language.

Need we now wonder at language having been ever regarded as something very sacred, as having had, in short, a divine origin?

There is a passage in the Anacalypsis (vol. ii. p. 6) taken from Georgius, according to which letters and superstition are in Thibet so closely allied as to be found inseparable, so that neither can be examined or inquired into without bringing in the other. As the rays of light flow from the nature of the sun, even so do the natives of Thibet believe that letters have emanated from the Deity. And, adds Georgius, the Indians entertain a belief somewhat similar about the Veda of Brama and the book of Atzala Isuren. Respecting the letters of their alphabet, the Thibetans revere them as wonderful gifts sent down from heaven[4]. And referring to this passage Higgins observes: " The truth of the observation respecting the close connexion between letters and superstition cannot be denied; and thus this beautiful invention, which ought to have been the greatest blessing to mankind, has been till lately its greatest curse. But if at first it forged the chain, it will break it at last."

There is something like inspiration in what Higgins here says about letters breaking at last the chain of superstition; and of this he would have had still less doubt had he known any thing of their real origin; but he makes a great mistake when he calls letters a *beautiful invention.* To consider them as an invention, would be, as I have already said, and as M. Max Müller has also since repeated, " to place a human being almost on a level with God Himself, to raise his wisdom to an eminence immensely beyond its reach[5]."

The Chinese also hold letters in religious veneration, and when they have done with any writing, burn it with peculiar ceremony[6].

---

[4] " Ex his, quæ mecum inter viam communicarunt laudati PP. Cappucini e Tibetanis Missionibus reduces, protinus intellexi tam arcto et inseparabili vinculo apud eas gentes duo hæc, litteras et superstitionem, inter se cohærescere, ut alterum sine altero nec pertractari, nec cogitari queat. Ut enim video, quem admodum defluunt radii a natura solis, sic litteras ab ipsa Dei substantia defluxisse concipiunt. Simile quiddam de Vedam Bramhæ, deque Atzalla Isureni libro, opinantur Indi. Aliud quid longe majus atque præstantius de litterarum suarum natura, ac dignitate Tibetani opinantur. Istas uti prodigiosa quædam munera e cœlo demissa venerantur."—Georg. Alph. Tib. Præf. pp. ix, &c.

[5] See M. Max Müller's Lectures, vol. i. p. 3.

[6] Alvarez, Hist. China, p. 34.

It is not now to be wondered at that the ancients adored a being called the Word. "In the Zendavesta," says Bishop Marsh in his Michaelis, " we meet with a being called ' *the Word,*' who was not only prior in existence, but gave birth to Ormuzd, the creator of good; and to Ahriman, the creator of evil. It is true that the work which we have at present under the title of Zendavesta, is not the ancient and genuine Zendavesta; yet it certainly contains many ancient and genuine Zoroastrian doctrines. It is said, likewise, that the Indian philosophers have their Λόγος, which, according to their doctrines, is the same as the Μονογενής."

That is to say, their Λόγος, or Word, is taken in the sense of the *Only Begotten* of St. John. But whence did St. John derive his Λόγος? I must not say whence, since if I did, every narrow-minded religionist might accuse me of blasphemy, and so do every thing to prevent my discovery being made known; and such too would be the pitiful plea of all such philologists as cannot allow any one to be equal to or superior to themselves, for never bringing it into notice. I must not therefore dare to offer an opinion as to whence St. John derived his knowledge of the WORD; but I cannot surely be censured if I quote what a very learned and pious Christian Bishop says on the subject: " Since St. John," observes Bishop Marsh in his Michaelis, " has adopted several other terms which were used by the Gnostics, we must conclude that he derived also the term Λόγος from the same source. If it be further asked whence did the Gnostics derive this use of the expression ' WORD '? I answer, that they derived it most probably from the Oriental or Zoroastrian philosophy, from which was borrowed a considerable part of the Manichean doctrines."

To a certainty, if Bishop Marsh had lived in the time of Calvin, and if this holy Christian got him within his power, he would have had him roasted alive like Servetus on a slow fire; and which merciful sentence would have been highly approved of by all his followers, nor last nor least among these would be the gentle Melanchthon. To trace the Evangelist's doctrine of the WORD to an idolatrous source, would have been judged as anti-christian as any thing the unfortunate Servetus wrote about the Trinity.

Now this undoubted fact, that in ancient times the WORD was revered as a Divine Being, must confirm still more and more the bold assertion that language grew, as I have shown, out of the name of the sun; this object having from the beginning been adored as God. Hence it cannot, according to Bishop Marsh, be wrong to assign to this source the opening of the Gospel of St. John: "In the beginning was the Word, and the Word was with God, and God was the Word." A religious heathen could not receive these words but as literally true, they being in perfect accordance with his own belief.

And has not a Grecian philosopher cried out, on reading this opening of John's Gospel: "By Jove, this barbarian is one of ourselves;" or, "This barbarian believes as we do." I quote from memory; but as the passage is well known, the reader will admit, if he should recollect it, that I do not mistake as to the sense, though I may do so as to the exact words.

CHAPTER X.

THE ALPHABET.

Origin of the signs a, a, and A.

How does it happen that the O is not a very prominent character in many alphabets? The cause of it is this: the O first meant the sun, but from the sun appearing always alone, it was made to signify *one;* and in order to know when it had the latter meaning, the figure 1, which was then, as at present, represented by a finger, was put by the side of the O thus, O1; and from each of these signs having precisely the same meaning—that of *one*—an alphabet might have been made from either of them, or from both united. And this has really happened, as the following will serve to show: " It has been the opinion of some of the most enlightened writers on the languages of the East, that the Pali, or sacred language of the priests of Boodh, is nearly allied to the Shanscrit of the Brahmins. The character in common use throughout Ava and Pegu is a round Nagari derived from the square Pali or religious text. It is formed of circles and segments of circles, variously disposed and combined, whilst the Pali, which is solely applied to purposes of religion, is a square letter, chiefly consisting of right angles[7]."

The round Nagari here referred to, and which is composed of circles and segments of circles, must, in the beginning, have been the O; and as to the Pali, which is

---

[7] Rees's Cyclopædia, art. Birman.

a square letter, chiefly consisting of right angles, it was, no doubt, made out of the hieroglyph I, which represented a finger, and like the O, meant also one, even as it does still. But the O and the I (the latter being merely explanatory of the former) could not have gone for ever side by side without having, with some people, coalesced, and made a single sign, such as *a*, in which it is easy to perceive both an O and an I. And in this sign a, it is also easy to perceive an O and an I when we look closely at any large form of it. And what have we in this sign A? An I and an I joined by a hyphen; that is to say, it is composed of two signs, each meaning *one*, which is also the meaning of the two signs composing *a* and a. From this it would appear that the sign A is less ancient than the sign *a*, and that because the parts composing *a* (that is, O and I) have each the meaning of *one*, A does, for this reason, mean double one, the hyphen by which the one is joined to the other having here no more value than the hyphen of any compound word; such, for instance, as in ‘ink-stand.”

We have thus seen that an alphabet has been made from the O, since such an alphabet is still extant; and that an alphabet belonging to the same language has been made from the I, which, as an explanatory sign, was first placed by the side of the O, showing that the latter meant then one, and not the sun.

Now, as this language, with its two alphabets, is, in the opinion of some of the most enlightened writers on the languages of the East, nearly allied to the Sanskrit, it follows that the alphabet of the latter may have first been composed of an O only, and at a later period, of an O and an I, each standing apart from the other, but not meaning more than a single sign ; this arising from the I being merely explanatory of the O. Now, if we suppose the Greek alphabet to be derived from that of the Sanskrit, the derivation must have taken place when the alphabet of the latter was in a rather primitive state. As we now see it, its characters are inconceivably artificial. They have all the appearance of having been formed by a body of learned pedants, such men being never satisfied with whatever appears plain and natural. Could any two alphabetical signs be more plain and significant than O and I? But how are these signs represented in the Sanskrit alphabet? The O is made thus ओ and the I thus ई. Such characters are, when compared with O and I, the very types of pedantry ; and all the other signs of this ugly alphabet are equally so.

In the passage quoted above from Rees's Cyclopædia, we are told that the round Nagari is derived from the square Pali ; but it cannot have been so, for the former is the O, and the latter has been formed from the I, which cannot have been in use as an articulate sound until some time after the O, which must have been man's first word. Here we see the cleverness of the priests of Buddha ; they have succeeded in making not merely the vulgar, but, as we see from the passage just referred to, the learned also, believe that *their* alphabet is the original of the one made from the O.

From the O and the I having so often and so long stood side by side, it was thought, after a time, that they should never be separated. It was then, no doubt, forgotten why the I was first placed by the side of the O. No one, it would seem, any longer remembered that the I was so placed for the sole purpose of show-ing that the O then meant one, and not the sun. Hence, when either of these signs stood alone, the other was thought to be understood. This accounts for the dot over the I; it represents the O supposed to have been then left out. There was also anciently a dot in the centre of the ⊙, as if to signify the absence of the I. But this dot over the I has not remained in Greek, though it is still used in Latin and its dialects.

In some words the O and I appear to have never coalesced and made *a*, and this will account for one of these signs having been often dropped. Thus, in some dialect of the Latin tongue, the i of the *dig* of *digitus* must have lost its O, for it is preserved in the French *doigt;* from which we may conclude that the latter was not derived from the *digit* of *digitus*, but from such a form as *doigit.* If the O and i of this word became *a*, we should now, instead of *doigt*, have *dagt* or *dagit.* This has happened in Greek; for the *dak* of *daktulos* (a finger) must have once been *doik;* that is, before the two signs *o* and *i* had fallen together and made *a*.

This knowledge of the formation of the first alphabetical sign may often lead not only to the discovery of the primitive forms of words, but to their primitive meanings also. Let us take, as a single instance, the Latin word *fiber*, of which there are several very corrupt forms in different languages, but which could have never been, had not its primitive form been lost sight of, and along with it its primitive signification also. But the explanation just given of the original form of *a* may now enable us to discover both. In English *fiber* is written *beaver*, in French *bièvre*, in Italian *bevero*, in Spanish *biverio*, and in Swedish *behwer*, all of which appear to have grown out of *fiber;* and as this form does not tell us why this animal has been so named, and as the forms which have deviated from it are, in this respect, equally meaningless, we know no more of the primary signification of *fiber* than if it were a word belonging to the language of some other world than our own. And M. Littré's fine dictionary, which is allowed to be the best authority extant, adds nothing whatever to the above information, as the following serves to show : "Anc. Wallon, *buivre ;* du Celtique : Cornwall, *befer ;* ou de l'Allemand *biber.* Comparez le Latin *fiber*, castor. On a rapproché le Sanscrit *babhru*, rat, ichneumon." This is all M. Littré says of *fiber*, so that we are not now a whit more enlightened as to the primitive meaning of this word than we were before. But now, the mere schoolboy who has attended to the explanation just given of the origin of *a*, may see at a glance that the i of *fiber* has, as its dot indicates, O understood, and that this word is therefore for *foiber*, and consequently, as O and i make *a*, for *faber*; and as this word means a workman, and a mason as much as it does a carpenter, and as the animal in question is well known for the wonderful talent it displays in the building of its habitation, we may be sure that its name is but another word for mason. Hence Noel, as the schoolboy will find on consulting his dictionary for the meaning of *faber*, gives the following explanation of *faber œdium*, namely, *maître maçon*, that is, *master mason*. And such is the animal which is designated by the word *fiber*; and this is confirmed by its other name, that of *castor*, of which the root *cas* is also the root of *casa*, a house. And as *maçon* and *maison* are in French radically the same, so are *castor* and *casa*. If we were, therefore, to invent a word literally expressive of *beaver* or *fiber*, we should say that it ought to be called *the houser*; that is, the house-maker.

Such an etymology as this can be always relied upon, because the sense obtained will apply, the beaver being remarkable for his skill as a builder. But however close the resemblance may be in form of any two words, the etymology should be regarded as worthless, unless the agreement between them in sense be equally striking. Let it not, therefore, be said that according to my principles a word can be made to have whatever meaning the etymologist may choose to give it, for it is not so. Take as an instance, the words *wick* and *wicked.* In form they are radically the same. This may be also said of *mèche* and *méchant* in French; but as there is no relationship whatever between the wick of a candle and wickedness, we cannot suppose that either idea was named after the other. The radical identity in form of two such words in two different languages is, however, startling; but of which we shall see the cause farther on.

CHAPTER XI.

HOW AN ENTIRE ALPHABET HAS BEEN MADE OUT OF O AND I COMBINED.

LET us now show how an alphabet has been formed from O and I combined, and not from each of these signs taken separately, as the two alphabets belonging to the language spoken in the Birman Empire, throughout Ava and Pegu, have been made. We have already seen how the two parts composing *a* have each the meaning of one, though both combined mean no more, this arising from the I being merely explanatory of the O, which, without this explanation, must, in the beginning, have always named the sun. When we do therefore meet with O in old English used in the tense of *one*, we should regard its explanatory sign, the I, as having been dropped, so that O, though alone, is to be considered as equal to OI, and consequently to *a*, *a*, or A. The English reader will find instances of O meaning *one*, in Halliwell's valuable edition of the " Voiage and Travaile of Sir John Maundevile, Kt.," and also in Wycliffe's translation of the Bible.

The following passages from the first of these two works may be here quoted.

" And *o* partie of the crowne of oure Lord, wherewith he was crowned, and *on* of the nayles, the spire heed, and many other relikes ben in France, in the kinges chapelle " (p. 12).

" But men han departed hem in two parties : of the whiche, *o* part is at Parys, and the other part is at Constantinoble " (p. 13).

" And thei scyn that there scholde be but *o* masse seyd at *on* awtier, upon *o* day " (p. 19).

In two of these passages (the first and the third) *on* is used for O, because it precedes words beginning with a vowel. There is, therefore, the same difference between *o* and *on* that exists between the two forms of the indefinite article (*a* and *an*) in English. But I should here state one of my rules, which, as the reader will see, I shall often have occasion to apply ; it is the following : Every vowel may take a nasal sound ; that is, be followed by *m* or *n*. Or should the sense, in the analyzing of words, require it, the nasal sound of a vowel may be dropped ; that is, lose its *m* or *n*. There is therefore no difference between *o* and *on*. And as O means both the

sun and *one,* even so does *on.* If we except the eupho-
nical tendency which prevails for making *o* and *a* become
on and *an* before words beginning with a vowel, the
sole cause of giving to the latter signs a nasal sound is,
that some persons are accustomed to pronounce them
through the nose, whilst others are not.   Hence, as there
is no difference in meaning between such a word as
educatio in Latin, and *education* in French and English,
neither is there any difference in meaning between *O* and
on.   And that *on* is a well-known name of the sun, the
following will serve to show : " Various derivations are
given of the word on, but they are all unsatisfactory.
It is written in the Old Testament in two ways, אוּן
aun and אן *an.*   It is usually rendered in English by
the word *on.*   This word is supposed to mean the sun,
and the Greeks translated it by the word ἥλιος, or sol [8]."
The circumstance of on having been so translated by the
Greeks, must remove all doubt as to its real meaning.
And from the identity of *o* and *on,* we thus obtain the
most undoubted proof that the O must have been also a
name of the sun, there being no more difference in meaning between *o* and *on* than there is, as just stated, between *educatio* and *education.*   The following, from the
authority quoted above, affords of this fact another
very plain proof : " The O in Syriac or Pushto
(which we have found is the same as Tamul) was the
emphatic article THE [9]."   This is, I say, a very plain
proof that the O means both one and the sun, for
every article, whether definite or indefinite—no matter
to what language it may belong—means *one.*   And as
it is only conventionally that such articles differ in
meaning, it follows that if the indefinite article means

one—and every body is aware that it does—such, too, must be the meaning of the one called the definite. In Cornish, a very ancient British dialect, the word *an* stood for *the* [1]. But I shall be told that if O meant *one,* and if it was also the definite article in any language whatever, it follows that I, which at present means *one,* may have been also, in some language or other, the definite article, since, according to what has been thus far shown, it cannot differ in meaning from O. And that I has been so used I learn from the respectable authority last quoted, who says, "I was the ancient emphatic article of the Saxons [2]."

It is thus made self-evident that O and I have each the meaning of *one;* and as this is allowed to be the meaning of the indefinite article, it is equally evident that the sole difference in use, not in meaning, between every two such words is merely conventional.

This knowledge enables us to account for the definite article being so often a name of God. The author of the Anacalypsis alludes to this fact as something *very remarkable,* but he could not possibly tell how this happened; for this it was necessary to know that the O was the first name of the sun, and consequently of the supposed creator of the world, this grand object having been anciently revered as such; and that, from its always appearing *alone* in the heavens, it served as a name for *one,* which is also the meaning of the definite or emphatic article, as we have just shown. But Higgins might state more than he has done respecting the identity of this name and that of God; he only observes as follows: "It is *very remarkable* that the emphatic article should so often be the name of God:—Arabic, Al; Coptic, Pi;

---

[1] The Gaelic of *the* is also *an*.   [2] Anacalypsis, vol. ii. p. 199.

Hebrew, ה (*e*), and I, and II[3]. " He might have also observed that the radical part of the Greek *The*os (*the*) and the *de* of the Latin Deus are also two emphatic articles, the former being our *the* and the latter, which cannot differ from *the* any more than *burthen* can from *burden*, being the same word in Dutch. Parkhurst gives also to *al*, as a Hebrew word, the meaning of *the*. And the following, which Higgins quotes from Parkhurst, is very important, inasmuch as it serves to confirm all I have thus far said of the sun and the article :—"AL or EL was the very name the heathens gave to their God Sol, their lord or ruler of the hosts of heaven[4]."

To the above I beg to add the following from the same authority :—"Parkhurst says, that the word Al means God, the Heavens, Leaders, Assistance, Defence, and Interposition, &c. ;" and according to a quotation given from Whiter, " Al, Al, means Deus optimus maximus[5]."

I have thus shown how it happens that the same word means God, the sun, one, and the ; and that this know-ledge has been obtained from having discovered the origin of human speech, is now made self-evident.

But how can such a word as the English article *the* have grown out of O ? In order to see how this has happened, it will, I perceive, be here necessary to state one of the rules that have grown out of my discovery of the origin of human speech, namely, that initial vowels may be aspirated; that is, have an *h* pre-fixed to them. Hence the exclamation O ! has become ho ! But when O served, not as an interjection, but as an article, it meant *one ;* and such must have been the sense in which it was taken when it signified *the* in Syriac, as

[3] Anacalypsis, vol. ii. p. 200.   [4] Ibid. vol. i. p. 67.
[5] Ibid. vol. i. p. 65.

we have just seen. But even in this language, O must have been often aspirated, just as in English many persons at the present hour pronounce *ho* instead of O, so great is the tendency to aspirate initial vowels. Hence it is that the definite article in Greek is ho (ὁ), that is, O asperated. But there must have been a time when this O had not the sign which represents *h* put over it, all persons not being equally addicted to aspirate initial vowels, though many are accustomed to do so. Now, what is the difference in meaning between ho (ὁ) and its feminine, *hē* (ἡ)? There is no difference whatever in meaning; their difference in gender is but conventional. Hence ho (ὁ) might as well have been hē (ἡ), or ἡ might as well have been ὁ.

How can we now prove ho and hē (ὁ and ἡ) to be equal to *the?* By showing what is well known, namely, that the sign which Greek scholars call the *spiritus asper*, or rough breathing, and which is nothing more than the sign *h*, is sometimes represented by *th*, that is, by this sign, θ. Thus, Donnegan, under Theta, has the following :—" θ seems to have sometimes supplied the place of the spiritus asper, the rough breathing, as θαμὰ instead of ἁμὰ, and θάλασσα, formed from ἅλς." According to this view, the masculine and feminine definite article ὁ and ἡ (ho and hē) is equal to *tho* and *thē;* and here the O and *ē* can no more differ from each other than they do in *older* and *elder*, or than they do in *show* and *shew;* by which it is shown that both ὁ and ἡ are but other forms of *the.* The Greek definite article might have therefore been θη instead of ὁ. And as ὁ cannot differ from O, and as O was the first name of the sun, and as the sun was then revered as the supreme divinity, it follows that *the* might have served as a name for the sun, and consequently for God. And this has happened, for θέος must have first been ος θε, and then have by transposition become θέος; just as the two Italian words *il sole* (the sun) have in French become *soleil;* by which we see that the ος of θέος must, like the *il* of *soleil,* have once been an article.

These latter etymologies confirm what we have already shown, namely, that the word signifying the sun meant *one*—hence *sol* and *solus*—and that *one* has been also, in all languages, the meaning of the definite article *the,* which accounts for this word being also either exactly or radically the same as the name of God, as we shall see more fully in the proper place [6].

There is another very plain proof that ό and ή cannot differ from *the,* and which is this : the spiritus asper, or *h,* is often represented by other signs, as by *s* for instance, besides θ; witness έπτά (seven) becoming *septem* in Latin, and ύδωρ (water) being the original of *Sudor,* sweat. Hence ό and ή are equal to *so* and *se;* and though the definite article is, as in English, represented in Saxon by *the,* it is represented by *se* also; and this proves the equality of two such words as ή and *the,* and consequently of ό, which does not differ from ή but conventionally, since both words have each the meaning of *one.*

But has not *se* in Saxon the meaning of *sea* also? It has, with several other meanings besides; and for all of which the reader will be well able to account farther on, though their origin has been hitherto unknown. As to the neuter of ό and ή, that is τό, it is equal to σο, this other

---

[6] Cicero does therefore mistake, when he derives sol from solus (De Natura Deorum, lib. ii.); for sol is the original of solus, and not its derivative.

form of ό; and as S and t are in Greek as the same sign—witness σύ and τύ, γλῶσσα and γλῶττα—it follows that the neuter το is but another form of the masculine σο, which, from the spiritus asper being so often replaced by S, must, in one or more of the Greek dialects long since forgotten, have been used for ό.

The origin of *a* and *an* have not perhaps been made sufficiently evident. Let us therefore notice them again. As O has i understood, and as O and i when they coalesce make *a*, it follows, since O means *one*, that such too is the meaning of *a*. And as O when used as an article before words beginning with a vowel, as shown above, became for the sake of euphony *on ;* and as the O of this word has, as well as the O of *a*, its i understood; and as *on* is therefore equal to Oin, it follows, that by the joining of its *o* and *i* (making *a*) it is the same as *an*. *O* and *on* must have therefore been the earliest forms of *a* and *an*. It has, however, been supposed, since the corresponding words of several other languages end with *n*, that *an* is the original of *a*. But this happens to be a mistake.

But here the reader may beg me to observe that there is a wide difference in form between such names of the Deity or the sun as Al and Pi, for instance, and their assumed original, the O. This is very true; but it is not in this place, but farther on, so considerable a difference in form can be accounted for. The reader must be first brought acquainted with a few more of the rules that have grown out of our discovery, and especially with the origin of the roots of language.

CHAPTER XII.

THE REMAINING VOWELS.

HAVING now sufficiently accounted for a, i, and O, we may notice the remaining vowels, and then the consonants. If it be true that all the signs of an alphabet have grown out of man's first articulate sound (the O), we should regard the *e* of the Latin word *tres* as an O ; and as O was so often attended by I, as an explanatory sign, that when absent it was thought to be understood, and that it should, for this reason, be supplied, it follows that *tres* cannot differ from *treis*, and which is confirmed by this form being the Greek of *tres*. But as *e* is less ancient than O (man's first word), *tres* must have once been *tros*, which, when the i understood is supplied, will become *trois*. If this word, which is the French of *tres*, be derived from the Latin, the derivation cannot have taken place from the Latin now extant, but from one of its ancient dialects, long since lost and forgotten. If the O and the i of *trois* had coalesced, the French of *three* would not now be *trois*, but *tras*. In this form, e, of the vowel we are accounting for, it is not difficult to perceive a modification of the O, and which is also apparent in its Greek representative ε. As to the capital E, it is nothing more than the half of the Greek *eta*, which is made thus, H. And as H is equal to an I and an I joined by a hyphen, we see that its parts may be said to mean double one, which is also the meaning of the parts comprising *a*, a, and A. In the small form of eta, which is made thus, η, it is also easy to perceive a double one.

The next vowel to be accounted for is U, which has been also made thus, V, though this sign is now a consonant. But in each of its forms it is easy to perceive double I, especially in V. U is therefore equal to the parts composing *a*, that is, to O and I. Hence, in some dialect of the Latin tongue, such words as *crux* and *nux* must have once been written *croix* and *noix*, as they are at present in French. And that U is, like Oi, equal to *a*, we see by comparing *fu*rther and *fa*rther, ex*u*lt and ex*a*lt, and the German *mutter* with its Latin equivalent, *mater;* and also the German *und* with its English form, *and*.

As W and Y are vowels at the end of words and syllables, they should be also noticed. In W, as its English name implies, we have a U or V doubled, so that it is but a repetition of the fifth vowel, already accounted for. As to Y, it is, as every one knows, equal to the Greek ypsilon, that is, to *u;* and hence it is that *syllaba* in Latin, or *syllable* in English, is sullabē in Greek, and of which there are many other instances. From y being thus the same as U, it must, like this sign, ·be equal to Oi. This will account for U in Greek being sometimes changed by the Æolians, as Donnegan observes, for *oi*. For the same reason y in English becomes sometimes Oi in French, this arising from y being the same as U; witness *my*self and *thy*self, in which y is the Oi of *moi*-même and *toi*-même. And that the O and *i* of *moi* and *toi* are equal to *a*, we see on allowing them to meet, as *moi* and *toi* will then become *ma* and *ta*, which shows how they have been converted into posses-

sives, from having first been datives. In *me* and *te* we
have still the same words; for as their C is for O, and
as O has i understood, *me* and *te* are precisely equal to
moi and *toi*. Moi-même and toi-même might have therefore been me-même and te-même; and, for the same
reason, so might *myself* and *thyself* have been *meself* and
theeself. But if *moi* and *toi* be equal to *ma* and *ta*, how
are we to account for their masculine forms, *mon* and *ton* ?
By observing that from moi and toi the i was dropped,
and that then the O took the nasal sound, as every
vowel may or may not do.

M. Littré in his etymology of *me*, says that it is the
same as *moi;* and this is very true. But he cannot have
known that if these two words are identical, it arises
from *me* being for mo, and consequently for *moi*, the *i*
being understood with O. And in his etymology of *moi*,
the same high authority says, "La forme ancienne est *mei,*
mi, à côté de *moi*; ce qui exclut l'accusatif Latin *me*."
This cannot be; for as O is more ancient than *e*, so is
moi more ancient than *mei*, from which *mi* does not
differ but from its *e* having been dropped. The Latin
me is still the same word, but less ancient than *moi*,
which must have belonged to some Latin dialect or
patois, of which perhaps no trace now remains beyond
some words in French and other modern idioms. And
thus it must often happen, that words supposed to be
corrupt forms of their parallels in Latin, are, on the
contrary, their originals, having come down to us, not
from this language as it is at present, but as it may have
once been. For the reason that O—man's first word—
must be older than *e*, it follows that the Latin words
me, te, and *se* must be less primitive than *moi, toi,* and
soi. But we are not hence to suppose that French is

older than Latin, but that it is so in many of its words[7].

We see by this short notice of the vowels, that it is not a difference in either sound or form can prove that there are different letters. Thus, as an instance, if I write *show* with an *o* or with an *e* (*shew*) the meaning will be the same. And if there were to be a difference in meaning between two such words, it would be only conventional. Hence it is that letters do constantly interchange, which could not be if a difference in either sound or form constituted different letters. In these three signs, A, *a*, a, we have not three different letters, but the same letter shaped differently; and if it had fifty other shapes, it would be still the same letter. And though this first alphabetical sign is allowed to have four very different sounds, as heard in the words *a*le, *a*ll, c*a*t, and b*a*r, it is never on this account regarded as four different letters, but still as the same letter pronounced thus differently; and if it were to be pronounced in as many other ways, it would be still no more than the same single sign. But if letters differed as much in power from one another as do the ten numeral signs, 1, 2, 3, 4, 5, 6, 7, 8, 9, 0, then indeed it might well be said that there are some twenty-four or twenty-six letters in an alphabet, each, like the ten numerals, with a value peculiar to itself; but for the

---

[7] It may be thought that *moy* and *toy* are, because no longer in use, more ancient than *moi* and *toi*; but it is a mistake to think so. It must have been from the sounds of i and y being similar, that y was formerly used for i, even as it is still. Thus many forms of words are supposed to be old, whilst they are, when compared with those which replace them, really modern. And as it is with words, even so is it with our present fashions. The grand lady of our day prides herself upon wearing what she imagines had never been thought of before; but her grandmother will undeceive her by assuring her that when she was a girl her bonnet or her gown was made in precisely the same way.

reason that they replace one another, this cannot be said. It were, therefore, as difficult to prove that there are even so few as two different letters in an alphabet, as to find the quadrature of the circle or perpetual motion.

Before we now proceed to account for those signs called consonants, it may be necessary to draw the reader's attention to a very important fact. He has seen how each vowel is equal to not only every other vowel, but even to such combinations as *oi, io, ei,* or *ie.* Thus he has seen how the Latin of three, that is, tres (and which is but a different form of tros), is not only equal to *treis* (its equivalent in Greek) but to *trois* in French. And what does this serve to show? It serves to show that if the single sign O has been the first name ever given to the sun, this object may afterwards— that is, when the O took its explanatory I—have been named *oi, io, ei,* or *ie.* And if I, who make this statement, can find no instance in proof of its reality, there are, most likely, many others who can. But I have an instance. Thus Parkhurst, referring to *ie* (and which is the same as IO), says: " יה ie is several times joined with the name יהוה *ieve,* so we may be sure that it is not, as some have supposed, a mere abbreviation of that word. See Isaiah xii. 2; xxvi. 4. Our blessed Lord solemnly claims to Himself what is intended in this divine name יה *ie,* John viii. 58: *Before Abraham was, ΕΓΩ ΕΙΜΙ, I AM* (comp. vv. 24, 28). And the Jews appear to have well understood Him, *for then took they up stones to cast at Him.* From this divine name יה ie, the ancient Greeks had their *Ιη, Ιη,* in their invocations of the gods, particularly of Apollo *i.e.* The Light. And hence ‪אי‬ (written after the oriental manner, from right to left), afterwards EI, was inscribed over the great door of the Temple of Apollo at Delphi [8]."

The above passage serves to show that IE (which is the same as IO) and EI (which is the same as OI) served not only as a name of the true God, but of Apollo or the sun also; and so must the O itself have done before the I had been yet joined with it. But Parkhurst mistakes when he allows us to understand that it was from IE (the name of the true God) the Greeks took their name of the sun; for the first object of worship over the world was that great orb which appeared to animate all nature.

Before attempting to account for the different forms of the consonants, we should not forget that there must have been a time when they were all represented by "circles and segments of circles variously disposed and combined," as they are at present in the alphabet of the language spoken in the Birman Empire, "throughout Ava and Pegu." Hence, such letters as *b*, *c*, *d*, &c., which are now so very different from the O, were first, like all the other consonants, represented by modifications of this sign. But when the O and its explanatory sign (the I) coalesced, and were regarded as the O had been before—that is, as a single sign, though composed of two—then letters took such forms as they have at present in the languages of Europe, having been all made to represent the single compound sign *a*, or one of its two parts, the other, when not expressed, being then understood.

---

[8] Lexicon, p. 128, ed. 1778.

CHAPTER XIII.

THE CONSONANTS.

B. THE account to be given of this sign may be long; for, as it constitutes the principal part of the auxiliary verb to *be*, it will necessarily suggest several observations, and probably some new etymologies relating to this important word; and as nothing deserving of particular notice during such an inquiry should be lightly treated, digressions of some length, before our noticing in regular order the other consonants, appear inevitable.

As the first form of A, *a*, or ᗩ was O I, as I have shown, so must it have been (the two signs having changed places) the first form of B also, which is composed of an I and an O, the latter being thus modified, Ɛ; that is to say, it is the O divided in two. The parts composing B did, therefore, previously to their having coalesced, stand thus, I Ɛ, apart from each other; and as the I is here but explanatory of the other part (Ɛ), the latter must, by itself, have long served for B.

And for the reason that this earliest form of B is an O divided in two, we should regard it as a vestige of the old alphabet, which must have been composed of circles and segments of circles. Other vestiges of this alphabet may be discovered by giving to this ancient form of B, that is to Ɛ, other positions. When it is, for instance, put thus ᗰ, it is an M; and when put thus ᗯ, it is a W; and when thus Ɛ, it is an E. Even in S, it is easy to perceive the same sign, the upper and the lower part of this letter being each the half of an O.

Let us now take advantage of this knowledge, and see to what it will lead. When we regard this second part of B, that is 3, as but a different form of S, we perceive that B is composed of I and S, so that it is the word IS, which is an inflection of the verb to Be. Let us now observe that from I being supposed ,to have always O understood, the word IS cannot differ from OIS, that is, when the O and I meet and make *a, as,* which is in Sanscrit the verb Be. And as the O of OIS is the same as e, it follows that ois cannot differ from eis, in which, when the i is dropped, we have *es,* and this is the root of the Latin *esse.* In *eis* we see also, since S contains the parts composing the Saxon ᴔ (ᴀ) the ειμ of the Greek ειμι, and also the English word *am,* which represents the ειμ of ειμι, the ει of this word being for *oi,* and *oi* for *a.*

In the two parts composing B (that is, in 3) we have also IƐ, that is, *ie,* which was, according to Parkhurst, a name both of the true God and the sun; and as the latter was adored as the author of existence, this explains why the verb to Be, which implies existence, should have obtained a name not different from that of the sun. And we must not forget that Parkhurst, as shown above, referring to Ie under its Hebrew form יה (*ei*) and its Greek form Iη, expresses himself thus :—" From this divine name יה (*ie*) the ancient Greeks had their Iη, Iη, in their invocations of the gods, especially of Apollo, *i. e. The Light*[9]."

And the light was the sun.

And as Ie is the same as IO, and as the I is here

---

[9] Lexicon, p. 128.

only explanatory of the O, the latter sign should be regarded as the genuine root, and as having long preceded IO or IC as a name of the sun. Hence, under its Hebrew form ה, that is *C*, Parkhurst explains it thus: " Prefixed to a noun, it is emphatical, and may be rendered *The* or *This*. It answers to the Greek ὁ, ἡ, το." And he further adds that it is also, when prefixed to a noun, vocative or pathetic. Thus השמים, *esmim*, that is, *heavens;* and הארץ *earj*, which means *earth*, the ה, *e*, is in both words rendered by O; thus, O heavens! O earth [1]!"

This is worthy of observation, for we see by it that the same word means both *The* and *O*, and that it is the very root of the word which means both the true God and the sun; while it is also the root of היה, *eie*, which is the Hebrew of the verb to Be. The intelligent reader may remind me that the above is still deserving of observation for another reason, namely, it confirms the statement made farther back, that the definite article is in many languages the same as the name of God, and which word was also, as we shall see, a name of the sun.

When we now call to mind that IS and the Sanskrit *as* are one and the same word, we discover, since one of the forms of S, as shown above, is ᴍ (M) that neither IS nor OIS can differ from *am*, which is not only another inflection of the verb Be, but it is this word itself; for the root of *Be* is B, that is I 3, and as 3 when put thus ᴍ, is the Saxon M, it follows that the two signs I 3 are not only equal, as already shown, to IS but also to Iᴍ, that is, IM, and as the I of IM has, as usual, O understood, IM cannot differ from OIM, that is, as the O and I make *a, am*. Hence, as already shown, there can be no dif-

[1] Lexicon, p. 122.

ference, except conventionally, between two such expressions as "if I *am*" and "if I *be*." It is, therefore, only by chance that in English we have *am* instead of *as*, there not being a shade of difference in meaning between these two forms. This view is confirmed by *asmi* in Sanscrit, which those who are learned in this language explain by *I am;* the part *as* being for *am*, and *mi* being for *ma*, and *ma* for I.

When we now make the sign ⌒ take this position 3, we bring it equal to the second part of B, and so perceive that when B is placed thus ⌒, it is an M. Hence, in Greek Μορτος is the same as Βροτος, and in English Brine is the same as Mrine; that is, Marine, radical part of *mariner*, French of to pickle or put in *brine*. In the same way we discover the primary sense of *bride* (hitherto, as well as brine, unknown), and see that it is for Mride, that is *Maride*, which does not differ from married; and the French of bride is *la mariée*, that is, the married one. We now see why *Beugler* is the same as *Meugler*.

That B and W are also often used for each other, is made evident by comparing the names Bill and Will, which are used indifferently for William. Na*b*ob is also written Na*w*ab. And that the *by* of "good *by*" is for *way*, is shown by the locution "by the *by*," since this is as frequently written by the *way;*" the second *by* of these phrases is therefore for *wy*, which, when the vowel understood is supplied, becomes *way*. Hence, when we say "good *by*" to a person, we wish him a *good way*, that is, a good journey; and this too is confirmed by the "bon *voyage*" of the French.

And that in M and W we have the same sign in different positions is shown by such a word as Mind, which has, under this form, no meaning; but when we make M take its form of W, we discover the primary sense of Mind, on perceiving that it is Wind. And this etymology cannot be called in question since the Hebrew רוח *ruh,* the Greek πνευμα, and the Latin spiritus, each of which means mind, are but other words for wind or breath, and of which the learned have been well aware, though never suspecting that *Mind* is the word *Wind* itself. This Etymology is also confirmed by the word Wit; for as every vowel may, as we shall see farther on, either take or lose a nasal sound, it follows that wit is equal to wint, that is, *wind,* t and d being here as the same sign.

Another plain instance of the identity of M and W is afforded by the German word *Mensch* being our word Wench.

When, years ago, I pointed out the identity of M and W, and was ridiculed for my pains, I little thought that the truth of my discovery could be made evident by the Sanskrit language, of which the W is often represented in Latin by M. Thus, in a work lately published, of very great learning and merit, I find the following : " La naso-labiale M remplace *souvent* en latin la labiale douce prolongée aryaque W; ainsi nous trouvons *Mare,* mer, au lieu du Sanskrit Wari; de même encore les terminaisons thématiques latines en Men, Min, Ment, &c., sont pour des organiques Wan, Want (Sanskrit van, vant), &c.[2] "

We have thus seen how out of IO have grown the several signs B, M, W, and S, and to which we may add X, for this sign is also made thus X, in which we see the two parts composing S, and which, when they

[2] La Langue Latine étudiée dans l'Unité Indo-Européenne, &c., par Amédée de Caix de Saint Aymour, p. 77.

are placed thus ᴍ, make the Saxon M, and, on being placed thus ᴡ, they are as evidently a W. The Latin *vox* is therefore the *vow* of *vow*el ; and though we do not write *bloxom*, it were, however, as correct as *blossom* or *bloom*. And in the verb to *blow*, as flowers do, we have also *blom*, that is, bloom ; and this is confirmed by the following from Webster, under the word *blow :* "A flower, a blossom. This word is in general use in the United States. In the *Tatler* it is used for blossoms in general."

It is scarcely necessary to observe that *flos* (Latin of flower) and the *bloss* of *bloss*om are one and the same.

We have also seen how the combination IO is the same as IE or EI, a name, according to Parkhurst, both of the true God and the sun. Our notice of IO has also led to the origin of the verb to Be, and to its two inflections IS and AM, as well as to its Sanskrit form, AS. And as this verb takes in Hebrew the form היה *eie ;* and as, according to Parkhurst (p. 127), the final *e* may be here omitted ; it follows that in Hebrew the name of the true God, and of the sun, and the verb to *be*, make, when radically considered, the same word. And it is reasonable to suppose that it should be so, the sun being worshipped at the time as the author of existence. But the primary signification of the verb to *be* has been hitherto so little known, that Victor Cousin, in controverting Locke's opinion that ideas apparently immaterial may be traced to material sources, chooses the verb to *be* as a proof that this opinion cannot be true. These are his words : " Je ne connais aucune langue où le mot français être soit exprimé par un correspondant qui représente une idée sensible [3]."

To which M. Renan replies : "Le verbe être, dis-je,

---

[3] Cours de 1829. Leçon 29.

E

dans presque toutes les langues se tire d'une idée sensible [4]."

In support of this opinion he refers to the verb *to be* in several languages, and concludes by tracing it to words signifying to breathe or to stand, and hence shows that it is not an abstract idea. But this does not give us the origin of either to breathe or to stand, though it serves to confute Cousin's opinion. Philologists imagine that when they find two words alike, one of them must be the original of the other, whereas they may be no way related, as the cause of their being alike may arise from their being both traceable to a source to which very different ideas may belong. How does it happen that the verb to *be* may be expressed by two words so opposite in meaning as to breathe and to stand? We shall see presently how this happens. But M. Renan should have attempted an explanation of what thus appears to be inexplicable, and his admitting that such an anomaly could not be accounted for, might lead him to confess that of the origin of the verb to *be* he was still ignorant, though well aware it cannot be an abstract idea.

But from our having shown that the earliest form of the verb to *be,* namely IO, was also the name of the sun, and that this object was regarded as the author of all existence, we at once see that the verb to be was called after the sun, and we know why it should have this name.

But why should the verb to *be* and to *stand* be expressed alike? Because to stand means to be upright, so that it is the contrary of being low; and as it is to lowness or the being down, the idea expressed by *dead*

[4] De l'Origine du Langage, p. 129.

or *death* is, as stated farther back, to be traced, it follows that to stand must, from its having the opposite
meaning, imply existence, that is, the not being down,
the not being laid low.

Now also we can account for the verbs to *be* and to
go having been originally the same; for 'Εἰμί in Greek
means not only *I am*, but also *I go*. We see that this
arises from existence implying motion; and according
to this view, any other kind of motion might, as well
as that of *going*, be expressed by the verb to be.
Hence *je suis* means not only I am, but also I follow.
And so might it have meant *I come* or *I go;* for these
two ideas (come and go) might have been also expressed alike. Hence it is that in Hebrew בא *ba* means,
according to Parkhurst, both to *come* and to *go;* and
in Sander's Hebrew and French dictionary בוא *bua* has
also both these meanings. But in all languages
instances are no doubt to be found of the same verb
meaning both to go and to come; and every such
word may have also often served as a name of the sun,
as well as all those in any way significant of motion,
such as *air, wind, breath, flying, flight, flowing, running,
walking,* &c., for it is only conventionally, as I shall
often have occasion to show, that words expressive of
such ideas differ in meaning.

But as words very different from those signifying
motion must have named many other ideas called
after the sun,—such, for instance, as light, heat, fire,
&c.,—may not the verb to be and such ideas be
expressed alike? This cannot but happen. Thus, in
Hebrew אש *as* means *fire;* whilst in Sanskrit it is the
verb to *be*. For this the reader can now very easily
account. He must know that it does not arise from

the verb to *be* having been called after fire, or fire after the verb to *be*, but from both ideas being traceable for their origin to the sun—fire as well as existence. Let us hear what Higgins says of the verb to *be*, under its form IS. " I apprehend the word IS to be a word of the most ancient language : in English ıs, in Hebrew שׁ *is*. It means *existens*, or perhaps hypostasis. As *existens* it meant self-existent or the formative power ; and as this power, or the creator, was the preserver, the word יֶשַׁ *iso*, the saviour and Isis came to be formed from it. In the Hebrew language it has exactly the same meaning it has in English. It is also to be found in the Mexican language, which bespeaks its great antiquity [5]."

If Higgins had been aware that the O, when not expressed with the I, is always then understood, and that both signs when joined make *a*, he would have seen that IS cannot differ from the Sanskrit *as* (to be), and that for the same reason יֶשַׁ *iso*, the Saviour, is the same as *aso*, and that from the root of this word being, as we have seen, a name of the sun, such too must be the primary signification of saviour. But was the sun, I shall be asked, ever called a saviour ? He was, as the following passage serves to show, and in which a very silly reason is assigned for his having received such a title : " That the sun rising from the lower to the upper hemisphere should be hailed the Preserver or Saviour, appears extremely natural ; and that by such titles he was known to idolaters cannot be doubted [6]." Joshua literally signifies the preserver or deliverer ; and that

[5] Anacalypis, vol. i. p. 532.

[6] " The sun, according to Pausanias, was worshipped under the name of Saviour at Eleusis."

this preserver or deliverer was no other than the sun in the sign of the ram or lamb, may be inferred from many circumstances. It will be observed that the LXX write Ἰησοῦς for Joshua, and the lamb has always been the type of Ἰησοῦς[7].

Let us now see what Parkhurst says of אש, *as*, meaning fire: " May not this word be a derivative from יש *is, being, substance,* and so eminently denote the substance or matter of the heavens, *i. e.*, subsisting in atoms without cohesion or such-like accidents? for אש *as* is plainly used as a formative or derivative from יש *is*[8]."

Now Parkhurst knew nothing of Sanskrit, and he never so much as alludes to it; yet a Sanskrit scholar could not have suggested a more evident truth when he here asks if אש *as* (fire) may not be a derivative of the verb יש *is*, that is, of the verb to *be*. When he put this question he never so much as suspected that this word *as* (the Hebrew of fire) is in Sanskrit the verb to *be* itself.

But Parkhurst could not tell why the verb to *be* and fire are in Hebrew expressed alike. He could never suppose that the sun was the source to which these two very different ideas are to be traced.

Another proof that the sun and the verb to *be* were anciently expressed alike is, as we have already seen, given by Parkhurst (pp. 127 and 128) when he admits that EI or IE served once to name both the true God and the sun; for he shows that the same word under its form *eie* means to *exist* or to *be*. And two words so different in both form and sound as the Hebrew יש *is*,

---

[7] Drummond, Œdip. Jud. p. 195.   [8] Lexicon, p. 34.

and הי IE, cannot be accounted for but by knowing that
the form of the sign O must have been once thus
modified, Ɛ (and then it was an E); and also thus, S, in
which we still see two segments of the O, but placed
differently from those comprising the sign Ɛ, which is
the Greek epsilon. The difference between O and S is,
however, so very considerable, that the philologist who
has not the power of divesting his mind of the opinion
he has entertained all his life respecting the dissimilarity
of these two letters, must find it rather difficult to
admit that such a sibilant as S can be the Ȯ modified.
This modification cannot, however, be denied, since the
alphabet of the language still spoken throughout Ava
and Pegu, and which is entirely composed of circles and
segments of circles, must have in one of its letters a sign
representing S.

The sign B and the verb Be do still suggest so many
observations and digressions, that to notice them all
might lead too far from the account we have yet to give
of the remainder of the alphabet, of which we shall find
every sign but a representative of OI, or, which is the
same thing, of ᘣ or B.

C. This sign was anciently pronounced K, which is
composed of an I and a C, joined thus, IC. C is therefore the half of K, but it represents the whole sign.
Hence in C and K we have only one letter; and this
accounts for C being unknown to the Greeks and K to
the ancient Romans; for as the one sign represented the
other, there was no necessity for both signs in each of
the two languages. Now, knowing as we do that every
letter stands for IO, we may safely regard the parts
composing K, that is, I and C, as being for IO. This
origin of K, and consequently of C, is confirmed, beyond

all doubt, by the following: " The letter Κόππα, which exists on ancient coins of Corinth and its colonies, especially Syracuse and Crotona, was received into the Samian, or Athenian alphabet: its form was Ọ, and thus in form and power the same as the Latin Q. or the Phœnician or Hebrew Koph ף [1]."

Now, though Donnegan knew nothing of the origin of language and its signs, he has here given a very convincing proof of the reality of our discovery. It is thus made evident that K, since it was anciently an O and an I thus joined Ọ, must, as well as C, be deduced from OI. Donnegan does not mistake when he says that this sign, Ọ, was "in form and power the same as the Latin Q;" for what is Q if not an O with a tail attached to it, and which tail represents the I. The letters K and Q have therefore parts precisely equal to those composing *a*. How clearly this is shown by the form of Q made thus, q; for what is this but an O and I, the latter being lengthened for the sole purpose of distinguishing q from *a?*

We have thus accounted for C, K, and Q, and consequently for such signs as interchange with them, as we shall have occasion to show as we proceed.

D. This sign is also composed of an O and an I, and it is consequently equal to OI or *a*. And the observation just made respecting the small form of Q, that is q, which could not be distinguished from *a* if its I had not been lengthened; will also apply to the small form of D, that is, to d, which does not differ from *a* but by the length of its I. But how does it happen that there is no O in the Greek D (delta, *Δ*)? It is as if I were asked, why is there no O in this sign A; for the two

---

[1] See Donnegan under Κόππα.

signs *Δ* and A are precisely equal to each other, each being composed of double I joined by a hyphen, the hyphen in *Δ* not differing from the hyphen in A, but by joining the I and the I at the base instead of doing so near the top. The *Δ* does not therefore differ from A in meaning, nor consequently from *a*, of which each part means one, as we have already seen. But in the small form of *Δ*, which is made thus, δ, it is easy to perceive an O, just as it is in its Roman representative d, which is but a modification of it.

Now, as the small forms of B and D, that is b and d, do not differ from each other but from the O of each sign being put, for the sake of distinction, on a different side of the I, it follows that in the parts of which they are composed, the b and d are exactly equal.

It would appear that B and D were anciently often pronounced alike. Witness *uber* in Latin and *udder* in English; and the *verb* of *verb*um and *word* in English; not to mention the *herb* of *herb*a and the *verd* of *verd*ure; and *barbe* and *beard*. By knowing that *b* and *d* are thus equal to each other, we are led to discover why *bellum* and *bonus* have been written also *duellum* and *duonus;* it must have arisen from *bellum* and *bonus* having been pronounced by some persons as if written *dellum* and *donus*, but in order to show that the real form of each word was *bellum* and *bonus*, the *b* was allowed to remain with the *d*, so that *bellum* and *bonus* must have then become dbellum and dbonus; and at a later period, from the interchange of b and v, dbellum and dbonus must have become *dvellum* and *dvonus*, and finally, from the identity of v and u, *dvellum* and *dvonus* must have become duellum and duonus. It is therefore a great mistake to suppose that *duellum* and *duonus* are the elder forms of *bellum* and *bonus.* But when a word ceases to be in use, etymologists at once believe it to be much older than the form which replaces it. Thus, Apello is thought to be older than Apollo, because known under this form to the ancient Romans; but as O is the elder form of e, so is Apollo a much older form than *Apello.*

But we cannot, I may be told, suppose *duellum* and *duonus* to have come from dbellum and dbonus without supposing b to be not only equal to u, but to be replaced by it. And it may be said of b that it is equal to u, not only because it ought, in conformity with our system, which deduces all letters from one sign, to be equal to it, but because it is so. Thus, does not every body admit that aufero and aufugio are the same as abfero and abfugio? and is it not equally evident that the u of the Spanish word ausente is the b in *absent?* And here it may be observed, that as b is the same as u, and u the same as a (compare further and farther), this will go to prove that a and b are, as already shown, the same letter differently formed and pronounced.

It is, I now perceive, more necessary than I imagined, to know that, from b and d being the same sign, they often replace each other. I find in M. Anatole Bailly's very learned work a positive statement to the effect that d does not replace b. Thus he says: "On ne voit pas que le d s'altère de manière à se changer en la moyenne labiale ou b. Quelques mots sembleraient, au premier abord, offrir la preuve de ce changement, le latin *bis*, par exemple, comparé au grec δίς (deux fois). Mais en réalité l'altération de la consonne initiale dans le mot latin s'explique par une évolution semblable à celle que nous avons signalée dans l'étude du son *gu* ou *gv*, devenant *gb* et finalement b: le b du latin *bis* corresponde de

même à un *v* primitif, *bis* procédant d'une forme anté-
rieure **dbis*[2], par durcissement du *v* de **dvis, duis*, forme
primitive. En grec ce *v* est tombé, comme il arrive
presque toujours, on le verra, lorsqu'il est précédé d'une
dentale ou d'une sifflante, et de là la forme δίς pour **δϜίς.
Le mot latin *bis* n'est pas d'ailleurs le seul qui se soit
ainsi transformé, et l'on peut vérifier la régularité de ce
changement dans bellum (*guerre*) pour *dbellum*, forme
altérée de **dvellum, duellum*, conservé par Horace:

<blockquote>" Græcia barbariæ lento collisa *duello*[3]."</blockquote>

But apart from the several instances which I have
already given between Latin, French, and English, showing *b* and *d* to be the same sign and to interchange;
other instances (but from Greek) may be also produced :
witness βελφίν being, in the Æolic dialect, for δελφίν;
and in the same dialect σάνδαλον being for σάμβαλον,
and ὀδελός being for ὀβελός[4]. Had this been known to
M. Anatole Bailly, he might have been led to derive the
Latin *bis* from its Greek equivalent δις, or, from *b* and *d*
being the same letter, to regard *bis* and δίς as one word.
As to the etymology of δίς, I believe it to have first
been δύο εἰς, and to have then meant *two-one*, that is,
double one, or rather *two-ones*. For the same reason I
should say that its English form *twice* is for *twa-ace*.
And that *twa-ace* or *twa-eis* might be abridged to *twis*,
just as *duo-eis* has been to *dis*, is shown by the English
word *twist*, of which the primary sense is *doubled*, *twis*
being its radical part. *Twain, twin,* and *twine* are kindred
words, each having for its literal meaning *double one* or

----

[2] The author uses the asterisk to signify what is ancient or con-
jectural.

[3] Manuel pour l'Étude des Racines Grecques et Latines, p. 68.

[4] See Donnegan, under B and Δ.

two ones, and of which the analysis *twa-ein*, that is, *twa-ane* or *twaone* is very plain.

D is used for several other signs besides B, all serving to prove still more and more that there can be only one letter in the alphabet, differently formed and pronounced. In the Doric dialect it is used for g, ἀμέρδω being for ἀμέργω, and δα for γα; it is used for Z, as Δεύς for Ζεύς, and also for k, as δαίω, καίω; and even for S, οδμή for οσμή, βαδός for βασμός; not to mention others. But the most usual change for *d* in all languages is *t* and *th*. Witness mo*d*er, ma*t*er, and mo*th*er; and padre, pater, and father.

But when learned men prove to us, by comparing words, that letters interchange, they should show us the great advantage of this knowledge, which they very seldom do. Indeed they *never* do so by telling us that it must be a proof of all letters having sprung from a single source; but they might by this knowledge discover sometimes the primary signification of a word. Thus, Donnegan, who knew very well that *b* and *d* interchange, ought by this knowledge to find out the primary sense of βίος, life. But he derives βίος from βιόω, which means to *live*, by which derivation I am no wiser than I was before, since he does not tell me after what it was men first signified the verb to *live*. To tell me, as this eminent Greek scholar does, that βιόω is the original of the Latin *vivo*, is still to keep me in the dark respecting the primary sense of life, for if *vivo* comes from the Greek verb βιόω, and if I happen to know nothing of the origin of βιόω I can know nothing of the origin of *vivo*. I consult other Greek authorities; but they are all equally perplexing, and allow me to perceive that of the origin of the idea expressed by βίος they know nothing whatever.

But Alexandre's great Greek Dictionary, which is thought by Frenchmen to be the best in the world, is not only, in the present instance, as deficient of information as the others, but rather more perplexing; for this authority sends the student, in a round-about way, from *Βίος* to the verb *Βιόω* as its root, and for the root of *Βιόω* the student is sent back to *Βίος.* This manner of explaining reminds me of an anecdote told of a child, who, wanting to know the meaning of the word *fellowship*, is told by his dictionary to see *partnership;* but not knowing the meaning of *partnership*, he looks out for it, and, on finding it, is now sent back by his dictionary to see *fellowship.*

But knowing, as we now do, that in *b* and *d* there is only one letter under different forms, and that these two signs often interchange, as we have seen, we need only, instead of *Βίος* write Dios, in order to discover the origin of *Βίος*; for *Dios* is the same as Deus, indeed it is the Spanish of Deus. And what can be more natural than to call life after the author of life—that is, after God? But we must not forget that Deus, Theos, Zeus, Dios, and all such words, were anciently but so many names of the sun, the then supposed author of life.

F. This sign, which is the same as the digamma of the Greeks, does not differ in form from the first half of the aspirate H, which accounts for its often serving as a substitute for this sign. Thus, the Spanish words *Hernando, huir,* and *hacer* are the same as Fernando, the French word *fuir,* and the Latin word *facere;* this, too, accounts for the present French word *hors* having been anciently *fors.* F is also used for *b* and *g*: witness *frater* and *brother,* and *fero* and *gero*; and it is also the same as V, as we see by comparing life and live, strife and strive, &c. This much serves to show that F, from its being equal to H, may be also said to mean double one, like every other sign thus far noticed.

G is, in form, nearly the same as C, and this brings it equal to K. Hence, *cat* is the *gat* of the Italian gatto, and *partake* is *partage* in French. And as we have shown K to have been anciently an I and an O (♀), it follows that G is also for I and O, for the reason that it often replaces K as now shown by *partage* and *partake.*

H. As this sign is both an aspirate and a vowel, it affords powerful proof that letters the most dissimilar in both sound and form may be all traced to one another, and consequently to a single sign. Though H is now a vowel in Greek, it was anciently in this language an aspirate, just as it is at present in English. Hence a learned authority admits as follows:—"The letter H, in the old Greek alphabet, did not sound what we now call η (that is Eta), but was an aspirate, like the English H. This was proved by Athenæus, and has been further evinced by Spanheim, from several ancient coins; and there are no less than four instances of it in the Sigean inscription[5]."

In Hebrew, also, H is often used for E. Hence the similarity of their forms, H being made thus ח, and E thus ה. The sole difference between them is this: the hyphen or connecting line is in the Hebrew characters at the top, instead of being, as in H, at the middle.

Donnegan observes, that "when the Greek H was adopted to note the breathings, its form was separated—Thus ⊣ marked the soft breathing, F the rough; for these were substituted ɔ and c." And from this I am

[5] Shuckford's Conn. vol. i. b. iv. p. 225, quoted by Higgins, Anacalypsis, vol. ii. p. 204.

induced to believe that H, when an aspirate in Greek, must have been also made thus ꜂-ꓛ. According to this view, the Latin *cornu* must have first been ꜂-ꓛornu, when, by the dropping of the first half of ꜂-ꓛ, it took its present form. The same observation may apply to the Latin curro (to run); for when we write ꜂-ꓛur for its radical part *cur*, we obtain the *hur* of the English word *hurry*, and to *hurry* is to *run*. But if *horn* and *hurry* be, as to their radical parts, older than *cornu* and *curro*, this does not go to prove that Saxon or English was the original of Latin; it serves only to show that some words of a dialect may retain their primitive forms, when these forms are to be found no longer in the original language.

The aspirate H is a most important character, as I shall often have occasion to show, as we proceed.

I have now, I believe, noticed, more or less, all the signs of an alphabet, excepting the following : L, P, R, T, Z. And these are, like those we have just accounted for, all traceable to the same source.

Thus the parts composing L are equal to double I, and so are the parts composing 𝖚, so that we need not wonder at finding L and 𝖚 so often replacing each other. Witness the French words faucon, saumon, and veau, being in English falcon, salmon, and veal. The best orthoepist of modern times, having no suspicion that L and U could be the same sign under different forms, makes the following very erroneous statement :—" L is mute between l and k in the same syllable, as balk, chalk, stalk, talk, and walk[6]."

The l is not here silent, for if it were, these words, balk, chalk, stalk, talk, and walk, would be then pro-

---

[6] Walker's Principles of Pronunciation, Dict. p. 5. Ed. 1847.

nounced as if written bak, chak, stak, tak, and wak; and no native has ever pronounced them so. But foreigners may very well make such a mistake, for this rule of Walker's is, I have no doubt, copied into their grammars; at least I find it in a work of this kind, and which is, as I learn from the title page, "Autorisé par le conseil de l'instruction publique."

Walker gives in the body of his dictionary the pronunciation of these words very correctly, and so far contradicts his own rule. Then why did he ever lay down such a rule?. because he could not suppose that l and u are one and the same letter. It is worthy of remark that in the words just quoted, the L, though it retains its usual form, is sounded like *u*, or, which amounts to the same, like w, for between two such words as *bauk* and *bawk* there is no difference in sound. This affords a plain instance of a single sign serving as if it were, at the same time, both a consonant and a vowel.

L is the same as several other signs, as I shall have occasion to show while analyzing words. Its small form (l) is an i lengthened, and hence equal to double i.

'P. In this sign it is not difficult to perceive an O and an I; and that it is like OI or *a*, the same as double I, is shown by its Greek form π. It often replaces B (of which it is but a different form) and consequently such signs as come nearest to *b* in sound, such as f and v. Its other substitutes will appear farther on.

R. In the parts composing this sign it is also easy to perceive those composing B, so that it is, like this sign, equal to I O, and consequently to all the signs already noticed. Its form in Greek does not differ from that of the Roman or English P. It is replaced by S, as is shown by arbor and arbos, honor and honos, and in French by *sur* and *sus*, and *chaire, chaise*. The Chinese, having no such sound in their language, always represent it by L, and so do many persons, but especially children, in both England and France; that is, in their manner of sounding this letter.

T. No letter is more clearly composed of double I than T; yet that it is the same as signs widely different from itself, in both form and sound, is shown by comparing pat and paw, spit and spew, water and wasser, better and besser. In Greek especially the identity of t and s is very frequent, as we shall see.

Z has been often regarded in Greek as a double letter, but this is to be ascribed to the way some persons pronounced it. Thus, such persons as pronounced Ζεύς as if written Σδεύς, considered Z as two letters, though in reality only one. So might we in English consider G as two letters, because it is often sounded *dj* : witness gentle, gender, &c.; but it would be a mistake so to consider it. In English, this sign is now mostly replaced by s, such words as were not long since written surprize and *analyze* being now surprise and analyse. Zeer is the old English for year; by which we see that Z is the same as Y; and when we compare the Greek word Ζυγόν with its English form yoke, we obtain another instance of the equality of Z and Y. And when we now compare Ζυγόν with its Latin equivalent, Jugum, we see that Z may be also J. Hence it is that children in France do frequently pronounce j as if it were z, allowing us to hear *ze* for *je*.

If we are to regard the parts composing Z—and of which there are three—as being like those composing all the other signs, for double one, we should take the short line above and the short one below as making a whole line, which, when added to the other line, will give two lines, or double one. But the Hebrew Z, which is made thus, ?, is composed of an I, or straight line, with a knob on the top of it; and it may, for this reason, be considered as equal to this sign, Ọ, which is for IO; and it was, as we have seen, a very ancient form in Greek of the letter K.

This account of the origin of letters will apply to all alphabets that have been allowed to remain in a primitive state; but such of them as have, like that of the Sanskrit language, been tampered with by the learned, lie far beyond the power of human intelligence to investigate. If the Hebrew, Greek, Roman, and Saxon alphabets have not *wholly* escaped being also meddled with, enough, however, of their primitive state remains to show us what they must have once been.

CHAPTER XIV.

ORIGIN OF THE ROOTS OF LANGUAGE.

HITHERTO there has been no means of discovering how the roots of words, and consequently words themselves, were first formed. Of all the mysterious parts of language, these, its earliest elements, must have ever appeared to the philosophical inquirer by far the most hidden. The prefixes and suffixes have been almost seen, as it were, to move and attach themselves to the bodies of the words to which they at present belong. But nothing like this can be said of the roots, of which no one has

F

been hitherto able to divine the origin, nor even, since the birth and growth of language, to invent so much as a single new one in addition to the original stock. The following passages from M. Barthélemy Saint-Hilaire's review in the "Journal des Savants" of 1862, of M. Max Müller's great work, are very well worth the reader's attention. They are admissions clear and forcible, that, with regard to its roots, nothing in language has been up to the present more astonishing and unknown: "On voit que les racines sont nécessairement monosyllabiques; et toutes celles qui ont plus d'une syllabe ne sont que des dérivés qu'on peut toujours ramener à l'embryon d'où elles sont sorties" (p. 538). "Dans le chinois tout mot est une racine et toute racine est un mot" (p. 540). "Le point de départ de toutes langues, du chinois jusqu'à l'anglais, a donc été monosyllabique; et le problème de l'origine du langage se transformant, il ne reste plus qu'à savoir comment les racines ont pu naître. Les inflexions, avec toute leur diversité, sont très-intelligibles une fois les racines données. Mais les racines elle-mêmes, d'où viennent-elles? À quelles conditions l'esprit humain a-t-il pu les enfanter, quand la parole, encore novice, a essayé ses premières articulations? C'est à résoudre cette question, autant du moins qu'elle peut être résolue, que M. Max Müller a consacré ses deux dernières leçons. On doit les regarder comme les plus importantes de tout son livre; et sans croire que la solution tant cherchée soit obtenue enfin, on doit convenir c'est avoir rendu un grand service que de l'avoir circonscrite aussi étroitement. La combinaison des racines après qu'elles ont été créés, est une œuvre tout à fait humaine; et dans une foule de langues, à prendre d'abord celle même que nous parlons, nous pouvons observer directement les progrès incessants de cette œuvre. Les langues néo-latines, surgissant et vivant sous nos yeux, nous disent assez comment les choses se passent pour ces produits de seconde formation. Mais, chose étonnante ! ces langues n'ont pas inventé une seule racine ! Elles ont changé de mille façons toutes celles dont elles héritaient ; mais sous un autre rapport, elles n'ont rien ajouté à la tradition ; leur stérilité en racines nouvelles a été absolue ; et fécondes à tant d'autres égards, elles ont été à celui-là d'une impuissance invincible " (p. 597).

And what does M. Max Müller himself say of these very mysterious little things, the roots of language ? These are his words : " Roots may seem dry things, compared with the poetry of Goethe ; yet there is something more truly wonderful in a root" [the writer means even in one single root] "than in all the lyrics in the world[7]."

This is very true ; and had M. Max Müller written a whole volume of several hundred closely printed pages on the mysterious origin of the roots of language, he could not have impressed his readers more truly nor more powerfully with an idea of his astonishment at the way of their first coming into existence having been so long and so completely buried in the depths of oblivion, and the likelihood of their so continuing to the end of time. Any one impressed with his strong belief in the impossibility of man's first word being ever discovered, may well exclaim, that a single root is truly wonderful, more wonderful than all the poetry in the world. Had the origin of the roots been hitherto discovered, philologists would not be ignorant of the origin of language.

For these admissions, made by M. Barthélemy Saint-

[7] Vol. i. p. 395.

Hilaire and M. Max Müller, I cannot but feel very grateful, though they were never intended for me. Emanating as they do from men who have looked shrewdly into language, and who appear to have made it a long and serious study, they must greatly enhance the value and importance of my claims whenever they are found real. But in what way soever they may be now received, my own convictions cannot but remain unaltered. It is not in the power of either praise or censure to add to or take from what these convictions compel me to feel and believe. All I have already obtained, as well as all I can still obtain through the use of the means now at my disposal, is too certain, too conclusive, to allow me to entertain a doubt respecting the results to which, sooner or later, the application of these my principles must finally lead. I even sometimes indulge in the fancy that I can foresee, as it were far away in the distance, new systems of grammar, new systems of lexicography, and of logic, and of philosophy, and even of religious creeds, growing out of my discovery of the origin of the roots of language, and consequently of the origin of language itself; for neither of the two can be discovered without the other.

We need now scarcely show the intelligent reader how all the roots of a language came into existence, which is the same as showing the origin of language itself, every root being in the beginning a word and every word being a root, as it is in Chinese at the present hour, and ever has been. He can easily conceive that every consonant attached to the O, whether it be put before or after it, must give both a word and a root, so that if we suppose nineteen consonants in an alphabet, we shall obtain nineteen words or roots from those preceding the O, and as many more from those which follow it, making in all thirty-eight words or roots : for instance, *bo, co, do, fo,* and so on to the last of the nineteen consonants; and then by having the same consonants after the O, thus, *ob, oc, od, of,* and so on to the last consonant. As each of the four remaining vowels (*a, e, i, u*) will also give thirty-eight words or roots for the nineteen consonants preceding and following in the same way each vowel, it is evident that the five vowels and nineteen consonants will yield in all five times thirty-eight words or roots, that is, one hundred and ninety roots and words.

The difference in the form of these roots arises from the different organs of the mouth that happen to be used, whether immediately preceding or immediately following the vowel sound. Thus the root *bo* is obtained from the lips meeting as the O is about to be sounded, whilst the root *ob* is produced by their meeting just as the O is sounded. And it is precisely in this way all the roots above referred to have, in the beginning, been produced, their difference in form being still due to the different organs used in connexion with each vowel sound. In other words, the difference in the formation of these roots is to be ascribed to the nineteen consonants that both precede and follow the vowels. And here we see, even if we were to proceed no farther with the roots, how the consonants themselves were first obtained. Thus, the *b* must have been produced by the meeting of the lips, and the *d* by the meeting of the teeth, whether the sounds so heard immediately preceded or immediately followed the vowel to which either consonant was attached. And it must have been in this way—that is, according to the organs of speech employed at the time,

whether labial, dental, guttural or nasal—that the consonants first came into existence, but being ever, like
the vowels, subject to change in both sound and form,
this arising from both classes having grown out of the
same single sign.

Let us now take the following diphthongs, ae, ai, ao,
au, aw, ea, ee, ei, eo, ey, ie, oa, oe, oo, ow,
eu, ew, ia, io, oi, ou, oy, ua, ue, ui, in all twenty-
five, and put each of the nineteen consonants before and
after each of them, as done above with single vowels, and
we shall obtain a large amount of roots, as many as
twenty-five times thirty-eight, that is, 950; which, when
added to the 190 obtained from the vowels and the
nineteen consonants, will yield 1140 roots; which number is susceptible of a vast amount of combinations, and
is consequently a great deal more than is necessary for
composing the richest language ever spoken.

Hence, however scanty the number of vowels and diphthongs belonging to a language may be, there must have
been always found enough of them to produce a large
amount of words, this arising from the numerous combinations that might be obtained merely from so few as
a hundred roots. After what has been now shown, we
need not allude to the roots that might still be acquired
by placing the nineteen consonants before and after the
triphthongs, of which, however, there are not many in
any language.

So much for the origin of the roots of the words out of
which all the languages ever yet spoken over the earth
have been formed; and they are every one of them traceable to the O with its explanatory I, itself being the first
word and root, and parent of all the others.

The following etymologies are such as have not, I perceive, been hitherto known ; nor could it be otherwise, seeing that the requisite knowledge was needed—I mean the knowledge of the origin of language and of the rules thence derived. If the author could suppose that what he has already advanced under this bold title were sufficient to bring home conviction to every understanding, there would be no necessity for the additional proofs he is now about to submit to the reader. But there are persons less susceptible of belief than others—I ought, perhaps to say less *capable* of belief—persons who, even among the learned, are so destitute of ideality and respect for their own private opinions as not to own a sufficiency of that intellectual daring called moral pluck, for enabling them to accept a new discovery however evident it may appear; whilst others—but of minds more largely endowed by nature—could not entertain a doubt respecting the reality of any such discovery. Hence the necessity for those additional proofs. And when I observe that nearly all the words of which I intend, through the help of my discovery, to show those original meanings, hitherto unknown, have been already examined by the highest authorities among living philologists, but who have ever failed to trace such words to their earliest sources, ought not this circumstance to serve greatly to prove that my theory—to give it no prouder name— must be unerring, and cannot but repose upon a solid foundation ?

As to the rules that have grown out of this discovery of the origin of language, it may be here necessary to set them down in full, though some two or three of them have been already sufficiently explained.

Every vowel is not only equal to every other vowel, but even to every combination of vowels; and hence it is that all such signs, whether single or compound, do constantly interchange, as every one knows.

Every initial vowel may, or may not, be aspirated; that is, it may have an h prefixed to it if it should not have one, or this sign may be removed if it should have it. The sense will always direct to the right application of this rule.

The aspirate sign, or h, has several substitutes, of which *b, f, v, w,* and *s,* are the principal ones; and as these signs interchange with others, it follows that signs not coming direct from the aspirate as its substitute, may however be traced to it, but indirectly.

As the aspirate *h* should never be regarded as belonging to the radical part of a word, it may always, in the analyzing of words, be left out.

As all words were not in the beginning composed of more than one syllable, just as they are at present in Chinese, it may be often necessary, in order to discover the original meaning of a word, to divide it into the several parts of which it is composed.

The common endings, in all languages, of nouns and adjectives, must have first been pronominal articles, and have then gone before the words behind which they afterwards fell, and, on having coalesced with them, became what the grammarian now calls their suffixes.

Two consonants without a vowel may take one between them, when the sense requires it.

Every vowel may or may not take a nasal sound, that is, have an *m* or *n* put after it; or when a vowel has the nasal sound, its *m* or *n* may be sometimes dropped.

CHAPTER XV.

BARRACKS AND TRANQUIL.

As far back as the year 1844 I discovered the original meaning—until then unknown—of two words in very common use, namely, *barracks* and *tranquil.* When I now call to mind how little I then knew of the origin of language, I am astonished at having made such a discovery. Both these words are to be found in a work I then published, and which bore the very modest title of " Discovery of the Origin of Language !!! " They are true etymologies, though surrounded by many very bad ones, as bad as any ever made by Horne Tooke.

I knew then, it would seem, that all letters were one and the same letter under different forms; and, taking advantage of this knowledge, I was led to perceive that *barracks* was for *war-oikos,* that is, *war-house,* oikos (οἶκος) being the Greek of house, this arising from B being equal to W, and *acks* being for *oiks,* and *oiks* for oikos.

This is a true etymology; and it is the more valuable as it accounts for the *s* in barracks, which is left out by Dr. Johnson and Webster, and all the lexicographers who follow in their track. In no part of the world, however, where English is spoken, does any one ever make use of such a word as *barrack* for *barracks,* unless it be some learned philologist. And the reason why a philologist may do so, must be ascribed to his being unable to account for this noun barracks, which is singular, having, in its *s*, the sign of the plural.

Dr. Johnson gives, as the original of barracks, *barracca,* which he explains thus: "Little cabins made by the Spanish fishermen on the sea-shore; or little lodges for soldiers in a camp."

But the meaning of *barracca* is *sea-houses,* for its B is not more equal to W than it is to M, so that its part *bar* is for *Mar,* and Mar is the Spanish of sea; and the *acc* which follows, is for the root of oikos, that is, for *oik.*

And that Mar cannot differ in meaning, any more than in form, from War, is shown by its being the radical part of Mars, the god of war. And as Mars will become Mors (death) when the *i* of its *a* is dropped, we thus discover the primary signification of both War and Mars.

Of this etymology we shall see a very curious proof farther on. It is to this effect: two learned authorities show that *Balsab*—an old Irish word—means Dominus Mortis or Lord of Death; but another learned authority says this cannot be, for the reason that Balsab means rather Mars, or the god of war. Thus, neither of these authorities suspected that in War, Mars, and Mors we have one and the same word.

Let us now show how the word Mars obtained its present form. From M being a common substitute for B, and from B being a common substitute for the aspirate H, which sign is never to be counted as belonging to the root of a word, it follows that *Mars* is reducible to *ars;* that is, when the vowel here due between *r* and *s* is supplied, *ares,* in Greek, Ἄρης. This etymology serves to show that the A of Ἄρης must have been once aspirated by many persons, though it is not so at present; otherwise there would not now be an M in Mars, a B in barracks, or a W in war. But had Ἄρης, or Mars, I may be asked, no other meaning than that of death? As the names of all the heathen divinities once served to designate the sun, and as the name Mars makes no exception to this general rule, it cannot have always meant death, that is, the being *low* or *down,* but *highness* as well, and consequently greatness, nobleness, and all such ideas. In short, it is like *altus* in Latin, which means both *high* and *low.* Hence the *ars* of Mars happens to be the Saxon of the Latin podex ; whilst under its Greek form ἄρης, it may be said to mean the highest, the noblest, the bravest ; for it cannot differ from the αρις of ἄριστος, which may be so explained. An instance of these two opposite meanings of the same word is also afforded by the Greek ἀρχὸς, which is not only expressive of dignity and highness, since it means a chief, a leader, but of lowness also, since it is rendered into Latin by *anus, podex,* and into English by the breech or fundament.

TRANQUIL. Though this word has come to us from the French *tranquille* or its Latin equivalent, tranquillus, its form is, however, older than either of these originals. I showed in the year 1844 that its literal meaning is, *to be upon one's keel,* that is, *to be seated.* Its two first letters, *tr,* are equal to *it re,* which means *the thing* or *the being;* and this does not differ in signification from the French *étre* or *estre.* As to the *an* which follows, it is the root of the Greek preposition ἀνὰ, and the same as *on* or *upon* in English. When we now observe that *quil* (the remaining part of tranquil) is equal to *qu-il,* that is, when the article *il* returns to its first place, *il qu,* we see that the entire word is for *the being upon the qu,* or buttocks. The last of these several words is now written with a *c* instead of a *q.*

We confirm this etymology by remarking that *sedate*, which implies tranquillity, is radically the same as *seat*, as we must admit on comparing *sedes* and *sedatus*. To be tranquil is therefore to be seated. Hence, in one of the remote French provinces I have been told that the peasant will sometimes say *tranquillisez-vous* instead of *asseyez-vous*. The idea of tranquillity is to be therefore traced to lowness; so that any word expressing this idea might have served for this purpose as well as the one that has been chosen by the Latins. This is confirmed by Ποδὸς, genitive of πούς, the foot, for it is radically the same as podex, Latin of breech. And this will account for the *quille* of the French tranquille having not only the meaning of *keel*, but also, when analyzed, that of *ille qu*, or, *the bottom*. It will also account for Ποδόστημα signifying the under part of a ship; for it is only conventionally that this meaning differs from that of keel. Greek scholars do not therefore mistake when they derive this word from Πούς and ἵστημα, and which two words may be said to have the literal meaning of *foot* and *being*; that is, *being* at the *foot*, or low part.

When we now observe that the *quille* of tranquille is the French of *keel*, we are led to perceive that *cul*, which is often used in the sense of bottom, must have first been *cu il*, or rather *il-cu*, the word *il* having then the meaning of *the*. The *cul* of the Latin *culus*, is therefore the same word; and it must have also been at first *il cu*.

But though I regard a consonant and a vowel as a root, I cannot help believing that at first every such root began with a vowel or a combination of vowels. Thus, taking the *qu* of *quille* as its root, the *u* must in the beginning have gone before the *q*, instead of being after it, or some other vowel must have done so. And if such a vowel was then aspirated, and if the aspirate was then replaced by one of its substitutes, and if, from every such substitute being a consonant, it took a vowel before it, as initial consonants frequently do,—such a root as *uq* would then be composed of five letters instead of two. I am, therefore, led to regard the *υχ* of *ἥσυχος* (Greek of tranquil) as its root, and as not being different from the *qu* of tranquillus, the latter being equal to *uq*, and consequently to such a form as *uc, ug, uk,* or *uch.*

Now, though another root might, as well as *qu* or *uq*, have signified *low*, and consequently the idea tranquil; such as *ub*, for instance, which is the root of *sub;* the Latins have, however, used this root on more than one occasion for signifying the idea expressed by the word tranquil : witness *quies, quietus, quiesco,* &c., whence the English *quiet.* The primary signification of every such word being the hinder part, bottom, or foot; in short, *low.*

The English *squat* might have also expressed quietness, for its root is *qu*, the S being here euphonic, as it often is before certain consonants; so that the primary signification of this word is *qu-at* that is, *at qu* or, on one's bottom. Webster derives *squat* from *quatio* in Italian, which serves to show that the *s* is now, as I say, euphonic.

M. Max Müller tells us in his Lectures (2nd Series, p. 341), that "Tranquillity was calmness, and particularly the smoothness of the sea." Tranquillity is certainly calmness; but what does M. Max Müller know of the primary signification of either word? Nothing whatever. He little suspects that the *cal* of *calm* is the *quil* of tranquil, and that it does not differ in the least from the French *cul*, or the *cul* of the Latin *culus*, and that it is, when analyzed, *il cu*, just as *quil* is *il-cu*. And if M. Max Müller knew that men first expressed the idea *calm* or *tranquil* by words signifying to be down, to be upon one's bottom, he would never think of saying that tranquillity "was particularly the smoothness of the sea." There was in the beginning, when men first gave names to their ideas, no more relationship supposed to exist between tranquillity and the smoothness of the sea, than there is at present between tranquillity and the smoothness of velvet, or any other sort of smoothness whatever.

But it would seem that the original meaning of *smoothness* is also unknown; but it is easily discovered when we observe that its radical part, *smoo*, must have once been *soom*, which is but a different form of *same*, and it is not difficult to conceive that *smoothness* is *sameness*. And as the S of *soom* is for the aspirate, which must never be counted, it follows that *soom* was at first *oom;* and *oom* cannot differ from *oon*, nor *oon* from *on*, nor *on* from one; so that *smoothness* and *sameness* are each traceable to the same source—to that of *unity*. Hence *uni*—French of *even* or *smooth*—is radically the same as *unus*, *un*, and *one*. And when we observe that *v* is *u*, and that *even* is therefore equal to *euen*, we can perceive that *even* is but another form of *un* and *one*, not to mention the German *ein*, and its Greek equivalent, *ἑv*. Hence, to be *even* or *smooth*, is to be all *one*. In the locution "*one* and the *same*," the word *same* is therefore a pleonasm ; and so is *idem* in "*unus et idem*." The French language is too mathematical to allow of such a phrase as *un et le même*.

CHAPTER XVI.

USE AND ADVANTAGE OF KNOWING THAT INITIAL VOWELS MAY TAKE THE ASPIRATE H.

HOWEVER well acquainted M. Max Müller may be with Sanskrit, it is only reasonable to suppose that he must know his own language somewhat better. This knowledge has not, however, prevented him from making the following erroneous statement: "Nobody would doubt the common origin of German and English; yet the English numeral '*the first*,' though preserved in *fürst* (princeps, prince), is *quite different* from the German *der erste*[8]."

Now, when a child calls to mind the rule, that initial vowels may or may not be aspirated, and that the aspirate (that is, the sign H) may be replaced by other consonants, and that *f* is one of the most common substitutes (witness *H*ernando and *F*ernando, *hacer* in Spanish, and *facere* in Latin; and *hircus* and *fircus* in the latter tongue, with many others), it will not be difficult for him to correct M. Max Müller's mistake, even though as ignorant of German as I am myself.

Thus, the child will begin by prefixing an *h* to *erste ;* but finding that *herste*, thus obtained, makes no sense, he will take away the *h* and put *f* in its place, which will give *ferste ;* and as all the vowels are equal to one another, he will soon perceive that *ferste* is for first. And as one vowel is not only equal to any other vowel,

---

[8] Lectures on the Science of Language, vol. i. p. 194.

but to any combination of vowels, it follows that neither *ferste* nor *first* can differ from *fürst*. We have thus shown that the English numeral " *the first*," is not, as M. Max Müller states, *quite different* from its German representative, *der erste*, but that *first* is the word *erste* itself.

But this etymology, I now perceive, leads to several others. The English word *erst* must be also for *first ;* and as a vowel is often understood between two consonants, *erst* is equal to erist, which, from the interchange of *e* and *a*, becomes *arist*, and *arist* is the radical part of *aristos* (ἄριστος) used as the superlative of ἀγαθός, *good ;* and though *best* is, in English, the superlative of *good*, it is easy to perceive that such an idea might serve as a synonym of *first*, though not derived from it.

Another word which is radically the same as *erst* is *ere ;* and from knowing that *ere* means *before*, we discover, by aspirating its initial *e*, that it is equal to *here*, and consequently to *fere ;* that is, when the *e* following next after *f* takes its form of *o*, *fore*, which, as it was anciently used for *before*—and is so still in such words as *foresee* and *foretell*—allows us to perceive that the word *erst* must, from its meaning time past, be radically the same as *formerly*, the *for* of this word being for *fore*. According to these views, the literal meaning of *aristos* should be the *foremost*, and not the *best*, which is traceable to *goodness*, whilst such an idea as *first* or *foremost* relates to precedency.

These etymologies suggest others, but of which I wish to notice only three. In the *her* of the Latin *heri* (yesterday), and in the French of *heri*, that is *hier*, we have two words signifying time gone by, for it is only conventionally they mean the day just passed. This is confirmed by the peasantry of Normandy using *hier* to signify a time preceding *yesterday*, as well as the time expressed in English by this word, *yesterday*, itself. And as we have shown the English word *ere* to be for *fore*, that is, *before;* so may we now, when we give to the initial *e* of this word its aspirate h, prove *heri* not to differ from it, this form *here* having been anciently used for heri. And as in the *hester* of *hester*nus we have the *yester* of *yesterday*, this serves to show that *h* may not only be replaced by f, as shown above, but by y also; and this proves that the old English word *yore* is the same as *fore* (before), and that it does not differ from it in meaning, but conventionally. Another proof that the *h* of the French *hier* is equal to y, is shown by *yr*, which, according to M. Littré, means *hier* in the Catalonian dialect. · In Spanish also the y is to be found instead of *h*, *ayer* being in this language the word for *yesterday*. The literal sense of *ayer* must therefore be *afore*, that is, *before*.

Supposing now that a German wanted to see if the English word *first* was in any way related to *erste*, he would soon, from a knowledge of our rule, reduce *first* *irst*, for initial consonants must be often no more than substitutes for the aspirate *h*, as is shown by the *f* of first; and the difference in both sound and form between *erste* and *irst* is so very slight that he could not help perceiving they made only one word.

Let us now give a single instance of the advantage to be derived from the knowledge thus obtained. Frenchmen cannot tell how it happens that the first person singular and present tense of the verb *être*, that is, *je suis*, does not differ from the *je suis* of *suivre*, though the one means *I am, I exist*, or *I am in being*, whilst the other

G

means only *I follow*. The Latin *sequor*, infinitive *sequi*, is referred to by all philologists as the sole original of *suivre*. But *sequor* does not mean *I exist*, though, like existence, it implies motion. *Je suis* differs, however, so considerably from *sequor* that it is rather difficult to regard the words as one and the same; and hence we feel inclined to look out for another original of *suivre*, for one that will account for *je suis*, I follow, not being different from the *je suis*, I exist. Let us, therefore, apply our rule showing that the aspirate to which initial vowels are subject, is often replaced by other consonants. Now, as one of those substitutes for the aspirate h is an s (witness *hudωr* in Greek and *sudor* in Latin, and also, in these two languages, *hepta* and *septem*), we should leave it out as no part of *suivre*, but as a substitute for the h, which must have been once prefixed to the u of this word; so that *suivre* is by this means reduced to *uivre*, of which the u being the same as v, shows this word to be *vivre*, in Latin, *vivere*; and as *vivre* or *vivere* means to *live*, and consequently to *exist* or to *be*, this accounts for *je suis* (I follow) not being different from *je suis*, I am; that is, *I exist, I live*, I am in *being*. And this has not been hitherto known, no one having suspected that in *suivre* and *vivre* we have the same word. But it is so, because *suivre* implies *motion* and motion implies existence. So much for the rule by the applying of which this discovery has been made. But in order to render it still more evident that *suivre* is equal to *vivre*, and does not differ from it in meaning save convention-ally, we need only conjugate *suivre* while omitting the s (because, from its being a substitute for the h, it can be no radical part of this verb), and then, instead of *je suis, tu uis, il suit; nous suivons, vous suivez, ils suivent*, &c., we shall have *je vis, tu vis, il vit, nous vivons, vous vivez, ils vivent;* the *v* being here the same as the *u* in suivre. Every one is aware that until a comparatively late period *u* and *v* were regarded as the same sign.

Suivre and *vivre* being both irregular verbs of the same conjugation, we cannot expect them to correspond in all their forms, but they do correspond in so many of them that there can be no doubt but they are radically the same word. Thus, in the imperfect and future tenses the identity is evident: witness *suivais* and *vivais*, and suiverai and viverai, not to mention other tenses; and though the difference in form between the past participles *suivi* and *vécu* is considerable, this cannot be said of the present participles, *suivant* and *vivant*. And as *suite* also comes from *suivre*, so does *vite*. And as a vowel may or may not be doubled, it follows that *suite* is equal to *suvite*, that is, *swift*, which happens to be the English of *vite*. And as *vite* and *vita* are radically the same, we thus see how life implies motion. Hence *vivere* and *vivus* in Latin; and *life, live,* and *lively* in English.

Judging from this etymology, we may expect to find, at least sometimes, if not very often, such ideas as have been called after life, expressed by words bearing a close resemblance to *suivre;* not, however, from their having been called after this idea, but after its original, which is *vivre.* The supposed original of *suivre* is the Latin *sequor* and *sequi.* But life is not the meaning of *sequor,* or of its infinitive *sequi,* though these ideas (*sequor* and *sequi*) are traceable to that of *life;* and why so? Because they have been called after motion, and motion after life. In the same way other ideas may be traced to *life* without having been called after it. Witness the French word *fuite,* of which the *f* does here but represent the aspirate *h*, just as the *s* does in *suite;* so that both words (*suite* and *fuite*) are reducible to *vite*, this other form of *vita*, life. Thus, by different substitutes for the aspirate h, the same word can have different meanings, as we see by comparing *vite, suite,* and *fuite,* which are all traceable to *vita,* that is, to *life.*

When we now leave out the aspirate substitute of *s* in *sequor,* we shall have *equor,* which is but a different form of *æquor,* and this word means *water.* Its eldest known form is *sequo;* that is, when the S, as in *sequor,* is left out, *equo;* and as the *e* is here for *o,* and *o* for *oi* or *a,* and as the *o* at the end is, from its *i* being understood, also equal to *oi* or *a,* it follows that *equo* is exactly the same as *aqua.* By analyzing in the same way, we shall find in *sequi* (infinitive of sequor) the word *aqua* itself. But why should *water* be signified by a word meaning *life?* because, from its serving to support *life,* it was called after this idea; and so was *viande.* Hence *la vie* is a synonym of *les vivres,* and *les vivres* and *victuals* have the same meaning.

This must lead us to infer that words for *water* will be found to signify motion, though not called after this idea, but after that of *life.* Hence, when the *a* of *water* receives its nasal sound, this word will become *wanter,* which cannot differ from *wander.* And as the *w* of this word should not be counted, because only representing the aspirate, *wander* is therefore the same as *ander,* and *ander* cannot differ from *andare,* Italian of to *go,* any more than it can from its Spanish form, *andar.* These observations suggest many others, of which a few may, because of their importance, be submitted to the reader.

We have now seen that the verb to *be* is expressed— as in French—by a word not different from one signifying

motion: *je suis*, I am, and *je suis*, I follow, being equal
to each other. And as the *suis* of *je suis* is, when its *s*
(here representing the aspirate *h*) is left out, reducible
to *uis*, that is, *vis*, we obtain another form of the *vais*
of *je vais*, I *go;* and this is confirmed by the verbs to
be and to *go* being in Greek the same word. And
as we have found that the idea *water* has been called after
life, and that the word by which it is expressed does
not differ from one for motion, we see that the *vais* and
vas of *aller* to *go* are each the same as the *was* of the
German *wasser*, this word *was* itself being an inflection
of the verb to *be*. Hence *wasen*—Saxon of *to be*—is
radically the same as the German *wasser*.

But though *suivre* and *vivre* make, as we have seen,
only one word, the English of *suivre* (follow) seems to
bear no resemblance to a word signifying either *existence* or *water*. But *fol*, which is the radical part of
follow, cannot differ from *fel*, nor *fel* from *pel;* and
pel is the radical part of πέλω, which means both to
be and to *move*. And as *flow* is *follow* contracted, and is
the same as *flux* and *fleuve*, we see that this word also
means *water;* and so might any word signifying motion.
Witness *current, runlet*, and *stream;* of which the two
first need not be explained, so clearly do they signify
motion; and when we observe that *ream* (the radical
part of stream) is letter for letter the same as *roam*, we
see that this word is as significant of motion as *current*
itself, which means *running*. In the *rom* of the German
strom (stream) we have but another form of *roam*.

I have now an important observation to make, which
must confirm all I have said respecting the origin of
the name of *water*. This confirmation is unwittingly
afforded by M. Littré, from whom I learn that

in Berry there are several places called after *water*, and that this idea is then expressed by *esse.* This statement, of which neither M. Littré nor any member of the Institute appears to have seen the consequence, is given under the article *eau.* It is as follows: " *Esse,* signifiant *eau,* se trouve dans le nom de plusieurs localités du Berry." This is to tell us in very plain language, that *water* and the verb to *be* were once named alike; and this leads to our conclusion as shown above, that *water* was—because so essential to the support of animal existence—called after the verb to *be.*

These are only a few of the many observations suggested by our notice of *suivre* and *vivre;* but as words signifying *being, water,* and *motion,* must be often referred to again as we proceed, no more needs be said for the present of such ideas.

Yet the reader will, I hope, excuse one or two other etymologies suggested by those just noticed. As the signs *b* and *v* do constantly interchange, there can be no difference in form between the Latin verbs *bibere* and *vivere.* But why should this be? I am going to tell why. Every word, as I shall have occasion to show, meaning *drink* or to *drink,* can be traced to one meaning—*water;* and *water,* because it supports life, even as *meat* and *bread* do, has been called after *life;* and *vivre* means to have life, that is, to *live,* in Latin, *vivere.*

Now, though *bibere* does not signify motion, we see that it might have had this meaning, which arises from its having been called after *water,* and *water* after life. But where is, I shall be asked, the word for *water* in *bibere?* If we regard the initial *b* of this word as representing the aspirate *h,* the radical part (not the root) of this word should be *iber,* and *ib* be the root;

and this root cannot differ from *oib, ab, eb,* or from *oip, ap, ep,* or from *oif, af, ef,* or from *oiv, av, ev ;* not to mention many others. M. Littré gives, under *eau,* more than twenty different forms of this word; and among them I find two which are equal to the *ib* of *bibere,* namely, the Gaelic *ab,* and the Sanskrit *ap.* And when we now notice *iber* as the radical part of *bibere,* we see that it cannot differ from *iver* or *ivre ;* and *ivre,* as a French word, means to be *drunk;* so that *drunkenness* must have been called after *drink,* and *drink* after *water,* and *water* after *life,* and *life* after its supposed author, the *sun.* If we now aspirate the *ibre* of *bibere,* or its other form, *iver,* we shall have *hiber* and *hiver ;* and as the latter is the French of *winter,* we may be sure that the former must have also had this meaning, since the verb *hibernare* signifies *to winter,* and the adjective *hibernus* may be said to mean *wintry.* Now, why should a word meaning *winter* be traceable to one meaning *drink ?* Because *drink* was called after *water,* and *winter* is a *watery* season. But to judge from the word for *winter* in Saxon, English, and several other languages, it would seem that this season was called after *wind,* and not after *water.* But according to one of my rules (already mentioned) every vowel may or may not have a nasal sound; hence, when we do not allow to the *i* of *winter* its nasal sound, this word will become *witer,* which, from *i* having *o* understood, and from *o* and *i* making *a,* becomes *water.* According to this etymology, *water* and *wind* are here but different forms of the same word. But why should this be? Because *water* has been called after life, which implies *motion,* and *wind* or *breath* is also significant of both *life* and *motion.* As to the original sense of *winter,* it appears to have been *water* and not *wind,* since its Greek form, χεῖμα, has, as Donnegan states, "properly the same sense as χεῦμα, and means a gush, a pouring, a pour of rain, and hence winter." The Latin *hiems* is the same word, which serves to show that χ or *ch* is reducible to *h*.

Our knowing that the idea *water* is traceable to life or motion, must guide the philologist to many new etymologies. Thus, he will see that *quake* is but a repetition of *aqua* abridged; and that *quick* can be also traced to *aqua*. Even *ague*, though not called after water, cannot differ from *aqua*; but as it is an illness attended with *shivering*, we may be sure that it was from *shivering* or *trembling* it took its name. Hence the Gaelic of this word, which is *crith*, is thus explained in my Gaelic dictionary: "trembling, tremor; a fit of ague." And if we could suppose that *aqua* is not precisely equal to *agua*, our doubt would be removed by the simple fact that the Spanish and Portuguese of *aqua* is *agua*. Hence, the e of *ague* being the same as o, and consequently as *oi* or *a*, *ague* is the word *agua* or *aqua* itself.

The ancient names of rivers will also bear out these etymologies; for the words *Rhine*, *Rhone*, and *river* are but other words for motion, and must, when radically considered, have meant both *water* and *running*. But of the root of these names we have only the *r*. In Hebrew, *ar* means to flow, and also *river*; and it means, when written *aur*, light, which is but another word for the sun, and consequently for life and motion. *Ar* is therefore, like the root of *aqua*, another word for *water*; and so may we say is *ab* in Gaelic, as well as *ap* in Sanskrit, which are to be found among the words given by M. Littré under *eau*. The r of *Rhine*, *Rhone*, and *river*, is consequently the same as the Hebrew *ar*, to flow, &c.

Another very plain instance of the name of a river being radically the word *aqua,* is the Latin *Sequana;* for the S of this word is for the aspirate, so that it is no part of its root; and as to the *equa* following this S, it cannot differ from *aqua;* so that *Sequana* means simply, the water; for the *na* with which it ends is for *una,* the *u* having been dropped; and this *una* must at the time have had the meaning of a definite and not an indefinite article.

The objection to this etymology may be, that the *Sequana* is now the Seine, in which there is no appearance of *aqua.* But let us observe that the word *Seine* must have had many other forms, and that *seigne* must have been one of them, which can no more differ from *Seine* than the *soigne* of the French verb *soigner* can differ from its noun *soin;* and when the S is here dropped, as in *Sequana, eigne* will remain, and *eigne* cannot differ from *eiqune,* which, since *ei* is equal to *oi,* and *oi* to *a,* is the same as *aqune,* and from this we deduce the *aqua* discovered in *Sequana.*

This explanation leads to another etymology. The *seigne* here noticed is but another way of writing the *saigne* of *saigner* (to bleed); and as the noun of *sainger* is *sang,* and as *sang* means *blood,* it follows that this idea has been called after water. And why should not the word *blood* have had this origin, since it signifies a fluid, and a fluid *flows,* even as water does? Hence *blood* is the same as *flood,* and a flood is a flow, and a flow is a *fleuve.*

By this knowledge, and the application of two of our rules already applied, we can now give the etymology of the Latin *sanguis,* blood. When we drop its S, as in the analysis of *Sequana, anguis* remains, which, when we leave out (according to rule) the nasal sound, becomes *aguis,* that is, *aquis*, and this is but another form of *aqua*. But sanguis is written also *sanguen*, and as the two rules just applied will reduce *sanguen* to *aquen*, we obtain a form precisely equal to the *equan* of *Sequana*.

These etymologies are confirmed by the names of the rivers *Sangarius* and *Sanguinum*, which words, though they here mean water, might as well mean blood.

Another very plain instance that the ancient names of rivers were but other words for water, is afforded by the German river *Weser*, this word being but a different form of *wasser*, water.

CHAPTER XVII.

OTHER OBSERVATIONS RELATING TO THE VERB BE IN HEBREW, SANSKRIT, AND GREEK; WHENCE THE PRIMARY SIGNIFICATION, HITHERTO UNKNOWN, OF SEVERAL IDEAS, SUCH AS LIGHT, HEAT, LOVE, ETC.

HAVING now shown the use and advantage of the rule respecting the aspirate h, I wish to know why the Sanskrit verb to *be* (*as*) should end with an S more than with any other consonant; and I answer this question of my own by declaring that I cannot tell why. But it seems to me that it might as well end with any other consonant in the alphabet. And why should I think so? Because I regard every personal pronoun in the singular number as having, when radically considered, exactly the same meaning as the Sanskrit *as*; and to which may be added every definite and indefinite article. Thus *il* (root

of the Latin *il*le) which is in French a pronoun, answering to *he* or *it* in English—and is in Italian the definite
article, as it was anciently in French—cannot, from its i
having O understood, and from O and i making *a*, differ
from a̱l; and as l and r interchange, and r and s also,
as I shall have occasion to show, it follows that the
Sanskrit *as* might as well have been *al* or *ar;* or its *a*
might have any other consonant after it as well as either
of the signs l and r, for all such monosyllables must
at one time or other have each served as a name of the
sun, and have consequently meant existence, and hence
the verb to be.

This opinion is confirmed by the Hebrew *al'* (אל),
which, according to Parkhurst, means both *the* and *that*[9]
and the same authority adds, in the same page, that אל *al*
was a name of the true God ; and that " the heathen worshipped their arch-idol the heavens under this attribute
אל *al* or the plural אלים *alim*." But why, it may be asked,
has not *al* served to signify the verb to be in Hebrew ?
Because there is in this language another name of the
Deity and the sun, as I have already shown; and which
is יה IE or EI [1]; and יה *ie* with an ה *e* prefixed, thus, היה
eie, is the verb to be.

It is thus self-evident, that anciently every word
naming the sun served also for the verb to *be*. But how
could it be otherwise, since the sun was believed to be
the author of existence, and this is also the substantive
meaning of the verb *be ?*

But the Greeks appear to have had *al* for the verb to
be ; for *el*, which is the same word, is the root of πέλω,
and this word means both to be and to move. But
why should the p be left out ? Because it does here

but represent the aspirate h, so that ελ alone should be considered as the entire word. When I give the etymology of *pater*, hitherto unknown, the reader will have an instance of the p of this word having served as a substitute for h.

The French might have also had *al* for their verb to *be*, for it is the root of *haleine* which means *breath*, and hence being or existence. And as the *el* of πέλω signifies motion, even so does *al* in French, for it is the root of *aller*, to go; and to *go* and to *be* are in Greek expressed alike.

In English also we have this *al*, as is shown by *hale* and *health;* and which can be seen more clearly when we observe that *hal* is the Saxon of *hale*, for the aspirate of *hal* being left out, *al* alone remains. But considered as a French word, *halé* means *sun*-burnt. In the *hal* of *halé* we have also the *hal* of *hal*ios, which is in the Doric dialect the same as Ἥλιος, the sun.

In the *sal* of *salus* (health) we have still this *al;* for the S of this word is but a representative of the aspirate. Nor can the *sal* of salus differ from *sol*, and Sol was Apollo, the god of medicine, the preservative of health.

Nor can *sol* differ from the *hol* of *holy*, nor from *hal*, which is the root of *halig*, Saxon of *holy*, and also of *halios*, Doric of *Helios*, the sun, as stated above. It is hence made evident that the first meaning ever attached to *holy* was that of *sunny;* and which is proved by what no one denies, namely, that *sun*day means the day of the *sun*, and that it is also a *holy* day, but primitively and literally a *sunny* day, that is, a godly day, because the sun was anciently worshipped as God.

According to Bryant, "The most common name for

the sun was *san* and *son;* expressed also *zan, zon,* and *zaan*[2]." The first of these forms gives the root of *sanus* and *sanitas* (healthy and health), so that in meaning it does not differ from *sol.* And when we drop the S (which represents the aspirate) of such forms as *son* and *sun,* the remainder of each word (*on* and *un*) is for *one,* which corresponds with the *sol* of *solus,* because, when the sun appears, he is *solus,* that is, alone, and consequently *one.*

And as *l* and *r* do constantly replace each other, it follows that neither *as* nor *al* can differ from *ar,* that is, when aspirated, *har,* which is the root of *haris;* and respecting this word Higgins observes: " Volney says, ' The Greeks used to express by X or the Spanish Jota, the aspirated Ha of the Orientals, who said *Haris:* in Hebrew חרש (*hrs*), *heres,* signifies the sun, but in Arabic the radical word means to guard, to preserve, and Haris *a preserver.'* And again, ' if *Chris* comes from Harish [Haris] by a Chin [name of the Hebrew ש *s*] it will signify artificer, an epithet belonging to the sun[3].' "

This passage from Volney confirms the one from Drummond already quoted, showing that the sun had anciently the title of *Saviour;* for " *a preserver* " is a *saviour.* This passage confirms also what I have already stated more than once, namely, that the sun was revered as the creator or *maker* of all; for an " *artificer* " is a *maker.*

And Parkhurst explains *ar* (אר) thus : " To *flow.* This is the idea of the word, though it occurs not as a verb simply in this sense; but as a noun אר *ar* is a river, a flood." And under its form *aur* (אור) he explains it thus :

---

[2] Holwell's extract of the Analysis of Ancient Mythology, p. 364.
[3] Anacalypsis, vol. i. p. 587.

" *The light,* so called from its wonderful fluidity ; for it is not only a *fluid,* but one of the most *active* and *perfect fluids* in nature[4]."

This is a mistake. *Light* was not named from its fluidity ; it is but one of the names of the sun modified. Fluidity implies motion and nothing more ; and every such idea is traceable to the sun, the supposed author of life and motion. It is not conceivable that at the remote period when language was being formed, and when the world was yet in a very rude and unenlightened state, any one could have supposed light to be a fluid. But for the reason I have just given, every word for *light* may also signify motion ; hence *lumen, flumen,* and *flow ;* and *lux* and *flux,* and *light* and *flight.*

But how, I may be asked, did *lumen* become *flumen,* or *lux* become *flux,* or *light* become *flight ?* By the l of these words having been aspirated[5]. Hence there was a time when *lumen* must have been *hlumen,* and *lux* have been *hlux,* and *light* have been *hlight ;* and then, when the aspirate was replaced by f, as it has often been, these words became *flumen, flux,* and *flight.* But if the aspirate had been dropped, as it might have been, then there would have been no means of distinguishing *lumen* from *flumen,* except by some slight difference in the pronunciation, such as there was in Saxon between *blác* and *blac ;* that is, white and black. And this serves to prove, since the aspirate should *never* be regarded as belonging to the root of a word, that there is not, as to their primary signification, the least difference between two such words as *lumen* and *flumen.* And when we compare *loaf* with its Saxon *hláf,* we see, since we do

---

[4] Lexicon, p. 29.
[5] Bosworth says that " th L was sometimes aspirated."

not write *hloaf*, that the l of *flumen, flux, flow,* and *flight* might have been left out.

But if the aspirate had been dropped from *flow*, we should have *low;* and as in *flux* and *flow* we have the same word, it follows that *low* is for *lux;* so that we are to consider its O as for *Oi*, and *Oi* as for U (witness *croix* and *crux, noix* and *nux*), and its W as X, this sign being composed of a V and a V placed thus $\frac{V}{A}$, and so allowed to meet. And as V is for five, so is X, or double V, for ten. And this etymology is confirmed by Dr. Johnson's definition of *low-bell,* which he explains thus: " A kind of fowling in the night, in which the birds are wakened by a bell and lured by a *flame* into a net. *Lowe* denotes a *flame* in Scotland, and to *lowe* is to *flame.*"

And what is the etymology of flame? Its root is *lam* (the aspirate f being dropped), and *lam* cannot differ from *lum* any more than *farther* can from *further;* and *lum* is the radical part of *lumen.* And as M is W in a different position, as shown farther back; and as W is the same as X, it follows that *lum* is the same as *lux.*

These latter etymologies serve to show how ideas the most dissimilar may be traced to the same source. Thus, to *blow* and to *flow* have very different meanings; but each of them implies motion, and this accounts for their being traceable to the sun, the supposed author of life and motion. And when we regard the *b* of *blow* as representing the aspirate *f*, and consequently as no part of the root of this word, we shall obtain the primary signification of the verb to *low,* as cattle do. And as, according to Dr. Johnson, to *lowe* means also to *flame,* this shows how a word synonymous with *fire* might be equal in form to one meaning *breath.* It shows also,

since W and V interchange (witness *wind* and *vent, wine*
and *vin*), that *lowe* cannot differ from *love;* and if this
derivation be true, to be in *love* means literally to be in
a *flame.* Hence, when animals are in love, they are
said to be in *heat—en chaleur,* as the French have it.

But what is the root of such a word as *flame?* It
can be no other than *am.* Then how is its l to be accounted for ? As the remains of such an article as *il* or
al; and that such, too, must be the l of *lux* and *lumen,*
the roots (*ux* and *um*) of these words being but different
forms of each other. Hence the *l* of *l*ustre and the *il*
of *il*lustrious; and hence the *il* of *il*lume and *il*lumine,
and the *al* of the French *allumer.* And as the roots
am, um, and *ux* must have once been but different names
of the sun, so must all such endings as replace them.
Thus, the *er* of *eros,* Greek of love, should be regarded
as the *am* of·flame and of *am*or. A similar view should
be taken of *love,* in Saxon *luf;* the *ov* and *uf* of each
word being equal to *om, um,* or *am.* But though such a
form as *love* or *luf* cannot differ from *life,* we are not
hence to infer that either of these ideas was called
after the other. The agreement in sense between two
such words should be closer. Their similarity in form
should be ascribed to their being traceable to the same
source. The ideas they express—*heat* and *existence*—
belong equally to the sun. These observations suggest
many others—too many to be noticed here.

I cannot, however, help quoting the following from
M. Müller's " Lectures on the Origin of Language[6]:"—
" *Etre* is the Latin *esse,* changed into *essere* and con-
tracted. The root, therefore, is *as,* which in all the
Aryan languages has supplied the material for the

---

[6] Vol. ii. p. 349.

auxiliary verb. Now, even in Sanskrit, it is true, this root *as* is completely divested of its material character; it means to *be* and nothing else. But there is in Sanskrit a derivative of the root *as*, namely, *asu*; and in this *asu*, which means the vital breath, the original meaning of the root *as* has been preserved. *As*, in order to give rise to such a noun as *asu*, must have meant to *breathe*, then to *live*, then to *exist*; and it must have passed through all these stages before it could have been used as the abstract auxiliary verb which we find, not only in Sanskrit, but in all the Aryan languages. Unless this one derivative, *asu*, life, had been preserved in Sanskrit, it would have been impossible to guess the original material meaning of the root *as*, to be."

This passage serves to show the advantage of knowing the origin of language. M. Max Müller was not aware that the ideas expressed by the words *be, breath, breathe, live,* and *exist*, are all but so many modified forms of the name of the sun. Thus, the *hal* of *hal*ios, the Doric of *helios* (the sun), is the *hal* of the Latin *hal*itus and of the French *hal*eine, and is but a different form of the word *sol*, of which the root is *al* or *ol*. And though the aspirate in *hal* is replaced by the S of *sol*, it might just as well have been represented by *b*, which proves *hal* or *sol* to be equal to *bal* and *bol*, each of which is a well-known name of the sun, while it is also equal to a word meaning *breath*, that is, to the *hal* of *hal*itus, and also to the *hal* of *hal*eine, French of breath. And that *bal* and *bol* have each the meaning of *breath*, is shown by their being radically the same as *bellow*; and that *wind* or *breath* is the primary sense of this word, is shown by the instrument named *bellows*, since this is in

H

French a *soufflet*, and in this language *souffle* means *breath*. The verbs to *bellow* and to *blow* are also radically the same; and to which may be added *bleat* and *blatant*; for, as *b* and *f* do constantly interchange, such a form as *blat* cannot differ from the *flat* of *flatus*, *wind*, and of which the verbal form *flare* means to *blow*.

Let us now observe that the root of such names of the sun as Bal, Bel, and *Bol* is *al*, *el*, and *ol*, the *b* of each word having grown out of the aspirate. And as *b* and *p* interchange very often, we discover in Bel the *pel* of πέλω, I am; and also the *pel* of Apello, which is another way of writing Apollo, and he was the sun[7]. But how are we to account for the A prefixed to the *pel* of Apello and to the *bel* of Abelion? We are to consider it as a definite article, or as a vowel before the initial consonant, for which, as already stated, there is a euphonic tendency.

The following from Baxter, quoted by Dr. Johnson under the word *ball*, throws considerable light on the name Bal: " Bol, Danish; bol, Dutch. *Bal*, diminutively Belin, the Sun or Apollo of the Celtæ, was called by the ancient Gauls *Abellio*. Whatever was round, and in particular the head, was called by the ancients either *Bâl* or *Bel*, and likewise *Bol* or *Bŭl*. Among the modern Persians, the head is called *Pole*; and the Flemings still call the head *Boile*. Πόλος is the head or poll, and πόλειν is to turn. Βόλος signifies likewise a round ball, whence *bowl*, and *bell*, and *ball*, which the Welch term *bél*. By the Scotch also the head is named *bhel*. Figuratively, the Phrygians and Thurians, by

---

[7] He was, says Bryant, " the same as the Abelion of the East. The old Romans called him Apello."

Βαλλὴν understood a king. Hence also, in the Syriac dialects, Βααλ, Βηλ, and likewise Βωλ, signifies lord, and by this name also the sun ; and in some dialects, Ηλ and Ιλ, whence Ιλος and "Ηλιος, Γηλιος and Βηλιος, and also in the Celtic diminutive way of expression Ελενος, Γελενος, and Βελενος signified the sun ; Ελενη, Γελενη, Βελενη, the moon. Among the Teutonics, *hol* and *heil* have the same meaning : whence the adjective *holig* or *heilig* is derived, and signifies divine or holy ; and the aspiration being changed into s, the Romans form their *sol*."

This passage affords ample proof, that in *Bal, Baal, Bel, Bel,* and *sol,* there is only one word under these different forms, and to which we must add *Abellio, Apello,* and *Apllo,* &c. ; the root being always *al, el,* or *ol,* and which, on being aspirated, become *hal, hel,* and *hol,* whence *sol,* and the *hel* of *hēlios* and *helenē,* the sun and the moon, in Greek. And as what was round took its name from the sun, or from something else thence called, we may be sure that in the *Apell* of *Apello* (ancient form of Apollo) and in the English word *apple,* we have the same word, and consequently the German *apfel* and its representatives in several cognate languages. It has not, however, been hitherto suspected that *Apollo* and *apple* make but one word. It has been equally unknown that the *ēl* of the Greek Μηλὶς and the *om* of the Latin *pomum,* each meaning apple, were ancient names of the sun ; yet these two words (*El* and *Om*) must have once served as such.

But how are we to account for the *M* of the Μηλ of Μηλὶς? When the *Hel* of Hēlios was alone in use, its aspirate appears to have been first changed for *b,* and then *b* for *m,* which sometimes happens, as is shown by the French word *beugler* being also written *meugler*, and the Greek Βροτὸς being Μορτὸς. The p of the *pom* of pomum is to be accounted for in the same way ; its root *om* must have first become *hom*, then *fom*, and finally *pom*.

But if it were true, which it is not, that the first meaning attached to *as* (the Sanskrit *be*) was to *breathe*, we are still at a loss to know how *as* happened to have this meaning, or after what such a verb as to *breathe* was called. According to M. Max Müller's origin of *as*, the verb to *breathe* was first named, and then the noun *breath*. But this is taking the derivative for the original. There can be no greater mistake than to derive nouns from verbs. The first words in use must have been the names of things, and verbs are nothing more than names used verbally. The Sanskrit *as* (Be) could not in the beginning be distinguished from one of the names of the sun, but by some slight difference in sound; and it must have then meant life, being, or existence, and not to breathe, which idea must have come long afterwards, and have been the word *as* itself, slightly modified for the sake of distinction. The same may be said of *asu*, breath ; but whatever form the verb to *breathe* obtains in Sanskrit, it will, I have no doubt, be found to be radically the same as the auxiliary *as*. M. Max Müller, who is reported to be well acquainted with Sanskrit, should have given us this verb.

But what is the radical part of the English word *breath ?* It is *br*, between which two consonants any vowel may be inserted, so that *br* is equal to *bar, ber, bir, bor,* or *bur*.

And if we now consider the *b* of these words as having

grown out of the aspirate, what remains (*ar, er, ir, or,* and *ur*) will be the real root of *br*. Nor can such forms as *bar, ber,* &c., differ from *bal, bel,* &c., any more than the *terr* of *terra* can differ from the *tell* of *tellus,* this arising from *r* and *l* being the same sign differently formed and pronounced. If this be true, I shall be told that *bar* and its different forms may have been also names of the sun, as well as ideas called after it. And so has it been. Higgins[8] speaks thus of *bra* : "It is singular that Parkhurst gives us the verb *bra,* to create, but no noun for creator. But though it may be lost now, it cannot be doubted that the verb must have had its correspondent noun. I have before observed that this word *Pr* or *Br* is said, by Whiter, always to mean creator." And the sun was, as I have already observed more than once, styled the Creator. But Higgins, in his second volume, p. 243, says, that "Bra means *factor* and *fecit,*" that is, it is, like many other words, both a noun and a verb; he does not, however, give an instance of its serving as a noun. But when we observe that *b* serves as a substitute for the aspirate, and that *bar* (whence *bra*) must have once been *har,* we discover the noun of the verb *bra,* and see that it has not been lost, but only concealed under one of its more ancient forms; for *har* is the radical part of such words as *hara, haris,* and *heri.* And hara means God, and heri means Saviour[9]; and as to haris (in Hebrew חרם *hrs*), it means, according to Parkhurst, " the solar light[1],"and according to Drummond[2], faber,

[8] Anacalypsis, vol. i. p. 431.

[9] "Hara Hara is a name of Muha-Deva, which is Great God; Heri means Saviour." Ibid. i. p. 313.

[1] Lexicon, p. 201.   [2] Orig. vol. iii. p. 192.

artifex, machinator; and the same authority says it
" may be sounded *choras, chros,* and *chrus.*"   This serves
to show that the aspirate may be represented by *ch* as
well as by *b* and other consonants[3].

The reader will please to bear in mind that in *al* and
ar, that is, in the roots of such names of the sun as Bal
and Bar, we have but other forms of the Sanskrit *as* (Be);
so that if *as* had, like *al* and *ar*, taken the aspirate, it
would be now composed of three letters instead of two.
And what would its form be?   It would first be *has,* and
there is no knowing what it would be afterwards, as the
aspirate might be replaced by many different signs, such
as *f, b, v, w,* or their equivalents.   On consulting my
Bosworth, I find that the aspirate has in Saxon been
replaced by *w,* the infinitive of the verb to *be* in this
language being *wesan,* of which the root *es* is, like the *es*
of the Latin *esse,* precisely equal to the Sanskrit *as,* for
its *e* being the same as *o,* and *o* having *i* understood,
and as the two signs *o* and *i* make *a, es* is thus brought
equal to *as.*

So much for the verb to be; it was named after
existence—in other words, after the sun.   And how far
etymologists have been from knowing any thing of its
real origin, may be supposed by M. Max Müller's deriving
it from the verb to breathe.   But what does this learned
gentleman mean when he says that the French imperfect
j'étais and the participle *été,* both derived from the Latin
stare, " show how easily so definite an idea as to *stand*
may dwindle down to the abstract idea of *being*[4] "?   If
these words have any meaning, they imply that the verb
to *be* must have had for its original the verb to *stand,*

---

[3] See Higgins, Anacalypsis, vol. i. p. 587.
[4] Lectures, vol. ii. p. 350.

and not the verb to *breathe*, as M. Max Müller has already stated; for if a word be nothing more than the dwindled-down form of another word, it is evident that it must have come from that other word of which it is, as it were, but a shred.

But etymologists not having hitherto known any thing of the origin of human speech, it has not been in their power to tell why the ideas to *stand* and to *be* are expressed alike; so that, whenever an attempt is made to account for such a relationship, etymologists are sure either to contradict statements previously advanced, or to give utterance to what neither themselves nor any one else can understand.

When, farther back, I had occasion to show how all the words of a language fall naturally of themselves into three chief divisions, I then found that death was called after lowness or the being down, and that the being upright or standing having the opposite meaning, it served to signify life; and this it is which accounts for the verb to *be* and the verb to *stand* being expressed by the same word. Hence, when a philologist talks of the verb to *stand* dwindling down to the verb to *be*, his words have really no meaning.

A very plain proof that the idea expressed by such a word as *standing* may also serve to signify existence, is shown by the name given to the quarter of the heavens where the sun rises; for, though it is written *east*, it cannot differ from *est*, its form in French, and which is also the radical part of *estre*, now *être*, for the *east* is also the *levant* or *rising*, just as the *west* is the not-rising or the being-down; and hence in French the *couchant* means the *west*.

Now, what is the etymology of *west*? No one can

tell, except my humble self. All the Germans know of
it is this, that it bears the same form in their language
as it does in Saxon, and that it is nearly the same in
several other languages. But this is only telling me that
the etymology of *west* is *west*, and this is no etymology.
Let us now analyze the word. It is equal to *ou* and *est*,
its *w*, when not representing the aspirate h, being equal
to *ou*. Thus, as the *w* in the English pronoun *we* is pronounced like the *ou* in the French affirmative *oui*, this
shows *w* and *ou* to have the same sound, *we* and *oui* being
pronounced alike. This is confirmed by *ouest*, which is
the French of *west;* and the two words are also alike in
sound. What now remains, since *ouest* is for *ou* and *est*,
but to know the meaning of *ou?* And is it not easy to
suppose that *ou* must be a negative, and that *ou-est* is
for *not-east;* that is, not *standing*, not *rising*, and consequently *down*, or *couchant*. Hence it is that the Greek
word οὐ means *no* or *not*. Every French philologist
must therefore, I shall be told, know the etymology of
ouest; it is, however, a mistake to think so; he knows
no more of the origin of this word than any one else.
Thus, De Roquefort says it is Teutonic, and is written
west. This is no etymology. Nor is M. Littré's any
better, as the following serves to show: " Allem. *west;*
Isl. *vest;* Sued. *vester*. Il y a en Pictet (t. 1) une dissertation très-ingénieuse sur l'étymologie de *west*, rap-
porté à *vastum*, désert, mer, parce que le désert et le
Caspienne étaient à l'ouest des Aryas qui devinrent les
Germains."

Nor do French philologists know any thing more of
the origin of *est* (east) than they do of *ouest*. Here is
all M. Littré says of it: " Mot germanique. Allem.
ost; Anglais, *east*."

From what M. Littré says above, under his etymology of *ouest*, it is clear that he imagines a relationship in meaning to exist between *mer* and *désert ;* but there is none whatever, as I shall have occasion to show farther on, when I come to notice M. Max Müller's very faulty etymology of *mare*, the sea.

CHAPTER XVIII. '

IDENTITY IN MEANING OF THE VERB TO BE AND THE PRONOUN I.

In the foregoing account of the formation of alphabetical signs, I was, in order to be brief, obliged to suppress many observations suggested during that inquiry. These observations relate chiefly to the verb to *be* and the personal pronoun *I*, neither of which has, I am sure, been hitherto fully accounted for. The investigation which is now to follow, will require from the general reader rather more than ordinary attention, for the subject is not a very simple one—it is not what we can call "reading-made-easy." But that I may be understood by all—by the slow thinker and observer as well as by the reader who catches every thing at a glance, but who often forgets it as soon—I intend not to shrink, especially in the beginning of this inquiry, from a repetition of some things already told, and perhaps more than once.

The reader will please to recollect that I have already shown IO to have been the earliest form of this sign, B, which is composed of I and this character, 3, the

latter being a substitute for the O. Nor can the reader
have yet forgotten that this second part of B, that is
3, may be either S or ᵐ , the latter, which is a Saxon
form, being now made thus M. By this we see that
the same character may, according to the position of its
parts, be either an S or an M. Nor should this surprise us, since, as I have already stated, M is in Greek
what it is in Latin, English, and many other languages,
whilst, when made to take this position, Σ, it is in
Greek the capital S. By this we see that the earliest
form of B, namely, IO, is equal to both IS and IM,
and that there is not a shade of difference between these
two forms, each of them being an exact representation
of the sign B. And as O is understood before the I of
both IS and IM, according to the rule stated farther
back, it follows that IS and IM are each equal to
OIS and OIM; that is, when here the O and I coalesce
and become *a, as,* and *am.* And as these two words
are also precisely equal to each other, it follows, since
in Sanskrit *as* means *be,* that such too must be the
meaning of *am* when regarded as the same verb in any
other language ; hence, when in English we say, " If
I *be* " instead of " If I *am,*" the meaning is exactly the
same, so that it is only conventionally that such locutions
are sometimes used differently. And though it is now
considered very vulgar to say " I *be* " for " I *am,*" it were,
however, very correct so to express ourselves, did custom
only allow it.

But in the IO which we have now shown to be equal
to the sign B, and also to the words IS, *as,* and *am,*
we see the Italian of the personal pronoun I; and this
circumstance deserves to be noticed. If this pronoun be
the same as the verb to *be,* its literal meaning must

be a *being*, conventionally a being of the first person singular. And if we grant this, we may be sure that such too is the meaning of the corresponding word in all languages. According to this view, there can be no difference in meaning between two such words as *I* and *am;* so that the word for *I* in one language may be the word for *am* in another. We should also observe that each of these words has several other representatives; that I is not only equal to IO, but also to *OI* and *a*, as well as to *u*, *ie*, *ei;* and of which each may be abridged to an *i*, an *o*, or an *e*. Hence, when we drop the O of IO or of OI, we obtain the English pronoun I, which, as I learn from M. Littré, is also the representative of *je* in the French province Nivernais. The same authority gives also *IO* not only as the Italian of *je*, but as a provincial form of this pronoun. But if M. Littré knew that *IO* is the elder form of *Ie*, he could scarcely help discovering—since I was anciently used for j—that in Io, Ic, and je we have but one and the same word under these three different forms.

The form *am* is also equal to *oim*, *um*, *eim*, and, by contraction, to *om*, *em*, or *im*. And now, while bearing in mind that *am* and its several forms are but modifications of OI or IO, we may state what we have to observe respecting the first person singular of the verb to *be*. *Asmi* (its form in Sanskrit) is for *as-ma*, that is, *am I* in English; for, as I has O understood, and as O and I make *a*, the I of *as-mi* is for *a*, and as *ma* has the meaning of I in Sanskrit, the learned make no mistake when they explain *asmi* as they do. They cannot, however, have known by what means *ma* became i. I am going to tell them how this has happened. It did not arise from the *a* of *ma* having, when under this form, been abridged to *i*, but when *a* appeared thus, Oi, its O was dropped, so that i alone remained. Hence the earliest form of this pronoun must have been *moi*, which, by the dropping of the O, became *mi;* but those who spoke Sanskrit differently having allowed the *a* and i to meet, made both *moi* and *mi* become *ma.* We have not, however, in *ma* and *am* two different words, but the same word read differently; so that in one province of the same country *ma* may have been for *I,* whilst in another province it may have been for *am,* or some modified form of this word, such as *oim, eim, um, im,* or *em.* Thus, in Hebrew the word for mother is *am;* but when read from right to left, it is the *ma* of *mamma;* and *ab* (Hebrew of father), when read in the same way, becomes *ba,* and this is the *pa* of *papa;* for *p* and *b* are but different forms of the same letter, and they constantly interchange.

Another form in Sanskrit of the pronoun I, is *aham.* How is it to be accounted for? By the applying of one of my rules, which says, that every initial vowel may or may not be aspirated, that is to say, it may take an *h* before it, or it may not; or, if having the *h* it may be deprived of it. The right use of this rule is to be confirmed by the result obtained. Hence, granting *am,* which is the same as *ma* (I), to be the root of *aham,* and then allowing *am* to become, according to the rule just stated, *ham;* and then, from the tendency there is to sound a vowel before initial consonants, *ham* will become *aham.* But as the aspirate *h* is frequently replaced by other consonants, and of which *s* is a very usual one (compare *hepta* in Greek and *septem* in Latin), it follows that *aham* is equal to *asam;* and this form cannot differ from *azem;* and in Zend this word represents *aham.*

We have thus shown how two such forms as *aham* and *azem* are to be derived from IO or OI. But in what does *aham* differ from *ma,* which is its other form? Since *ma* is the same as *am,* we may say that there is no difference whatever between *aham* and *ma ;* for the aspirate prefixed to *am* is no radical part of this word, so that *ham* is the same as *am.* And as to the *a* prefixed to *aham,* it does not, any more than h, belong to *am* : the cause of its being prefixed to *ham* arises from the euphonic tendency that often prevails, of prefixing a vowel to an initial consonant. Nor are we to account for the *em* of *azem* but as a different pronunciation of *am.* This *em* must have therefore become *hem ;* and *hem* cannot differ from *sem* (compare the *hem* of *hemi*sphere and the *sem* of *semi*circle), because h is often replaced by *s ;* and *sem* has, from the tendency to prefix vowels to initial consonants, become *asem,* which is *azem* differently pronounced.

If we now take the O of *ego* in Greek and Latin, as the original form of this word, it may be also very easily traced to *IO* or *Oi ;* for, referring to g, Donnegan observes that in some dialects "it is prefixed to words as a mark of aspiration, thus δοῦπος becomes γδοῦπος, and αἶα, γαῖα." Hence when Ō (ω) is aspirated by g, it becomes gō ; and from the euphonic tendency to prefix a vowel to initial consonants, go will become εγω, whence the Latin *ego.*

We may now assume that two such forms of this pronoun as the Gothic *ik* and the German *ich* are but modifications of the *eg* of ego. In Picardy, *ege, ej,* and *enj* are, according to M. Littré, the forms in use, and which are also the same as *ego,* as it is not difficult to perceive.

But under whatever form the pronoun I may appear, we shall find it not to differ in meaning from the verb to *be*, and that it is also but a modified form of this word. Hence, to know the primary signification of the verb to *be*, is to know also that of the pronoun I.

If we were therefore to say "*I* a Roman," every one would conceive such a locution to mean " I am a Roman;" and if, instead of " I a Roman," we were to say " *am* a Roman," the meaning would be still the same. This arises from *I* and *am* having each the same primitive meaning; and we can conceive that anciently, when words were few, *I* or *am* must have been often used to signify *I am*. How then are we to explain the Latin *sum?* It must have first been only *um*, of which there are several other forms, such as *oim, am, eim, om, em*, or *im;* and, granting this, as many persons must have aspirated the *u, um* must have become *hum;* and as *h* was frequently replaced by other consonants, and especially by S, as shown above, *hum* would become *sum*, and the meaning be either *I* or *am*. According to this interpretation of *sum*, " *Sum Romanus*" may be explained either by " *I a Roman;*" or " *am a Roman.*" Hence, though *sum* represents the Sanskrit *asmi*, it is not this word contracted; that is to say, it is not composed of two words, but of one, and which one may mean either *I* or *am*, but, literally considered, it does mean both *I* and *am*.

But Sanskrit scholars account for the origin of *sum* otherwise. They say it must have been *esum*, and that *esum* must have been *esumi;* and that the *u* of the latter —as if no part of the root of *sum*—is only a euphonic link, here serving to connect *es* and *mi;* and this analysis they confirm by the Sanskrit *asmi* and the Æolic form of εἰμί, that is, ἐσμί. Such is, I apprehend, an exact representation of the following passage : " Le mot *sum* est une forme réduite de *esum*, lui-même pour *esumi*, avec intercalation d'un *u* euphonique pour *esmi*, comme le prouvent le Sanscrit *asmi* et le Grec *ἐσμί* (éolien), devenu dans la langue commune *εἰμί*."

The above [5] is taken from a work of very great merit, entitled, " Manuel pour l'Etude des Racines Grecques et Latines, par Anatole Bailly. Ouvrage publié sous la direction de E. Egger, membre de l'Institut, professeur de la littérature grecque à la Faculté des Lettres de Paris."

In two other parts of his work this authority refers again to sum ; but no more than the following needs be quoted : " s-u-m, pour *es-u-m*, es-u-mi (l'*u* est une voyelle de liaison [6].)"

Before quoting another learned authority who argues to the same effect, I beg to call the reader's attention to this single fact, namely, that *ἴω* is in the Bœotian dialect for egō, and that this same word *ἴω* is also allowed to be one of the radical forms of *εἰμί*, to *be*. We thus see fully confirmed what I discovered farther back by the application of these principles; that to know the meaning of the verb to *be* is also to know the meaning of the personal pronoun *I*, in no matter what language. And though the first person singular, present tense, of Latin verbs end in *o, eo* or *io*, they are all one and the same, so that *o* and *eo* are each for *io*. And as IO, as I have already shown, is the original of IM, and consequently of OIM, just as OIM is of *am*, it follows that the *o, eo*, and *io* might as well have been *am*. This is confirmed by the second *am* of *amamus*, for it is evidently for the *o* of amo ; and so may we say that the *em* and *im* of

such plural endings as *emus* and *imus* are also for *am.*
Hence there is no difference in meaning between inqu*io* and
inqu*am,* the *io* of the former being correctly represented
by the *am* of the latter. Sanskrit scholars do therefore
mistake when they suppose that *inquam* is for *inqua-mi,*
which mistake is to be ascribed to their not knowing
that every such pronominal ending of a verb as *am* or *em*
is but a different form of the Sanskrit pronoun *ma* (I),
which must have first been *moi,* and then *mi,* its *O* having
been dropped with some persons, and its *O* and *i* having
with others been allowed to coalesce, and so make *a.*

But Sanskrit scholars make a stranger mistake when
they suppose that the Latin verbs present tense ending in
O must have first been *omi,* not supposing that every such
verbal ending in Latin is as genuine a pronoun as the
Sanskrit *ma* or *mi.* And this mistake is made still worse
by *sum* and *inquam* being referred to as proofs that these
verbal endings in Latin can be nothing less than the
diminished forms of the Sanskrit pronoun.

That this statement is no exaggeration, and that the
censure I have already passed on the faulty etymology
of *sum* has been equally just, the following passage, taken
from another learned work, will, it is presumed, fully
certify :—

" Le MI caractéristique de la première personne, si bien
conservé dans le Sanskrit, le Lithuanien, et le Grec, est
reduit d'abord à la consonne initiale M, ce qui nous fait
perdre le signe de rapport I ; mais ce n'est pas tout :
cet M, précieux reste du pronom MA (moi) organique,
ne nous est parvenu que dans Es-u-m (pour AS-mi),
plus tard S-u-m, et dans *inqua*-M pour *inqua*-MI. Par-
tout ailleurs, la notion de la première personne s'est
attachée à la voyelle Ō remplaçant la voyelle Ā organique

précédant immédiatement la terminaison, mais ne la constituant en aucun façon.

" C'est ainsi que l'organique Iaksa-MI, en Latin organique legō-MI est devenu legō, après avoir sans aucun doute, été legō-M (comparez su-M et inqua-M).

" De même, Man-aya-MI, *je fais penser,* après avoir été Man-eo-MI, est devenu mon-eō-M, puis *mon-eo.* De même encore Kam-aya-MI, *j'embrasse, j'aime,* après avoir été Kam-aō-MI, puis Kam-ao-M, et Kam-o-M est devenu (K)amo. Le k aryaque, conservé en Sanskrit, est tombé en Latin."

This is a mistake; *amo* has never had the k here referred to, and it cannot therefore have lost it. But we are not hence to infer that the *Kam* of *Kam-aya-mi* is not the *am* of *amo.* If an Englishman were to request the first ten persons that happened to pass his door to pronounce the word *amo,* five of them might, in all probability, aspirate its *a,* and consequently read *amo* as if it were written *hamo.* And so has it been, with regard to the aspirate, in all languages over the world. And this aspirate has been replaced by several different signs : witness *h*orn, *c*ornu, and *Képas,* in which words the *h, c,* and *k* represent one another. Now, as an initial k is not such a letter as can be easily dropped, we may be sure that if the *am* of *amo* is to be derived from the *Kam* of Kam-aya-mi, the derivation must have taken place when this Sanskrit word was written am-aya-mi; that is to say, when its initial *a* had not yet been aspirated.

And as the O of am*o* is for the assumed pronoun IO, the endings of the second and third persons, that is, *as* and *at* (*amas, amat*) are also to be regarded as genuine pronouns, and not as corrupt forms of the corresponding words in Sanskrit. But M. Amédée de Caix de Saint-

I

Amour (author of the passage just quoted) is of a different opinion, as the reader will find on consulting this
author's very learned work, entitled "La Langue Latine
étudiée dans l'Unité Indo-Européenne," p. 192.

What has been now said of the verb to Be and some of
the personal pronouns, suggests several other observations, of which a few may be here set down at random.
What difference is there in meaning between the verbal
pronominal endings *o, as, at,* as in am*o,* am*as,* am*at ?*
There is none whatever; for it is only conventionally
they differ as to person, so that each of them might have
been either of the other two.   Then what is the primary
signification of every such pronoun ?   It is that of *one,*
and it does not, for this reason, differ from either the
definite or indefinite article, nor from any word that did
anciently serve as a name of the sun.

Every such pronoun is also equal in meaning to the
verb to *be ;* hence the *as* of am*as* is this verb in Sanskrit,
and from which the English verb *is* cannot differ.   The
Latin pronoun *is* has still the same meaning, and so have
its feminine and neuter forms *ea* and *id ;* to which we
may add *he, she,* and *it* in English ; these and all such
words not being different from one another in either use
or meaning, save conventionally.

Now, as the personal pronoun and the verb to *be* do
not differ from each other in meaning, it may not be
always easy to tell, when both words from their having
coalesced make only one, which is the pronoun or which
is the verb.   Thus, if *eom* in Saxon means not only *am*
but *I am* (Ic eom), which of its two parts, if we analyze
it thus, *eo-am,* is for the verb or the pronoun ?   As the
English pronoun *I* appears to have been once pronounced
oi, the Saxon *eom*—supposing it to have been for the

pronoun and the verb—would be then for *oi-m*, that is,
I'm, instead of *I am*. But in the *em* and *am* of the
potential mood in Latin (am*em*, doce*am*) we have not
verbs but two pronouns, each representing ego.

We may now well doubt if *am* has been always in
English an inflection of the verb to *be* and never a pronoun. As *m* and *n* do constantly interchange, *am* cannot
differ from *an*, which means *one* in English (*an* apple, *an*
egg, that is, *one* apple, *one* egg) as it does in Saxon;
and from *a* and *u* being the same sign, *an* cannot differ
from *un*, root of *unus*, and the French of *one*. From *am*
having this meaning of *one*, such too must be the meaning
of the pronoun I, since, when a verbal ending, *am* stands
for I. The Hebrew word אני *ani*, written also אנה *ane*,
is the pronoun I[7]; and the root of this word (that is,
אן *an*) is a name of the sun[8], after which, as already
stated, both unity and existence have been called. Hence
the pronoun I means *one* and a thing existing, conventionally the first person. Nor can *an* differ from *as*
(French of ace), which therefore means *one* as well as it
does in Sanskrit. And as the aspirate of εἷς forms no
part of the root of this word, εις is the same as *eis* (one),
and consequently as *ois* or *as*.

If we needed other proofs that the personal pronoun I,
in no matter what language, does not differ in meaning
from the verb to be, and that it implies both unity
and existence, we might not go beyond εἶναι, the infinitive of εἰμί; for the radical part (*ein*) of this word
is not only equal to *oin*, *an*, and *un*, but it is the German
of one.

And in Lithuanian, "a language still spoken," says M.
Max Müller, "by about 200,000 people in Eastern Prussia,

and by more than a million of people in the conterminous parts of Russia," the pronoun I is, according also to M. Littré, expressed by *isz*. And as this word cannot differ from the verb *is*, it affords a plain proof that the pronoun I and the verb to *be* are in meaning one and the same. " And there are in this language," says M. Max Müller, " some grammatical forms more primitive and more like Sanskrit than the corresponding forms in Greek and Latin [9]."

I have been thus as particular and as close as I could possibly be, in endeavouring to show the identity in meaning of personal pronouns and the verb to *be*; for though the learned no longer regard the verb to *be* as an abstract idea, but as having had a material origin, yet their notions of this origin are very imperfect; and as to the personal pronouns, they cannot imagine how they have come into existence, or what they literally mean. This will be confirmed by the following, which I transcribe from M. Max Müller's Lectures on the Science of Language, vol. ii. p. 347.

"*Victor Cousin*, in his Lectures on the History of Philosophy during the Eighteenth Century[1], endeavours to controvert Locke's assertion by the following process :— ' I shall give you two words,' he says, ' and I shall ask you to trace them back to primitive words expressive of sensible ideas. Take the word *je*, I. This word, at least in all languages known to me, is not to be reduced, not to be decomposed, primitive; and it expresses no sensible idea, it represents nothing but the meaning which the mind attaches to it; it is a pure and true sign, without any reference to any sensible idea. The

---

[9] Lectures, vol. i. p. 219.   [1] Paris, 1841, vol. ii. p. 274.

word *être*, to be, is exactly in the same case; it is primitive and altogether intellectual. I know of no language in which the French verb *être* is rendered by a corresponding word that expresses a sensible idea; and therefore it is not true that all the roots of language, in their last analysis, are signs of sensible ideas.'"

Little as I know of Hebrew, it would seem that Victor Cousin, if at all acquainted with this language, knew still less, for, according to Parkhurst, this verb is more significant of substance than of ideality. "It is joined," says this authority, "with both genders and numbers. It seems to have rather the nature of a noun than of a verb, taking after it several of the same suffixes as nouns."

Parkhurst explains it also as meaning, under its form שׁ *is*, "*substance, reality, the true riches.*" And also, "a *being*, or *thing subsisting* or *existing;*" and with a formative א *a* which makes שׁ *is* become שׁא *ais*, it is explained, "*a person, a man*[2]."

But does not the noun *être* in French also mean a person, a man? I am sure that it does, and that every French dictionary will tell me I am right. Hence *being* is in English not only the participle present of *be*, but it is also a noun, just as *être* is in French.

Referring to Cousin's opinion of *je*, M. Max Müller says, "Now it must be admitted that the French *je*, which is the Sanskrit *aham*, is a word of doubtful etymology. It belongs to the earliest formations of Aryan speech; and we need not wonder that even in Sanskrit the materials out of which this pronoun was formed should have disappeared. We can explain in English such words as *myself* or *your honour*, but we could not

[2] Lexicon, p. 251.

attempt, with the means supplied by English alone, to analyze *I, thou,* and *he.* It is the same with the Sanskrit *aham,* a word carried down by the stream of language from such distant ages, that even the Vedas, as compared with them, are but, as it were, of yesterday. But though the etymology of *aham* is doubtful, it has never been doubtful to any scholar that, like all other words, it must have an etymology; that it must be derived either from a predicative or from a demonstrative root. Those who would derive *aham* from a predicative root, have thought of the root *ah,* to breathe, to speak. Those who would derive it from a demonstrative root, refer us to the Vedic *gha,* the later *ha, this,* used like the Greek *hóde*[3]."

The reader cannot have yet forgotten my etymology of the French *je;* I have shown it, he may recollect, to be for IO, between which and IE there is no more difference than there is between show and shew in English; nor is there any more difference between IE and JE than there is in French between *jour* and its elder form *iour.* I have also had occasion to show that IO and its form IE was a name both of the true God and the sun, as Parkhurst testifies. It would seem as if the author of the following passage knew something of the primitive meaning of this personal pronoun, though how he could have come by such knowledge, I cannot imagine :—

"Jean Paul, in his Levana, p. 32, says, I is—excepting God, the true I and true Thou at once—the highest and most incomprehensible that can be uttered by language or contemplated. It is there all at once, as the whole realm of truth and conscience, which, without 'I,'

---

[3] Lectures, 2nd series, p. 348.

is nothing. We must ascribe it to God as well as to unconscious beings, if we want to conceive the being of the One and the existence of the others [4]."

The author of the above seems to have taken the pronoun I as a name of the Deity; and if so, he did not mistake.

Farther on I shall have occasion to notice M. Max Müller's etymology of the Sanskrit verb to be, *as*.

From what this learned Professor says of *aham*,—in Sanskrit, the pronoun I,—it is evident that the etymology of this word is wholly unknown; and this admission he confirms still further by the following :—

" I thought it possible, in my *History of Sanskrit Literature*, p. 21, to connect *ah-am* with Sanskrit âha, I said, Greek ἤ, Latin *aja*, and *nego*, nay, with Gothic *ahma* (instead of agma), spirit; but I do so no longer. Nor do I accept the opinion of Benfey (Sanskrit Grammatik, § 773), who derives *aham* from the pronominal root *gha* with a prosthetic *a*. It is a word which, for the present, must remain without a genealogy [5]."

Had the learned known any thing of the rule illustrated under the article headed, "*The use and advantage of knowing that initial vowels may take the aspirate II*," they would have long since discovered the etymology of *aham*. But this rule the learned could not know without having first known the origin of language, out of which knowledge all the rules thus far applied have grown.

---

[4] Quoted by M. Max Müller, Lect., vol. ii. p. 349.
[5] Lectures, vol. ii. p. 148.

CHAPTER XIX.

HAND.

LET us now show how the names of things very diffe-rent from any of the attributes of the sun can, however, be traced—but indirectly—to the same source as those expressive of *being* and *goodness*.

As many words are indebted for their origin to such as served to signify the *hand*, we can conceive that such words should never be taken as the primitive forms of names designating this member. Thus, the idea expressed by *hold* must have been called after the *hand*; and the latter should not, for this reason, be traced to the verb to *hold*, but this verb should be traced to a word for the *hand*. Hence, when we make the *l* of hold take its form n (compare *l*uncheon and *n*unchion), we shall, instead of *hold*, have *hond*, which is one of the forms in Saxon for *hand*. But I shall be told that *to hand* does not mean *to hold*, but, on the contrary, to pass or transmit some-thing from the hand. But it is only conventionally that *to hand* has this meaning. In the beginning, *to hand* must have been used for *to hold*. Thus, in such a sentence as "let me go; I do not wish you to hand me;" the meaning of *to hand* would be *to hold*. And this view is confirmed by the verb *to unhand*, which is literally *to unhold*; that is, *to hand not*. But though *to unhand* is still in use, to *unhold* is not. But why so? because there is no necessity for it; if *unhand* did not exist, we should have *unhold*. We thus see, by comparing *to hand*

and to *unhand*, that the former verb must have once meant *to hold* as well as to transmit, the latter being the only sense in which it is now used.

On looking into my Johnson, I find these views of mine confirmed by his simply informing me that the verb *to hold* is haldan in Gothic and Saxon, and *henden* in Dutch, to which he might have added the German *halten*. Now, as in these several languages we have the same word for *hold*, written somewhat differently, it follows, that if any one of them can be shown to be the same as *hond* or *hand* (both of which exist in Saxon) that the others must be also the same as these two words. There is one of them, *henden*, of which its root, *hend*, can no more differ from *hond* than *shew* and *show* in English can from each other; or than *elder* can from *older*. And when instead of this *hend* of *henden*, we write *hond*, to which it is equal, and then give to its o its i understood, and so obtain *hoind*, we bring this form equal, by joining its o and i, to hand; which, though not so old as *hoind*, is certainly older than *hond*, oi being the first form that *a* must have ever had.

Let me now take the liberty of showing the reader how, from knowing this much, he may learn something more. Now, when *hoind* was in existence, as it must have once been, if then the o was dropped instead of the i, *hind* would remain, and this happens to be the radical part of the verb to *hinder;* and to *hinder* a person from doing any thing, is to *hold* him from it; by which we see that the idea of hindering is to be traced to the hand, but indirectly, because called after an idea (to hold) which has been named from the hand. Now, to tell me that the verb to *hinder* is very like another word in one or several of the Teutonic languages, were to tell me very little, and this is all that has been hitherto known of this idea; but to trace it as we have just done, is to show how man must have first reasoned with himself when making his words; and this is knowledge not to be despised, but greatly valued; at least Locke thought so.

But there is another source to which the idea of hinderance can be traced, and of which—it being so very evident—no one seems to be ignorant. I mean *impede*, in the radical part of which (*pede*) we see the ablative of *pes* (the foot); so that to *impede* has, when we regard *im* as a negative equal to *un* (witness *im*poli in French and *un*polite in English), the literal meaning of to *unfoot*; that is, not to allow to one the free use of his feet.

There are several etymologies suggested by those just noticed to which it is scarcely necessary to draw the reader's attention—such as to *halt*, as soldiers do after a march; or to halt, from being lame. It is evident that in each case *halt* means to *hold*. When the soldier is ordered to halt, he is ordered to hold himself from marching; and he who is lame holds himself, as it were, from advancing, at every step he takes. Halter also, as it is used for holding certain animals, seems to have taken its name from the use made of it. Dr. Johnson refers it to a word in Saxon meaning the *neck, hals.* And though the Latin word (*capistrum*) refers it to the head, the French of *licou* is, in meaning, literally a *neck-tie; li* being the root of both *lier*, to tie, and *lien*, a tie; and *cou* or *col* being for neck. Hence, every time a French gentleman calls for his *cravate*, he is, inasmuch as the primary meaning is concerned, calling for a *halter;* for a cravat is a neck-tie.

But what is the etymology of *cravate?* French philologists cannot in my humble opinion tell; for it is not

reasonable to suppose that so refined a people as the
French did not wear cravats before 1636, at which time
they are said to have borrowed this ornament from the
Croatians. Such is the origin of *cravate,* according to De
Roquefort; and I am rather surprised at finding so distinguished a philologist as M. Littré to be of the same
opinion. De Roquefort's words are, " C'est en 1636
que nous avons emprunté cet ornement des Croates,
lorsque la France était en guerre avec l'Allemagne[6]."
And M. Littré says, " *Cravate ;* parce que cette pièce
d'habillement fut dénommée d'après les Cravates ou
Croates qui vinrent au service de France ."

Let us now, in order to discover the real etymology of
cravat, bear in mind that it is taken in the sense of a
neck-tie; that is, something that fastens to the neck.
The radical part is *crav,* which cannot differ from the
clav of *clavus,* Latin of *nail,* nor from the English word
claw, which means both the nail of a bird or of a beast, as
well as of its foot. And as a nail is what fastens, and as
to *tie* has this meaning, the *crav* of cravat may be therefore said to mean a *tie,* conventionally a tie for the neck.
And that I have taken no undue liberty in changing
the *crav* of *cravat* for *clav,* one of the following words
given by M. Littré from several dialects and languages
as different names of *clou* (French of nail) will serve to
show : " Picar. cleu ; Bourguig. clo; Wallon, clâ; Rouchi,
clau ; Provenc. clau; Espagn. clavo ; Portug. *cravo;* Ital.
chiavo; du Latin clavus, de même radical que clavis "
(key). Thus we see that in Portuguese the word for
nail is not *clavo,* as it might have been, but *cravo,* of
which the radical part, *crav,* is also the root of the French

Dict. Etymologique.

cravate, which might as well have been *clavate*, l and r being but different forms of the same sign.

Are we now to suppose that a cravat was called after a word for *clou* or *clavus?* By no means; but after a word meaning to tie or fasten, but which word is to be traced to *clou* or *clavus*, just as *clou* or *clavus* is to be traced to *claw*, and *claw* to a word for the hand—conventionally, the hand of a beast or bird. As there are, however, many ways of tying a cravat—as many, I am assured, as thirty-five—the cravat may, from its knots bearing some resemblance to the claws of a beast or bird, have thence taken its name; but the radical sense will be still the same. Dr. Johnson's definition of the word *claw* is, therefore, perfect : " The foot of a beast or bird armed with sharp nails; or the pincers or holders of a shell-fish." The following (from an abridged edition of Webster) is perhaps still better : " The sharp hooked nail of a beast, bird, or other animal. The whole foot of an animal armed with hooked nails. The hand, in contempt." I beg to draw the reader's attention to the meaning of " pincers or holders;" and that a *claw* may mean either a *nail* or the whole foot. Pincers have so evidently the meaning of holders, that it is rendered into French, not only by *pincettes*, but also by *tenailles*, literally *holders :* witness *teneo* and *tenir* in Latin and French, as well as *tenaculum*, that which holds. As *tenere*, and *tenir* mean each to *hold*, and as *hold* is for *hond* or *hand*, it must follow that the Latins had once such a word as *ten* for both *hand* and *finger*, or that they borrowed this word from a people who in their language used it so; and of this there can be no doubt. Hence, *dextra*, a Latin word for hand, even the right hand, has for its root *dex*, which can neither differ from the *dek* of *deka*, Greek of ten, nor from the *dec* of the Latin *decem* (which was pronounced *dekem*), nor from *dix* in French. And the *dak* of daktulos is still the same word; and such too is the *tak* of *take* in English, as well as *touch* and the *tick* of *tickle*, and the *tang* of *tangere* in Latin, which was also *tago*. Donnegan does not therefore mistake when under *deka*, he says, "δέκω, δέχομαι, is related to δέκα, viz., from the ten fingers, to ' grasp, hold.' "

We thus see how words grow out of one another, though all be referable to a single source. Only witness the word *grasp*: when we drop its S, we get *grap*, root of grapple; in *grap* we have *groip*, that is, *grip* and *gripe*. But if we consider the r in *grasp* as the l in *clavus*, *grasp* will become *glasp;* that is, from the interchange of c and g (witness *gatto* in Italian and *cat* in English), *clasp;* and a *clasp* is what ties or closes. In grip we have also, from the interchange of p and f (witness pater and father), *grif*, that is, *griffe*, which is the French of *claw*, and, as we now see, but a different form of it. Yet in *griffe* and *claw* there is not a letter in common!

These three Latin words, *anguis, unguis,* and *angus*, root of *angusto*, are all one and the same. The first means a serpent, the second a nail (of the hand) and the third is significant of tightness, since angustere (infinitive of angusto) means to tighten, close, &c. We may now show how these different ideas are to be traced to the hand. But let us first call upon the rule which says that every vowel at the beginning of a word may or may not take the aspirate h, which arises from some people in all countries sounding an h before a vowel when they ought not, or from their leaving it out when it should be used. Hence, the word *anguis* cannot, because equal to *hang*, differ from *fang* (a claw) ; this arising from the interchange, so very frequent, of h and f, as we see from *Hernando* and *Fernando.* As the *ung* of *unguis* (a nail) is equal to the *ang* of *anguis*, just as further is to farther, we see that it has the same root, and is consequently not different from *fang*. The same observations apply to the *ang* of *angusto*, to tighten ; so that it is also but another form of *fang*, just as fang is of the *fing* of *finger*. And as *f* cannot differ from *p*, the *fing* of finger is, from its being the same as *fang* or *foing*, not different from *poign* in French. And if it be objected that this word means the *fist*, it should be observed that *fist* cannot differ from *fast, firm, tight*, &c., ideas called after the hand. But as *poignée*, in which we have *poign*, means both a handful and a handle, there can be no doubt about the original meaning of *poign*. In this French word we see also the *poign* of *poignant*, and even *pang*, a pain proceeding from a *bang* or blow ; for *pang* and *bang* are equal to each other. And may we not also say that in *anguis* (a serpent) we have *anguish ?* not that the latter idea was named from a serpent, but from the circumstance of its root *ang* being not different from *fang*, an idea called after the hand, with which a blow is given, and hence a *bang*.

But, as a serpent has neither hands nor claws, why should its name be traceable to such an idea ? Simply because, like a *crab*, which may be said to have hands or claws, it creeps ; and hence its name, which I shall most likely have occasion to notice farther on, it being a very important word, as it has given rise to a great deal of superstition over all the world. But I must be cautious ; superstition has always been a dangerous thing to meddle with, not only in times long gone by, but even in our own days.

And though the *serp* of *serpent,* which is its radical part, differs so widely from the *clav* of clavus (a nail) yet the same meaning can, without its being in the least far-fetched, be deduced from it. Thus, in Greek *herpō* means to creep as a serpent; but its radical part, *herp,* is not only, from the interchange of h and s (witness hepta in Greek and septem in Latin), equal to s, whence the *serp* of *serpent;* but also to this sign $)-($ an ancient form of H, and of which a c is the half, and so may represent the entire letter. Hence, *Horn* is the *corn* of *cornu* in Latin, and is the same as *corne* in French; and as c is equal to k, this too accounts for *ker,* root of *keras,* Greek of horn, being so written; for this *ker* cannot differ from *cor,* which has also the meaning of horn in French, as we see by *cor de chasse,* a hunting horn. Hence, the s of *serp* is shown to be equal to c; but which we might see by merely comparing the English words practi*s*e and practi*c*e. The *serp* of serpent is therefore brought equal to *cerp,* which, from the common transposition of vowels preceding r, becomes *crep,* equal to both *creep* and *crap,* in the latter of which we have the root of *crap*aud (a toad) and a form of precisely equal value, namely, *crab.* And as we have seen the *clav* of clavus under the form of *crav* in Portuguese, it follows, since b and v are the same, that *crab* is also equal to crav, and consequently to the *clav* of *clavus.* And here we light accidentally upon the word *crave,* of which the primary sense has been hitherto unknown. As it is traceable to the hand as its source, we see that it must have the meaning of holding out the hand in supplication, as a beggar does. Hence it is used in the sense of supplicating earnestly. "I *crave* your pardon" and "I *beg* your pardon," are therefore synonymous. This etymology is confirmed by dektĕr, the Greek of beggar, and of which the root, dek, is also the root of deka, ten.   But as C is equal to O, and as O has i understood, giving, by its joining with O, *a*, it follows that the *beg* of *beggar* and the *dek* of *deka* are equal to *bag* and *dak*, of which the former means a *bag*— a thing which *holds*, an idea called after the hand; and the latter is the root of daktulos, Greek of finger, an idea also called after the hand.   In *dak* we see also the *dag* of *dagger*, an arm for striking with, and consequently named from the hand, and which is confirmed by *poignard* and *poignée* in French, as the former means a dagger and the latter a handle and handful.   In this *dak* we see also the *tag* of *tago*, elder form of the *tang* of *tango*, to touch.   In *tickle*, *touch*, and *take*, we have also ideas called after the hand, and but different forms of the *dak* of daktulos and the *dek* of deka, with others too many to mention here.

I nearly forgot to account for our word *nail*.   If we drop the ᵷ of its German form, nagel, we obtain nael, which, as one combination of vowels is equal to another, cannot differ from *nail*.   Hence, the word nail was obtained by pronouncing the German nagel or its Saxon form, næged, without allowing the ᵷ to be heard.   In nail we have also, as in the words above noticed, the name of a creeping animal, as we may see by writing it with an S, producing *snail*; for this S is no part of the word snail, any more than it is of *sneeze*, which is for nooze; that is, nose.   This is confirmed by the Saxon of sneeze being niesan, and not sniesan.   There is a tendency thus to pronounce an S before several consonants, as we shall see as we go on.

Nor is the *ong* of *ongle* (a nail of the hand) more equal

to the *ang* of *anguis* in Latin, which has the same meaning, than it is to the *nag* of its German form, nagel; for, as the latter cannot differ from nogle, this becomes, by the ll passing over the O, *ongle*. The *ang* of *anguis*, a serpent, is still the same as the nag of nagel and the *ong* of *ongle*. And in the *nag* of nagel, what do we see but another form of *nak*, as g and k do constantly interchange? And as the ll, as shown above, often takes S before it, what is this *nak* but *snak*; that is, *snake*, but of which the radical part is nak? And what is *snake*, but another word for serpent? By which we see that the same idea may be expressed very differently. But what is the word for serpent in Hebrew? It is, according to Dr. Adam Clarke, who was, as every one knows, a great Hebrew scholar, Nachash; which cannot, as ch is equal to k, differ from *nak*ash; that is, as S may be, and often is, expressed before ll, as already shown, snakash. By which it is shown that this word snakash is the same as the English word snake. But German philologists say that there is no relationship whatever between English and Hebrew. And if this be true, of which I have my doubts, it proves still more forcibly that all languages have grown out of one single sign, there being a great many words in Hebrew radically the same as in English.

By these different forms of the word, we have seen how things the most insignificant may be traced up to the name of the sun. Thus, a nail, from its belonging to the hand, has thence taken its name; and as it is with the hand that things are made, this member has been thence called a maker, just as the sun has been called the maker of the world. Hence, so insignificant a thing as the nail of a man's finger does not differ from a name

K

of the sun, though not called after it. And a snail is still the same word, not from having been called after the hand, but from its creeping like things (such as a crab) which may be said to have claws or hands. This accounts for things the most trivial having been worshipped as gods; which arose from its being perceived that they had names similar to one or more of those by which the sun was designated, though they were never called after this object, but after something, such as the hand, which happened to have a name not different from that of the sun. We need not, therefore, wonder at the serpent having been worshipped all over the world long previous, not only to the birth of Christ, but even to the birth of Moses. It has never until now been supposed that it was the identity in meaning of the two names, serpent and maker, that first led to so gross a superstition. Hence Calmet, in his " Dictionary of the Holy Bible," explains thus the cause of this ancient and universal worship : " The worship of the serpent is observed through all Pagan antiquity. The devil, who tempted the first woman under the shape of a serpent, takes a pleasure to deify this animal, as a trophy of his victory over mankind."

If this be true, and no good Christian can for a moment doubt its being so, it follows that the devil cannot be suffering so much as we are told ; for there is not one of us who could or would, if rolling in a lake of fire, think of any thing but our own cruel sufferings. I once knew a husband and wife who, in Paris, during the revolution of 1830, suffered dreadfully from an explosion of gunpowder. The wife was saved, but not so the husband. The poor woman confessed to me, on asking her how she felt for her husband at the time her own torture was so excruciating, that she could not think of any thing else than her torture, not even of her husband's sufferings, though she loved him dearly. Yet what were her sufferings compared to those which the devil is, we are taught to believe, ever enduring.?

But the true cause of the serpent's having been worshipped through all Pagan antiquity is this: From its being an animal that creeps, it was called after claws or hands, though having neither; and as it is with our hands that we *make,* this member was consequently called a maker; so that the serpent's name and that of the hand were the same. And as the sun also was believed to be the great maker or creator of the world, the serpent was also, thanks to its name, revered as such. But this superstition could not have begun to prevail when the serpent was first named, but long after. And why so? Because when any thing was first named, the meaning of the word by which it was then designated was well known, and it could not for this reason be *then* the cause of superstition. But when the origin of the name was after a time forgotten, and when it was found not to differ from one of the many titles of the sun, that which it then served to signify, whether man, beast, or inanimate object, received divine honours, the belief then being that it must, on account of its name, have once been the sun.

But why was the serpent believed to be the wisest of all animals? Because its name happened to be, under one of its forms, significant of wisdom.

Thus, *ophis,* a name of the serpent in Greek, cannot, when we make its O take the rough instead of the soft breathing, differ from *hophis,* which, as the aspirate is constantly replaced by S, is equal to *sophis,* that is,

sophos, and this is the Greek of wise. The serpent could
not therefore fail, on account of its name, being thought
very wise, though it is not half so wise as the fox, perhaps not even so much so as the ass.

Thus, whatever crawls or creeps, even though having
neither claws nor hands, will be found to have a name
traceable to that of the sun ; and, however stupid it may
be by nature, the word by which it is designated may be
also found to be significant of wisdom. But *worm,* I
shall be told, has no such meaning in either Greek, Latin,
or English. But this is no proof that it has not had
such a meaning, and that the word then used has not
been replaced by one of the titles of the sun, whose
name, when he is called Buddha, is allowed by the
learned to mean wisdom. It is languages in a very
primitive state, or which died out when they were so,
that should be examined in order to see how far this
opinion of mine may be true. In the Hebrew language,
for instance, in which, from its having died, as it were, in
its infancy, the word for *worm* (orm) is, with other meanings, explained " wise, prudent, ready-witted [7]."

And as to this Hebrew word *orm,* it is easy to perceive
when we make its O take the aspirate, and then call to
mind that this sign has been often replaced by the
digamma (F) and the digamma by such other signs as
b, f, v, w, p, and frequently by s, it follows that when
we take of those signs the one most suitable, we shall,
instead of *orm,* obtain *worm;* which is the same as the
German *wurm,* and not different from the radical part of
vermis in Latin.

The root of such words as *vermis, worm,* or *wurm,* cannot differ from such a form as *bar,* nor *bar* from *bra,*

[7] Parkhurst, Lexicon, p. 507.

which means in Hebrew to create; and the sun was believed to be the creator or maker of all things. The root of *bar* is *ar*, which, as *r* takes often an *n* after it (witness *tour* and *turn*) is the same as *arn*, *arm*, or *orm*, which, with the aspirate, makes *worm*.

But how are we to account for the English word *eel* or its German form *aal?* They make but one and the same word, and each means a kind of serpent; and by merely dropping a single vowel of each name we obtain both *el* and *al*, which were, according to Parkhurst, two well-known names of the sun with the heathen, and also, as shown farther back, with the ancient Jews, as names of the Deity. And when we remark that the nasal sound has been represented not only by *n* but by *ng*, *al*, the reduced form of the German *aal*, will be found equal to *angl*, and consequently, by means of the aspirate and its being replaced by the digamma, to *fangl*, in which we see the word *fang*, though the *eel* has none.

These words suggest too many other observations to be noticed here.

CHAPTER XX.

HAND, SECOND NOTICE.

BUT the ideas named after the hand are still so numerous and so very dissimilar, that a few more of them should be submitted to the reader's notice.

In *son* we see a form not different from *soin*, which is the French of *care*, and this idea has been called after the *hand*, since it is by its use we take *care* of whatever we wish to be careful of. As *n* may be represented by *gn*, it follows that *soin* (care) is equal to *soign*, and this is confirmed by *soigner* being the verbal form of *soin*. But this *soign* cannot differ from the *sogn* of *besogne*, and *besogne* means work, and work has been called after the hand, since it is with our hands that we work. If we now give to this *sogne* of *besogne* its other form of *soin*, we shall, instead of *besogne*, have *besoin*, which means *want*; and this idea was, it would seem, first signified by extending the *hand*. If we do therefore regard the *w* of *want* as representing the aspirate *h*, there will be no difference between *want* and *hant*, that is, between *want* and *hand*. But as many persons must have dropped the *h* of *hand*, it must have been reduced to *and*, which by transposition becomes *nad*, that is *naed*; and this being the Saxon of *need*, we discover in *hand*, *want*, and *need*, three different forms of the same word.

A word very different in form from any of these, but similar in meaning, is the Greek word *dektēr*, *dektēs*, or *dektōr*, which means a beggar, a mendicant. But the radical sense is the *hand*, the latter idea being in this instance signified by *dek*, root of *deka*, meaning the ten fingers. Another word equal in form to *dektēs*, *dektēr*, or *dektōr*, is *deiktēr* or *deiktēs*; but how different the meaning, since it signifies one who *indicates*, and not one who *begs*. But the original source is still the hand. The French word *mendiant* (a beggar), and its Latin form *mendicus*, and the French *mander* to show with the hand, are also radically the same as *manus*. Nor has the *beg* of beggar a different origin, for it is equal to the form *bag*, and a *bag* is that which *holds* or *contains*; and to hold or contain has been called after the *hand*. In *bag* we have also but a different form of *mag* that is, *mak*, or *make*;

and this idea also has been called after the hand, as every one must, from what has been already shown, admit. In order to see how *bag* is the same as *mag*, the reader has only to recollect what he has seen farther back, namely, that *brine* and *bride* are for *marine* and *married,* this arising from the interchange of B and M, as *brotos,* and *mortos* in Greek; and to which we may add, as an etymology hitherto unknown, the Latin words *binus* and *manus;* for as the i of *binus* is for *oi* or *a,* we see that *binus* is the same as *banus,* and consequently as *manus,* after which the idea *double* was *in this instance* called. I say, in this instance, for the idea *two,* as already shown, must have been first signified by a repetition of the idea *one,* and *two* and *double* are radically the same. If the reader cannot easily conceive how the i of the latter words is equal to *oi* or *a,* he may be convinced that it is so by comparing *bind* and *band,* in which it is easy to perceive the same word, a *band* being that which *binds.* But in this instance the B should not be considered as replacing the m of *manus,* but as being for the *h* of *hoind* (hand) which became *boind,* and then, by the dropping of the o, *bind,* and afterwards, by the coalescing of o and i, *band.*

This much will serve to guide the reader to many other etymologies. Thus the word *bag* (noticed above) being equal to *mag,* and this being the root of *maggot* (a worm) we see that the thing so called must have been named after the idea *creep;* and as in creeping we make use of our hands, just as we do when *making* any thing, we thus see how ideas so dissimilar as *making* and *maggot* can be traced to the same source.

But as an instance of two words equal in form, yet traceable to very different sources, we may refer to *bag;*

for though it cannot differ from *big*, neither of these words can belong to the same class of ideas. When we regard *mag* as the root of *magnus*, we can connect it with *big*, these ideas, greatness and bigness, having at first been expressed by the same word ; and yet they do not belong to the class of ideas called after the hand, but to the one called after the sun, then revered as the *greatest* of objects. Another instance of this kind is afforded by *caput* and *capio*, for the former being traceable to height, belongs to the ideas called after the sun, whereas the *cap* of *capio* (to seize) is referable to the hand, and it is not different from the *hab* of *habeo*, its c being for the aspirate *h*, just as it is in cornu, of which the elder form must have been *hornu*, whence *horn*.

Farther back I had occasion to show how the Portuguese word for *nail* (an idea belonging to the class called after the hand) is *cravo ;* but from the r appearing under its form of l, *cravo* becomes *clavo* in Spanish : in the same way we can show *creep* to be equal to *cleep*, and this is but a different form of *clip*, to cut—an idea called after *two*, or *dividing*, and consequently belonging to the class called after the hand, though not in any other way related to the idea *creep*. Another form of both *clip* and *creep* is *crop*, to cut.

If we now give the nasal sound to any of these latter forms, we shall obtain a word equal to *climb*. Witness *grimper* in French, and of which the etymology is confirmed by what M. Littré admits under *grimper*, namely, that "On trouve griper pour grimper, et *grimper* pour *gripper ;*" and that the high German for *grimper* is *klimban*. But M. Littré does not seem to suspect that every such idea is to be traced to the hand ; and still less does he seem to think that the root of all and each of these words is *cheir*, the Greek of *hand*. And yet it is so.

And because wanting this knowledge, MM. Littré and Diez are both at a loss to account for the origin of *gravir*. This word is, however, but another form of both *gripper* and *grimper*. M. Littré's definition of *gravir* is, like all his other definitions, very correct. It is as follows : "Monter avec effort à quelque endroit escarpé en s'aidant des pieds et des *mains*." But he regards its derivation as *uncertain*, and, while rejecting, as he well might, the etymology given of it by Diez, he offers none of his own. These are his words : "Origine incertaine. Diez pense qu'il vient d'une forme *gradire*, qui est Italienne, et qui dérive du Latin *gradus*, pas, *gra-ir*, du *gravir* par l'intercalation d'un *v*, comme dans *povoir* de l'ancien *pooir*. Mais à coté de *gravir* est la forme de *graver*, qui ne se prête pas bien à une telle explication."

The *graver* here referred to, is but another form of *gravier ;* but though M. Littré is well aware that *graver* and its Greek equivalent *grapho* are radically the same word, yet the difference in meaning between writing and climbing is so considerable, that he could not conceive their being in any way traceable to the same source. Hence the necessity for these three classes, into which all words have, from the very birth of language, been divided. Another instance of the advantage to be derived from this knowledge, is afforded by *maggot* and *grub* having the same meaning. A child acquainted with the principles which have grown out of this dis- covery of the origin of language, must know that it arises from both these words having for their source the class of ideas belonging to the hand; and that *grub* is not only equal to *grab* (to seize with the hand) but also to the *grav* of the French *gravir,* to climb ; and the *grav* of *graver* and its Greek equivalent, namely, the *graph* of graphō ; not to mention several others, such as *gripe, grip, grapple, cripple, griffe,* and the *scrib* of scribo and scribble, and the *scriv* of scrivener, in which latter forms the S is merely euphonic, and the C for *g*.

From C having thus the power of *g*, we see that *clove* (the name of a spice) cannot differ from *glove;* and this can be easily accounted for. Thus we know that *clove* is for *clou,* this spice having been so called from its resemblance to a nail or *clou;* and this idea being traceable to the hand, as shown farther back, accounts for the identity in form of *clove* and *glove,* notwithstanding how widely they differ from each other in meaning. And the word *glaive* (a sword) is also to be traced to the same source, because the name of that which cuts, and consequently divides—an idea called after two, or the hand. Hence, in the *find* of the Latin *findere* and the *fend* of the French *fendre* (each meaning to cleave) it is easy to perceive a form equal to *hand,* the f of each word being a substitute for the aspirate (h), and which is made evident by the Spanish of findere being *hender.* Here too we discover the origin of the idea to *find;* for what we *find* we have in *hand.* And as it is by our *hands* we defend ourselves, there can be no doubt but the ideas expressed by such words as *hindering, defending, defence, fender,* and *fence* are also to be traced to the same source.

And this knowledge must lead to many other etymologies of which I have myself no idea. Let us only remark that, according to my principles, there being no difference between *rep* and *rap,* the ideas expressed by *repo* (to creep), and *rapio* (to carry off) must belong to the same class of ideas; and as we make use of our hands in *creeping* and also in carrying off, this will account for words so different in meaning as *repo* and *rapio* (creeping and carrying off) being equal (in form) to each other.

And as the English word *rap* means a *blow*, and as it is with the hand that a blow is usually given, this accounts for two ideas so different as carrying off and giving a blow being expressed alike and being traceable to the same source. We are hence led to suspect that in the *frap* of the French word frapper, *rap* must be the root. But how are we to account for the *f* of *frap?* In the same way we have accounted for the *f* of *findere* in Latin and its French form *fendre;* that is to say, we are to consider it as representing the aspirate *h*, according to which view *frap* must have been once written *rhap*, and then, by transposition, *hrap*, which, from the constant interchange of *h* and *f*, became *frap*. This is confirmed by Webster, from whom I learn that the Saxon of the verb to *rap*, is *hrepan, hreppan,* and *repan*. The English verb to *rip* is also written in Saxon with an *h*, witness *hrypan*, but it is also written in this language without the *a;* and as it means to *divide* by cutting or tearing, and hence to make two of one, this shows it to belong to the class of ideas named after the hand.

But we should not leave unnoticed our etymology of *frapper*, as Frenchmen are not aware that such an idea is to be referred to the hand for its primary sense. Here is all M. Littré says of its origin : " Bourguign. *fraipai;* Provenç. *frapar;* anc.Cat. *frappar;* Ital. *frappare;* d'après Grangagnage, du Hollandais *flappen,* souffleter; Ang. to *flab,* battre de l'aile. Diez, qui donne aussi de l'attention à cette étymologie, incline pourtant vers le haut Allemand, *hrappa*, insulter, attribuant à *frapper* le sens primitif d'injurier, sur ce fondement que, dans le patois Anglais, *frape* a le sens de dire des injures, et que le mot n'y peut venir que du Français. Malgré cette autorité, l'étymologie par *flappen* paraît mériter la préférence. Du reste, nous n'avons, dans l'historique, d'exemples que du XIVième siècle."

The above notice of *frapper* suggests several observations; but as they might lead to others, I must pass them by. I cannot, however, help giving another instance of the advantage to be derived from knowing that words of very different meanings, but similar, or even alike, in form, can be traced to the same source.

Let us notice *plough*, but under the better and more intelligible form of *plow*. We know from the identity and constant interchange of p and b, that *plow* cannot differ from *blow*. But why should this be? Because a *plow* is an instrument that *cuts* (the ground); and a *blow* and a *cut* have been expressed alike. Thus the French word *coup* means not only a blow, but also a *cut*, witness *coup* and the verb *couper*. Hence in *plowshare*, we have a repetition of the same idea, and which has been occasioned for the purpose of distinguishing *share*, a division, from its signifying that which *cuts* the ground. The French word *charrue* (a plow) is but a different form of our word *share*. But Frenchmen are so far from supposing this to be the derivation of *charrue*, that their etymology of it is a *car* with a *wheel*. Thus, M. Littré after giving the different forms under which this word appears in several languages and their dialects, concludes thus: " Du Latin curruca, voiture, dont le nom général a passé spécialement à la machine à *roue* dite charrue." But M. Littré must know that a plow with a wheel to it, is a modern invention. Most likely his grandfather never saw such a plow; I am pretty sure that mine never did. This derivation of *charrue* is, however, very plausible; for *char* means a *car*, and *rue* may very well pass for *roue*, a wheel. But *char* or *car* means to carry, as is shown by *charrier*; and *char* is but a different form of *cheir*, the Greek of hand, to which source the two ideas to *cut* and to *carry* must be traced. Frenchmen have, however, this very word *charrue* in the sense of tearing or dividing; but they cannot perceive it. I must therefore take the liberty of showing it to them. It is the *chirure* of *déchirure*. In the *chir* of this word we see *choir*, the *o* being understood with its *i*, and as *o* and *i* compose *a*, *choir* is equal to *char*. And as to the *ure* of chir*ure*, it is letter for letter the *rue* of char*rue*, and from this we may infer that *charrue* must have once been written *charure* or *chirure*, between which forms there is not a shade of difference. In the *chir* of *chirure* it is easy also to perceive the *chir* of *chirurgie*, that is, in Greek, *cheirourgia*, and, as M. Littré shows, *cheir* and *ergon*, in which we see the two words *hand* and *work*. Nor should we here omit to observe that in the *erg* of *ergon* we have but a different form of *cheir*, the idea expressed by *work* having been called after the hand. The *e* of the *erg* of *ergon* must have therefore been aspirated by some people, and from its having first been *herg*, have afterwards become *ferg*, and then *verg*, *verk*, *vork*, and *work*.

I may now be asked, What difference is there (radically considered) between *charrue* and *car*? I answer, None whatever; and yet a plow was never named after a *car*, nor a car after a plow. The cause of their identity arises from this, that the two ideas (carrying and cutting) belong to the same source; I mean to the class of ideas called after the hand.

What now may be the consequence of this identity? The consequence may be, that the words for *car* and *plow* may in two different languages be expressed alike. This may happen even in the same language, as is shown by the following, which I transcribe from vol. i. of M. Max Müller's Lectures, p. 288 : " In the vale of Blackmore a wagon is called *plough*, or *plow*; and *zull* (Anglo-Saxon *syl*) is used for *aratrum*."— Barnes' Dorset Dialect, p. 369.

Let us now observe that *wagon* is for *way*on, so that its primary sense is *conveyance*; but it is often expressed by the word *cart*; and the Greek *karrh*on means, according to Donnegan, either a wagon or a *car*. It must have, therefore, been from the word *plow* being referable to the hand, that with some people it means to *cut* and with others to *carry*, these two ideas, *cutting* and *carrying*, being traceable to the same source.

From the note just quoted, we see that *zull* is used for *aratrum* in Dorsetshire. But *zull* is, says M. Max Müller, *syl* in Anglo-Saxon ; but the form which Bosworth prefers to *syl* is *sul*; and as *u* is for *oi* (witness crux and croix, nux and noix) it follows that *sul* is equal to *soil*, which is often used for ground, land, or earth. I find also in Gaelic that *ar* is explained "ploughing, tillage, agriculture;" and as a verb, "to plough, till, cultivate;" and as an obsolete word, " *land, earth*." Thus we see that the Saxon word *sul* (aratrum) is equal to soil, though meaning a plow, and that this happens also in Gaelic. This would make it appear that the *earth* was called after a *plow* or a plow after the earth. Neither derivation would, however, be correct. Men must have

had a word for the *earth* long previous to their having
had one for the plough. Such an instrument is a modern
invention, when compared with the time when men lived
by the chase, and on the wild fruits of the wood. But
according to M. Max Müller [8], the earth " meant originally the ploughed land, afterwards earth in general."
This cannot have been, for the reason just given. But
let us hear what Parkhurst says of the word *earth:*
" ארע *aro*, Chaldee *low*, inferior. This word is used in
the same sense in the Targums [9]. As a noun, the earth
(Greek 'Eρα), either on account of its inferior situation,
or from Heb. ארץ *arj*, the same ע *0* being, as usual,
changed into ץ *j*, ארץ *arj*. It occurs, not as a verb, but as
a noun feminine ארץ, the earth, the dry land, so called
on account of its readily breaking to pieces [1]."

Here we see it admitted that *earth* means *low;* but
Parkhurst mistakes when he supposes that it may have
obtained its name from " its readily breaking or crum-
bling to pieces;" *lowness* is the only meaning it can at
first have had. But from the words signifying cutting
or breaking not differing from the one serving as a name
for the earth, the latter has been thence derived by
etymologists. *Ar*, or a form of equal value, must have
been the first word for *earth;* but when the *a* of this
form obtained its aspirate, and so became *har*, the *h* must,
in order to suit the sound it sometimes obtained, have
become *ch*, which brought *ar* equal to *char*; and *char*
is but a different form of the Greek *cheir* (hand), whence
the ideas of *breaking, cutting, tearing,* or *ploughing,* but
which have no relationship with the idea *earth*. No
word appears more likely to lead to the belief that the

---

[8] Lexicon, vol. i. p. 285.   [9] See Castell. Lex. Heptag.
[1] Lex. p. 33.   Ed. 1788.

earth must have been named after the plough than the now obsolete English verb to *ear*, which means to plough. But with the aspirate, *ear* becomes *hear*, and consequently, from the *h* being replaced, as it often is, by *s*, and *s* by *sh*, *hear* is brought equal to *shear*, which means to *cut*, and does not differ from *share*, *shire*, or the *char* of charrue, or the *chir* of *chirure*, radical part of *déchirure*. And if we allow this old verb *ear* to be preceded by such a pronominal article as *id*, *it*, *the*, or *to* (for these four are all one and the same), and then some such form to join with it, *ear* will become *tear*, in which we see the meaning we have assigned to *charrue*. But when the pronominal article preceding *ear* fell behind, then *ear* became *eard*, *eart*, or *earth*. But if the article preceding *ear* happened to be *is*, which has still the same meaning as each of the four just mentioned, then *ear* became, when this *is* fell behind, *earis*, contracted to *ears*, and afterwards to *ars*, whence *art*, from *arte*, ablative of *ars*. The idea *art* must have therefore been named after the *hand;* and the *tech* of the Greek *technē* (art) confirms this derivation, for it is equal to *tak* or *take*, and also to the *dech* of *dech*omai, to take, as well as to the dek of *deka* (ten), whence deko, to seize, to grasp. If we aspirate the *a* of *art*, we obtain *hart*, and here, by the common substitution of *r* for *n*, we get *hant*, which is the same as *hand*. But as *hart* is also equal to *hard*, it follows that *hand* may have been often so written. This view is confirmed by *hard by* having the meaning of *hand by;* that is, at *hand*, not distant. It is also confirmed by the *fard* of *fardeau*, which cannot differ from *hard;* and *far* (root of *fardeau*) is the *fer* of *fero*, to carry, to bear ; an idea called after the hand. In this word *hard* we have also the French *hardes*, which means clothes, either old or new. This word, *hardes*, serves to show how necessary it is to know to what class an idea must belong. Little do French philologists suspect that, radically considered, *hardes* does not differ from *cheir*, and that it is but a different form of the English words *bear* and *wear*. Several instances are, however, given by M. Littré, showing that *hardes* must be the same as *fardes*, and that the latter means clothing. This is clearly shown, both under the articles *hardes* and *fardes*. But the conclusion come to is, "*origine incertaine*." There could have been no uncertainty, however, if it had been known that such an idea is traceable for its origin to the hand, and that from *fardeau* meaning what is *borne*, so does it mean what is *worn*, and consequently *wearing* apparel.

Even *hard* (durus) must be referred to the hand; for it is with this member that we make *firm*, and consequently *harden*. Hence *durus* is explained by *firmus*. But *rudis*, though it is the same word, has not been called after the hand, but after *durus*. In the *rud* of *rudis* it is, however, easy to perceive a form equal to *hard*, and hence to hand, for *rud* cannot, as the r may fall behind its u, differ from *urd*, which is the same as *ard*, and (with the aspirate) as *hard*.

Form, which is an idea very different from any of these, must also be traced to the hand, for it is with the hand we give to things their *forms*; and this is confirmed by the Latin *formosus*, since it may be rendered into English by *hand*some. It is also confirmed by the Greek *charieis*, of which the root *char* is the same as *cheir*, the hand, and of which the meaning is also *hand*some.

The idea *abundance* may be also traced to the hand. Hence, *much* in English and *mucho* in Spanish cannot differ from *mach*, nor *mach* from *make*. But we are not to suppose that these ideas (*abundance* and *making*) are otherwise related than by their belonging to the same source. The radical identity of *many* and *manus* is also very apparent; and hence it is that *manus* in Latin is synonymous with *grex*, and *grex* and the Greek of hand (*cheir*) are radically the same word. And as grex means a *troupe, troupeau,* or large number, hence the French word *trop,* and of which the *turb* of *turba* (a multitude) is but a different form; and when we regard the *rop* of *trop* as its radical part, it is easy to perceive, since its *o* is for *oi*, and *oi* for *a*, that it cannot differ from the *rap* of *rapio;* nor can the *urb* of the *turb* of *turba* differ from either *rub* or *rob*, ideas which have been also called after the hand, but, like the *rap* of *rapio*, are not otherwise related to *trop* or *turba*. And as *grex* is used in the sense of *herd* (of cattle) we thus discover that *herd* is for *hand,* and nowise different from the *hard* of *hard by*, that is, hand by, at hand; nor from the French word *hardes,* an idea traceable also to the hand, as shown above.

As some words can be easily traced to the hand, such as *graphō* in Greek and *scribo* in Latin, of which the radical parts are equal to such forms as *grap, gripe, crib, rob, rap,* &c., they will lead to the etymology of others equal in meaning but so different in form as not appearing to be traceable to the same source. Thus, to *write,* which is the English of graphō and scribo, bears under its present form no resemblance to a word for the hand; but from our knowing that such must be its origin, we are at once led to its etymology. Thus, when we take the *w* of *write* as representing the aspirate h, we see that *write* cannot differ from *hrite;* and as this aspirate was, according to the different ways of pronouncing it, sometimes accompanied by *c*, and sometimes by *w*, it became *ch* with some people (as with the Latins and Italians), and with others (as with the Saxons) *hw*, now represented by *wh, ch,* and *wh.* These signs are therefore equal to each other, and also to *qu.* In *qui, chi,* and *who,* we have therefore only one and the same word under these three different forms. Hence, the *quan* of *quando* is equal to *when,* and *quoi* is equal to the *wha* of *what.* And as this proves *qu* and *wh* to be as one sign, it follows, since *qu* cannot differ from *ch* (witness *qui* and *chi*), that *write* or (as it might have been represented) *whrite* is equivalent to *chrite,* in the *chr* of which it is easy to perceive the Greek of hand, *cheir,* vowels being understood between consonants. And in *cheir* we see a form precisely equal to the *char* of *character,* which means an alphabetical sign. Hence, the Greek word χαράκτης is thus explained by Donnegan, " one who traces characters, a *writer,* a copyist."

Another word, which it would be difficult to trace to its real source, is our word *rend.* But as to *rend* means to *tear,* and as we have already traced this idea to the hand, we at once see that *rend* must be for *re-hand,* that is, to *double hand,* to make two of any thing, to divide it, and consequently to tear it. But to say that to *rend* is *rendan* in Saxon, is not to tell us any thing worth knowing, as I am not now a whit wiser respecting the primary sense of either word than I was before.

As an instance of this kind of imperfect acquaintance with the origin of words, I wish here to notice the etymology of *copy.* I learn from Webster that it is *copie* in French and *copy* in Armoric. I go to Johnson, and find the following : " copie, French ; copia, low Latin. *Quod cuipiam facta est copia exscribendi.* Junius inclines, after his manner, to derive it from κόπος, labour; because, says he, to copy another's writing is very painful and laborious."

I now go to De Roquefort, who derives *copie* from the Latin *copia*, abundance. Not satisfied with any of these, I consult M. Littré, from whom I transcribe the following derivation of *copie* : " Saintonge. *coupie;* Provenç. *copia*, du Latin *copia*, abondance, permission, d'où le sens restreint de permission de reproduire, de copie, contracté de *cum* et *ops*, richesse (voyez opulent)."

As I cannot perceive the least relationship between two such ideas as a transcript and abundance or opulence, I am obliged to refer to one of the principles of my own discovery, namely, that 0 has always i understood, and that 0 and i make *a*, which will give me *cap* for the *cop* of *copy* or *copie ;* and in *cap* I find the root of *capio*, which means to *take*, seize, &c., an idea called after the hand, and to copy any thing is to *take it off.* It is, moreover, easy to conceive that as a copy is a *transcript*, and as a transcript is a writing, and as to *write*, as shown above, has been named after the hand, so must the idea of copying be traceable to the same source. Hence, to copy is in Greek μεταγράφω, which corresponds with its Latin form transcribo. The Greek χαρακίτης means also one who copies or traces characters, and consequently a writer.

As to *copia*, it cannot differ from *copy* or *copie*, and hence, as M. Littré shows, *copie* is in Provençal written *copia*, which circumstance has been, most probably, the cause of his supposing that *copie* means abundance. But to what class of ideas does copia, abundance, belong? To those of the hand, most certainly; and hence *manus* is often taken in the sense of *copia*. It is, therefore, a great mistake, and one which I find in several Latin dictionaries as well as in M. Littré (under *copie*), to suppose that *copia* is composed of *cum* and *ops*. Even their word *beaucoup* might show Frenchmen that abundance should be traced to the hand; for as the *coup* of this word means a *blow*, its origin cannot be doubted. As to the *beau* here used, it does but heighten the signification of *coup*. *Beaucoup* may be therefore said to mean literally a *great deal*, *coup* and the *cop* of *copia* being the same word. The English word *deal* confirms the truth of these observations; for it is frequently used in the sense of *much*, as, a *deal* of money means, *much* money. A *deal* at cards may be also said to have the literal meaning of a *giving* at cards, and hence the French of this noun is *une donne*. And as a thing given means a gift, and as the Latin of *gift* is *munus*, this word cannot differ, save conventionally, from *manus*. These views are further confirmed by the Italian word *copia*, which means in this language not only *abundance* but *copy* also; and this was an additional reason for influencing M. Littré to derive *copie* from *copia*. But every philologist must *now* know why these two words are in Italian written alike. And it must be admitted, that but for the discovery that there is a class of ideas called after the hand, and of which a great many are expressed by names widely different in meaning; never could the identity in form of two such words as *copie* and *copia* be accounted for. But whence came this knowledge that there is such a division? It has, like the other two divisions of ideas, grown out of the discovery of the origin of speech, without which it could never have been acquired.

CHAPTER XXI.

RIVERS OF THE SUN.—WHY RIVERS STYLED RIVERS OF
THE SUN, HAVE BEEN SO CALLED.—ORIGIN OF THE
SUPERSTITION TO WHICH THE NAME HAS GIVEN
BIRTH.

CAN the reader account for the English noun *salt* being radically the same as the Latin verb *salto*, which means both to leap and to dance? He will answer, that by the use of our principles he can very easily do so. Thus, he knows that to *brine* is, as we have shown, to put in brine, that is, to *mariner*, as the French have it; so that, from the interchange of *b* and *m*, *brine* and *marine* make only one word; and *brine* is salt water, for *marine*, from which it cannot differ, is radically the same as *mare*, Latin of sea. And the sea, as we shall see, has been named after water, and water after life, whence motion; and such too is the primary signification of both leaping and dancing, these ideas not differing from each other in meaning, but conventionally. Hence, *sal* in Latin means both *salt* and sea water, and it is the radical part of *salt*, as it is also of ἅλς in Greek, which has still the same meaning. Thus, from *salt* having been called after the sea, and the sea after water, and water after life or motion, it follows, since to leap and to dance do each imply motion, that any word meaning *salt* may also mean to leap or to dance. But it may be remarked that *danse* in French and *dance* in English, do not in any way appear significant of water. But this is a great mistake. There is perhaps no word in the world more significant of water than *dance*. But how so? Because no word is more frequently used in the sense of *river*—which has been called after *water*—than *don;* and that this is the same as *dan,* is not only proved by our principles (O being the same as Oi, and O and i being the parts composing *a*), but it is also proved by the fact itself, as is shown by the Danube being in German written Donau ; that is, Don *eau,* or water of the Don, or Dan. Nor is the *ube* of Danube less significant of water than the *au* of the German Donau, the *b* being here what the *d* is in the Greek *ud,* which is the root of *udor ;* that is, with the aspirate, *hudor,* water. To this let us add, that in Sanskrit—of which Greek and Latin are regarded by the learned as no better than dialects—the signs "d and r are *always,*" according to Colonel Tod[2], " permutable ; " so that such words as *dan, don,* or *dun* cannot, especially when of Sanskrit origin, differ from *ran, ron,* or *run,* each of which forms is as significant of motion as rheō in Greek, which means to flow, and is radically the same as the names *Rhine* and *Rhone.* There are, as the author of the Anacalypsis observes, many rivers in different parts of the world known by the name of *Don.* And as *Don* means also Lord, and as it was a name of the sun, this were sufficient to account for rivers having obtained divine worship, and also for the sacredness of water, after which the idea river was called. But learned men—having no suspicion that this superstitious belief arose from water being, as already shown, traceable to the sun, then adored as the sole god of this world—have ever in vain sought for the cause of a circumstance apparently so extraordinary, as that many rivers and the sun should

[2] Col. Tod, Hist. Raj. vol. i. p. 51, note.

be designated alike. "When I find," says Godfrey Higgins[3] "widely separated countries, towns, and rivers
called by the same names, I cannot consent to attribute so
striking a coincidence to the effect of accident or of uncon-
nected causes. I feel myself obliged to believe that some
common cause must have operated to produce a common
effect. I find rivers by the name of Don in many
different countries, and under very peculiar circumstances.
Almost all great rivers have been called rivers of the sun.
May not the origin of this be found in the abstruse consideration, that they appear to be directly the produce
of the sun; and may they not originally have been thus
called as a sacred name?" "In almost all countries we
find sacred rivers. The priests of all countries wished to
have the river which ran through their territory sacred;
from this it is that we find so many rivers dedicated to
the sun, and called in the different languages by a name
answering to the word sun[4]."

In the same writer (vol. ii. p. 98) I find also the
following : "Tertullian, Jerome, and other Fathers of the
Church, inform us that the Gentiles celebrated on the
25th of December, or on the 8th day before the calends
of January, the birth of the god Sol, under the name of
Adonis, in a cave like that of Mithra; and the cave
wherein they celebrated his mysteries was that in which
Christ was born in the city of Bethlehem, or, according
to the strict meaning of the word Bethlehem, in the city
of the house of the sun."

And referring in a note to the name Adonis, here
mentioned, the writer adds : "And from this word, all
the rivers called Don have derived their names." But
this happens to be a great mistake. Never was a river,

---

[3] Anacalypsis, vol. i. p. 532.   . [4] Ibid. p. 529.

when first named, called after the sun, but after water, of which the name did not, because signifying life and motion, differ from that of the sun. And such was in ancient times the cause of the superstitious belief in the sacredness of water and of rivers. But when rivers were first named, they could not have given rise to superstition. And why so? Because it was then well known that each of their names meant water, and nothing more. But when this very simple and natural meaning was, after a time—perhaps a very long time—so entirely forgotten that the word at first signifying water appeared, through the change which language had in the interval undergone, no more as an appellative, but as a proper name; then must rivers, from their names and those of the sun being found alike, have first begun to be regarded as sacred—but not before. If we do therefore except the innocent worship of the sun, there appears to have been far less superstition in the world at the birth of language than there has been at any time since.

He who believes in the doctrine of ancient types, cannot fail to have noticed what has been just quoted, respecting the idol Adonis. I open my Parkhurst, who was, of all learned Christians, one of the most orthodox, in order to see how far so firm a believer in this doctrine approves of the instance I refer to. It appears that Adonis was called Tammuz also. To this, Parkhurst, referring, says, " Jerome interprets Tammuz by Adonis, and observes that in Hebrew and Syriac he is called Tammuz." " But still, what was meant by Tammuz or Adonis? Macrobius says, ' Adonis was undoubtedly the sun', and many other writers are of the same opinion.' " And Parkhurst further observes, " I find

---

* " Adonin quoque solem esse non dubitabitur."

myself obliged to refer Tammuz, as well as the Greek and Roman Hercules, to that class of idols which were *originally* designed to represent the *promised Saviour, the desire of all nations.*   His other name, Adonis, is almost the very Hebrew אדוני *aduni,* or Lord, a well-known name of Christ[6]."

Parkhurst refers, in a note, to another part of his Lexicon[7], where he expresses the same opinion respecting Hercules, regarding his labours "to have been originally designed as emblematic memorials of what the real *Son* of God and Saviour of the world was to do and suffer for our sakes :—

Νόσων θελκτήρια πάντα κομίζων.
Bringing a cure for all our ills."

I should have remarked sooner, that in the radical part of ἅλς (Greek of salt), that is, in *hal,* which, from the aspirate becoming S, gives the *sal* of salt, we have also the radical part of salvus (safe), and which is the same as *save,* and consequently as saver and saviour. Now, as *sol* cannot differ from *sal* (salt), and as salt has been always used for *saving* food, this too were sufficient to suggest the superstitious belief that the sun should be regarded as a saviour.

It is scarce necessary to observe that the hal of ἅλς (Greek of salt) cannot differ from *heal* in English, or from *hœlan* in Saxon; and to *heal* is to *cure,* and to cure fish or meat is to *save* it.   The root of *halig,* Saxon of holy, serves also to show that the sun must have been named *hal;* for it was at the time man revered him as God, that the idea holy was named after him.   Hence, the *hol* of holy and *sol* make only one word.

[6] Heb. Lex. p. 734.   [7] Ibid. p. 469.

CHAPTER XXII.

THE NAME OF THE SUN CAN HAVE NO ORIGINAL.—AN INSTANCE OF THE ADVANTAGE OF THIS KNOWLEDGE.—WHAT M. MAX MÜLLER, GRIMM, AND OTHER PHILOLOGISTS THINK OF THE WORDS GOD AND GOOD.

"There is perhaps," writes Max Müller, " no etymology so generally acquiesced in as that which derives *God* from *good.* In Danish, good is *god,* but the identity of sound between the English god and the Danish *god* is merely accidental. The two words are distinct, and are kept distinct in every dialect of the Teutonic family. As in English we have God and good, we have in Anglo-Saxon *God* and *gód ;* in Gothic, *Guth* and *god ;* in Old High German, *Cot* and *cuot ;* in German, *Gott* and *gut ;* in Danish *Gud* and *god*[8] *;* in Dutch, *God* and *goed.* Though it is *impossible* to give a satisfactory etymology of either *God* or *good,* it is clear that two words which thus run parallel in all these dialects without ever meeting cannot be traced back to one central point. God was most likely an old heathen name of the Deity, and for such a name the supposed etymological meaning of *good* would be far too modern, too abstract, too Christian[9]."

The mistakes in this passage would be unpardonable if its author knew any thing of the origin of language.

---

[8] Is this an oversight of the press ? The writer has just said that in Danish God and good are expressed alike.

[9] Lectures, 2nd Series, pp. 285, 286.

We see that he does not find fault with the etymology which derives God from good, but because such a meaning for the name of the Deity " would be far too modern, too abstract, too Christian." No, Sir; but it would be too absurd : it would be taking the derivative for the original. But we should still be at a loss to know the origin of the word *good;* whereas we are no way embarrassed when we take the name of the Deity for the original, and good for its derivative, nothing being more natural than to suppose that the idea of goodness was named after the author of all goodness. When M. Max Müller declares so positively as he does, that "it is *impossible* to give a satisfactory etymology of either *God* or *good*," he is, it appears, supported in this opinion by Grimm, whom all philologists (except *one*) look up to as an infallible authority. This I learn from the following passage : "The derivation of our English word God is doubtful; but I fear the *beautiful* belief, that it is deduced from *good* must be abandoned. Grimm[1] shows that there is a grammatical difference between the words in the Teutonic language signifying *God* and *good*[2]." Of course there is a difference, and which has been wisely made, and for the sole purpose of distinguishing the one word from the other. But this difference is sometimes so very slight as to make no difference at all. Witness *God* in Danish, which is in this tongue the name of the Deity, and which means also *good*. Witness also *God* and *gód* in Anglo-Saxon, of which the latter (meaning *good*) cannot be distinguished from the former but by the accent over the Ó.

Thus, by the application of our principles, and not by

[1] Deutsch. Myth. p. 12.
[2] Farrar, Origin of Language, p. 123.

any particular acumen of our own, we have here clearly shown the etymology of two very important words, which the highest judges in philology have hitherto thought *" impossible."*

That the idea of goodness must, as just shown, have been named after whatever was revered as the source of all goodness, I have now another very plain proof to submit to the reader. In Noel's " Dictionnaire de la Fable" I find the following : " Le Dieu Bon était le dieu des buveurs ; ce qui le fait quelquefois confondre avec Bacchus. Il avait un temple qui conduisait de Thebes au mont Ménale. Phurnatus donne aussi ce titre à Priape, et d'autres à Jupiter."

It is here stated that the heathen divinity named " le Bon," or the Good, was thought by some to be the same as Jupiter. But why so? Because Jupiter was anciently worshipped as the supreme God; that is, as goodness itself. But why should this divinity be confounded also with Priapus? Because the latter, though ridiculed by many, was, according to Bryant, " looked upon by others as the soul of the world; the first principle, which brought all things into light and being[3] " Priapus was therefore, in the opinion of many of his worshippers, equal to, if not above, Jupiter himself. But why was le Bon thought to be by some of the heathens the same as Bacchus? Because Bacchus was the god of wine, and in wine and the *bon* of bonus we have the same word, as we may perceive when we observe that the Greek of wine is οἶνος, but of which the root *oin* cannot differ from *hoin* (some persons having aspirated the O) nor *hoin* from *foin, boin, voin,* or *woin,* the aspirate preceding the *oin* of *oinos* having been often replaced by *f, b, v,* or *w,* so that *oin* became

[3] See Howell's Compendium, p. 351.

boin, and *boin* by the dropping of the i became *bon*. There must have therefore been a time when the *bon* of *bonus* was *boin*, and which is its correct form, for the reason that O is equal to Oi. Hence, from *boin* (the elder form of *bon*) having not only the meaning of good but of wine also, the belief prevailed with many that the divinity named the Bon was the god of wine, and consequently the same as Bacchus. In Spanish the word for wine is not only *vino* but *bino* also, which is the same as *boino*; and *boino* is, by the dropping of the *i*, not different from *bono*.

Judging from what we have already seen, the ideas wine and goodness are no way related, though they may have often been expressed by the same word. This arises from wine having been called after drink, and drink after water, and water, as already shown, after life. Hence the several ideas wine, drink, water, and life might be signified by the same word; so that from one of these ideas, life, having been called after its supposed author, the sun, it might be expressed by a word not differing from one meaning God or goodness; and so might wine, because but another word for drink, and hence for water, which was called after life, just as life was called after the sun, which, when worshipped, was believed to be the source of all goodness. M. Max Müller says : " God was most likely an old heathen name of the Deity." This is very true; but the Deity was then the sun.

In M. Max Müller's "Chips from a German Workshop," the ideas of *God* and *good* are again alluded to. It seems that Welcker, a great German scholar, is of opinion that God and good have the same meaning. But this too is a mistake. Professor Welcker should say that *good* has been called after *God*, and that its first meaning must have been godlike (*gutig*). Good is an adjective in the positive degree, having only some of the qualities of goodness; it is even less than *better* and *best*, whereas the word God takes in *all* the qualities—it is goodness itself; in other words, it is a degree even above the superlative. In Saxon, *gód* with the accent over its O means good; without the accent, it means God. There must have been —for the sake of distinction—a difference in pronunciation between the two words. The following is the passage in which M. Max Müller refers to Professor Welcker: "We should sometimes like to ask a question, for instance, how Professor Welcker could prove that the German word God has the same meaning as good. He quotes Grimm's 'History of the German Language,' p. 571, in support of his assertion; but we looked in vain for any passage where Grimm gives up his opinion, that the two words God and good run parallel in all the Teutonic dialects, but never converge towards a common origin [4]."

Yes, Professor Welcker mistakes when he asserts that there is no difference in meaning between God and good. There is, as I have shown, a wide difference. Grimm's mistake arises from his supposing that the name God must have had for its original some other word, which he and his admirer find "*impossible*" to discover. So far they are right. Such a discovery is *impossible*, but they know not why. I can, however, tell them how it happens, and so can, I am sure, every intelligent reader who has studied this discovery of mine and its principles. The name God, which was at first only the O, was a name of the sun.

It must have become *od*, by the O ending with a

---

[4] "Chips from a German Workshop," vol. ii. p. 150.

dental sound; and then by the o of od having been aspirated, and the aspirate having been replaced by g, God was obtained [5].   Now, from the name of the sun having been the origin of human speech, it follows that *it can have no original;* and this undoubted fact were of itself sufficient to prove the truth of my discovery.   M. Max Müller, however, derives the name of the sun—as do other philologists—from a source which it *cannot* have had.

Thus, in the second volume of his Lectures (page 353), he says: "From roots meaning to *shine,* to be *bright,* names were formed for sun, moon, stars, the eyes of man, gold, silver, play, joy, happiness, love."   Here are several mistakes; but for the present I wish to notice only his bold assertion that the sun took its name from roots meaning to *shine* and to be *bright.*   Then, after what, I should like to know, was the idea to *shine* called?   After the sun, certainly, and not the sun after such an idea. M. Max Müller tells us [6] that Moses was rightly stripped of his scientific knowledge; but if Moses has made the *sun* come several days after *light,* does not M. Max Müller commit as great a fault in deriving the name of the sun from the verb to shine?   But he is not the only one who makes this gross mistake.   Thus, Donnegan gives ἔλη as the root of ἥλιος, and his meaning of ἔλη is thus given: "The heat of the sun—sunshine; daylight," and to which he adds the following: "Etymon, this word is the theme of ἥλιος."

If this etymology had any truth in it, we should believe that which is impossible to believe, namely, that the heat of the sun as well as sunshine and daylight,

---

[5] " In some dialects G (Γ) is prefixed to words as a sign of aspiration." —*Donnegan.*   [6] Vol. i. p. 377.

must have preceded the existence of the sun itself. M. Regnier, an eminent Greek scholar, gives also, in his excellent edition of "*Le Jardin des Racines Grecques,*" ἔλη as the root of Ἥλιος.

In Alexandre's Greek and French dictionary, which is allowed to be the best that France has now to boast of, the same blunder is repeated, even in its eleventh and last edition, as the following serves to show : "ἥλιος, racine ἔλη."

And ἔλη is thus rendered : "chaleur du soleil; éclat du soleil; hâle."

This addition of *hâle* increases the blunder considerably. Thus, as *une figure halée* means a *sun-burnt face*, to derive the sun's name from such a source, is to make us believe that a man's face must have been reddened by the sun before the sun had yet appeared. But granting this, where or how, we beg to ask, was the word hâle itself obtained ? It is certainly but another name of the sun. But in order to show how this can be, let us first observe that *hâle* should not have been written *hasle*, as it sometimes was, and which is indicated by its circumflex. But, according to the different forms given of it by M. Littré, it has appeared oftener without the *s* than with it. *Hâler* has been even written *herle*. But both the *r* and the *s* are rejected by M. Littré, who says : "Quant aux formes en *s* ou en *r*, elles s'expliquent par la tendance de l'ancienne langue à intercaler ces lettres parasites." *Hâle*, which is the substantive form of haler, should be therefore written, as it often has been, *hale* and not hâle or hasle. And if we now give to Hēlios its fuller form, it will become *halios ;* for its e being equal to 0, and this 0 having, as usual, its *i* understood, and from 0 and *i* making *a*, hēl becomes *hal*, and this is, no doubt, the original of hâle, or, as it should be written, *hale*. The truth of this analysis is made evident by the fact that *halios* is, in the Doric dialect, for Hēlios.

Now, as *hâlé* means, when referring to the face, *sun-burnt* it cannot be a mistake to derive a word with this meaning from a name of the sun. But Diez, who is a great favourite with M. Littré, derives it from the Fle-mish word *hael*, which means dry (sec); and he confirms, as he supposes, this derivation by showing an adjective (*hasle*) which is used by Rutebeuf in the sense of *dry*. But it should be remarked that the idea of dryness may be signified by a word not different from one of the many names of the sun, which arises from every such idea being traceable to this source. But as a word meaning *dry* cannot be traced as directly to a name of the sun as one meaning sunburnt, we should consider hâle as having come *direct* from a name of the sun, and not from a word meaning dry, which idea must be traced *indirectly* to a name of the sun, as through some word signifying *air*, *fire*, or *heat*. But M. Littré, for whose opinion I have great respect, when referring to this derivation given by Diez, expresses himself thus in its favour : " Il prouve que dans hâle est non pas le sens de soleil ou de vent, mais le sens de dessécher." But there can be no better proof that this happens to be a mis-take of M. Littré's, than his own correct definition of hâler, which is as follows : " Rendre le teint brun et rougeâtre, en parlant du *soleil* et du grand *air*." And this definition of *haler* does not differ from the following by De Roquefort : " Action du soleil et du grand air sur le teint." And De Roquefort's derivation of the noun *hale*, which, as well as its verbal form, he writes without a circumflex, is as follows : " Du Latin *alea*, fait du Grec aléa, ardeur du soleil ; d'autres le dérivent de *halios* pour hélios, le soleil." I prefer the latter ; for as the participle *halé* means sunburnt, I cannot help believing but this idea has come *direct* from a name of the sun, and not from such a derivative as *ardeur*. But we should not omit noticing this word *ardeur :* its radical part is *ard*, of which the root is *ar*, and as *ar* cannot, from the constant interchange of *r* and *l*, differ from *al*, we thus obtain the well-known name of the sun with the heathens, and, as Parkhurst admits, of the Diety also with the true believers. But with the aspirate, *al* becomes *hal*, whence the hēl of hēlios, and consequently *sol* and *sun*, S being a constant representative of the aspirate h. But as *al* cannot differ from *au*, as every French school-boy knows (*au* roi being for *à le* roi), it follows that the *ard* of *ardeur* cannot differ from *aud*, and this, with the aspirate to which its *a* is entitled, becomes *haud*, that is, *chaud*, *h* and *ch* being equal to each other, as already shown. And in *haud* or *chaud* we see but different forms of *hot* and *heat* in English.

Though the intelligent reader may have now seen enough to feel assured that every ancient name of the Diety has grown out of the one that first served to designate the sun, the hieroglyphic O ; yet it may not, perhaps, be thought too much if we offer another instance of this fact, already so evident.

CHAPTER XXIII.

BUDDHA.

"Mr. Creuzer says, 'There is not in all history and antiquity, perhaps, a question at the same time more important and more difficult than that concerning Buddha.' He then acknowledges that by his name, his astronomical character, and close connexion, not only with the mythology and philosophy of the Brahmins, but with a great number of other religions, this personage, truly mysterious, seems to lose himself in the night of time, and to attach himself by a secret bond to every thing which is obscure in the East and in the West[7]."

A great deal of the obscure and mysterious in the accounts given of Buddha, has no doubt grown out of his name. "The Buddhists," says Godfrey Higgins, when they address the Supreme Being, or Buddha, use the word *Ad*, which means *the first*[8]."

But this name must have been preceded by *od*, and *od* by the hieroglyphic O, the sun; which by the teeth meeting at the close of this sound, od was obtained, whence came, by means of the aspirate and its changes, Hod, Bod, Pod, God, and a variety of other forms, according to the vocal organs employed on ending the sound of the O.

Faber gives sixteen different names of Buddha, of which many are clearly but different forms of the same word. Thus there can be no difference between *bod* and

---

[7] Anacalypsis, vol. i. p. 153.   [8] Ibid., vol. i. p. 199.

wod (root of Woden), nor between *wod* and God. Hence, a third class of his names is (as given by Faber) Gautamch, Godama, Godam, Codam, &c.[9].

Among these forms we see two (Godama and Godam) of which the radical part is God; and this word must, if there be any truth in my principles, have served to name the sun. Hence Higgins says: "Two facts seem to be universally agreed upon by all persons who have written respecting Buddha. The first is, that at last he is always found to resolve himself into the sun, either as the sun, or as the higher principle of which the sun is the image or emblem, or of which the sun is the residence. The second is, that the word Buddha means wisdom[1]."

Thus we find it admitted that Buddha is but another name of the sun; and as to this name meaning also wisdom, it might have still many other meanings, all and each of which would increase the fabulous history we have of this divinity, who was, say the learned, once adored as God over the whole world[2].

But I have an observation to make respecting the universal worship of Buddha. I wish, however, before making this observation, to draw the reader's attention to one of the meanings given by the learned to his name—that of *wisdom*. As it has not been hitherto known that every name of the heathen mythology can be shown, by the application of our principles, to have at least several meanings, learned men are, in general, satisfied with one; and they are so for the reason that it is not in their power to discover any more.

---

[9] Faber, Pag. Idol. b. iv. ch. v. p. 351.

[1] Anacalypsis, vol. i. pp. 154, 155.

[2] According to M. Barthélemy Saint-Hilaire, whose very learned and interesting work I am now reading, Buddha's most celebrated name means ' le Savant, l'Eclairé, l'Eveillé " (p. 73). This fine work is entitled " Le Buddha et sa Religion." Paris, 1868.

In a learned work which has just appeared (1868), entitled "*Grammaire Comparée des Langues Classiques,*" par M. F. Baudry, the name Buddha is said to mean *éveillé, savant*[3], which corresponds with the meaning *wisdom,* assigned to it by Higgins and others. But this divinity was never called after either *learning* or *wisdom;* nor does his name bear such a meaning among his worshippers at the present day, as we shall soon see. But even *sol* can be shown to mean *wisdom;* for, its l is but a different form of *u,* as is shown by the French coin named a *sou* having been anciently *sol;* and *sou* is the same as *sov,* and *sov* the same as the *soph* of *sophos* and *sophia;* that is, *wise, wisdom.* And such too is the *sap* of *sapientia* and the *sav* of *savoir,* not to mention *sage* and *sagesse.* Even the *hel* of *helios* of the Greeks and the *al* and *el* of the Hebrews, are all but different forms of *sol,* or *sol* but a different form of these—the O (the sun's first name) being the parent of them all.

But the learned should not suppose that the identity of his name and worship in various parts of the world was any proof of his being the same character. If we were to-morrow to discover another people who had ever lived unknown by themselves in some remote corner of the world, we might, on going amongst them, hear them call upon Buddha as their God, and we might find them having even in their history of him the leading events of his life as related in several other very different localities. And all this might very well happen without the least connexion having ever taken place between this people and the inhabitants of any other nation. And to what should we ascribe so wonderful a coincidence? To a very simple cause, namely, to this people having, while

[3] Page 90.

naming the sun, allowed a dental sound to be heard on their uttering O, instead of some other sound, such as a labial, a guttural, or a nasal. That is to say, the O with them would become *od* or *ot* instead of *ob*, *og*, *om*, or *on*; and consequently, from the O taking the aspirate (h) *od* would become *Hod*, which, from the constant interchange of H and F, would become *Fod*, and *Fod* might become *Bod*, and *Bod* become *Wod*, and *Wod* become *God* or *Got*, not to mention several other forms slightly differing from these, as having grown out of them.

According to a learned author, who writes under the name of Nimrod, Buddha is now worshipped under the form of a gigantic *foot*. The reader familiar with our principles will at once account for so gross a superstition by saying that his name must have so changed with time as to have lost its first meaning (that of the sun) and to have signified at last a *foot*. The sole of this gigantic foot is, says our author, "covered with hieroglyphics, and the lamas and emperors of the Buddhic creed delight in being called Feet and Golden Feet [4]."

The same learned authority continues thus: "The name Buddha, Baudha, Butus, Butta, Buduas, Buda, Battus, Padus, Boudha, Baouth, Boot, Boutes, Bod, Bud, Woden, Poden, and Pot, is varied in almost every possible combination; but its etymon and original meaning is that which the form of Buddha's symbol points out, ex pede Hercules. Our words *foot* and *boot* are his name, and the latter is the very way in which he is called at his ancient but ruined temple of Bactra or Boot-Bumian."

Let the reader please to observe what this learned authority admits, namely, that "our words *foot* and *boot* are his name." He saw not the consequence of this ad-

[4] Nimrod, vol. iv. p. 217.

mission.   He little suspected, when writing these words,
that he was then giving very powerful proof of the origin
of language, one day to be discovered.   How could the
worshippers of Buddha have our two words *foot* and
boot, they who had never heard a word of English ?   It
arose from all words, belonging to no matter what people,
having, as already shown, grown out of one word, the root
and parent of them all.   As to *boot*, it has been named
after that to which it belongs, namely, the *foot.*

But why should Buddha, he who was once revered
every where as God, have obtained a name not different
from such words as *boot* and *foot ?*   Buddha's name does
not, radically considered, differ from *boot*, because this
was, as just said, called after *foot*, so that we have only
to discover why his name and *foot* are so much alike.
Fot, which is the Saxon of foot, and but another of its
forms, is equal to *foit* (i being understood with O); and
foit cannot, when its O is dropped, differ from *fit*, nor *fit*
from the *vit* of *vita* (life), whence *vite*, the French of
quick; and quick has also the meaning of lively, life,
and living; witness the *quick* and the dead.   By this we
see that *foot* has, because the member with which we
move, been called after *motion*, and motion implies life,
and life was called after its supposed author, the sun ;
and all admit that Buddha was the sun.   *Foot* is also
equal to the word *food*, which, because supporting existence, was called after life, and it is therefore to be traced
to the sun.   In the noun *living*—as the *living* and the
dead—we see also a synonym of food, for a man's food is
his living.   Another idea very different from any of
these, but which is traceable to the foot, and consequently to life, and from life to the sun; is expressed
by the word kick, which, from the identity of k and qu,

cannot differ from quick. Hence to kick is to strike with the foot.

We have still an important observation to make respecting the name Buddha when appearing under the form of the word *boot,* or a form precisely equal to it. And this is our observation: *boot* cannot differ from *goot,* nor *goot* from *good,* and *good* was called after *God ;* and this is the root of *Goduma,* one of Buddha's many names given by the learned Faber, as already shown. I say this is important, because it serves to show that there is no difference between *boot* and goot or good, and that consequently *good, better, best,* is equal to *boot, booter, bootest.* From the learned having hitherto had no idea of the origin of language, they have been led to suppose that the word *good* could not have belonged to the same language that had *better* for its comparative, and *best* for its superlative, this mistake arising from its not having been known that *good* is equal to *boot,* and *better* to *booter,* and *best* to *bootest.* The author of the " VESTIGES OF CREATION " has made this mistake, and so has Webster, in his invaluable dictionary, in which I find the following : " The word *good* has not the comparative and superlative degrees of comparison, but instead of them better and best."

I cannot close this brief notice of Buddha, respecting whom a great deal more might be said, without stating my firm conviction that his name is legion ; that it has appeared under numerous forms—as numerous as the names of the sun, or, if you will, as numerous as the roots of language, of which every one may have served at different times, and in all parts of the world, to designate a Buddha. He who is therefore writing the life of such a character, is, though it may be unknown to himself, writing the lives of thousands, and of whom not so much as one has, any more than their sole parent the sun, ever existed; that is, as a being either human or divine.

Here, before proceeding any farther, I consider it necessary to refer to a few of the many faulty etymologies of the learned, to the end that much of what is yet to follow may be the more easily understood, and the reality of my discovery be fully confirmed.

CHAPTER XXIV.

AN INSTANCE OF THE ADVANTAGE TO BE DERIVED FROM KNOWING THAT THERE IS ONLY ONE LETTER IN AN ALPHABET. — M. MAX MÜLLER'S ETYMOLOGY OF THE WORD SOUL.

This eminent philologist makes, I am sure, a rather serious mistake in his attempt to discover the primary sense of the English word *soul.* He says: " *Soul* is the Gothic *saivala,* and this is clearly related to another Gothic word, *saivs,* from a root *si* or *siv,* the Greek *seio,* to shake. It meant the tossed-about waters, in contradistinction to stagnant or running water. The soul being called *saivala,* we see that it was originally conceived by the Teutonic nations as a sea within, heaving up and down with every breath, and reflecting heaven and earth on the mirror of the deep[5]."

This is certainly a very fine and learned bit of writing,

---

[5] Lectures, vol. i. p. 423. Ed. V.

though not so very clear towards the end. What its author means by "the soul heaving up and down with every breath, and reflecting heaven and earth on the mirror of the deep," I cannot, for the life of me, make out. But the fault must surely be mine; for who can suppose that such a work in its fifth edition, "carefully revised and corrected,"—which has been translated into several languages, and has come under the notice of the most eminent reviewers in England, France, Germany, and Italy,—can have been allowed to retain until now an incomprehensible passage? The fault must therefore be mine in not being able to discover what it means. I am well aware that there is, at times, something both grand and pleasing in the obscure, which arises, no doubt, from its being understood by perhaps a hundred readers in as many different ways, and from each of them taking it in the sense most agreeable to his own fancy. There must be, I am inclined to suspect, a great many such beautiful passages in Goethe, Klopstock, Dante, and Byron, and which might lose a considerable portion of the praise they have obtained if they were a little less incomprehensible. But as ambitious writing (I mean the obscure) does not suit in a work on philology, of which the style and sentiments cannot be too clear and simple, it is only fair to suppose that M. Max Müller, who, from his being a learned instructor of youth, is surely well aware of this fact, and must have embodied in the passage above quoted some very precise meaning, and that it is no fault of his, if I am so obtuse as not to be able to make out what that meaning may be.

But there is one portion of M. Max Müller's etymology of the word *soul* very plain; namely, "that this immortal part of man was originally conceived by the Teutonic nations as a sea within, heaving up and down with every breath." That is to say, the soul was called by the Teutonic nations after the sea. Now, as this etymology appeared to me rather startling and far-fetched, I had, on its first coming under my notice, recourse to the leading principle of my discovery (that there is only one letter in an alphabet) in order to see how far I might be justified in not receiving it as being evidently genuine. And this is how I went to work. But though there is only one letter in an alphabet, yet there are some of them that interchange with one another more frequently than they do with others, when the interchange is not direct, but indirect. Now, as no signs replace each other oftener than u and v, I therefore took from the word *soul* its u, and put v in its place, by which means I brought *soul* equal to *sovl;* but as this alteration gave no meaning, I tried another change. Being well aware that the v in such words as *live, give,* and *strive* is the *f* in their substantive forms, *life, gift,* and *strife,* I therefore replaced the v of *sovl* for *f,* by which change *sovl* became *soft;* but not knowing any such word as *soft,* I directed my attention to its o, replacing it by *a,* then by e, and then by i, without obtaining a significant word. But on changing the o of *soft* for u, I got *suft,* which, it was easy to perceive, cannot differ from *sufft,* that is, from the radical part of the Latin *sufflatus;* and as this means air or breath, I had no doubt that such too was the meaning of the English word *soul,* of which the parallel form in Hebrew, Greek, and Latin has, as every one knows, the same meaning.

And as one vowel is equal not only to any other vowel, but even to any combination of vowels, it is easy to perceive that, from o being consequently equal to *ou,* there can be no difference between the *suffl* of sufflatus and *souffle*, which has still the same meaning in French.

We can now very easily discover the primary sense of *seele*, which happens to be the German of soul; for as one combination of vowels is equal to any other, there can be no difference between *seele* and *soole*, any more than there is between *bleed* and *blood*, *feed* and *food*, or *breed* and *brood*; and still, for the same reason, *soole* cannot differ from soule any more than *troop* in English can differ from *troupe* in French. And *soule* is but an ancient form of *soul*.

Now, if German philologists had hitherto known that *seele* is but a different form of souffle, M. Max Müller would have also known it, and so have escaped the rather serious mistake of supposing that the Teutonic nations regarded the *soul* " as a sea within, heaving up and down with every breath, and reflecting heaven and earth on the mirror of the deep."

But M. Max Müller does not mistake when he allows his readers to understand that the Gothic word for *soul* is radically the same as a word meaning the *sea* and also as one meaning to *shake*, though he knew not why it is so, and I must not here anticipate so far as to point out the cause. We shall see it farther on. But this circumstance serves to show that one word being radically the same as another is not sufficient for proving the truth of an etymology, as a perfect agreement in meaning between two such words will be always necessary, to the end that every shade of doubt may be removed and the discovery be, when real, received as such. Nor is it any fault of mine if M. Max Müller has not received timely information on this important particular in philology; and this is my reason for thinking so: shortly after the appearance of my work on the origin of myths, I published a short exposition of its principles, in a *brochure* entitled " An Author his own Reviewer," and of which I took the liberty of sending a copy by post to M. Max Müller at Oxford.   In this little book I find (page 12), among other explanations, a passage which serves to show how the names of many different ideas may be finally traced to that of the same object (the sun) without having been called after it; and it is in the same way that a word meaning *soul* may be found to be radically the same as one meaning the *sea* or the verb to *shake*, without having been called after either of these ideas.   This is the passage : " That the first name ever given to the sun must have been O, and that all other words are traceable to this single one as their root, we have here such proof to adduce, as cannot, from its being so very conclusive, be called in question except by dulness itself, which, with regard to new discoveries, is too often the parent of scepticism. And our proof is this : the learned admit that all the heathen divinities—even without regard to sex— have, at one time or other, been taken for the sun, which, since their names were, as every one is aware, once common names, is telling us that there were anciently, and that there are consequently still, multitudes of words meaning radically the sun, if we could only but see them.   And if we can no longer perceive that all these words have [radically considered] this single meaning, it arises not only from their bearing no more the forms they once did bear, but also from their having now, as they ever did have, many other meanings as well as that of the sun.   It is, however, difficult to conceive how ideas relating in no manner to this luminary, can have names traceable to its name; as, for instance, such ideas as night and darkness. But when we say that the night must have been called after the moon, and the moon after the sun, we make these three ideas have, primarily considered, the same name. And when we say that darkness was called after night, and night after the moon, and the moon after the sun, we make these four ideas have, primarily considered, one and the same name. But it does not follow, as it is easy to perceive, that either night or darkness was ever called after the sun. In this way a thousand different ideas can be shown to have names traceable to that of the sun, without so much as one of them having been called after it."

M. Max Müller has evidently disregarded the lesson contained in the above passage, and this accounts for the mistake we have just noticed, as it will for some others, still more deserving of censure, yet to come.

Need I now show the original of *sufflatus* or *souffle*, that is to say, of the idea *breath*? It is scarcely necessary, for have I not already shown somewhere farther back that *breath* implies *life*, and *life*, as I have also shown, was called after its supposed author, the sun? Hence, as any combination of vowels may be reduced to a single vowel, there can be no difference between *soul* and *sol*. We may therefore safely assume that the root of any word meaning the *soul* must have first been one of the names of the sun, no matter how widely every two such names may now differ from each other in form.

CHAPTER XXV.

M. MAX MÜLLER'S ETYMOLOGY OF SEA.

IT is not safe, as I have, I think, already shown, to suppose that a word may have in one language a meaning very different from that which it obtains in several other languages; and it is not safe so to suppose for this simple reason, namely, that languages have been made after the same manner, which accounts for their identity on so many occasions. "The sea," writes M. Max Müller, "was called *saivs*, from a root *si* or *siv*, the Greek *seio*, to shake; it meant the tossed-about water, in contradistinction to stagnant or running water[6]."

It cannot be denied that the sea bears a name significant of motion, though, as I am now going to show, it was never called after this idea, but after one of which the name has this meaning.

Then, after what was the sea called? I answer, after water. How Bopp, who, though a very learned man, knew nothing of the origin of language, found out this, I cannot imagine, as I have not his work—of which there is an English translation—by me; but that he did find it out I am assured by his admirer, M. Max Müller, who disapproves of it thus: "Bopp's derivation [of the sea] from Sanskrit *vari*, water, is not tenable." I beg your pardon, Sir, it is tenable, and very tenable, as I am now about to prove to you.

[6] Lectures, &c., vol. i. p. 423. Ed. V.

Every word meaning water may also mean motion, as I have already shown. This arises from water having been called after existence, because necessary for the sustenance of life; and as the sea is composed of water, it has thence taken its name. That is to say, it is another word for life or motion, though not called after either, but after that element of which the name happens to have this meaning. M. Max Müller, from his not being acquainted with the origin of ideas as signified by language, on finding that the Gothic word *saivs* means the sea, and that *saivs* can be traced to a Greek word (*seiō*) meaning to *shake*, at once concludes that the sea was called after its violent motion; and so far is he from suspecting that it is but another word for water, that he even censures Bopp for his having assigned it such a derivation. But M. Max Müller does not mistake when he traces *saivs* to the Greek *seio*, to shake; for the root of the latter is *ei*, and *ei* is the same as *oi*, and *oi* is, as I have often shown, the same as *u*, and *u* is the root of the Greek ὕω, which means to produce or make water. *Seiō* and *huō* (ὕω) are therefore radically the same word, for the *s* of the former is a representative of the h or aspirate of the latter, just as the *s* of the Latin *sudor* is a representative of the h of ὕδωρ, water. And in sciō what have we, when its *s* is left out, but *eiō*, which is allowed to be the radical form (εἴω) of εἶμι to *be?* And as *being* implies existence, we thus discover in *seiō* (to shake) the very idea after which water has been called. We have also found *aqua* in our etymology of *sequor* because it is, like *seiō*, expressive of motion. Hence the *qua* of the Latin quatio (to shake) is, we may be sure, for *aqua*. And when we observe that the *sh* of *shake* is here but a representative of the aspirate, the

N

remainder of this word (*ake*) cannot differ from *aka*, nor *aka* from *aqua;* and this is confirmed by the Swedish tongue, in which *shaka* means to *shake*. By this we learn that words signifying motion do not differ from one another but conventionally; so that such different ideas as *walk, fly,* and *flow* might be expressed by three words radically the same. And this knowledge will lead us to the primary signification of many a word of which the origin has been hitherto unknown. Hence, when we regard the *s* of the French *secouer* (to shake) as representing the aspirate, and as consequently forming no part of this word, the *ecou* which follows should be considered as equal to *equa* and *aqua*, not that the idea of shaking has been called after water, though this might very well be, but after motion, and motion after existence, from which water, as already shown, derives its name. The root of every such word as *quake, quick, quaver,* and *quiver* is still *aqua*, so that they cannot be said to differ from *shake* but conventionally.

I expressed only awhile ago my astonishment at Bopp's having discovered that the primary signification of *sea* was water; but I have since learned something which has lessened my astonishment considerably. Bopp was very learned in Sanskrit, and in this language the word for water is *vari*, as M. Max Müller states; and I now learn from M. Amédée de Caix de Saint-Aymour[7], who is also a learned Sanskrit scholar, that the word for sea in the same language is *wari*. Surely it was not difficult for Bopp to perceive that in *vari* and *wari* there is only one word, no two signs being more evidently the same than *v* and *w* (compare *vinum* and *wine, ventus*

[7] See his work entitled "La Langue Latine étudiée dans l'Unité Indo-Européenne," p. 77.

and *w*ind). Now, if M. Max Müller knew no more of
Sanskrit than I do myself, I could easily account for
his failing to observe the identity of two such words ;
but believing, as every one else does, that he is deeply
read in this language, I am at a loss to account for
his making so light of Bopp's etymology of *sea*.

But I am now going to give other proofs that Bopp
has made no mistake in deriving the word for *sea* from
one meaning *water*. I open my Parkhurst[8], from
whom I learn that the Hebrew word ם *im* means *the
sea* or *a sea*, and that it has been so called "from its
tumultuous motion by winds or tides. It is used more
extensively than our English word *sea* usually is, as for
any large collection of waters, a lake—for the *large brazen
or molten vessel* in Salomon's Temple, for the *priests to
wash in*." And Parkhurst further adds, that this word ם
im means "*water* or *waters* in general, thus denominated
like ם *im, the sea*,—from their being so susceptible of,
and frequently agitated by, tumultuous motions."

I forgot to state that the first meaning assigned by
Parkhurst to ם *im* is "*tumult, tumultuous* motion."
But Parkhurst mistakes when he imagines that both
water and the sea have been so named from their being
so susceptible of being agitated "by tumultuous
motions." It never occurred to him that the sea was
named after water, and water after existence, and this
idea after the supposed author of existence, the sun.
If he knew all this, such knowledge would have prevented him from making another serious mistake
connected with ם *im ;* for, under its form םי *ium*, he
explains it thus: "*The* or *a day*, from the *tumultuous
motion* or *agitation* of the celestial *fluid*, while the sun

[8] Page 234.

N 2

is above the horizon[9]. A good telescope, says an excellent and pious philosopher, will show us what a *tumult*
arises in the air from the agitation of the sunbeams in
the heat of the noon-day. The heaven seems trans-
parent and undisturbed to the naked eye; while a
storm is raised in the air by the impulse of the light,
*not unlike what is raised in the waters of the sea by the
impetuosity of the wind.* It increases with the altitude
of the sun, and when the evening comes on, it sub-
sides almost into a calm[1]."

In the passages from Scripture here referred to by
Parkhurst, there is no allusion whatever to " the tumultuous motion or agitation of the celestial fluid."

Parkhurst has made a great mistake by supposing
that the day was named after this tumultuous motion
of the celestial fluid in the heavens. How could he
suppose that they who first made words knew any
thing of this tumultuous motion? To make such a
discovery, it was, we are told, necessary to have a
good telescope; but at the remote period referred to,
there were no telescopes either good or bad, nor for
thousands of years afterwards.

But what is here admitted by Parkhurst is well worth
knowing, namely, that ‏‎‏‎ם‎ *im* means not only water and
the sea, but, under its form ‏‎‏ם‎ *ium*, day also; for *day* is
the same as Deus, and Deus was one of the names of the
sun, after which existence was named, and after existence
water, which accounts for the names of the latter being
always significant of motion.

Another word in Parkhurst, similar in meaning to ‏ם‎
im, is ‏‎‏אר‎ *ar*, and to which I have already referred, for it

<hr/>

[9] Gen. i. 5. 18; viii. 22. Psalm cxxxvi. 8, et al. freq.

[1] Rev. William Jones, in his " Essay on the First Principles of Natural
Philosophy," p. 241.

means to flow, and as a noun, a *river*, a *flood*, which ideas have been called after water; and as under it; form אור *aur* it means *light*, Parkhurst makes the same mistake respecting the origin of this idea, that he has made when accounting for the origin of ים *im* under its form *ium ;* that is, he says light has been so named from its being a fluid[2].

I have referred thus twice to אר *ar* and אור *aur* for two reasons, namely, that the reader may see how in the same language the same idea may be expressed by different words, and how every monosyllable may have served as a name of the sun, and have hence signified both existence and motion as well as water.

. I forgot to take advantage of a statement made by Parkhurst under ים *im,* namely, that this word was also the name " of the large brazen or molten vessel in Salomon's Temple for the priests to wash in;" for this serves to show that things used for holding water were named after it. This knowledge will serve us farther on.

From what we have now seen, it will be reasonable to suppose that words meaning the sea must have also meant water. Thus, in *mare,* Latin of *sea,* we are induced to take *ar* as its root, and to regard this root as having first meant water. Hence, the French verb *arroser,* of which *ar* is also the root, means to *water;* but sea-water is not understood. In the French noun *rosée* we have still the same root, for this word must have been *arosée,* as no consonant can, without a vowel, be a word ; and *rosée* means *dew,* which is but another word for water, but not sea-water. Dew, when read as in Hebrew, gives *wed,* and *wed* cannot differ from *wet* nor from the *wat* of *water. Thaw* is still the same word;

[2] Page 29.

for it is equal to the *wath* of *wather*, that is, *water*. The
r of the Greek rheō, to flow, is also for *ar;* and so is the
r of ῥαίνω (to sprinkle or bedew).   In the same way we
can account for the *r* of the rivers Rhine and Rhone;
and as *ar* must have been their first name, this might
lead us to suppose that they were once designated by a
Hebrew word, since, according to Parkhurst, as we have
seen, אר *ar* means a river[3].   But under each of these
forms, יאר *iar*, and יאור *iaur*, he explains it thus, " a river,
stream, or flux of water."   And he concludes with saying
" Hence perhaps *yar* or *yare*, the name of a river in
England, and Jaar of one in Flanders."   I cannot say if
the two rivers here mentioned have been named after the
Hebrew of *river;* but this I can say, namely, that the
words יאר *iar* and yar, yare, and jaar are precisely equal
to each other.   But, for the reason that words of all
languages have emanated from the same source, the
names of rivers in very different parts of the world may
be sometimes found alike without there having ever been
the least intercourse between the countries to which they
belong.   Learned men, on perceiving this similarity in
the names of many places over the world, have, from their
total ignorance of the common origin of all languages,
often endeavoured to prove a close connexion in ancient
times between nations which had, in all probability,
never so much as heard of one another; and this is
confirmed by our article headed, " RIVERS OF THE SUN."
And the *r* of the word river itself is for *ar*, just as it is in
the names Rhine and Rhone.

We have even in English this word *ar* in the sense of
sea, but it is now hidden in the word *brine*, which is for
*bar*ine, that is, *marine*, as we must admit on comparing

[3] Page 29.

salt-water or pickle with its French equivalent *mariner* to pickle. The *bar* of barine is therefore the *mar* of the Latin *mare*. In Gaelic also this word *bar*, now obsolete, means the *sea ;* but it must at some remote period have meant water, for it is the radical part of *braon*, which in this language means dew, and dew is water. In this language I find also two words which, without being submitted to the least change, mean both sea and water. Thus, from among five Gaelic words for water I take these two, *muir* and *cuan*. The first is thus rendered into English, "The sea, a sea, an ocean ;" and the second thus, "a sea, ocean."

Here it is not said that these words mean water ; nor is it said, where I find them among the Gaelic words for water, that they mean either a sea or an ocean; which serves to show that they are not in either case to be taken in a metaphorical sense.

But what word can show more clearly that the sea means literally water than this word *sea* itself? For as its *s* represents the aspirate, which is *never* to be counted as a constituent part of a word ; the *ea* that remains should be regarded as its root, and in Saxon *ea* is thus explained by Bosworth : " running water, a stream, a river, water." Another form of *ea* is *eah*, which is explained " *a river.*" *Eg* is still another form of *eah*, though Bosworth does not give it as such; but he explains it " *the sea ;*" and as he gives *egland* for *island*, this serves to show that *eg* and *is* are equal to each other ; so that, from *eg* meaning the sea, such too must be the meaning of *is*, which is the verb to *be* ; and water, as we have shown, has been called after this idea.

Now *is*, this inflection of the verb to *be*, appears also, according to Bosworth, under the form *sé* ; and *sé*, writes the same authority, is for *sea*, of which another form is *sæ*. Hence the literal meaning of *island* may be either *sea-land* or, since *sea* means water, *water-land*. But that a word in any way significant of water might also serve to signify the sea, could, I believe, be shown by Saxon alone. Thus our word *lake* is in this language written both *lagu* and *lago*, and its explanation is "water, the sea, a lake;" and Bosworth explains *egor*, "the sea, water."

In the radical part of several of those words, it is easy to perceive a modification of *aqua ;* witness *lagu, lago,* and *lake*, of which *agu, ago,* and *ake* may be regarded as the radical parts, but not as the roots, which are *ag* and *ak*, just as *aq* is the root of *aqua*. In the *eg* of egor, just noticed, we also see this root; and which is confirmed by *eg* (the sea) which we have also just seen.

The noticing of these roots reminds me of the Gaelic word *cuan*, which, as shown above, means not only *water* and *sea*, but *ocean* also. Now, as every vowel may receive or lose the nasal sound, it follows that *cuan* is equal to *cua*, that is, when the vowel due before initial consonants is supplied, *acua*, which is precisely equal to *aqua*. But as any other vowel may, as well as *a*, be prefixed to the *c* of *cuan*, we discover, on substituting *o* for *a*, that this word is as equal to *ocuan* as it is to *acuan ;* and in *ocuan* it is easy to perceive a modified form of *ocean*, which is the radical part, but not the root, of the Latin *oceanus*, or, if you will, of its Greek form ὠκεανός, written also ὠγήν. And this serves to show that the primary signification of ocean is, like that of sea, *water*, and nothing more ; so that, however differently such words may be used, the difference between them can be no more than conventional.

Now, as the *aq* of *aqua* cannot differ from *ag*, and as *ag* is the root of *ago*, to act, and also of *agilis*, active, we thus see how *aqua* is, like every other word for water, significant of motion. Hence the ok of ὠκεανός is also the ok of ὠκύς, which means swift; nor can this root differ from the *ag* of *agilis*, nor *agilis* from *Achelous* ('Αχελώος), which, according to Donnegan, meant not only one particular river, but any river, and *water* also. Hence its radical part *ache* is equal to *aqua*.

But is not *Achilous*, I may be asked, very like Achileus (that is, Achilles)? The two words are so much alike that they may be regarded as one and the same. Nor do they differ in meaning; for this hero was, according to Homer, remarkably swift of foot: "ποδὰς ὠκὺς 'Αχιλλεύς." Hence in *Achilles* and *agilis* we have but different forms of the same word. There are other reasons for Achilles being made so *agile :* his father was Peleus, and this name is radically the same as πέλω, which means, says Donnegan, " to move, to be in a state of movement, and also to be;" and his mother was *The*tis, in which we see the radical part of θέω to run, and also of θεά (a goddess) ; and as θ is often replaced by Σ (witness θεῖος, godlike, being also σεῖος, and 'Αθάνα being 'Ασάνα) there can be no difference between θεά and the English word *sea*, and Thetis was the goddess of the sea. And the Saxon word *se* means not only *sea* but the article *the ;* and no article, whether definite or indefinite, can, as we have already seen, differ in meaning from the name of God or the sun. And *se* is also used in Saxon for *is*, so that from its thus signifying existence, we see why it should be equal to a name of the author of existence.

As to Achilles having been thought *light* of foot, it was no doubt from his name implying swiftness that such an epithet has been applied to him. And for his having had Peleus for his father and Thetis, goddess of the sea, for his mother, and for his having been dipped at his birth in a river, the cause must be the same; for these several words, Achilles, Achelous, Peleus, and Thetis have radically the same meaning. We may, therefore, conclude that Achilles, as he is described by Homer, is ane ntirely fabulous character: the origin of many things in the history we have of him, has, no doubt, been suggested by the several meanings of his name.

When we now observe that the S of the Saxon *se* (sea) does but represent the aspirate, and that the aspirate should *never* be regarded as any radical part of a word, we must admit that the single sign *e* is the root of *se ;* and that such too is the root of the article *the*, and hence of Thea, Theos, and Deus. But as one vowel is equal to, not only any other vowel, but to any combination of vowels, the root *e*, here referred to, may be represented by *o, eo, io, ie, ea,* &c.

And in these representatives of the sign *e*, the reader can recognize primitive forms (already noticed) of the verbs to be and to go, as well as (according to Parkhurst) of the true God and the sun.

These latter etymologies enable us to account for the origin of some ideas which learned men have hitherto endeavoured, but in vain, to trace to their real source. Thus, I learn from my Donnegan, under θεός, that " Herodotus derives θεοί from τίθημι, to lay, to place, from the gods having fixed and disposed of all things in the world;" but Plato's derivation is from θέω to run, because "the first notions of a divinity having been derived from observing the motions of the heavenly bodies." But what is Donnegan's opinion ? It leads to nothing ;

he only observes, "It is obvious that Ζεύς, Διός, and the obsolete nominative Δίς, the Latin Dis and Deus, have a common origin." No one doubts it; but we are not told what that origin is. I now consult Alexandre, which high authority derives θεός from θεάομαι, a word meaning to behold or contemplate with admiration.

I need scarcely tell the reader who has the least faith in the truth of the foregoing principles that these notions of the origin of such an idea as the one expressed by θεός or Deus, are very erroneous. It is true that such a word as θέω (to run) and θεός are radically the same; but though this is necessary for proving the truth of an etymology, it is not sufficient; something else is required: a perfect agreement in sense. The reader can now easily account for the radical identity of θεός and θέω. He knows that it arises from existence having been called after θεός (once a name of the sun), to which source or to ideas thence derived, those significant of motion are to be traced.

The θη of τίθημι and the θε of θεός are also radically the same; but τίθημι means to lay, that is, to lay *down*; and as such an idea implies lowness, even death, there is no relationship whatever between it and the sun. The identity of the radical parts of the two words θεός and τίθημι is to be accounted for in the same way as we account for altus meaning both high and low, and for the same word in Saxon meaning both *black* and *white*. The ideas night, darkness, lowness, and death have all and each the moon for their source; and as the moon has been called after the sun, the very different ideas just mentioned may, from their names being traceable to the name of the moon, be traceable to the name of the sun also. Hence the θη of τίθημι is also the θα or θη of θάνω or θήνω, in which we have the ancient verbal form of θάνατος, death. This will explain why there are certain hills in England called the *downs* instead of the *hills*. It will also explain why don and dom, titles of dignity, are radically the same as *down*. Indeed, when we remark that the *w* in Sanskrit becomes *m* in Latin, we see that *down* cannot differ from *domn*, that is, *domin*, radical part of *dominus*.

Alexandre has made a notable mistake in deriving θεός from θεάομαι; for the primary sense of this word is to see (conventionally to see with admiration); and the idea signified by seeing or sight is traceable to the eye, and thence to light, and through light to the sun; so that θεάομαι can be derived from the name of the sun, but the name of the sun cannot be derived from θεάομαι.

And so must it have been in all languages. The name of the sun being the first and sole original parent of human speech, all other words may be traced up to it either directly or indirectly, but this name can itself be traced from no word. The quadrature of the circle or perpetual motion may, perhaps, be one day discovered, but that word from which the name of the sun can be derived—*never*.

Wishing now to know to what source modern etymologists have traced the idea *ocean*, I open my Donnegan, and find under ὠκεανός the following: "If not derived from it, it has the same origin as ὠγήν—both *perhaps* from ὠκὺς νάω, I flow rapidly." Donnegan has done well to express his doubt on giving such a derivation of ὠκεανός. It must, however, be admitted that this word is radically the same as ὠκύς. But why so? Because ὠκύς means swift or rapid; that is to say, it implies motion and so does water, and the primary and radical sense of *ocean* is water. Hence it is very correct to trace ὠκύς to water or life, but very incorrect to trace water to ὠκύς. De Roquefort gives the same etymology of ὠκεανός as Donnegan, with this difference, that he does not allude to ὠγήν, which is radically the same word, for it has the same meaning.

Count de Gébelin gives the following derivation of Ocean : "Du primitif *ok, grand, an, cercle.*"

I need not say that this is another serious mistake.

Noel's derivation of *oceanus* does not differ from the one given by Donnegan and De Roquefort.

Quicherat and Daveluy's only etymology of *oceanus* is that in Greek this word is written ὠκεανός, which is no etymology.

Alexandre's derivation of ὠκεανός is simply ὠκύς, from which it appears that he believes it to have been called after the idea of swiftness. He does not seem to think that its name is in any way connected with water. He admits, however, that it is used in the sense of both the sea and water in general, but that this is only a poetical licence. The word *waters*, when so used, has, it is true, such an effect; but poetical expressions and allusions are often more real and primitive than the poet himself imagines. *Ocean* had at first, as it has still, the meaning of water. I was forgetting to observe, that when Alexandre gives ὠκύς as the root of ὠκεανός, he appends to this word a note of interrogation, which, as I learn from the explanation of the signs in his dictionary, implies doubt. Such a sign happens to be on this occasion an appendage very properly applied.

M. Littré supposes the original meaning of ocean is to surround, to enclose. These are his words : "L'étymologie très-probable de ὠκεανός est le védique açayana, épithète de Vritra, dans le sens d'entourant, enserrant, les eaux du nuage. Pour le changement de *α* en *ω*, comparez açu, qui est *ὠκύς*, rapide."

This etymology appears both improbable and far-fetched. There must have been a word for the ocean long previous to such a knowledge of natural philosophy as that which enabled men to know that " *les eaux du nuage* " were surrounded or enclosed.

We have now said enough of the words *water*, *sea*, and *ocean* in different languages to confirm Bopp's derivation of *sea*, and to prove, beyond all doubt, that M. Max Müller's etymology of the Gothic of *sea* cannot be relied on. But the learned Oxford professor takes now a different view of the word *sea*, as I am going to show.

Thus, whenever an etymologist finds two words alike in form, or nearly so, he is mostly always disposed to imagine that such words must express kindred ideas, though they may differ as widely in meaning from each other as those signifying day and night, or white and black. But if the etymologist knew how all languages have grown out of a single sign, he would be far from judging so hastily. The faulty etymology we have now noticed must be ascribed to M. Max Müller's want of this necessary knowledge of the origin of human speech, and of which I now beg to give, from the same author, another instance bearing a very close resemblance to the one we have just seen. And during this inquiry, which promises to be a long one, I shall have occasion to make, through the applying of my principles, a few other important discoveries in philology.

CHAPTER XXVI.

M. MAX MÜLLER'S ETYMOLOGY OF SEA UNDER ITS LATIN
FORM MARE.

FROM what we have just seen, M. Max Müller has
derived *saivs*, the Gothic of sea, from the Greek σείω to
shake, and not from a word meaning water, as he should
have done.   But on perceiving that *mare*, the Latin of
sea, is nearly the same as *mar*, which in Sanskrit means
to die, he is led to believe that the northern Aryans
must have called the sea after such an idea.   But words
may be very much alike in form and not at all so in
meaning, as I have already often shown.   In no language in the world can a people have named the sea,
which appears so full of life and motion, after death ;
but M. Max Müller thinks otherwise, as the following
passages serve to show.

" When the Romans saw the Mediterranean, they called
it *mare*, and the same word is found among the Celtic,
Slavonic, and the Teutonic nations[4].   We can hardly
doubt that their idea in applying this name to the sea
was the dead or stagnant water, as opposed to the running streams (*l'eau vive*) or the unfruitful expanse[5]."

He says again : " If in English we can speak of dead
water, meaning stagnant water, or if the French use
eau morte in the same sense, why should not the northern

_____

[4] Curtius, Zeitschrift, i. 30.   Slav. more ; Lith. marios and marés ;
Goth. marei ; Ir. muir.   [5] Lectures, vol. ii. p. 320.

Aryans have derived one of their names for the sea from the root *mar*, to die?" And he further adds, "If it is once established that there is no other root from which *mare* can be derived more regularly than from *mar*, to die, then we are at liberty to draw some connecting line between the root and its offshoots."

Really, if I did not know from report that M. Max Müller is very learned in Sanskrit, I should say his knowledge of this language is very limited, so much so that he does not know its word for the Latin *mare* is *wari*, and that its word for water is *vari*; for these two words do not differ any more from each other than the English and Danish words *water* and *vater*, which are alike in meaning. Then why, with his knowledge of Sanskrit, does he suppose that the northern Aryans named the sea after a word meaning death, when they had, we may say, one and the same word for both sea and water (*wari* and *vari*), and since water is the element of which the sea is composed?

Having already sufficiently shown that the sea has been called after water, it cannot be required of me to do so again; but its Latin form, *mare*, has, I perceive, induced more than one philologist to connect the idea it expresses with that of death. Thus, M. Littré, after giving the several forms of this word in different languages and dialects, concludes as follows: "Corssen et Curtius rapprochent *mare* du Sanscrit *maru*, le désert, c'est-à-dire, l'élément *mort*, stérile, ἀτρύγετος πόντος."

Great stress is laid upon this epithet *atrugetos*, as serving to show that the Latin *mare* is allied in meaning to the Sanskrit of desert; but as this word means *unfruitful*, it is applied to the air as well as to the sea, so that had there never been a desert, there would have been such an epithet as *atrugetos*. Nor does πόντος, or its Latin form *pontus*, mean a way; it is but another word for *sea;* and as *sea* means water, even so does *pontos*. When we do, therefore, leave out its nasal sound, as we may do (compare *tango* and *tago*), this word becomes *potos*, which, as an adjective, means potable, and, as a noun it is explained "a drink, a draught," &c. Potamos, a river, is radically the same word. But the latter observation is, I now perceive, unnecessary, for I learn from my notes that I shall have to notice pontos again.

When M. Max Müller says that "if there is no other root from which *mare* can be derived more regularly than from *mar* to die, then we are at liberty to draw some connecting line between the root and its offshoot." But he forgets that it is not *mare* he has to consider, but its Sanskrit form *wari*. I have already quoted a passage from M. Amédée de Caix de Saint-Aymour's learned work, serving to show that *wari* is *mare*. Here is another passage from the same authority (p. 148) : "Il importe encore de signaler le changement *si commun de W en M*, changement que l'on retrouve dans le Latin *mare*, originellement identique au Sanskrit *wari* et à l'Aryaque *wari*, &c. "

And since *wari* is the same as vari (water), to say that *mare* is derived from a word significant of death, is to say that such too must be the original meaning of *water;* for every word meaning the sea or the ocean, in no matter what language, must have been a word for water, and also for motion or life, which is the reverse of death.

Words meaning even standing water do not differ but conventionally from such as mean water in general. There may be one or two exceptions; such as *stagnum* in

Latin and *étang* in French; but an exception should not
be regarded as subversive of a general rule; it tends
rather to confirm it. At first standing water must have
been signified by two words. Hence, *stagnant* cannot
be used as a noun in English, nor can *stagnante* in
French. The English word *marsh*, as well as *marais*
in French, and which is but a different form of it, is
radically the same as *mare*, Latin of *sea*. In *mire* we
have also the same word; for as its i has, as usual, O
understood, it cannot differ from *moire*, that is, when the
O and *i* meet, making *a—mare;* and which is confirmed
by this very word *mare*, for though a synonym of
marais, it is the Latin of *sea*, and consequently a word
not differing in signification from *water* but conventionally, since sea is water.

It was only by altering the form of a word for water,
that it was made to signify a marsh, or a pool of standing water. Thus the radical part of *limus*, that is, *lim*,
is also the radical part of λίμνη; and the latter means
not only a marsh or a lake, but even sometimes a sea.
Yet it cannot differ, as shown farther back, from either
slime in English or *flumen* in Latin. And from knowing
that all such ideas are traceable to water, we are led to
discover that the French word *boue* must have first been
oue, its *b* being only a substitute for the aspirate, and
consequently no radical part of this word. And what is
oue, but a different form of *eau*, water?

There is another word in French for *slime*, namely,
vase; and yet it was never named after such an idea as
mud or *slime ;* for it is radically the same as the word
vessel, which was called after water. *Vase* and *wasser*
are also kindred forms, as it is easy to perceive.

Judging from what we have now seen, we may safely

assert, that in no language was the sea ever called after such an idea as dead or death. Even such an idea as we express by the word *marsh* has not the meaning of death, nor any other than that of water; but conventionally standing water.

CHAPTER XXVII.

OTHER INSTANCES OF THE ADVANTAGE TO BE DERIVED FROM KNOWING THE PRIMARY SIGNIFICATION OF THE IDEA WATER.

IF we now want to add other proofs of the advantage of our system to all we have hitherto produced, we need only open M. Littré's valuable dictionary, and transcribe, as one proof, his etymology of *ivre*, which, the reader will please to recollect, I have traced to the idea *drink :* " Ety. Berry, *ebriat;* Provenç. iber, ivre ; Espagn. et Portug. *ebrio;* Ital. *ebbro,* ebro; du Lat. *ebrius,* qui vient, d'après les étymologistes Latins, de *e,* hors, et *bria,* sorte de mesure : mot à mot, qui est hors de la mesure. Mais ce qui rend cette étymologie peu sûre, c'est que *bria* est un mot probablement étranger et recent, et peut-être douteux, car on lit aussi *ebria* et hebria au lieu de *bria.* Le Berry dit *ebriat,* qui paraît représenter le Latin ebriacus." Of course, *ebriat* represents *ebriacus,* and so do all and each of the above words represent both *ebriacus* and *ebrius;* but this is not telling us what the primary signification of any of these forms of the same word may be.   An attempt has, however, been made to give us the primary signification of *ebrius;* but it has been only an attempt, and a very silly one too; and it has been wisely rejected by M. Littré, though his reason for doing so is no proof that he knows any thing of the origin of language.   Allow me, dear reader, to tell him that every initial vowel may or may not be aspirated, so that one-half of his countrymen might pronounce *hebria* instead of *ebria;* which arises from the common tendency that prevails with almost all people to aspirate initial vowels.   Hence such an aspirate should *never* be regarded as belonging, in any way, to the root of a word.   But let us take advantage of what is here admitted, namely, that *bria* is also written *ebria;* for this confirms one of our rules, namely, that initial consonants have vowels understood before them.   When we do therefore prefix a vowel to words beginning with *b* that do in any way relate to the idea *drink,* we may find them to be but different forms of *ivre* or *ebrius.*   Witness *beer* in English, *bier* in German, and *bière* in French, none of which can, when *i* or *e* is prefixed, differ from *ivre* or the *ebr* of *ebrius.*   Thus, as every combination of vowels may be reduced to a single vowel or to any other combination of vowels, we discover in the French verb *boire* a form equal to *beer, bier,* or *bière.*

And this knowledge will greatly serve the etymologist, and enable him to detect some serious mistakes in the assumed derivation of certain words.   Only witness the following, which I transcribe from M. Baudry's learned work, entitled " Grammaire Comparée des Langues Classiques," p. 77 : " Οἶνος se rapporte en Sanscrit, soit, selon M. Kuhn, au Védique *vaina* (aimable), épithète du Soma; soit, selon M. Pott, à la racine *vjai* (tegere, texere) qui a fait le Latin vieo, d'où *vimen* et vitis, et a pu donner vinum de vitis. Le Grec ne compte de mots correspondants à vieo et vimen que ἴτυς (circonférence), ἰτέα (saule). L'absence de mot analogue signifiant 'vigne' en Grec, qui aurait été nécessaire pour donner lieu au dérivé οἶνος, nous fait donc pencher vers la première explication."

Here are several serious mistakes, made by three very learned men. Thus, M. Kuhn traces wine to a Sanskrit word (vaina) which is explained *amiable;* and M. Pott traces it to another Sanskrit word or root (vjai) which may mean in Latin either tegere or texere; that is, *wine* may, according to this view, be what covers, weaves, or knits, the reader being left to choose any one of the many widely different meanings allowed to *tegere* or *texere;* but the meaning of binding seems to be preferred, for the Sanskrit root (vjai) is regarded as the original of the Latin vieo, which means to bind with osier twigs, whence, we are told, come the nouns *vimen*, an osier twig, and *vitis*, a vine, and consequently wine. But M. Baudry, instead of rejecting both these explanations, feels inclined to accept the first, there being no word in Greek for vine corresponding with either *vieo* or *vimen*.

But as wine is a drink, and as we have proved this idea to be traceable to water, we at once perceive in the πίνω to drink a form no way different from the *vin* of vinum, because *p* and *v* do constantly interchange. And when we now apply to the *vit* of *vitis* (a vine) our rule which says that a vowel may or may not receive a nasal sound, we discover in this word *vit* the *vint* of vintage. In the *vit* of *vitis* we have also the *vit* of vita, Latin of

life, after which idea *water* has been called, just as drink
has been called after the idea water. In *vita* we also
see the French *vite*, quick, an idea of which we have
already traced the name to that of water. And as *vit*
is equal to *voit*, and thence to *vat*, we get in the name of
the latter a well-known vessel for holding wine and
other liquids; by which we see that it is but another
word for water, and that it has, like *vase*, been so called,
because of the use made of it. *Vat* is also the radical
part of *vater*, which in Danish means *water*. We shall
see in the proper place why this word *vater* means also,
as in German, father.

Even *uva*, a grape, can be traced to water, for it is
radically the same as *uvor*, which means humidity; but
the English word *grape* has a different origin; it is
allied to such ideas as *group*, *grab*, &c., and is therefore
traceable to the hand. Hence *grappe*, 'a bunch, applies
to currants as well as to grapes.

As to the Sanskrit word *vaina* (amiable), to which
idea M. Kuhn traces wine; we must admit that it is in
form radically the same as *vinea* and *vinum*, but not in
meaning, which is always required for confirming the
truth of an etymology. I can, however, account for
such an idea as is expressed by the French word *aimable*
bearing a close resemblance to one meaning wine. In
order to make this very apparent, let us observe that in
Spanish *vinum* is not only written *vino* but also *bino*,
which, from 0 being here, as usual, understood with i,
cannot differ from boino, nor *boino*, when its *i* is dropped,
from *bono*, which means *good;* and this idea is also often
represented by such words as kind and *amiable*. And if
we wish to know why wine and goodness should be
named alike, we need only observe that wine was called

after water, and water after life, and life after the supposed author of existence and of all that is good, that is,
after God, once a name of the sun. And if we now allow
the O and i of *bono* to coalesce, we shall obtain *a*, and
thus bring *boino* equal to *bano*, which is the Spanish of
bath; and this word, as we have already shown, means .
water, the idea to which wine is traceable. Another
word equal to *ban* is the Greek βαίνω, which implies
motion, since it means to walk, go, come, &c.; and water
also has this meaning of motion, and of which I have
given several very conclusive proofs.

The word *bain* just noticed, and shown .to be, like
bath, but another word for water, cannot differ from
the French *bien*, for the reason that one combination of
vowels is equal to another as well as to any single vowel.
But *bain* and *bien* are so different in meaning, that the
equality in the value of their form must be ascribed to
the circumstance of their belonging to the same division
of language. Hence, from *bath* being a word for water,
and from this idea having been called after life, and life
after its supposed author, the sun, we see how it might
be expressed by a word signifying God or good. And
this happens, since the *ben* of *benè* (Latin of *bien*) is for
the *bon* of *bonus*. And this etymology is confirmed by
the word *well*, which is not only the English of *bien* and
benè, but is also, like *bain*, expressive of water. We
may therefore regard the *p* of *puteus* (Latin of *well*) as
being here for the aspirate, by which *puteus* is brought
equal to *huteus*, and *huteus* to *hudeus*, that is, ὔδας, the
elder form of ὔδωρ, water.

Another form of *benè* is *bellè*, and here too we have the
English word *well*, since B is constantly represented by
W, witness Bill and Will, each the familiar of William;

so that the *bell* of *bellè* cannot differ from *well*. Another
form of *well* is *weal*, as is shown by the public *weal* being
the same as the public good, and this too is confirmed
by its Latin and French equivalents, *bonum publicum*, and
bien public. And as *Bon* was once a name of the sun,
then revered as God, even so was *Bel*.

We now see why *bain* and *bien*, though so different in
meaning, make only one word ; and which is confirmed
by *well*, when considered both as a noun and an adverb.

But I have still other proofs to add to the above,
and which serve to show that even *blood* is traceable to
water. In Gaelic *fuil* means *blood ;* but as its *i* must
be for *oi*, and as *oi* must, when these two signs coalesce,
be for *a*, it follows that *fuil* is equal to *fual*, and, on
looking out for this word in the Gaelic side of my
dictionary, for I know not what it means, I find it
rendered thus into English : " urine, water." We may,
therefore, conclude, that *fuil* and *fual* have not been
made to differ in form as they do—and the difference is
very slight—but for the sake of distinction.

I have still another proof that *blood* has been called
after water. In *blood* and *flood* (Saxon *blod* and *flod*)
we have two words precisely equal to each other in form,
for B and F do often interchange (compare *brother* and
frater) ; but equality in form is not sufficient, there
must be an agreement in sense to prove the truth of an
etymology. Now, Johnson gives the following definition of *blood:* " The red *liquor* that circulates in the
bodies of animals." In this word *liquor* it is not difficult
to perceive the Latin of water, for its radical part, *iquor*,
is the same as *œquor*, which is a general name for water,
and, as shown farther back, is radically the same as *aqua*.
Hence, from blood being a *liquor*, it is a *liquid*, and

consequently that which flows, and as a *flood* is a *flow*, it follows that, primarily considered, the two words *blood* and *flood* make but one.   This etymology is further confirmed by the Greek word βρότος, which is thus explained by Donnegan : " gore, clotted blood. Thema (ῥοτὸς) ῥέω, to flow, β, Æolian, for the aspirate."

Now, from βρότος having, through meaning clotted *blood*, for its root ῥέω, to flow, there can be no longer any doubt of its having at first been called after water; conventionally, *red* water.

I am now enabled to make an etymology which, without the knowledge just obtained, could never be known.   Greek scholars cannot find the root of ῥόδον, a *rose*. And why so ? Because no one could ever suppose it should have such a root as ῥέω, to flow, which implies that its origin is to be traced to water.   And what relationship could any philologist think of finding between a *rose* and water ?   These two ideas are, however, allied to each other in name, even as much so as are *rain* and *water*.   And this is how it happens : Wine, as just shown, has been called after water, and so has blood ; and this being, from what we have seen, undeniable, it follows that an idea called after blood must be designated by a word radically the same as one meaning water. Now *blood* is *red*, and so is a *rose;* and this flower has been named after its colour.   But roses, I shall be told, are also white, and this is very true; but they are so usually red that no one ever supposes that the poet, when he sings of *rosy* cheeks, means white ones.   When we now leave out the aspirate of *rhod* (radical part of *rhodon*) we shall have *rod*, and *rod* cannot differ from *red* any more than *show* can from *shew*.   Another form equal to both rod and red is the *rud* of our word *ruddy ;* and *rud* can no more differ from *ruth* than *burden* can from *burthen ;* and in *ruth* we have the radical part of ἐρυθός, Greek of red, and but another form of the *rhod* of ῥόδον And as *th* and *f* are equal to each other (compare θηρα and *fera*) *ruth* cannot differ from the *ruf* of *rufus.* And that the *ruf* of *rufus* is equal to the *rub* of *ruber*, is shown by each word having the meaning of red. And that the *d* of *rhodon* is equal to both *b* and *th* we see by comparing *udder, uber*, and their equivalent in Greek, *outhar.* Nor can any of these forms of the *rhod* of ῥόδον differ from the *rhut* of ῥυτός, which means streams, running water, &c.

But two such forms as ῥύδην and ῥυδόν show still more clearly that ῥόδον must have for its root ῥέω, to flow, since such is the root of these two adverbs, ῥύδην and ῥυδόν, as every one knows; and they have the same meaning, that of *flowing*, but conventionally, flowing abundantly, *affluenter.*

The reader needs not now be told why in *ros* and *rosa* we have the same word ; for he knows from what has been just shown, that *rosa* has been named from its colour, and consequently after blood ; and that from blood having been named after water, a *rose* is necessarily expressed by a word of the same meaning, and which is also the meaning of *ros* (dew) in all languages. How evident this must seem to the French student, since *la rose* means the rose, and *la rosée* means dew ; and since the verb *arroser* means *to water!* He can also easily perceive the identity in form between the Greek words ῥόος and ῥοῦς (a stream) and *roux* and its feminine *rousse,* each meaning red, as applied to hair, and of which *rouge* is but another variety. The identity in form between *roseau*, a reed, and *rousseau*, a *red*-haired man, is also very apparent ; but *reed* and *red* in English must appear still more so. And though the word reed does not signify moisture under its present form, we should observe that it cannot differ from rood any more than bleed can from blood, or feed can from food, or breed can from brood. Reed might have been therefore written rood, or, as it is in Saxon, *reod*, and from which such a word as *rhut* cannot differ; yet *rhut* is the radical part of *rhutos*, which in Greek means streams, running water, &c., as shown above; and its root is ῥέω, to flow. But as *reod* (Saxon of reed) cannot, any more than reed, differ from red, this were sufficient to show that reed implies moisture, since this is the primary sense of red, from the idea so named having been called after blood, and blood after liquor or water.

To these proofs that *reed* has been called after water, we should add the fact that its French representative *roseau*, and which bears so close a resemblance to *ruisseau*, is allowed by French etymologists to have been named after the element in which it grows. Thus De Roquefort says : " Roseau, plante qui croît dans l'eau et qui en prend son nom." Hence *reed* is correctly defined " an *aquatic* plant."

So much for the primary signification of ῥόδον, which is, I say, that of blood; a signification which must have been long since lost, for it is not to be found in Greek dictionaries, not even in M. Regnier's last edition of " *Le Jardin des Racines Grecs.*" And this learned Greek scholar is not one to shrink from attempting the etymology of a word, however difficult to find it may appear. Witness his giving ἕλη for the root of Ἥλιος; which is equal to his telling us that the sun was called after two of its own children, for light and heat, which is the meaning assigned to ἕλη, must have come from the sun, and not the sun from light and heat, which is taking two derivatives for the original, a common fault with all philologists. But I have, I believe, noticed this mistake already.

I learn from De Roquefort that Varro derives the Latin *rosa* from its Greek name *rhodon;* but he did not know that both words had ῥέω for their root, from their having been called after blood. But unless we allow the Latin tongue to be a mere dialect of the Greek, we cannot suppose *rosa* to be derived from rhodon. The Latins had, in all probability, a word of their own for the rose, long before they began to borrow any thing, in the way of language, from the Greeks. But the fact that Varro knew nothing of the primary sense of either *rosa* or *rhodon,* and that since his time no one has been any wiser, serves to show how long the etymology of a word may remain unknown. He died some twenty-six years before the Christian era.

This discovery of the origin of the idea *rose,* has, as the reader may recollect, grown out of my etymology of wine, which, it would seem, no one has thought of tracing to water. But such an origin for wine ought not to surprise us, when we find ardent spirits traced to the same source. Witness *whisky,* which, as every one knows, is both the Irish and Gaelic of water, *uisge.* Witness also the French *eau de vie,* literally *water of life,* in English *brandy;* the latter being a corruption of the two words *burned wine.* As to *rum,* it is, I have no doubt, also traceable to water. Webster gives no etymology of it, and Johnson admits that he does not know its origin. Here is all he says of this word: "rum, a kind of spirits distilled from molasses. I know not how derived. *Roemer* in Dutch is a drinking-glass." We now see the advantage of the discovery made farther back, namely, that vessels relating to drinks or liquids have been called after water; for if Johnson had happened to have this knowledge, he would have at once perceived, that from *roemer* meaning a drinking-glass, and from its radical part, *roem*, bearing so close a resemblance to *rum*, the spirit in question was called after water. And this he would confirm by the Greek ρῦμα, or, as it is also written, ρεῦμα, which means a stream, a current, a flowing, a flux, &c., having for its root ρέω, to flow. The *ream* of stream, and the *rom* of its German equivalent, *strom*, would also confirm the truth of such a derivation.

And as οἶνος means not only wine but several other kinds of drink, this ought to serve to prove that it must have once meant water, man's first and universal beverage. Donnegan explains it thus: "οἶνος, wine, also a kind of beer made from wheat, from barley; palm wine; a place where wine is sold. Etymon, with Ϝ, vinum, in Latin; and the name was given to liquors made from the juices of several fruits, as cider, &c." And as to this word *cider*, I have every reason to suppose that it is the Greek word ὕδωρ itself; that is, *water*, for it has been also written cyder, of which the c is for the aspirate or half of H, once made thus)-(; and y is, as every one knows, for the Greek ʋ. And cider has been also a word for drinks in general—conventionally, strong drinks. According to Donnegan, it was, with the Greeks, even a word for wine; but in England this drink was, it appears, an exception. Thus, Johnson's definition of it is, "All kind of strong liquors except wine. This sense is now wholly obsolete."

From all this it is made self-evident that the word wine is not, as Kuhn has been led to imagine, in any way related to a Sanskrit word (*vaina*) meaning *amiable;* nor to any of the different acceptations of *tegere* and *texere,* which is M. Pott's opinion; but that its primary sense was drink, and hence water.

The intelligent reader will now, I dare hope, admit, that whilst noticing M. Max Müller's second opinion of the origin of the idea *sea* under its Latin name *mare,* I have been so fortunate as to make several important etymologies. M. Max Müller's great mistake lies in giving to words for the sea very different meanings, whilst they have all but one and the same meaning—that of *water.* "θάλασσα," he says, "has long been proved to be a dialectical form of θάρασσα or τάρασσα, expressing the troubled waves of the sea, ἐτάραξε δὲ πόντον Ποσειδῶν[6]."

This learned gentleman does not seem to be aware that ἅλς and θάλασσα have precisely the same meaning, the aspirate in ἅλς having been replaced by the θ, so that it is by this means brought equal to θάλς, which, when the vowel due between λ and ς is supplied, becomes θάλας, and this, with the common ending α, becomes θάλασα, which when the s was doubled, as is usual, produced θάλασσα. It is therefore a mistake to suppose that θάλασσα is a dialectical form of either of the assumed words θάρασσα or τάρασσα. In common with all words meaning the sea, it signifies motion, for the reason that it has been called after water, and water after life, which always implies motion, agitation, &c., as we have already often shown. It was, no doubt, the verb ταράσσω (to stir, disturb, &c.) that first led Greek scholars to suppose that θάλασσα must have been at one time or other θάρασσα or τάρασσα; but had there never been such a word as ταράσσω, θάλασσα would be, both in form and meaning, just as it is at present. But is there any difference between the θάλασσ of θάλασσα and the τάρασσ of τάρασσω? None whatever; they are, because of the interchange of l and r, as equal to each other as the *sal* of *Sally* is to the *sar* of *Surah*. And this radical identity of two such words, the one meaning the sea and the other commotion, confirms what I have already shown many times, namely, that every word traceable to one meaning water, such as *sea* and *ocean*, must be significant of motion, for the reason that water has been called after life, which it serves, as well as bread, to support; and life is motion.

Πόντος, which is another word for *sea*, has also, from its resemblance to the Latin *pons* (a bridge) led M. Max Müller and other learned Germans to suppose that it meant originally a way across the sea, " a high road," in short. But when, according to the rule we have already often applied, the first O of πόντος loses its nasal sound, this word will become πότος, which means *drink*, an idea called after water, man's universal beverage. This etymology is confirmed by the Latin of πόντος, that is, *pontus*, which gives also, when the nasal sound of its O is dropped, another word for drink, namely, potus. M. Max Müller says also that *pontus* comes from the same source from which we have *pons*, a bridge. This is very true; but does he know why? No; for if he did, he would know the original meaning of πόντος and pontus. As a bridge is used for a passage over water, it has in Latin been called after water; and such also is the origin of its French equivalent, *pont*, formed from the ablative of *pons*. The English *pond* is still the same word, so that it might as well mean a sea or a river as what it does mean. Its Greek equivalent is some proof of the truth of this assertion, for it is λίμνη, which, as I had occasion to show farther back, cannot differ from *flumen*, a river. Λίμνη is even sometimes used in the sense of *sea*.

The Saxon of *bridge*, which is not only *bricg* but also *brig*, seems to confirm my etymology of *pons*; for brig is the name of a sailing-vessel, which idea has been called after water, whether meaning a vessel on sea or one for holding liquids, and of which the *pot* of *potus* (a drink) is a plain instance. We see even in *pot*, when it is read as in Hebrew, from right to left, the *top* of *toper*, a drunkard. These views are further confirmed by the subjoined observation made by Johnson under the word *brig*: " And possibly also brix is derived from the Saxon *bricg*, a bridge; which to this day, in the northern counties is called a brigg, and not a bridge."

But how are we to analyze *brig*, so as to make sense of it ? If we regard its *br* as equal to *ber*, which is the root of the Saxon verb *beran*, to bear; and its *ig* as equal to *ag*, root of *agua*, Portuguese and Spanish of *aqua*, we shall have the two words *bear* and *water*; so that a bridge may, according to this analysis, mean what bears on water. As the *ber* of the Saxon *beran* cannot differ from the *fer* of *fero* in Latin, which also means to bear, the signification of this analysis will be still the same.

The analysis of γέφυρα, Greek of *bridge*, lies on the surface. It meant originally, says Donnegan, " a dam, dyke, or mound ; the space between hostile armies; a wall—generally a bridge, an isthmus." And according to Damm, its origin is γέα φέρω ; that is, *earth* and the verb to *bear*. This is very good, for, as a *dam* is a mound of earth, and as it serves as a protection against water, *bridge* may have been very well called after it, as it also protects against water. It might be thought that this derivation would also apply to the Saxon *brig;* for γέα may have first been αγεα, vowels being often understood before initial consonants; and its root would then be *ig.* But as *brig* would, according to this view, be composed of a Saxon and a Greek word, we should obtain what can be seldom approved of, a mixed etymology.

The following, from M. Max Müller, calls for other observations. "The Greeks, who of all Aryan nations were most familiar with the sea, called it not the dead water, but thalassa (tarassô), the commotion, *hals,* the briny, pélagos (plazo), pontos, the high road[7]."

I have already disposed of *thalassa* and *tarassô;* but *hals* requires another observation in addition to what I have just said of it. We are, by what is here stated, allowed to understand that the Greeks called the *sea* after salt (hals) which no people ever did; but all nations have called *salt* after the sea; so that when *salt* is traced to its source, it may be said to mean water, since this is the original meaning of *sea.*

As to *plazô,* it is no way related to pélagos in meaning, though put in a parenthesis after this word; it means no more than to drive about or lead astray. But when we take the *pél* of *pélagos* as being the original of the πλε of πλέος and also of the *ple* of the Latin plenus, each of which means *full;* and when we then observe that the *agos* (the remaining part of pelagos) cannot differ from *aquos,* which must have been, as well as *aqua,* a substantive form of aquosus (watery); it follows, that pelagos will, when its parts are so explained, mean *full water;* or, if you will, *full sea* or *full ocean;* for there is no funda-

[7] Lectures, 2nd Series, p. 321.

P

mental difference in meaning, as I have already shown, between water, sea, and ocean.

Now, on having given the above derivation of πέλαγος, I have looked into several Greek dictionaries in order to see if in any of them I might discover an etymology of this word; but on this particular point I find them all equally silent. M. Regnier gives under ὠκύς, which means swift, rapid, &c., several of its derivatives, but he never alludes to ὠκέανος, though it is radically the same word; and it is for the reason that water implies motion, of which this fine Greek scholar was not aware, because not knowing any thing of the origin of language.

I find, however, in Alexandre's dictionary something very worthy of observation. Though he does not attempt to give an etymology of *pélagos*, his second explanation of it is *pleine mer*, which accords exactly with the derivation I have given of this word, though it did not occur to me while I was analyzing it, that *pleine mer* is the usual representation in French of the idea expressed by pélagos.

I learn also from M. Max Müller that the great philologist Bopp, assigned, as he does himself in common with other learned Germans, the meaning of high road to pontus. This is sufficiently shown by the following: " That high roads were not unknown [to the Aryans] appears from Sanskrit path, pathi, panthan, and pâthus, all names for road, the Greek πάτος, the Gothic fad, which Bopp believes to be identical with Latin pons, pontis, and Slavonic ponti [8]."

Now, to what are we to ascribe those mistakes, made by men who studied language so long and so seriously?

---

[8] " Chips from a German Workshop," vol. ii. p. 40.

Why, for instance, have they been led to confound such a word as *path* with one meaning water? For this simple reason, that a path is a passage. It has been named after the verb to pass, which, like water, implies motion. Indeed, *path* does not differ any more from *pas* or *pass*, than *doth* and *does* can differ from each other. A plainer instance than this is afforded by the word alley, which is also a passage, for its French equivalent is *allée*, of which the original is *aller*, to go. And to go implies motion. Hence the *bain* of the Greek word *bainô*, is the French of *bath*, whilst *baino* means to move, to come or to go. For the same reason there can be no difference in English between *bath* and *path*.

It is now very easy to perceive that *rue*, French of street, has for its root ῥέω, to flow, not because a street has been called after water, but because all words meaning water must mean motion also; and a street is a place in a town through which people move or pass, and it is consequently a passage. This etymology is confirmed by ῥύμη which means both a street and a current. The French and English words route and road have the same primary sense as *rue*. But French etymologists derive *route* from the Latin *ruptu*, and *rue* from route. The *rhut* of the Greek ῥυτός, which means running waters, &c., is still the same word, and it is justly traced for its root to ῥέω, to flow.

Very different in form from all these words is way, in English; but when we observe that its y is the same as *g* (witness its German equivalent *weg*), we see that it cannot differ from *wag*, which is the same as the vag of the old Latin verb *vagare* to wander; nor is it different from vague, French of *wave*. And as we have in *vague* and *wave* the same word, for *gu* is constantly repre-

sented by *w*, vague might have been *vawe*, and consequently vave or wave; whence it follows, from the *v* and
w being in these words but representatives of the aspirate, that *vague* (this other form of *wave*) is for *ague*, in
which we see both the *ag* of *ago* (to act) and *agua*, the
Italian of *aqua*. And since the Sanskrit W is often
represented by M in Latin (compare wari and mare, and
the English *wick* with its French equivalent *mèche*) it
follows that in *wave* and *move* we have the same word,
for between the *a* in the one and the *o* in the other
there is no difference.

Chemin, French of way, appears to offer an exception
to all and each of the above results; but when we observe
that its *ch* may be reduced to c (compare *chat* and *cat*)
and that its e is not only equal to o but to *oi* or *a*, we
prove *chemin* to be equal to the *camin* of the Italian
cammino, of which the *m* might not be doubled: and
the same may be said of *camminare*. Now, as the first
of these two words means a way, and as the second means
to walk, and as they are radically equal, we thus see how
the same word may signify a way, and also *to walk*. We
should further observe, that in the *camin* here noticed,
we have both the German *kommen* and its English equivalent *come*, each of which is expressive of motion[9]. But
where is the *water?* From all we have thus far seen
the water cannot be difficult to find. I have already
shown, more than once, that neither the aspirate *h* nor
any of its substitutes should be regarded as belonging,
in any way, to the radical part of a word. Now, as the
ch of *chemin* serves to represent the aspirate *h*, which
must have been so pronounced by some persons, we are

[9] *Chimney* and its Italian and French forms, *cammino* and *cheminée*,
are also but other words for way.

to leave it out altogether, and so reduce *chemin* to *emin*, which, from its C being equal to O, and O to *oi*, and *oi* to *a*, cannot differ from *amin;* and this is the radical part, but not the root, of *aminis*, at present written, from its first *i* having been dropped, *amnis*, Latin of river. Now the root of *amnis* is *am*, which, being another form of the verb *be*, implies existence or life; and after this idea, as I have often shown, water has been called. Be it also observed, that as *am* is the same as *oim*, we obtain by the dropping of its *i*, *om*, one of the thousand names of the sun and of Buddha, the supposed author of life. But when it is not the i of *oim* we drop but the O, we shall then obtain *im*, Hebrew of water, so called from its being a support of life. And though I have already often said and proved that every word meaning river must have first grown out of one meaning water, it may not be thought out of place if I do so again, as this may be shown very clearly from the word *amnis* itself, and not only by regarding *im*, Hebrew of water, as equal to *am*, root of *amnis*, but by showing how the word *amnis* itself has been used in the sense of water, and of which Quecherat quotes several instances. Thus, from Tacitus, *amnis fluminis*, the water of a river; even water poured into a basin, as shown from Virgil, *amnis labris fusus*. And as I have referred to the word flow as meaning both river and water, Quecherat gives an instance from Palladius, of amnis having also this meaning; thus, *amnis musti* is the *flowing* of new wine.

This instance of *amnis* being significant of flowing, confirms the truth of the statement made above, as to *amnis* having first been aminis, and which is according to one of my rules, namely, that when two consonants come together they have often a vowel understood between them; for the verbal form of *amnis* is *mano*, to flow, which, as an initial consonant may be preceded by a vowel, is equal to *amano*, and of *amano* the radical part, *aman*, cannot, as the vowels are all equal to one another, differ from the *amin* of *aminis*, now written *amnis*.

These few last etymologies have been suggested by that passage of M. Max Müller's, in which he shows that both himself and other learned Germans assign to πόντος in Greek and pontus in Latin the meaning of high road. The question now is, by what means could they have avoided making so gross a mistake? by merely knowing that words signifying water, river, sea, or ocean, may signify also road, way, or path; and sometimes a bridge, but not always, as we have seen by γέφυρα. But how could men who knew nothing of the primary signification of water, know that a road must have been signified in the same way? Their total want of this knowledge was the cause of their mistake. If they had known that water was called after life, which implies motion; and that a road, from its being that upon which people *go* and necessarily *move*, was called after its use, they could not help perceiving that these two very different ideas (water and road) must have been expressed by words that were, *in meaning*, radically the same, however widely they might differ in form.

CHAPTER XXVIII.

AN INSTANCE OF THE ADVANTAGE TO BE DERIVED FROM KNOWING THAT ONE VOWEL IS NOT ONLY EQUAL TO ANY OTHER VOWEL, BUT EVEN TO ANY COMBINATION OF VOWELS.—M. LITTRE'S FAULTY ETYMOLOGY OF THE NOUN BOUCHER.

THE general opinion seems to be, that the French of butcher (boucher) has been called after *bouche* (the mouth). But Renouard, and others before him, assign to *boucher* a very different origin—that of *bouc*, in English a buck-goat, and which so high an authority as M. Littré accepts with approval. Thus, after showing its different forms in several languages and their dialects, this celebrated philologist gives the following etymology of *boucher*. " Une analogie apparente semble d'abord indiquer *bouche* comme primitif de *boucher;* mais l'italien *beccaio* s'y oppose. Remarquant que *becco* en italien signifie *bouc*, et que la forme française et la forme provençale peuvent être sans peine rattachées à *bouc*, on acceptera cette étymologie, qui, indiquée avant Renouard, a été etablie par lui. Le *boucher* est proprement le tueur de *boucs* (la partie pour le tout). Ainsi, pour le mot *boucherie*, à coté de *bocaria*, le provençal avait brecaria qui, venant de berbex, signifie proprement la tuerie des brebis (encore la partie pour le tout). Bien qu'il semble très-étrange que le *boucher* ait été nommé d'après le bouc ou chevreau, cependant, étymologiquement, il n'y a aucun moyen d'écarter l'italien *beccaio*, ni de rapporter le provençal *bochier* et le français *boucher* à *bouche*."

According to this reasoning, a *boucher* was named after a *bouc* or *buck;* but M. Littré mistakes, as he will soon see. For the present I do not intend to notice the French of mouth, that is, *bouche*, in order to see if the two ideas (bouche and boucher) be any way related; but this I may do when I have shown that a *boucher* was never called after a *bouc*.

On first reading M. Littré's etymology of the noun *boucher*, I started, and felt just as I did on reading M. Max Müller's etymology of *soul*. And I said to myself, This cannot be orthodox. I could not, however, but admit that the words *bouc* and *boucher* are radically the same. But this, I knew, was no proof that either idea was called after the other. I therefore looked out for other words radically the same as *boucher*, to try if any of them was expressive of a similar idea. I saw that neither *bouchon* (a cork) nor *buche* (a log of wood) could be in any way related to the idea expressed by *boucher*, though they too are, as well as *bouc*, radically the same word. Nor could *biche*, any more than *bouchon* or *buche*, appear related to *boucher*. But on taking the word *bêche* (a spade), or, as it has been also written, *besche*, I was obliged to make a longer pause than when I tried how far any other word might suit. And why so? Because a *bêche* is that which cuts, and so is a butcher. Cutting or chopping is his constant employment. In order to prove the radical identity of two such words as *beche* and *bouche*, we have only to recollect that one vowel is not only equal to any other vowel, but to any combination of vowels, so that the *e* of bêche and the *ou* of .boucher have so evidently the same power that they cannot differ from each other in signification save conventionally. But there is, it may be remarked, no S in *boucher*, though there is one understood in *béche*, as the circumflex over its *e* serves to show. This should not, however, be regarded as an objection of any importance; for in French *ch* and *sch* are precisely equal to each other. Hence I find in M. Littré's dictionary the following passage: "Li rois une beche tenoit, qui d'autre mestier ne servoit."

Here there is no circumflex over the e of *beche*, to indicate the absence of an S. And in French of the sixteenth century M. Littré quotes also the following, under the verb *bécher*. "Ce soldat *bechoit* en la terre avec plusieurs autres, pour la porter sur les remparts." Here too is an instance of *ch* being used instead of *sch*, there being no circumflex over the e of *bechoit*. It is, therefore, evident that bêche has been written without an S as well as with it, just as *boucher* is at present. Hence the verb *boucher* (to stop a hole) has been also written *bouscher*, as M. Littré shows, though it is not so any longer.

Let us now show how *boucher* must, from its being radically the same as *béche* (a spade), have for its primary signification that of *one who cuts* or *chops;* in other words, a *cutter* or *chopper*.

Kreourgos (κρεουργός) is thus explained by Donnegan: "A cutter or chopper of flesh, a butcher." But this authority does not give the analysis of Kreourgos. It is, however, sufficient to know that it means a *cutter* or *chopper* of flesh, and consequently a *butcher*. According to this definition kreourgos must, when radically considered, be composed of two parts, one for flesh and the other for cutter or chopper. Hence the *kre* of kreourgos must be for kreas (κρέας), flesh; and the *ourg* of the second part, *ourgos*, must be for *orux* (ὄρυξ), genitive *urgos;* which is explained " a hoe, a spade." And as a hoe or spade is that which cuts, it follows that *kreourgos*, a butcher, means a flesh *cutter*. Another of the meanings assigned to ὄρυξ, is that of the *sword* fish, which is also a striking confirmation of the truth of these etymologies; for *spada*, which cannot differ from spade, is both the Saxon and Italian of sword; and in the Swedish and Danish Languages, spade is the word sword itself. In Spanish, too, *espada*, which is radically our word *spade*, means a sword; and that the original sense of sword is that of *cutting*, the words κόπτω and κοπίς sufficiently prove, for they are evidently one and the same word; yet the first means to cut, and the second a sword or dagger. This also allows us to perceive that the word dagger cannot differ from digger. And as a *digger* is one that cuts the earth with a spade, it follows that a dagger may be defined a *cutter*. Hence any word meaning to *cut* might have meant a butcher. The noun oruktēr (ὀρυκτήρ) signifies therefore a digger, and also a plough-*share*, and consequently a cutting instrument; and its radical part, *oruk,* becomes by transposition *ourk*, which is equal to the *ourg* of kreourgos. And this is an additional proof that the *ourgos* of kreourgos means a cutter. But may not the *ourg* of *ourgos* be another form of the ἔργ of ἔργον, which means *work?* It must be admitted that the *ourg* of ourgos is equal to the *erg* of ergon (work); and hence an eminent Greek scholar (Alexandre) has in his dictionary explained kreourgos (a butcher) as meaning a *flesh-worker.* But it is a mistake; and the cause of the ideas *cut* and *work* being in Greek expressed by words radically the same, must be ascribed to the fact that both come from the same source—the hand.

The Latin verb *lanio* means to *cut in pieces;* but when a noun, it means, as well as *lanius,* a butcher; so that in this language, as well as in Greek, a butcher is a cutter.

If we consult other languages, the result will be still the same. Thus *metzger* is in German a butcher, and its radical part *metz* means, according to Doctor Schuster's dictionary, "celui qui taille;" that is, he who cuts; in other words, a *cutter.* In *metzen,* to cut, we see the same word; and the reader is justly referred to *messer,* a knife, as a word to be compared with metzen, for they are evidently kindred ideas.

Fleischer and fleischhauer are two other words in German for butcher, the first having the literal meaning of *flesher;* that is, one who deals in flesh, and the latter one who *hews* flesh, and consequently a flesh-cutter; for hew—which is but another form of the word *hoe*—means to cut. And as in Spanish *cortador* means a butcher, it is also literally a cutter, for *cortar* is in this language the verb to *cut.*

In order to confirm these etymologies, we need refer but to one language more, namely, Flemish, in which there are three words for butcher: *slayter, been-hower* and *vleesch-houwer;* that is, literally, *slayer, bone-hewer,* and *flesh-hewer.*

Now it was not without a very considerable show of reason that *boucher* has been derived both from *bouche* and *bouc,* for it is not only in French that *bouche* and *boucher* are so much alike, but in Italian also. Thus, *becco* is equal to *bocco* (the mouth), and it means a *bouc* also. But there is another word in Italian for *becco* which means *bouc*, but not the mouth; and it serves to confirm all thus far said of *boucher*. This word is *beccone*, and it does not differ from *becco* but conventionally, its meaning being a large *bouc*. Hence both words are radically the same. But how does *beccone* confirm all we have hitherto said of *boucher?* By its having also the meaning of *eunuch*, and by *eunuch* being *spado* in Latin, and by its verbal form (spadare) meaning to *cut*, so that in primary signification it does not differ either from *spade* or *boucher*.

Nor does *becco* want the meaning of cutting, for it cannot differ from the *becca* of *beccamorti*, which means a digger for the dead, that is a grave-digger; and as a digger means one who *cuts* the ground with a *spade*, we see that a form equal to *becco*—the *becca* of *beccamorti*—means a *cutter*. But why have not the Italians *becca-carne*, that is *flesh-cutter*, since they have *becca-morti?* For a very good reason, namely, that they have this word under another form—that of *beccaro*, and of which *beccaio* is the same word softened; and *beccaio* means a butcher.

We shall see presently the original meanings of both *bouche* and *bouc*, and which have been hitherto unknown.

I have now done with the French noun *boucher*. When the person so called first received this name, every one must have known what it meant; but after a time this meaning was forgotten, and it has until now remained undiscovered. French philologists themselves have known no more of what it first signified than the learned of other nations. But a foreigner has taken what seems the *unpardonable* liberty of discovering it for them. And how has he dared to do this ? By the application of a very simple little rule, as he has shown. But some persons will assure me that the very little rule I refer to, and which I am pleased to call my own, has been long since known, and even by school-boys; for who does not observe, they will say, that one vowel is not only often used for another, but even for two or more vowels combined. And this I admit, and so do I admit that ever since the lid of a pot or a kettle, when the water was in a state of ebullition, has been seen to rise up, the power of steam has been admitted all over the world; yet this general observation of many ages has not, until a comparatively late period, been turned to account. From this it would appear that it is a little less difficult to observe than to take advantage of what we do observe, by drawing out of it something useful. But most discoveries and their results appear, when they become known, so very easy and simple as to be thought by none, save a few, scarce deserving of notice.

It is ever Columbus and his egg. Yet without this little rule, which, from its appearing so very simple, may be regarded with no slight share of indifference, never could the etymology of *boucher* have been discovered; for who could imagine there is any relationship whatever in meaning between the name of a butcher and that of a spade? I, at least, if I may be allowed to answer for myself, could never, I am sure, have perceived the least connexion in meaning between two ideas apparently so unallied. I might, it is true, have discovered the etymology of *boucher* if I knew the original meaning of *bouche* or *bouc;* but the etymology of neither word has been hitherto known, as I am now going to show, by tracing each word to its source.

CHAPTER XXIX.

ETYMOLOGY OF BOUCHE.

As *bouche* and *boucher* are radically the same word; and as a *boucher*, or *butcher*, means, as we have seen, a cutter; and as a *mouth* cuts its food; it follows that it may be also said to mean a cutter, or that which cuts; so that it does not, in this respect, differ from either butcher or spade, though it was never called after either of these ideas; nor was either of these ideas ever called after the mouth. Now, as the mouth has been named after the idea expressed by the word *cut*, and as to cut, as shown farther back, was named after the hand, it follows that an idea called after this member may be signified by a word not different from one called after the mouth, even when the latter is not taken in the sense of *cutter*. Witness *ward* and *word*, between which terms there can be no difference in form; for as the *o* of *word* has i understood, and as the *o* and *i* make *a*, *word* is thus shown to be equal to *ward*. Word was, however, called after the mouth; and *ward*, which is but another form of *guard*, was called after the hand, whether we take it as a noun or as a verb. And as *mot*, French of *word*, is equal to *moite* (i being understood with its o), and as there is a euphonic tendency to sound an s before such consonants as *m*, *n*, *p*, *t*, and *w*; *moite* cannot, for this reason, differ from *smoite*, which is the elder form of *smite*, an idea called after the hand, it being with this member that we *smite.* Another word equal to the French *mot,* is *moth ;* and as this is an insect that cuts into cloth, we see, from its being equal in form to *mot* in French, that so is it equal to mouth. This too is confirmed by the Saxon of mouth, which is *muth,* and this is the radical part of μῦθος, which in Greek means, not only a myth or fable, but a word also.

Even the English equivalent of *mot* in French and μῦθος in Greek, that is, *word,* serves to confirm all these etymologies ; for, as stated above, there is a euphonic tendency to prefix an S to several consonants, and of which, as we have shown, *w* happens to be one; witness *wet* and *sweat, wan* and *swan ;* by which addition of the euphonic S, *word* becomes *sword,* and a sword is an instrument that cuts; witness κόπτω, to cut, and κοπίς, which means a dagger, a sword, or a knife. But as S is no radical part of sword, this weapon must have once been expressed by *word* only ; and even by *ord,* as *w* does here but replace the aspirate. Hence, in the Swedish tongue *ord* alone means *sword.*

These etymologies will, I have no doubt, guide the philologist to a great many others hitherto unknown. Thus, as *th* may be replaced by *s,* as we see by comparing such words as *hath* and *has, doth* and *does,* it follows that *mouth* cannot differ from *mous,* that is, *mouse,* and which the Germans write *maus,* in Latin *mus.* By this we see that *mouth* and *mouse* are expressed alike ; and now every child can, while judging from what he has already seen, tell why it is so. He must know that it is to be ascribed to the fact that a mouse is a rodent animal; so that it may, like the *mouth* and a *moth,* be called a *cutter.* But how are we to account for the French *souris,* which means both a mouse and a smile? It is for *sou-rat;* that is literally *under,* inferior, or small rat; so that it does not differ in meaning from the Latin *mus,* but by the addition of a word (*sou*) to mark its inferiority. As to *souris,* a smile, we can easily perceive that it is for an under, small, or inferior laugh. Hence, the verb *sourire* is equal to *sub*ridere. We may therefore regard the English *smile* as for *small,* laugh being understood. But *laugh* and *ris* can be nothing more than two very different imitations of the sound produced by the action of laughing. Hence, *la! la!* is sometimes made to signify the repetition of a laugh; and so is *ri! ri!*

The etymologies given of *moth* and *mouse* I find thus confirmed: Dr. Schuster derives moth (in German motte) from the Gothic *matjan,* manger; and mouse (in German maus) is derived by F. G. Eichhoff and W. De Suckau from *meissen,* ronger. As to *rat,* it must be for the *rod* of rodere, to gnaw; the two forms rat and rod are precisely equal to each other.

The Greek of mouth, στόμα, must also confirm our etymology of *bouche;* for, as its *s* does not belong to its radical part, its place before *t,* as shown above, being purely euphonic, *tom* alone should be considered as the principal part of *stoma.* And as *tom* is the radical part of τομεύς, and as this word is explained "one who cuts, an instrument for cutting," &c., the agreement in meaning between it and *bouche,* or mouth, is perfect. And when we now observe that M represents the W in Sanskrit, we see that *tom* cannot differ from *tow,* nor *tow* from *two,* an idea called after the hand, of which member we happen to have two. Hence, the idea mouth can, because meaning that which cuts, be traced to the hand.

As the *mand* of the Latin *mandere*, to eat, cannot differ from *mund*, German of mouth, it would seem that to *eat* may be sometimes used in the sense of cutting, since such is the primary signification of mouth. Hence when we say that a mouse can *eat* a cable in two, our meaning is that a mouse can *cut* a cable in two. In Hebrew (ברה) *bre* means both to eat and to cut[1]; and under another of its forms, ברא *bra*, it means also to create. These are very different ideas; but their being expressed alike must be ascribed to their having been each named after the hand, with which we both *cut* and *make*, that is, divide and create.

M. Littré gives no other etymology of *manger* or *mandere* than the following, and which is certainly very bad: "*Manduco* est le fréquentatif de *mandere*, dont l'etymologie probable est ainsi donnée par Corssen, Beiträge, p. 246 : il le rapporte au radical *mad*, enivrer, être ivre, dont le sens primitif est mouiller, être mouillé ; de là madayâmi, enivrer, rassasier, de là aussi *madeo*, madidus, le Grec μαδάω, se dessoudre, se fondre, et μασάομαι, mouiller, mâcher. *Mandere*, avec insertion d'une nasale, aurait le même sens : humecter de salive, et de là manger."

This etymology is, I say, very bad, and very far-fetched, there being no relationship whatever between such an idea as to eat or to cut and that of being wet or drunk. But Corssen does not mistake when he connects the being *drunk* with the being *wet*. It confirms my etymology of drink and also of drunkenness, both of which I have derived, as the reader may recollect, from water. I knew nothing, however, at the time of Corssen's derivation. M. Littré should, in his fruitless

---

[1] See Sander and Trench's Dict. Heb. Franç.

endeavours to discover the primary signification of *ivre*, have paid some attention to the passage he has here quoted from Corssen under *manger*.

I forgot to observe that one of the many forms given by M. Littré of the verb *manger* is *mezer*, which, from its close resemblance to *messer*, German of knife, may be said to mean *cutter*.

This notice of *bouche* serves to show how closely it is allied to *boucher*, though neither of these ideas has been named after the other. *Boucher* was not called after *bouche* any more than it was called after *béche*; but it was expressed by a word—that of *cutter*—which does not differ in signification from either *bouche* or *béche*.

Another form equal to *béche* is *mèche*, as in *mèche* d'une chandelle, *wick* of a candle. And as a *béche* means that which cuts, a *mèche* means that which is *cut*, as a *cut* or strip of any thing. Hence the *wick* of a candle is a strip of cotton, but literally a *cut* of cotton. Now this word *mèche* has, from meaning that which is *cut*, obtained also the meaning of *spade ;* namely, that which *cuts*, a cutter. We can now clearly perceive the primary sense—hitherto unknown—of "*un méchant.*" We see that it must have been first used to designate one who *cuts* or *strikes* others, for *coup* a stroke, and *coupeur* a *cutter*, are radically the same word. And this knowledge enables us to account for *mèche*, which means a *wick*, being the root of *méchant*, which means *wicked ;* just as *wick*, which is the English of *mèche*, is also the root of *wicked*, which means *méchant*. We have here a plain instance of the identity of M and W, the M of *mèche* being the W of *Wick*. But how different the ideas expressed in English by the words *wick* and *wicked*, and in French by *mèche* and *méchant*. But every one can now account for ideas so different having been signified alike. It can be easily perceived that it arose from *mèche* and *wick* having each the meaning of a *cut* —as of cotton for instance; and *un méchant* or *wicked* (person) having had the meaning of a *cutter;* that is, of one who cuts or strikes others.

Now things bearing a resemblance to a *mèche* or *wick* may have been often called after it. This will account for the Latin *myxus* (une mèche or match) being radically the same as muxa (μύξα), that is, mucus or mucous, what hangs or flows from the nose. Hence *moucher* une chandelle is for *mecher* une chandelle. When a French woman says to her child *mouche-toi* (blow thy nose), the literal meaning is *mèche-toi*, that is, take away the *mèche* or *wick* from thy nose. A *mouchoir*, which is used for this purpose, is therefore for *mèchoir*, because it serves for taking away the *mèche* from the nose. And as a *mèche* means a *cut* or *strip* of any thing, it follows that *mouchoir* might mean that which *cuts*, because called after *mèche*. Now as the *e* of *mèche* is for *o*, and as *o* has *i* understood, this *e* is therefore equal to *oi* or *a;* so that *mèche* is equal to the *mache* of *macher*, which means to *chew*, that is, to *hew;* for the combination *ch* may be reduced to either of its signs, they having both grown out of the aspirate; and to *hew* is to *cut*. And when we now make the verb *macher* take its substantive form, we shall get *machoire*, and a *mâchoire* or jaw is a *cutter*. Hence the *chap* of *chaps*, which has still the same meaning, cannot differ from *chop*, and a *chop* is a *cut*, and but another form of the *coup* of *couper,* just as *coup* is but another form of the *cout* of *coutcau*. When we now give to the *a* of the *chap* of *chaps* its nasal sound, and which may be obtained by *m* or *n*, we shall bring *chap* equal to *champ*, and the verb to *champ* is rendered into French by *mâcher*, as every English and French dictionary will tell you.

It is now easy to perceive that the *muk* of *mukter*, Greek of nose, and the *mux* of *muxa* in the same language, and the *muc* of its Latin equivalent *mucus*, make only one word, and that none of these forms can differ from the *muk* of the Greek *mukos* (a wick), nor from the *myx* of its Latin form *myxus*.

I was forgetting to notice *mouche*, French of *fly*, and which is but another form of the Latin *musca*, just as it is of *mèche*, and consequently of *wick*. But why, it may be asked, should a fly have like *mèche*, the meaning of *cut*? Because it has a *sting*, which idea was, as we shall see in the next article, called after that expressed by *cut*. The English word *fly* cannot be traced to the same source, but to the action of *flying*.

Now as *mouche* is, from *ch* being the same as *k*, equal to *mouke*, we see that it is the same as the *muk* of the Greek *muk*ter the nose; and as neither *mouke* or *muk* can differ from the *muc* of *mucus*, nor from the English *muck*, we see that *mucus* and *muck* are as one and the same word. But the idea filth—in this instance signified by *mucus*, whence muck—can be traced to other sources as well as to the nose. Witness *soil*, which when its *o* and *i* meet, becomes *sal*, radical part of *salir*, French of *to soil*. And as *soil* has also the meaning of ground, not to mention another certain matter, we see that the idea *filth* may be traced to this source also. And as the *s* of *soil* does here but represent the aspirate *h*, and as this sign is represented as often by *f* as by *s*, it follows that in *soil* and *foil* we have the same word. And what is

foil but *foul,* combinations of vowels being all equal to
one another. And when we allow the O and i of *foil* to
meet and so produce *a,* we shall get *fal,* that is, *fall,* a
word expressive of lowness, and consequently of *soil* in
the sense of ground. But we may see more clearly the
identity of *soil* and *foil* when we give such an instance
as this; "a young bird will not *foul* its nest;" for here
foul may be replaced by *soil.* Nor is it difficult to perceive that *foil* is equal to *fall* in such an instance as
" truth *foils* falsehood;" that is, literally, truth *falls*
falsehood, it puts falsehood *down;* and of both *foil* and
fall, fail is but another form. Nor should I omit to
observe that *filth* is composed of two words, *foul* and *the;*
so that it must have first been *the foul;* and then by the
article having fallen behind, *the foul* became *foul the;*
whence *filth.*

There are still two words, one in English and the
other in French, which are highly expressive of filth; but
decency forbids me to name them, yet their radical parts
—which may be found when their initial consonants are
left out, because not belonging to the root of either
word—mean *earth* and nothing more; indeed, *erde,*
which is the radical part of the French word, happens to
be the German of earth. This much will serve to show
that there are other words expressive of filth besides
mucus, and of which another instance now occurs to me
—it is *dirt,* of which the radical part *ird* is but another
form of *earth.*

I have nearly forgotten to notice *nose.* Its radical
part *nos* is for *nois,* O having i understood; and as *oi* is
for *a,* we see that *nos* is the *nas* of *nasus;* and as S
cannot differ fron *sh*—witness *finis* and *finish*—it follows
that *nas* is the same as *nash,* and, from the interchange

of *n* and *m*, *nash* is equal to *mash*, and *mash* to the *mache* of the French *macher*, which means to cut, just as *mecher*—that is, *moucher*—does.　By this analysis we see that *s* is not only equal to *sh* but to *ch* also, and consequently to *k* or *ck*; and hence *alas* is the same as *alack*.　To what source should we now trace the *nas* of nasty and nastiness?　To the *nas* of *nas*us certainly! just as we should trace muck (filth) to the *muk* of *mukter*, Greek of nose.

Let us now show why *bouche* and *bouc* bear so close a resemblance to *boucher*, and thereby discover the cause of the mistake of the two different classes of philologists —those who regarded *bouche*, and also those who regarded *bouc*, as the original of *boucher*.

CHAPTER XXX.

ETYMOLOGY OF BOUC OR BUCK.

Bouc is certainly equal to *bouche;* but how can *bouc* have the same meaning—that of *cutter?* Does a goat ever cut?　It does not do so like a spade or the mouth, but it has horns, and a horn is an arm for attacking and defending, and it can pierce as well as a sword.　And has not this word *sword* come up in our etymology of *bouche*, when we found *word* to be its radical part, and accounted for its being so?　Now there is a sharp-pointed instrument of which the name bears so close a resemblance to that of goat as to seem the same word; it is *goad.* In Saxon the resemblance is equally close ; witness *gat*, a goat, and *gat*, a goad. I find also in Eichhoff and Suckau's Vocabulaire Comparatif des Racines Anglaises et Allemandes, *geiss* or *geis* for goat, and *geiss* for goad; but in Dr. Schuster I cannot find *geiss* in the sense of goad, but *geissel*, which is radically the same word. According to this authority it means, " un instrument dont on se sert pour stimuler les animaux." But its usual meaning appears to be a whip. The Greek of goat is *aix* (αἴξ) ; but this cannot, from the interchange of X and *g*, differ from *aig*, and which is confirmed by *aigos* being the genitive of *aix*, and not *aixos*. I make this remark because *aig* happens to be the radical part of *aiguillon*, which is the French of *goad*. Now, it is easy to perceive that *aiguillon* and *aiguille* (a needle) do not differ from each other but conventionally ; and as *acus*, the Latin of needle, is still radically the same as *aiguillon* and *aiguille*, it follows that *ac, ag, ak*, or a form of equal value—such, for instance, as *uc, ug*, or *uk*,—may be regarded as exactly equal to *aἴξ*, Greek of goat. And this being granted, we see that such a root as *uc* can, when the aspirate to which its *u* is entitled is replaced by *b*, become *buc*, that is, *bouc* or *buck*. If a goat, when bearing such a name as buck, was called after its horns and its horns after sharpness, this must have been done as just described. And that such a root as *uc, uk*, or *ak*, may signify what is sharp or pointed, is shown by the Greek word ἀκή, which is explained " a point, an edge, the point of a sword." In ἀκίς we see the same root, and three of its meanings are, " a pointed instrument, a thorn, a sting," &c. And as the point of any object is its highest part, we see that sharpness may be also expressed by height. Hence, the *cap* of *caput* is also the *cap* of *caper*. In ἀκμή we see also a word signifying height, point, edge, sharpness, &c. ; so that if a goat has been called after its horns, it may have been often expressed by a word signifying head or height. Hence, *chef* and the *chev* of *chèvre* are equal to each other; though *chef* in French means head or chief, and *chèvre* means a goat. Nor does our word *head* differ from the *hæd* of *hædus*, a goat. But the identity of two such Greek words as ἐλέφας and ἔλαφος is still more apparent; yet the one is the name of the elephant, an animal remarkable for its lofty stature, and the other means both a *stag* and a *hind*. This instance serves to show that an animal called after its great height may have a name not different from the one signifying a horned animal. This is further confirmed by what Parkhurst says of an animal of the beeve kind, named *ram* (ראם), and which word means, according to the same authority, " to be raised up, exalted, elevated[2]."

Now, the English word *ram* does not name an animal of the beeve kind, nor is such an animal so remarkable for its height as it is for its horns. Donnegan, though he cannot have known the primary signification of *horn*, does not, however, mistake when he derives κριός, a ram, from κεραός, " horned." And κέρας means not only a horn, but when differently accented (κεράς), " a female horned animal, a she-goat, a sheep two years old, a hogget." From this it would appear that several animals have taken their names from their being horned. This is shown still more fully by Parkhurst, according to whom[3] " איל *ail* means not only a ram, but also a stag, hart, deer, hind, or doe. Whether masculine or feminine the LXX render the word by

---

[2] Lex. p. 613.   Ibid. p. 14.

ἔλαφος, which denotes both a stag and a hind. Dr.
Shaw[4] understands איל *ail*, Deut. xiv. 5, as a name of
the genus, including *all the species of the deer* kind,
whether they are distinguished by *round horns*, as the
stag, by *flat ones*, as the *fallow deer*, or by the *smallness*
of the branches, as the roe."

As אל *al* is the root of אלף *alp*, a bull, and as it
cannot differ from איל *ail*, just noticed, this is another
proof that any horned animal, however low in size,
may have a name not different from one designating
the elephant or the bull. In Hebrew height is still
implied, whether we allow the *a* of ראם *ram* to its first
place before the r, or to come after it. Thus, ארם *arm*
means a palace; and when its *a* is dropped, the רם *rm*
which remains is explained "to be lifted up, exalted,
elevated[5]."

Now, as the root of ארם *arm* is *ar*, so is it the root
of ראם *ram*; and to which we may add the *ar* of *aries*,
Latin of ram. The ερ of κέρας, a horn, and of κεράς, a
female horned animal, is therefore the root of either
word, k being only for the aspirate, and which is not to
be counted any more than the ending ας; and as the ε
of ερ is for o, and as i is understood, this root becomes
oir, and consequently *ar*, when the o and i unite,
making *a*.

Parkhurst's article on ראם *ram* is very long. The
learned are divided in their opinion as to what kind of
animal it was; but they agree in supposing it to be of
the beeve kind, and remarkable for its great strength and
size. Thus Parkhurst says, "remarkable for his strength,
and of the beeve kind. In short, the name seems to

---

[4] Travels, p. 414, 2nd ed.   [5] Parkhurst, Lex 633.

denote the *wild bull*, so called from his height and size,
in comparison with the tame[6]."

But this animal being, as Parkhurst does himself admit,
of the beeve kind, why should he, as he does, derive
from its name the English word ram? for no other
reason, I suppose, than that the two words are exactly
the same. Parkhurst was not aware that a horn was
first signified by a word meaning what was pointed, and
that from a point being the topmost part of an object, it
must have been expressed by a word for head or height,
and consequently for strength, which idea also has been
called after height. This knowledge would, if he had
it, enable him to perceive that a horned animal might,
however small, have a name not different from that of
the elephant; that is, if named after its horns, and
judging from what we have already seen, and especially
from the passage quoted above by Parkhurst from Dr.
Shaw, it would seem that horned animals have in general been named after the idea horn.

And what is the root of this word horn? It is *or*,
for its aspirate is not to be counted: and as to the *n*
with which it ends, there is a euphonic tendency to
sound it after *r* (witness *tour* and *turn*, spur and spurn),
so that it must not be counted any more than the
aspirate. And this root *or* cannot, from its being equal
to *er*, differ from the ερ of κέρας (a horn), or from the
ερ of κεράς, a horned animal. Nor does this root *er*
differ in the least from the root of the Hebrew of horn,
which is קרן *krn*. We may even say that there is no
difference whatever between *krn* and horn; for a vowel
being understood between the k and r of *krn*, and as this
vowel may be O, it follows that *krn* is the same as korn;

[6] Lex. p. 613.

that is, since k is for the aspirate, horn. The *corn* of
cornu is still the same, the c being now for the
aspirate.

And as the French word *corne*—which is to be accounted for in the same way—is also written *cor*, this
confirms the statement just made, namely, that the *n* of
horn should not be counted.

There are still other proofs of what has just been said
of such words as signify goat and horn. We have
shown goat to be the same as goad, and a goad is an
aiguillon, of which one of the meanings is a *sting;* and
as the *aig* of *aiguillon* may be said to be a word for
goat, since it does not differ from the *aig* of *aigos*, genitive of αἴξ, Greek of goat; even so is *sting* a word for
goat, as we can thus show : as its i is equal to *oi*, and
consequently to *a*, we see that *sting* cannot differ from
stang, which since its nasal sound may be dropped—
witness, *tango* and *tago*—is the same as *stag*.

And if we make no other alteration in sting than to
give to its *g* its common form of k—witness partage
and partake—it will become stink; and the Latin *hircus*
has this meaning as well as that of stag.

And this offensive odour is the same—or very nearly
the same—as that of the arm-pits. Hence *axilla* is for
aix-illa, which, as *aix* is for αἴξ, may be said to have the
literal meaning of *the goat.*

If we now drop the nasal sound in stink we shall have
stik, and of which *stick*, *stake*, and *steak* are other forms.
And as a *stick* ends in a point, this accounts for its
having, when used verbally, the meaning of to pierce;
and such ideas as we now express by the verbs *sting*,
stick, and *pierce*, were also taken in the sense of to cut.
Thus the German *stich*—and which cannot differ from

stick—may, according to Dr. Schuster, mean to stick
with a sword as well as with a needle : and *stechen*,
which is radically the same word, means to sting. Nor
does the *stech* of *stechen* differ from the *stach* of *stachel*,
which means also a point or that which stings. And if
we give to the e of the *stech* of *stechen* its nasal sound,
we shall have *stench*, and which is but another form of
stink.

The English word *stitch* is but another form of those
just noticed. But it should be written *stich*, as in German. Its second *t* has not been here inserted but for
preventing the *ch* to be sounded like k, as in monarch.
That stitch means a *point*, can be thus very easily shown :
mettre un *point* à un habit, is literally to put a *point* in
a coat; but the meaning is, to put a *stitch* in a coat.
And as a *stitch* in the side is rendered into French by
un *point* de coté, this is another plain proof that *stitch*
means a *point*.

Nor can the word *stack* differ from *stitch*; but why
so? Because a stack means, according to Webster, " a
large conical pile of hay, grain, or straw;" and a cone
ends in a point, and a stitch, as just shown, is a point.
We thus see, by the applying of our principles, how it
happens that ideas the most dissimilar are signified alike.
There is some little difference, I hope, between a stitch,
as in a coat or in the side, and a *stack*, as of corn or hay;
and yet the same word is used for expressing those different ideas. But as other roots and forms might be
employed, the words might be no way alike.

If we now notice the French word *piqûre*, which means
a *sting*, we shall find it to have the same root as sting,
though this cannot be so easily perceived. But the root
of piqûre is *iq*, which is equal to *aq* and *ak*, and this is

the *ak* of the Greek ἀκή, which means a point; and so is it of ἀκίς, which means a thorn, a pointed instrument, and a sting. As to the p of *piqûre*, it is for the aspirate, and its *ure* is an ending common to many other words, and it appears under various forms, such as *eur, or, er, ir,* &c. Now, as the root of sting is, when the nasal sound is dropped, *ig*, and as *ig* cannot differ from *ik*, nor *ik* from *oik*, nor *oik* from *ak*; we thus find the root of *piqûre* and of sting to be one and the same. But what difference is there between the p of piqûre and the t of sting? There is none whatever; for these signs often interchange. Witness σπάδιον and σπόλας being also written σταδιον and στολας. But how are we to account for *piqûre* having no s, whilst there is one in *sting?* There has been always with many people a strong tendency to prefix in pronouncing their words the sound of an s to several consonants, and especially to *p* and *t*. Hence *pike* and *spike* have, primarily considered, the same meaning; and so have piqûre and sting. We may even regard *pique* as the word *sting* itself. Let us now try to turn the knowledge thus acquired to some account.

When we write pike—this other form of pique and spike—in full, we shall have poike; that is, when the i is dropped, *poke;* and the verb to *poke at* means, according to Webster, "to make a thrust at with the *horns.*" This word must have, therefore, once served to name a horned animal; just as *sting* has, under a different form, been the same as stag. But since *poke* and its other equivalents cannot, as just seen, differ from sting, it follows that *poke* is equal to the word stag itself. By knowing this we are led to the discovery of another word for stag; that is, to *poke*. And what is the *poik* of *poike* but *puk;*

that is, *buk*, and of which *buck* and *bouc* are other forms. It is in this way that words grow out of one another.

Now an animal that *pokes*, that is, which strikes with its horns, may very well be called a *poker ;* so that it does not differ in name from the instrument with which we stir the fire.   And when we read the *pok* of poker, as in Hebrew, this word will become *koper*, and consequently *koiper*, *kaper* and *caper ;* in the third of which forms we have one equal to *couper*, to cut, as well as another form of *buck* and *bouc*.   But why should such an instrument as a poker have a name not different from that of a goat ? because it is a bar, and ends in a *point ;* and is, for this reason, the same in use as a goad, which is but another word for goat.

The equality of goat and goad is as evident in Saxon as in English.   Thus in this language a *goat* is *gat* and a *goad* is *gad*.   And when we remark that the Danish of *goat* is *geit*, we see confirmed what we have already often stated ; namely, that one vowel is not only equal to any other vowel but even to any combination of vowels ; for it must be clear to every one that in *goat, geit,* and *gat* we have the same word.   And have we not in *geit* proof of what has been also often stated, namely, that *ei* is equal to *oi*, which when its two signs coalesce makes *a ;* for this shows *geit* to be exactly equal to its Saxon equivalent *gat*.

And as *gat* cannot differ from cat (witness the *gat* of the Italian *gatto* and its English form cat), nor *cat* from *cut*, nor *cut* from the *cout* of the French *couteau*, nor this *cout* from the *coup* of *couper ;* we see again confirmed what came up during our analyzing of *bouche ;* namely, that the mouth was called after the idea *cut ;* and thanks to its horns, such too is the original meaning of *bouc* or *buck*.

But something else, I may be told, came up during our analyzing of *bouche* of which nothing similar during the present inquiry has yet been shown; witness, word and sword; word having been called after the mouth, which can be easily conceived; and sword after the idea expressed by cut, because the mouth cuts its food. But all this has too been shown in our notice of bouc; for is not *spike* equal to *speake*, a single vowel being equal to a combination of vowels? and speak has, I am sure, been often written *speake*, not to mention its several other forms to be met with in old English.

This allusion to *spike* suggests another rather curious etymology, and which must confirm all we have just seen. When we give to the i of *spike* its O understood, we shall have *spoike*; that is, when the O and i coalesce, *spake*, preterite of speak, and from which it does not differ but conventionally; and if we drop the *i* of *spoike*, we shall have spoke, which is now used instead of *spake*, the latter form having become obsolete. But this is not the etymology to which I allude; this one has not come up but incidentally, while on my way to the other, and which is this: we have seen how *spoike* is, by the dropping of its i, equal to *spoke;* and what are the *spokes* of a wheel? Every one will answer, from what has been just shown, that they must be its *spikes.* And so they are; and they do not for this reason differ from a stick, a rod, or a bar; and every such object, however thick or blunt it may be at the end, is to be regarded as being pointed, even as much so as if it were a needle or a sword.

I have heard all my life those bars in the wheel of a car called *spokes*, but never until now could I tell why they had such a name. And who could ever suppose there was any relationship between the spoke of a wheel, the mouth, and the past time of the verb to speak? But how have I at length been able to account for what appears so unaccountable? By merely knowing that when *i* is not expressed with the o it is then understood. This knowledge has allowed me to perceive that *spoke* is equal to *spoike*, and that the *spokes* of a wheel are consequently its *spoikes*, and this is how the natives of Yorkshire pronounce such a word as *spikes* at the present hour. And it is genuine; our present pronunciation is a corruption of it. Now when the *spoke* of a wheel was written *spoike*, as it must have once been, its *i* after a time was dropped, so that *spoike* was reduced to *spoke*, a word which, in this case, had no meaning. But if the o instead of the i had been dropped, *spike* would remain, and this would be significant, for every one knows that a spike is something pointed. How unfortunate that of the o and *i* in *spoike* the i instead of the o should be left out! But it has happened otherwise with the name of the fish called a *pike*; every one sees that it must have been so designated from its pointed snout: but when it was named a *poike*, as it must have first been, if its i happened to be then dropped instead of its o, it would be now called a *poke*, in which case no one could tell why it had such a name, or what this name then meant.

The French of *pike* is *brochet*; and as this word means also the *pointed* kitchen utensil called a *spit*, we thus see further confirmed our etymology of the noun *spoke*.

This word *brochet* suggests another etymology. Its radical part *broche* is, I find, equal to *forche*, and so is *forche* equal to both *fourche* and *fork*. Then where is the relationship between a forked instrument and one that is, like a brochet or spit, straight and pointed? The relationship must be traced to the circumstance that a fork was named from its being *pointed*, and not from its prongs or divisions. When the epithet *forked* was first applied to lightning, it was the prongs or divisions at the end of a fork that suggested the comparison, and not the circumstance of the fork itself being a pointed instrument. The definition of the word fork should therefore be, a pointed instrument with two or more prongs. And as its prongs are so many points, this only proves the more fully that a fork is a pointed instrument.

But as the name of the goat can be also traced, as we have seen, to a word for *point*, might not, I may be asked, this animal's name and that of a *fork* have been sometimes expressed alike? This may have very well happened sometimes, or it may not, for the reason that two roots very different in form, though not so in meaning, may have been used to express the same idea. Thus though the words goat and fork are no way alike in form, yet they have each the meaning of *point*. But let us write fork in full, and see what we shall obtain : its O having i understood brings it equal to *foirk ;* that is, when we drop the O, *firk ;* and when we now observe that the Italian *forca* is in Spanish *horca*, it must be admitted that *firk* cannot differ from *hirk,* *f* and *h* being two signs that do constantly interchange ; and the *firk* thus obtained cannot, we now see, differ from the *hirc* of *hircus,* a goat. In short, any word signifying a point may, since the point of an object is its highest part, signify also any other object not only remarkable from its being pointed, but also from its being high. Thus there is some difference between a fork and a hill or

R

a mountain, yet they may have been often named alike,
or they may not, for the reason above given; namely,
that the same ideas can be expressed by roots of different forms though alike in meaning.   Thus I find
that, according to Bosworth, *firgen* means in Saxon a
hill or a mountain; yet its radical part *firg* cannot
differ from the *firk* just noticed, and shown to be the
same as *fork*, any more than it can from the *hirc* of
hircus, a goat.

I cannot find in my Littré any observation intimating
that a fork—that is, a *fourche* or *fourchette*—took its
name from its signifying a point, but, on opening my
dear old Johnson, I find two admissions that this word
has such a meaning.   The first instance is shown by
the following from Shakspeare, to which we are thus
introduced : " It is sometimes used for the point of an
arrow :—

> " The bow is bent and 'drawn : make from the shaft.
> Let it fall rather, though the fork invade
> The region of my heart."
>
> (*King Lear.*)

The second is thus headed :—

" A point," and the quotation, which is from Addison,
is as follows : " Several are amazed at the wisdom of
the ancients that represented a thunderbolt with three
forks, since nothing could have better explained its triple
quality of piercing, burning, and melting."

But if M. Littré does not give an etymology of fork,
he shows the forms it takes in several languages, and
this is always of service.   It is from him I have known
that the Italian of fork (*forca*) is *horca* in Spanish.

I learn from Webster also that *fork* means a *point*;
but there is no instance given; my copy of this fine
dictionary being unfortunately, as I learn from its

editor, "A revised and enlarged" edition. What an advantage it would be to the whole world if the editors of certain great works would only leave them just as they find them, and be satisfied with the glory of seeing their names in the title-pages coupled with those of their authors!

Every intelligent reader must, while bestowing a serious thought on the latter etymologies, find proofs of his own that bear out mine; at least I am led to think so every time I return to what I had finished a little before, and then imagined to be made sufficiently evident. Thus I now perceive that *speck* and *speak* are the same as *beak*, and *beak* the same as *bouche;* and that none of these forms can differ from *peak*, which is thus defined by Webster: "The top of a hill or mountain ending in a *point*. A point; the end of any thing that terminates in a point," &c. And there is this word *point* of which the radical part *poin* is equal to pain, one combination of vowels being equal to any other; and from thus knowing that *poin* is the same as *pain*, we see that un *point* de coté (a stitch in the side, or rather a *stick* in the side) is a *pain* in the side.

And there is my etymology of the *spoke* of a wheel. The Latin word is *radius*, but what does radius mean besides the spoke of a wheel? I find in Quicherat and Daveluy, among its several other meanings, the following: "A cock's spur, a *stake*, a *rod*, and a *thorn;*" all of which mean objects that are pointed.

And there is *speiche*, the German of the noun *spoke;* is it not easy to perceive that it is letter for letter the elder form of spoke, that is, *spoike*, since its *ei* is equal to *oi*, and its *ch* to *k !*

And there is *béche*, a spade; by the noticing of which

I was first led to discover the etymology of *boucher*. This word has in Swedish the very meaning it has in English; but *spader*, which is radically the same word, is *pike*, that is *poike*, and with the euphonic *s*, *spoike*, and consequently the noun spoke; by which means we show the identity, in primary meaning, of spade and spoke.

And there is *stag*, which, when we drop its euphonic *s*, becomes *tag*; and a tag is a *point*, but, as Webster says, " a metallic *point* put to the end of a string." Hence, in the word for so insignificant a thing as a *tag*, we see the name of that noble animal, the stag; and which we further confirm by reading *tag* from right to left as in Hebrew, since tag will then become *gat*, which is the Saxon of goat, and a stag is a goat.

But something as insignificant as a tag is a *pin*, and yet, because it happens to be a pointed instrument, it is in French the name of the pine-tree. Even a *thorn* might have had such a name; for the *th* of this word is for the aspirate (witness ἅμα being the same as θαμά, and the αλ of ἅλς being the original of the θαλ of θάλασσα), and the Hebrew of the pine is אֹרֶן *arn*, which, with the aspirate, is equal to *harn*, that is, horn; and when the aspirate of horn is represented, as just shown by *th* (θ), this word becomes thorn. And it was after its horns, which are pointed, the goat was called.

By the knowledge thus afforded, we may often show how words alike in meaning, but very different in form, can be traced to one another. Thus *or*, which is the root of thorn, being equal to *oir*, and *oir* to *poir*—because p often represents the aspirate—can be shown when *poir* takes the euphonic s, not to differ from *spoir*, whence *spire*, and even spine, for the reason that r and n interchange; and spine is in Latin *spina*, which has also the

meaning of thorn. Thus a spire cannot, because it terminates in a point, differ, as to its primary meaning, from
a pin or a thorn. And when we make the *oi* of *poir*
take its form of u (witness *croix* and *crux*), we shall have
spur instead of *spoir* or *spire*. Hence this instrument
has been so called from its being pointed. Spear is but
a different form of the same word, and it is so for the
same reason, that of being pointed.

And as in the *poir* of *spoir*—original of *spire*—we have
the word *poire;* even so have we in *spear* when we drop,
as in *spoir*, the euphonic S—the English of *poire*; that
is, pear.

Now if the inquisitive reader consults dictionaries in
the hopes of discovering the primary meanings of the
words to which I have just drawn his attention, he will
lose his time—be told nothing more than what he knows
already, and what every schoolboy knows. Thus, take
as an instance the meaning and etymology of so common
a fruit as a *pear*. M. Littré defines it; " fruit à pepins,
de forme oblongue, et plus grosse à la partie inférieure."
And his only etymology of it is: Berry, *poire, pouese,*
Genev. *un poire;* Ital. *pera;* du Lat. *pirum.*"

The reader cannot, from this etymology, tell why a
pear was named as it is. M. Littré not being aware that
the *pir* of *pirum* must have once been *poir*, i having o
understood; and it being equally unknown to him that,
from the euphonic *s* being used, *poir* cannot differ from
spoir, nor *spoir* from such forms as *spoine, spine, spina,*
nor any of these from *pin*, or *pine;* he could never, for
the want of this necessary knowledge, suppose that a
pear might have been signified by the names of any of
the above-mentioned objects.

Take the word *pine*, for instance. Could he ever suppose that such a tree and a pear were named alike? Never.

They have each, however, a conical appearance, being broad below and pointed above. But after which end were they named? After the one terminating in a point. Witness a boy's spinning *top*. It has also, like the pine-tree or a pear, the form of a cone; but its name *top* tells us that it was called after height and not after lowness. Its name should not, therefore, differ in meaning from that of the pine, which has the form of a cone, being broad at its basis and pointed at its top. Hence it is that the Greek word κῶνος means both a cone and a boy's spinning-top.

But might not *top* mean either high or low? Certainly it might; but as we now have it, lowness is never implied. When its O takes i understood, top will be *toip*, and *toip* becomes when the O is dropped, *tip*, which is significant of height; but when read as in Hebrew, it will be significant of lowness, as it will then be *pit*. In Greek, however, this word *pit* means what is high, since it is the radical part of πίτυς, which is the name of the pine-tree. When we now give to *pit* its fullest form—that is, supply the O understood with the *i*; it will be *poit*, that is, when we give to the combination *oi* its nasal sound, *point*. Hence the point of any thing might be called its *tip*—its very highest part. We have, therefore, in *top, tip, pit,* and *point* one and the same word.

An instance similar to the opposite meanings of *top* and *pit* is also afforded by the Hebrew words שׁיח *tis* and שֵׁת *sit*, of which the first means a he-goat (hircus), and the second is thus explained by Parkhurst: "That part of the body upon which men *sit, the buttocks* [7]."

Having already shown that the name of the goat is but another word for height, and as that " part of the body upon which men sit" implies lowness, it follows that

[7] Lex. pp. 724, 743.

we have in the Hebrew *tis* a word for height, and when read in the contrary direction a word for lowness also, just as we have in *tip* and *pit*.

Another instance of the same kind is still afforded by שית *sit*; to which Parkhurst gives also the meaning of *thorn;* for as *thorn* is, as we have seen, the same as *horn,* after which the goat was called, it follows that it now means what is high; and which is further shown by its being what is pointed, the point or tip of any thing being its highest part. The word *thorn* might have therefore served as a name for the goat, and so might it for the pine-tree; its radical part *orn* being the same as *arn,* in Hebrew ארן *arn,* the pine[8].

CHAPTER XXXI.

THE CROW AND THE RAVEN.

On these words and their different forms in Sanskrit, Greek, Latin, Saxon, French, and English, M. Max Müller has a very long article. His main object appears to be the discovery, if possible, of the original meaning of the word *raven;* and though he has, like all of the German school, failed in this respect, his endeavours are not the less deserving of praise; for the mere form of a word is no etymology. The philologist should, like M. Max Müller in this instance, try to find out why an idea obtained the particular name by which it is known more than any other. A father

[8] Parkhurst, p. 636.

once told me that his child was continually asking him why were things named as they are; why was a cat called a cat, and a mouse called a mouse? But the child could not be satisfied, because its parent knew no more of the philosophy of language than if he were some very learned academician, or some great philologist of the German school.

M. Max Müller having, in common with every one else, observed that the cuckoo and the cock must have been each named from its note, begins thus his article on the raven :—

"Let us now examine the word *raven*. It might seem at first as if this was merely onomatope. Some people imagine they perceive a kind of similarity between the word *raven* and the cry of that bird. This seems still more so if we compare the Anglo-Saxon *hræfn*. The Sanskrit *karava* also, the Latin *corvus*, the English *crow*, and the Greek *korōnē*, all are supposed to show some similarity to the unmelodious sound of Maître Corbeau. But if we look more closely we find that these words, though similar in sound, spring from different sources. The English *crow* can claim no relationship whatever with *corvus*, for the simple reason that, according to Grimm's Law, an English C cannot correspond to a Latin C. *Raven* on the contrary, which in outward appearance, differs from *corvus* much more than *crow*, offers much less real difficulty in being traced back to the same source from which sprang the Latin *corvus*. For *raven* is the Anglo-Saxon *hræfn* or *hræfen*, and its first syllable *hræ* would be a legitimate substitute for the Latin *cor*. Opinions differ widely as to the root or roots from which the various names of the crow, the raven, and the rook in the Aryan dialects are derived.

Those who look on the Sanskrit as the most primitive form of Aryan speech are disposed to admit the Sanskrit *karava* as the original type, and as *karava* is by native etymologists derived from the *ka + rava*, in which the initial interrogative or exclamatory element *kâ* or *ku* is supposed to fill the office of the Greek *dys* or the English *mis*, are so numerous as they are supposed to be in Sanskrit. The question has been discussed again and again; and though it is impossible to deny the existence of such compounds in Sanskrit, particularly in the later Sanskrit, I know of no well-established instance where such formations have found their way into Greek, Latin, or German. If, therefore, *karava, corvus, korōnē,* and *hræfen* are cognate words, it would be more advisable to look upon the *k* as part of the radical, and thus to derive all these words from a root *kru*, a secondary form it may be of the root *ru*. This root *kru*, or, in its more primitive form, *ru* (*raiti* and *ravīti*), is not a mere imitation of the cry of the raven; it embraces many cries, from the harshest to the softest, and it might have been applied to the note of the nightingale as well as to the cry of the raven. In Sanskrit the root *ru* is applied in its verbal and nominal derivatives to the murmuring sound of birds, bees, and trees, to the barking of dogs, the lowing of cows, and the whispering of men. In Latin we have from it both *raucus*, hoarse, and *rumor*, a whisper; in German *rumen*, to speak low, and *runa*, mystery. The Latin *lamentum* stands for a more original *laviventum* or *ravimentum*, for there is no necessity for deriving this noun from the secondary root *kru, krav, krâv,* and for admitting the loss of the initial guttural in *cravimentum*, particularly as in *clamare* the same guttural is preserved. It is true, however, that this root *ru* appears under many secondary forms. By the addition of an initial k it is raised to *kru* and *klu*, well known by its numerous off-shoots; such as the Greek *klyo*, *klytos*, the Latin *cluo*, *inclitus*, *cliens*, the English *loud*, the Slavonic *slava*, glory. By the addition of final letters, *ru* appears as the Sanskrit *rud*, to cry, and as the Latin *rug*, in *rugire*, to howl. By the addition both of initial and final letters we get the Sanskrit *krus*, to shout, the Greek *kraugē*, cry, and the Gothic *hrukjan*, to crow. In the Sanskrit *sru* and the Greek *klyo* the same root has been used to convey the sense of hearing; naturally, because, when a noise was to be heard from a far distance, the man who first perceived it might well have said, " I ring," for his ears were sounding or ringing; and the same verb, if once used as a transitive, would well come in in such forms as the Homeric *klythi mey*, hear me, or the Sanskrit *srudhi*, hear !

" But although, as far as the meaning of *kárava*, *corvus*, *korōnē*, and *hræfen* is concerned, there would seem to be no difficulty in deriving them from a root *kru*, to sound, I have nowhere found a satisfactory explanation of the exact etymological process by which the Sanskrit *kárava* could be formed from *kru*. *Kru*, no doubt, might yield *krava*; but to admit a dialectic corruption of *krava* into *karva*, and of *karva* into *kárava*, is tantamount to giving up any etymological derivation at all. Are we therefore forced to be satisfied with the assertion that *kárava* is no grammatical derivative at all, but a mere imitation of the sound *cor cor*, uttered by the raven? I believe not; but, as I hinted before, we may treat *karava* as a regular derivative of the Sanskrit *káru*. This *káru* is a Vedic word, and means one who sings praises to the gods, literally one that shouts. It comes from a root *kar*, to shout, to praise, to record; from which the Vedic word *kíri*, a poet, and the well-known *kírti*, glory, *kirtayati*, he praises. *Káru*, from *kar*, meant originally a shouter (like the Greek *kéryx*, a herald), and its derivative *kárava* was therefore applied to the raven in the general sense of the shouter. All the other names of the raven can be easily traced back to the same root *kar: cor-vus* from *kar*, like *tor-vus* from *tar; koróne* from *kar*, like *chetone* from *har; korax* from *kar*, like *phylux*, &c. The Anglo-Saxon *hræfen*, as well as the Old High-German *hraban*, might be represented in Sanskrit by such forms as *kar-van* or *kur-van-a;* while the English *rook*, the Anglo-Saxon *hroc*, the Old High-German *hruoh*, would seem to derive their origin from a different root altogether, viz., from the Sanskrit *krus*.

"The English *crow*, the Anglo-Saxon *cráw*, cannot, as was pointed out before, be derived from the same root *kar*. Beginning with a guttural tenuis in Anglo-Saxon, its corresponding forms in Sanskrit would there begin with the guttural media. There exists in Sanskrit a root *gar*, meaning to sound, to praise; from which the Sanskrit *gir*, voice, the Greek *gérys*, voice, the Latin *garrulus*. From it was framed the name of the crane, *geranos* in Greek, *cran* in Anglo-Saxon, and likewise the Latin name for cock, *gallus* instead of *garrus*. The name of the nightingale, Old High-German *nahti-gal*, has been referred to the same root, but in violation of Grimm's law. From this root *gar* or *gal*, *crow* might have been derived, but not from the root *kar*, which yielded *corvus*, *korax*, or *kárava*, still less from *cor cor*, the supposed cry of the bird.

"It will be clear from these remarks that the process which led to the formation of the word *raven* is quite distinct from that which produced *cuckoo*. *Raven* means a shouter, a caller, a crier. It might have been applied to many birds, but it became the traditional and recognized name of one, and of one only. *Cuckoo* could never mean any thing but the cuckoo, and while a word like *raven* has ever so many relations, *cuckoo* stands by itself like a stick in a living hedge[9]."

I beg to draw the reader's particular attention to M. Max Müller's asserting so positively as he does in the above passage that, " The English crow can claim no relationship *whatever* with *corvus*, for the simple reason that, according to Grimm's law, an English C cannot correspond to a Latin C."

This is indeed a "simple reason." Every philologist should learn to think for himself, but they all follow in the wake of their idol Grimm, who knew no more of the origin of language or letters than any one else. It was this great man who declared, as we saw farther back, that it is impossible to give a satisfactory etymology of either God or good; and he having said so, M. Max Müller, *for this simple reason,* says so too. But neither of these gentlemen being aware that *God* was a name of the sun, and that it was from such a word, when yet only O, that all other words emanated; it was not in their power, nor in any man's power, to give the original of a word that was itself the origin of all words. But *good* could be easily traced to *God,* which though only the sun, was supposed to be the author of all goodness.

As to Grimm's law respecting the English c, it is far from being orthodox, as I am now about to show.

But let me first take the liberty of bringing M. Max Müller acquainted with something respecting the letter

[9] Lect. Science of Lang., v. i. pp. 400 to 405.

C of which he does not seem to be aware. The Saxon and English word *horn* may not be so old a word as *cornu,* but in form it is much older, for the c of the latter does here but serve as a substitute for the h of horn. There must have been therefore a time when instead of *cornu* the Latins had *hornu;* the h having then been made thus Ɔ-Ϲ, of which the second half still serves in Greek for the whole sign; that is, for the *spiritus asper.* Now in the *hund* of hundred what have we? the *cent* of the Latin *centum;* and what has been just said of *horn* and *cornu,* will apply here; namely, that the *hund* of *hund*red is, at least in form, much older than the *cent* of *centum.* When we do therefore write *cent* in full we shall have *hoint,* and *hoint* is the same as *hunt* or *hund,* and *hunt* the same as *hant,* and *hant* the same as *hand,* after which idea that of a great many and hence a *hundred* was anciently called, just as at present we have *many* for *manus.* Another word older in form in English than in Latin is hurry, of which the *hur* is the *cur* of *curro,* to run, and which must have first been *hurro,* and its infinitive *currere* have been *hurrere.*

These instances serve to show that c in English has often served to represent *h,* and that of the two signs *h* is the elder. But if Saxon or English be less ancient than Latin, it is not difficult to conceive that the forms of many of its words should be older? This is not so difficult to conceive as at first sight it appears to be. Thus, supposing one language to have borrowed some words from another language, the borrowing may have taken place at a very remote period; and though such words may not have undergone any change in their new place, they may, some time after they were borrowed, have been considerably altered in their own language. Thus

if in English, such words as *feast, haste* and *forest* come
direct to us from the French, we might suppose their
forms to be modern compared with their originals. Yet
it is not so; for they are much older than *fête, hâte,* and
forêt, as every one will admit.

Now granting, as shown above, that *h* was, at least
on some occasions, the elder form of *c,* the *harmon* of
harmonia having been the original of *carmen,* just as we
have found *horn* to have preceded *cornu;* it follows that
c in English cannot be always distinct from itself in
Latin, the relationship of the two signs *h* and *c* being as
close as that of parent and child. Hence the *c* in such
words as *care, cross,* and *cruelty,* is as evidently the same
sign in *cura, crux,* and *crudelitas,* since these words are
in the two languages but different forms of one another.

Let us now see if, in opposition to Grimm's law,
corvus and *crow* are radically the same word. I have
already had occasion to show that vowels preceding r
do frequently fall behind it; witness *forst* in Saxon and
frost in English; hence the *corv* of *corvus* cannot differ
from *crov,* nor can *crov,* because of the interchange of
v and w, differ from *crow.* And as this interchange is
not more frequent than that of b and v, as every one
knows, it follows that the *corv* of *corvus* is the same as
the *corb* of *corbeau,* the famous bird immortalized by La
Fontaine in France, and by Poe in America, in English
called a *raven.* Hence in *corvus, crow,* and *corbeau,* we
have radically the same word, though we know not yet
why such a bird was so called; but we shall, no doubt, ·
find it presently by the applying of our principles. Let
us first, for this purpose, notice *corbeau* again. As its
eau is an ending common to many words, it must, as
such, have once been *eal* or *el; u* and *l* being, as we

have often shown, the same sign (hence *beau* and *bel*) ; and it must, when under such a form as *eal, el* or *il*, have served as an article first standing before the noun *corb*, behind which it must have afterwards fallen, just as the *il* of *il sole* fell behind *sole*, whence the French *soleil*. This is confirmed by M. Littré, who shows that in old French one of the forms for *corbeau* was *corbeil*.

The *corb* of *corbeau* or *corbel* is all we have now to notice of this bird's name.

As two consonants have, in general, a vowel understood between them, *corb* is equal to *corab*, and this is confirmed by the Sanskrit of raven, which is, according to M. Max Müller and M. Littré, *kârava*, and the *karav* of this form is precisely equal to *corab*, the o of the latter being for *oi*, and *oi* for *a*; and the *b* at the end being the same as *v*, as shown above. As the c of *corab* is for the aspirate, so is the k of its Sanskrit *karav*, because it does here but represent the c; and as the aspirate cannot any more than one of its substitutes be regarded as belonging to the root of a word, it follows that *orab*, or *arav*, is alone to be accounted for. Now as in the *ab* of *orab* and the *av* of *arav* we have the same word, and as the *av* of the latter cannot differ from the *av* of the Latin *avis*, a bird, we are naturally led to suspect that the *ar* by which it is preceded must be a word serving to express the quality of *avis*. And granting this, what must be the meaning of the *ar* of *arav ?* We know that it cannot, any more than the *or* of *orab*, differ from *oir*, its *a* being equal to *oi*, which combination makes·a part of *coirba*, and this word happens to be— according to M. Littré—the name of the raven in Wallon. But its c is here, as in the *corb* of *corbeau*, for the aspirate ; and as this *coir* of *coirba* has not, under its

present form any meaning, we are free to change its c
for some other substitute of the aspirate until we find a
word that will apply when prefixed as an epithet to *avis*.
When *s*, which is a common substitute for the aspirate, is
prefixed to the *oir* of *coirba*, it will produce *soir*, which
cannot differ either from the *ser* of *serus* (late) or from
the *ser* of *serum*, evening.   But the raven is not a late
bird, nor is it ever called an evening bird.   The ideas
expressed by *late* and *evening* can, however, be traced to
those belonging to night; and as night implies darkness,
and consequently blackness, it follows that the Wallon
word for raven, that is, *coirba*, cannot, from its being
equal to *soirba*, differ in meaning from the *dark* or *black*
bird ; and such epithets as these will apply to both the
crow and the raven.   I was forgetting to observe that
the *a* of *coirba* must have first gone before its *b*, whence
ab and the *av* of *avis*.

Let us now confirm this etymology.   The Hebrew of
the verb to fly is עף *op*, and of which עוף *oup*, a bird, is
but a different form ; nor can either of these differ from
the *av* of the Latin *avis*, a bird.   And this is so evident,
that Parkhurst referring to עף *op* says, " Hence Latin
avis, a bird [1]."

Now as the fuller form of the *orb* of *corbeau* is, as
shown above, *oir-ab*, this combination of two words may
be said to have, since *oir* is for *soir*, the literal meaning
of *dark* or *black* bird.   But when these words *oir-ab*
coalesced, they became, by the dropping of the *a*, *orb*, in
Hebrew ערב.   Now this word has, according to Parkhurst [2], these several meanings : " The evening ; to be
darkened, duskily obscured ;" and also this very important meaning, " A crow, a raven from its dark colour [3]."

---

[1] Lex. p. 492.   [2] Lex. p. 501.   [3] Lex. p. 502.

This etymology cannot be called in question; it is too evident for that. But Parkhurst has failed to observe that the ב *b* of ערב *orb* (corbeau) is for *ab*, and consequently for the *av* of *avis*. Hence the *or* of *orb* is the real word for both evening and darkness, and its fuller form *oir* is not only the root of the French *soir* but of *noir* also. When M. Littré gave the Wallon *coirba* for *orbeau*, he little thought that this word contains in tself the several meanings of *evening, darkness,* and *bird;* ıd from his not knowing this, it has not been in his power to tell his learned countrymen why the *corbeau* was first named as it is. He could not, however, help perceiving that the name of this bird, in several languages, bears a very close resemblance to the word by which it is signified in Hebrew, and, according to him, this Hebrew word is *harab.* Parkhurst does not, however, give such a form for raven as *harab,* but *orb* ערב only. Sander and Tremel's dictionary gives also *orb,* and quotes the passage in Genesis viii. 7, which says, " And he sent forth a *raven;*" and here, too, the Hebrew is ערב *orb.* But *orb* cannot, as our analysis of it has shown, differ otherwise from *harab* than by its wanting the aspirate *h,* to which its initial vowel is justly entitled. We have, therefore, it may be said, in *orb* and *harab* the same word, for the *h* should not be counted.

If Parkhurst has failed to perceive that the *b* of *orb* is for *ab,* and that *ab* is for the *av* of *avis;* the philologists of other languages seem to have failed not only in this respect but in all others. Thus Greek scholars do not perceive that the κορων of κορώνη (the crow) means the blackbird.. This arises from their not knowing that the *k* of this word is for the aspirate, and that ὁρῶν is alone to be accounted for. And if they knew

s

this, they would have still to learn that the οr of ὁρῶν is, as just shown, equal to *oir*, and *oir* to *soir*, and *soir* to the *ser* of *serum*, which has the same meaning in Latin as *soir* has in French—that of evening, and consequently of darkness. They would have also to learn that the ων of κορώνη is for bird, and this is confirmed by its being taken in this sense in οἰωνός, the literal meaning of which is *lone* or *single bird*, οι being for οἶος, single or alone, and ων for bird; whence *omen*, such birds as fly alone having been preferred by augurs to all others for divination. And that the ων of οἰωνός has here this meaning of bird is further shown by ὠόν, Greek of *egg*, which idea was called after bird. I find also in Gaelic that *eun* means a bird, and such a form cannot differ, except conventionally, from either ὤν or ὠόν.

Now what difference is there between. the ων of οἰωνός and the οp of ὄρνις, which is the usual word in Greek for *bird?* There is none whatever, and yet there might be a very great difference. And why so? Because ων and οp are two roots, and here they have each the meaning of *bird;* but this is only conventional, for they might have many other very different meanings, but still conventionally. We should bear in mind that the roots of a language have all emanated from the same single source—man's first word; and though they may, for this reason, be regarded as making only one root, yet they have, by universal consent, obtained not one and the same meaning, but a great many; just as the letters of an alphabet, which, though representing a single sign, have also obtained many different forms and powers. There may have been once in Greek many dialects long since forgotten; and each of them may have had, for aught we know, a particular word of its own for signifying *bird*.

Of the several words for crow or raven, in Greek and
Latin, perhaps the most difficult to explain are κόραξ
and *cornix*, to which I would give the assumed forms of
κόρακος and *cornicus;* for X is a compound letter, having
the power of *ks*, which, with the vowels understood,
is equal to *akos* or *icus*, the roots *ak* and *ic* being now
each of them for bird; for the k of *lukos*, as shown
farther back, is equal to the p of *lupus;* and for this
reason so is *korakos* the same as *korapos*, of which the *ap*
is equal to the *av* of *avis*. As to the *n* of *cornix*, it is
now merely euphonic, as it often is when following r.

The difference in meaning between the words *crow*
and *raven* is only conventional; and the same may be
said of these words and the Latin *merula* and its French
form *merle*, the *mer* of each form having now the meaning of *black*, and being equal to the *maur* of μαύρος,
to the French *maure* and *noir*, as well as to the English
word *moor*, a black, and the *mur* of *murky*. Hence the
English of *merula* or *merle* is literally a *blackbird*. The
ul of *merula* should be now considered as having once
meant *bird*. When we do therefore give to *merula* its
elder form of *mervla*, we see in its *vl*, with a vowel
supplied, the *vol* of *volo*, to fly, whence *fowl*, a bird, just
as in Hebrew עף *op* is for the verb to *fly*, and עוף *oup* is
for bird; all such ideas and their names being traceable
to the same source.

It is now easy to perceive that the initial consonants
of the words for raven given by M. Max Müller in
fræfn, *kraban* and *karava*, do but represent the aspirate
h, and that they should not, for this reason, be counted.
Hence when they are left out, the remainder of each
word will be found to be but another form of *raven*.
And in order to see the radical identity of raven and

its Hebrew equivalent *orb*, we need only remark that the *rav* of raven becomes *arv* by transposition, and that *arv* cannot differ from *arb*, nor *arb* from *orb*. The *rab* of the German *rabe* is to be traced to *orb* in the same way.

Now since *high* and *low* are often signified alike, and since *white* and *black* are to be traced to the same source as *high* and *low*, I may be here asked if the word for raven and dove may not be expressed alike in different languages? This may very well happen, just as it happens in Saxon that *blàc* means not only white, but black also. Hence the English word *dove* which must have meant *white*, cannot differ from *dubh* in Gaelic, and it is, I believe, the same word in Irish; yet *dubh* means *black*. Hence the two birds mentioned in the history of the deluge may, at the remote time an event so awful, and according to science so incredible, was first made known, have been signified by the same name. Or, we may say, that if at first there was only one bird mentioned, at a later period there may have been two, which would arise from the same word meaning both *white* and *black*, and consequently *dove* and *raven*.

It has only now occurred to me that in my work on the Origin of Myths, published in 1856, I had occasion to give the etymology of both the *raven* and the *dove*. But though my discovery of the origin of language and myths was then as real as it is at present, I had not yet made myself acquainted with all its principles; so that I am now, on consulting The Myths, really astonished to perceive that my etymology of the *raven* made some fourteen or fifteen years ago was in substance what it is at present. I even perceive that I gave then the origin of *rook*, which, on the present occasion has been overlooked. Thus referring to the *cor* of *corb*[4], I showed that when read after the Hebrew manner, it was *roc*, and that *roc* is the same as *rok*, and consequently as *rook*.

I beg also to draw the reader's attention to the subjoined passage, published in 1856 :—

"The following will serve to show how little the learned Gesenius knew of the various forms of the Hebrew word *orb*, raven : ' No root is to be sought in the Phœnicio-Shemetic languages, but to this answers the Sanskrit *karawa*. The letters *b* and *w* are shown not to belong to the root by the Greek *korax*, and apparently the Latin *cornix*.' He means that the *b* of *orb* is no part of its root, and so far he is right; but in what way it came to belong to *or*, making this word become *orb*, of course he cannot imagine, his knowledge of its not being here radical having been obtained not through any rule or principle, but merely by comparing *orb* with *korax*. As to the Sanskrit *karawa* (raven), it appears to have a meaning more than Gesenius suspected. Its *w* is, of course, no part of the root meaning *raven*, this being expressed by *kar;* but it is, however, a root; for *awa* is equal to *ava*, and *ava* to *avis*, the Latin of *bird;* and the meaning of the whole word *karawa*, or, as we might write it, *kar-ava* or *karavis*, seems to be blackbird, *kar* being for black, and *awa* for bird; so that *aw* is the root of *awa*, and it must have once meant bird, or a form very similar to it [that is, to *aw*] ; such as *av*, *ou*, *ouv*, or still, *ap*, *op*, or *oup*, must have had this meaning. In Hebrew both *op* and *oup* mean a bird ; they are but different ways of writing the same word. Though I cannot help considering the Greek *korax* (raven) as meaning only *black*, yet I strongly suspect that *korōnē*

[4] Myths, vol. ii. p. 396.

(a crow) means both black and bird; its non-radical part being merely *e*, its *kor* being, like the *kor* of *korax* for *black*, and its *ōn* being the same as the *iōn* of *oiōnos*, which means bird[5]."

This passage, published in 1856, though somewhat different from any of those by which we have to-day shown the primary signification of raven, leads, however, to the same result; namely, that the word *raven* has, in no matter what language, the literal meaning of *blackbird*, and not the *shouter*, as the learned Sanskrit scholar and correspondent of the Institute, M. Max Müller, asserts, in a work for which he obtained the prix Volney.

I sent, however, in 1856, as a competitor for the prix Volney, the two volumes from the second of which I have just transcribed a considerable portion of my etymology of raven, sufficient to show that I had even then discovered the primary signification of this bird's name in Sanskrit, Hebrew, Greek, Latin, and French. But did the body of the very learned, honourable, and conscientious gentlemen, who were commissioned to examine my work, ever read my etymology of *raven?* No; they never did. But how do I know? I have found it out in this way : having my suspicions that my work had never been carefully gone through, I paid a visit to the Institute last year, and requested to be shown my two volumes, as if I wanted to copy something out of them; but this was not my real object. When they were presented to me, I saw that the whole of the leaves of the first volume had not been cut open, and that this favour had been granted to only a few pages at the beginning of the second volume; so that towards the end,

---

[5] *Myths*, vol. ii. p. 399.

where my etymology of *raven* happens to be, all appeared as completely intact as when it came from the
printer. Now, as M. Littré was elected member of the
Institute in 1839, and as his honourable colleagues
consider him a very high authority in all matters
relating to philology, he may have very well been on
the committee for the prix Volney in 1856, just as he
was last year; and if so, we need not be surprised at his
being even still totally ignorant of the etymology of
corbeau; for to give us only the different forms of this
word in several languages is no etymology, and M.
Littré does no more.

Now, if every tame raven throughout France were to
be christened *corbeau* by his keeper, he would soon find
out that this was his name, and he would answer to it
accordingly. But his knowledge of the word would go
no farther—he could not divine its original meaning;
hence there is not, in this respect, a shade of difference
between the great Sanskrit scholar, M. Max Müller, and
Maître Corbeau. But I may be told that M. Max Müller
knows the word for raven in several languages, which
Maître Corbeau does not. And this, I must admit, is
very true. On such knowledge I do not, however, set
much value; nor is it the kind of knowledge I allude to.
What I want to know is this: why was the bird called
a raven distinguished by this name more than by that of
cat or dog, or any other name? Can M. Max Müller
tell me why? No. Can M. Littré tell me why? No.
Can any member of the French Academy or the French
Institute tell me why? No; for M. Littré, who is perhaps more learned in philology than any of them, cannot
tell me why. Can any of the German school tell me
why? No; for M. Max Müller, who is a learned Ger-

man, cannot tell me why, and yet he knows all that has been ever written or said relating to the word *raven* in his own language.

I must therefore conclude that, from the learned men and learned bodies of men here alluded to, not knowing the original meaning of the word *raven*, they are not, in this respect, as I have already declared, and as I do again declare, a shade more enlightened than Maître Corbeau himself.

But might not, I shall be asked, the Hebrew scholars of France and Germany have discovered the original meaning of *raven* on merely consulting a Hebrew dictionary? Certainly they might; but that would have been considered as something very low; for Hebrew appears to be with philologists no longer in the fashion, whilst Sanskrit is, to use a vulgar phrase, " all the go." And yet, strange to say, I have not yet met with a single pretended etymology made through a knowledge of Sanskrit, that did not prove to be, like the etymology of *raven*, not merely a mistake, but, on my soul, a very gross blunder; and of this I have, I dare assert, given in the foregoing pages some very palpable proofs; but others—philologists less difficult to please—philologists with no principles whatever to guide them—may be more fortunate than I have been.

Has not, I may be asked, Parkhurst's etymology of *raven* greatly served me? It has served me so far as to confirm my own; for if I knew not a word of Hebrew, my etymology of *raven* would have been just what it is. But does Parkhurst's etymology deserve to be so called?

As the same word in Hebrew may be said to mean both darkness and raven, no ingenuity was needed for perceiving that the raven must have been named after his dark colour. But where a little ingenuity was needed, Parkhurst displayed none; I allude to the *b* of *orb,* which this authority has failed to observe is for *ab,* and *ab* for the *av* of avis; a vowel being frequently, but not always, understood between two consonants.

What has so long kept etymologists from discovering the original meaning of *raven* was the belief that this bird was called after its *croak* or *cry*; whilst it was the idea expressed by the word croak that took its name from the bird, and not the bird from its croaking. Hence the Greek κρωγμός, the Latin *crocitus,* the French *croasse-ment,* and the English *croak,* are all imitations of the same sound—of the cry of crows and ravens. There is, therefore, no resemblance between such a sound and that of such names as ערב *orb, rabe, raven,* and the *corb* of *corbeau.*

The raven was not therefore called after its croaking or shouting, but after its colour; so that the literal meaning of its name is *blackbird,* and nothing else; and from the *corb* of *corbeau,* a raven, being equal to *corw,* and from this being the word *crow* itself, we see that the name of the crow does not differ in meaning from that of the raven; hence the common comparison, "as black as a crow;" and hence in his description of a beautiful woman the poet says, "Her hair was the raven's wing."

CHAPTER XXXII.

PYRAMID.

THE reader must be now, from all he has just seen, well prepared to discover the primary signification—hitherto unknown—of the word *pyramid*, which happens to name one of the wonders of the world. Many learned philologists have tried, but in vain, to find out what this word means. Its radical part, *pyram*, is the same in both Greek and Latin; and as this radical part cannot differ from *pyrum*, or, as it is also written, *pirum*, and as *pyrum* or *pirum* is the Latin of *pear*, and as this fruit was, as shown above, called after its conical figure, even so was a pyramid. Hence so great an object has not, because ending in a point, obtained a prouder name than the one assigned to a pear or a boy's spinning top.

There is in De Roquefort a long article on the word *pyramid*, too long for insertion here. But it is in substance to this effect; that Lancelot and Daviler derive it from *pur* (Greek of *fire*), because a flame ascends in the shape of a point. But Volney supposes *pur* to be for the Egyptian word *bour*, which means an excavation in the earth, and that the *amis* of *pyramis* may be for *amit*, which means *du mort* (of the dead); so that pyramid, or *pyramis*, would, according to this authority, signify a sepulchre, or place for the dead. This etymology has not prevailed, because no one could suppose *pyramis* to have had for its original the Egyptian words *bour* and *amit*.

Donnegan gives the following under πυραμίς : " The old grammarians derive the word, some from πῦρ, fire, flame having a conical appearance, others, from πυρός, a heap of corn, either very improbable : most likely, as Passow supposes, an Egyptian word."

M. Littré's etymology is as follows : " πυραμίς. Ce mot qu'on s'attendrait à trouver dans l'Égyptien, mais qu'on n'y retrouve pas, a été rattaché par les Grecs tantôt à πῦρ, parce que la flamme se termine naturellement en pointe, tantôt à πυραμίς, gâteau conique qu'on offrait aux morts. , D'après Brunet de Presle, les Grecs ont comparé la pyramide à ce gâteau conique, de même qu'ils avaient nommé ὀβελίσκος, *brochette,* les obélisques. Πυραμίς, gâteau, vient de πυρός, froment."

This etymology, in which there is more than one mistake, serves to confirm our own. From it we learn that the Greeks, as well as other people, named objects after their forms. Thus, as an obelisk ends in a point they gave it a name of similar import ; that is, they called it after a word signifying *pointed.* Now a *brochette* or little spit happens to have this meaning in Greek just as it has in French and English ; but it does not follow that the Greeks were thinking of such an instrument as a *spit* when they first named an obelisk. The word, no doubt, then signified *pointed ;* and from its having this general meaning, it must, under different modified forms, have served as a name for many other objects ending in a point. The Greeks are allowed to have had a cake called a *puramis,* long anterior to their having seen a pyramid ; what, then, let me ask, was the meaning of *puramis ?* The cake so named was called after its form ; that is, it meant the *pointed ;* and there is nothing to show that the Greeks were thinking of such a cake when they gave the same name to a pyramid. As well might we say that the *pit* of *pitus* (the Greek of the pine) is derived from the kitchen utensil called a spit, both words being radically the same, and having the same primary signification, that of *pointed.* Or as well might we say that *broche* (the French of spit) took its name from *brochet* (the French of the fish called the pike), for the reason that the latter has a sharp snout.

We do therefore conclude that a pyramid did not first mean a place for the dead, nor was it called after fire, a heap of corn, or a *cake;* in short, after no particular object whatever ; but that it was like a *pear*, the *pine-tree*, or a boy's *spinning top*—designated by a word that had the meaning of *cone.*

CHAPTER XXXIII.

M. LITTRÉ'S ETYMOLOGY OFPITCH, POISSARD, POISSARDE, ETC.

THE following forms of the word *pitch*, taken from different languages and their dialects, are given by M. Littré : *pége, pegue, pes, pez, pece, picean, πίσσα,* and the Sanskrit *piccha.*

Now all these words for *poix* are but so many modified forms of the Greek name of the tree (*pitus*) which yields *pitch;* but to this M. Littré never alludes; and we cannot, for this reason, imagine why *poix* or *pitch* was named as it is. He may say that it can be traced even to the Sanskrit *piccha,* which is only telling us that there is in Sanskrit a word having the meaning of *poix*; it does not let us know after what either *poix* or *pitch* was called, and this is what the philosophy of language requires of every philologist. But how can this knowledge be acquired if philologists know nothing of the origin of speech? M. Max Muller says, "We know not yet what speech is."

This French word for *pitch* (*poix*) has, from its resemblance to the *poiss* of *poissard* and *poissarde*, been the cause of a serious mistake. M. Littré quotes under *poissard, poissarde*, in the *partie historique* of his dictionary, relating to this word, the following passage: "XVI. Siècle. *Poix* dont vient *poissard* pour un larron, Rob. Estienne, Gramm. Franç. p. 108, dans Lacurne." This etymology, which is very faulty, is accepted by M. Littré, who says, "Poix, comme on le voit par l'historique, a le sens propre de *poissard*, et veut dire fripon, vaurien, voleur, dont les doigts se collent aux objets comme de la poix; il s'est particularisé pour exprimer la grossièreté, et, encore davantage, pour exprimer la grossièreté des halles. Mais *poisson*, malgré l'apparence, n'y est pour rien; seulement la persuasion qu'il y était pour quelque chose a determiné le sens que *poissarde* a aujourd'hui."

This happens to be a great mistake. *Poisson* is for *every thing* in *poissarde*, whilst *poix* or *pitch* is for *nothing at all*. *Poissarde* must have first been *poissonarde*, and have then been contracted to *poissarde*, when it literally meant *fishwoman*, just as *poissard* must have meant *fishman*. When at a later period dealers in fish were found to be remarkable for their coarseness of language and manners, ill-bred persons, on being compared to them, were often called after them. But never at first did any such name as *poissard* or *poissarde* imply thieving, nor had it then any relationship whatever with the idea expressed by the word *poix* or *pitch*. Farther back I had occasion to show that a fish was called after the element in which it lives, that is, after water, and that *poisson* and *boisson* are traceable to the same source; this arising from *boisson* also having been named after water, man's universal drink. But *aqua* (water) and *piscis* (a fish) bear so slight a resemblance to each other in form, that when the latter took the name it has now, the word for water must have been very like it. Hence the Latin *piscina* and *piscis* are radically the same word; and *piscina* means not only a reservoir for fish, but for preserving water; it signifies also a place for bathing or swimming, and sometimes, as Quicherat states, a sea. As to the *pisc* of *piscis*, it is but another form of the *poiss* of *poisson*; and *pois* is, by the joining of the O and i, equal to *pass*, and *pass* to *vass* or *wass*; in the latter of which we have the *wass* of *wasser*, German of water. If we drop the O of the *pois* of *poisson*, we obtain another well known word for water; and that it is the same as the *pisc* of *piscis* (fish) is shown by the *pisc* of the Italian *pisciare*, which has the same meaning as the *poiss* of *poisson*, when the O of this radical part of the French word for *fish* is left out. Hence *poissarde* cannot differ from such a form as *pissarde*. The reader must know why the latter word, which is not French, might have very well replaced *poissarde*. It might have done so, he will say, because its radical part means water, conventionally animal water; and though a *poissarde* or fishwoman did not take her name from water of any kind, but from fish, this will account, since fish has been called after water, why *poissard* might as well mean a waterwoman as a fishwoman.

CHAPTER XXXIV.

ETYMOLOGY OF ANIMAL WATER.

Now, though the word in both French and English for animal water is well known to mean a certain kind of water, yet, strange to say, philologists are ignorant of its etymology; that is to say, they know not how it has obtained the name by which it is known. M. Littré's etymology of this word is as follows :—

"Wallon, *pihi;* Prov. *pissar;* Cat. *pixar;* Ital. *picciare* [*pisciare*]; Valaque, *pisà;* Allem. *pissen;* Sued. *pissa;* Angl. *to piss. On ne connaît pas l'origine de ce mot. Diez remarque qu'il n'est pas indigène sur le sol Germanique; il le croit d'origine Romane, et il incline à penser qu'il provient d'une onomatopée; ce qui est vraisemblable.*"

When we regard the p of this word as a substitute for the aspirate, and its *er* as the common ending of all French verbs of the first conjugation, its root *iss* will alone remain, and as the consonant should not now be doubled, *iss* must be reduced to *is;* that is, since i has here O understood, *ois,* which, from O and i composing *a,* makes *as.* But when the O of *ois* was dropped, *is* became the root. Our word for animal water may have therefore appeared at different times, under three forms, namely, *ois, as,* and *is,* which, when the aspirate *h* was represented by p became *pois, pas,* and *pis.* In the second of these three roots, *ois, as, is,* we see the Sanskrit of the verb to *be*, and of which *is* became a contraction; and this confirms our etymology, since the verb to *be* and *water* are, as we have already often seen, expressed alike.

We have now only to observe that all the roots of a language are, like the letters of an alphabet, equal to one another, and that they never differ in meaning save conventionally; and we can then account for the roots of such words as signify water ending with different consonants. The *aq* of *aqua* must be therefore considered as equal to the *as* of *wasser*, of which the W does here but represent the aspirate *h*, so that *as*, or a combination of equal value, must have once had in German the same meaning *wasser* has at present. This remark will also apply to the English *water*, of which *at* is the root.

Now, from knowing as we do that a fish was first called after the element to which it belongs, its name in different languages should be regarded as so many words for water. Fish is therefore the *wass* of *wasser*, and so is the *pisc* of *piscis*, as it is easy to perceive; and *vish, vash* and *wash*, may have been other forms of it. Every one must admit that the German *wasser* and *wash* in English are expressive of kindred ideas, so that if such a form as *fish* can be equal to that of *wash*, it cannot be less so to that of *wass*, radical part of *wasser*. And it is so easy to conceive a close relationship between two such ideas as fish and water, that every one, except a very learned philologist, may well ask if the etymology of fish has not been hitherto known? We answer that it has not; for to give a great many of the words by which it is signified in different languages is not to tell us why a fish was, when first named, called a fish.

M. Littré quotes under *poisson* many of its equivalents in other languages besides French ; but this is all he seems to know of its origin. The last of the words which he gives for *fish* is the Gaelic *iasg*, and this form differs but very slightly from the *uisg* of *uisge*, which in the same language means both water and whisky. But why should a fish have a name not different from that of whisky ? Because whisky is a liquor, and every such idea as liquor or liquid was at first called after water, as we saw farther back. But the more any one is learned in philology as this science has been hitherto known, the more difficult it will be for him to admit the reality of a new etymology. All old philologists should therefore be born over again, and think like little children.

CHAPTER XXXV.

A CHILD'S ETYMOLOGY OF ANIMAL WATER.

I WAS once crossing a bridge with a French family, when a little boy, not yet three years old, was raised by his father to the parapet. The child on beholding the water, exclaimed, " Oh ! *pipi !* " which happens to be the French word used in the nursery for signifying animal water. Upon hearing this child so express itself, I said to the father, " There is an etymology for you ! and one which, in all probability, one of your most learned academicians could not make." And has not the truth of my observation been confirmed by M. Littré's attempt, as we saw a while ago, to discover the original

T

meaning of the word for animal water, and of which *pipi* is the diminutive? But of this diminutive M. Littré does not attempt the etymology; all he says of it is, that it is the "terme enfantin pour designer l'urine. Faire *pipi*, pisser."

The child here referred to is now a brave military man; and if I were to ask him after what *pipi* was first called, I am sure he could not tell, even though it were to save him from being shot. He told it, however, when little more than a baby, and that too without the least effort. Men must, therefore, when they first began to give names to things, have found the task far less difficult than we now imagine; and they would, no doubt, find this task still very easy if they could only bring back the days of their childhood, and always try to think as they did then, while engaged in signifying their thoughts by articulate sounds. As children unchecked are now accustomed to reason with themselves when making words of their own, even so were full grown men accustomed to do at the birth of language. They could not, like the learned philologists of our day, be ignorant of the primary signification of so simple a word as *pipi;* they could as easily tell after what this idea was called, as the child we have referred to has done.

We can now discover many of the words first signifying water by merely knowing the ideas called after it, and of which one or two instances may now be given. We have already shown how in *piscis, poisson* and *fish,* words signifying water may be found; and to these we may here add the same ideas as they are expressed in Hebrew and Greek.

CHAPTER XXXVI.

ETYMOLOGY OF DAGON. A MYTH.

THE Hebrew of fish is signified by these two signs דג *dy*, which, with vowels supplied, are equal to *de-ag*, or *id-ag*, and here, as in דבר *dbr* (word), which is allowed to be for *debur*, the *de* or *id* may be regarded as an article, and as having the meaning of *the*. According to this analysis, the *ag* of *de-ag* is the root of this word, and is for *water;* so that the literal meaning of דג *dg* or *de-ag* is *the water*. In *ag* it is easy to perceive a form equal to *ak* or *aqu*, in the latter of which we have the root of *aqua*. But as every article, whether definite or indefinite, means *one*, as we have shown; *de-ag* may, when it first signified a fish, have meant *one-water;* that is, one belonging to water, or the *water-one*. אג *ag* or a form of equal value must have therefore, as well as ם' *im*, meant *water* in Hebrew, or in one of its dialects.

We should not neglect to notice a myth that has been suggested by the Hebrew of *fish*. The radical part of Dagon is Dag, which is equal to דג *dg*, a *fish ;* and Dagon was, says Parkhurst[6], "The Aleim of the Philistines, mentioned Judg. xvi. 23, 1 Sam. v. and al." And the same authority adds : "From 1 Sam. v. 4, it is probable that the lower part of this idol resembled a *fish*, and it appears plain from the prohibitions, Exod. xx. 4, Deut. iv. 18, that the idolatry in those parts had

Lex. p. 105

anciently some fishy idols, as it is certain they had in later times."

This very gross superstition of worshipping a fish as God, must have arisen from the same word having served to designate both a *fish* and the *sun* at a time when the latter was revered as the supreme divinity. Hence the *dag* of Dagon cannot, from the interchange of g and y, differ from *day*, as is shown by the German *tag*; and *dies* (Latin of day) and Deus are but different forms of the same word. When we do therefore read the *dag* of Dagon from right to left, we get *gad*, which was, according to the learned, one of the names of the sun, as the following will suffice to show: "Meni approaches most nearly to a word used by the prophet Isaiah, which has been understood by the most learned interpreters as meaning the moon. 'Ye are they that prepare a table for Gad, and that furnish the offering unto *Meni*,' Isa. lxv. 11. As Gad is understood of the sun, we learn from Diodorus Siculus that Meni is to be viewed as a designation of the moon[7]."

CHAPTER XXXVII.

WHY FISH AND SAVIOUR HAVE BEEN EXPRESSED ALIKE.

AND that the idea *fish* must have been regarded with favour by the chosen people of God, would seem from the following: "And the head of Dagon, and both the

[7] See Dr. Jamieson's Dictionary, article "Moon."

palms of his hands were cut off upon the threshold; only the *stump* of Dagon was left to him [a]."

According to the marginal note in the Bible, the word *stump* is here used instead of the *fishy part;* by which we are allowed to infer that the part of Dagon which resembled a *fish* was respected. But why so? Because a fish was called after water, and water after life, of which it is a principal support; and life after the sun, the supposed author of existence, and which was anciently, as we have shown from the admissions of the learned, called a Saviour. Hence a fish, though not called after *Saviour,* may have often had a name not different from the one expressing this idea.

Higgins has the following: "Calmet has observed that this word *Dag* means *preserver,* which I suppose is the same as Saviour [b]."

Preserver has, of course, the meaning of *Saviour,* since *preservare* means to *save.* Hence Dagon, whose name does not differ from that of a *fish,* was revered as a Saviour, and for which he might thank his name. Had the word Dagon resembled the one signifying a bull, a horse, or a serpent, he would have been worshipped under the form of one of those animals.

Salt has also suggested many superstitious notions; and why so? because it took its name from the sea, which has been called after water, and because it is constantly used for *saving* or *curing* flesh. It may have therefore been often expressed by a word not different from that meaning *water, fish, saver,* or *saviour.* Holy water, which I once saw made, is nothing more than salt and water blessed by a priest. There are few Roman Catholic families without it in their bed-rooms. Need

[a] 1 Sam. v. 4.　　　　[b] Anacalypsis, vol. i. p. 639.

we now wonder at the primitive Christians having signified their belief in a Saviour, and the faith in which they died, by the figure of a fish on their tombstones. Their faith was also signified, says De Roquefort, by the two first letters of ἰχθύς (a fish), being the initial signs of Jesus Christ.

Calmet also says, in his Dictionary of the Holy Bible, " Among the primitive Christians the figure of a fish was adopted as a sign of Christianity; and it is sculptured among the inscriptions on their tombstones, as a private indication that the persons there interred were Christians. This hint was understood by brother Christians, while it was an enigma to the heathens [1]."

And is not Christ himself somewhere called a *fish*, and were not most of His first followers fishermen, and does not the Pope at the present hour style himself a fisherman ?

Great stress appears to have been laid on the circumstance of Christ having been called a *fish ;* only witness the following : " Jesus is called a fish by St. Augustin, who says he found the purity of Jesus Christ in the word *fish*. ' For He is,' says the saint, ' a fish that lives in the midst of waters.' Paulinus saw Jesus Christ in the miracle of the five loaves and two fishes, ' *who is the fish of the living waters.*' Prosper finds in it the sufferings of Jesus Christ, ' *for He is the fish dressed at His death.*' Tertullian finds the Christian Church in it. All the faithful were with Him; so many fishes bred in the water, and saved by ONE GREAT FISH. Baptism is this water, out of which there is neither life nor immortality. St. Jerome commending a man that desired baptism, tells him that, like the son of a fish, he desires to be cast into the water [2]."

---

[1] See Fragments, No. cxlv. p. 105.   [2] Anacalypsis, vol. i. p. 636.

But the sole cause of this must be ascribed to the circumstance of the three ideas *water, fish,* and *saviour,* having been expressed by the same word. Other causes have, however, been imagined. Thus the author just quoted says, " But I ask, what has Jesus Christ to do with a fish? Why was He called a fish? Why was the Saviour *IHΣ*, which is the monogram of the Saviour Bacchus, called 'Iχθύς. Here are the Saviour, the cycle, and the fish, all identified. The answer is, because emblems of the sun, of that higher power spoken of by Martianus Capella, of which the sun is himself the emblem; or, as Mr. Parkhurst would say, they were types of the Saviour [3]."

It is no such thing. We shall see when we come to consider the name Bacchus, that it does not differ from any word meaning *water* or *fish,* which accounts for this divinity having been called a saviour, and for his having the same monogram as Christ. Bacchus may well be regarded by all true Christians who believe in religious symbols, as a genuine type of the Founder of their holy religion.

CHAPTER XXXVIII.

UNIVERSAL BELIEF IN THE SACREDNESS OF WATER ACCOUNTED FOR.

JUST as we have accounted for a fish having been once revered as a God, even so are we to account for the ancient belief in the sacredness of *water.* I am therefore com-

[3] Anac. p. 636.

pelled to regard the following very profound explanation of this apparent mystery as another great mistake. The real solution of this question is uncommonly simple; taken as a myth, it lies on the surface: " Among all nations, and from the earliest period, *water* has been used as a species of religious sacrament. This, like most of the other rites of the ancients when examined to the bottom, turns out to be founded on very recondite and philosophical principles, equally common in all countries. We have seen that the sun, light, or fire, was the first preserver at the same time that he was the creator and destroyer. But though he was the preserver and the re-generator, it is evident that he alone, without an assistant element, could regenerate nothing, though that element itself was indebted to him for its existence. That element was water. Water was the agent by which every thing was regenerated or born again. Water was in a peculiar manner the great agent of the sun : without the sun, either as light, heat or fire, water would be an adamantine mass.

" Without water the power of the sun would produce no living existence, animal or vegetable. Hence, in all nations, we find the Ἔρως, the Dove, or Divine Love, operating by means of its agent water ; and all nations using the ceremony of plunging, or, as we call it, baptiz-ing for the remission of sins, to introduce the hierophant to a regeneration, to a new birth unto righteousness[4]."

And so this very erudite reasoner continues to account for the ancient and universal belief in the sacredness of water. But when this element was first named it was called after that of which it was a principal support—life. And when this first signification was lost sight of, and when the word for water was perceived to mean not only

[4] Anac. v. i. p. 529.

life, but also *save*—because life was called after the sun, and because the sun had, as we have seen, for one of his many names, that of Saviour—then water was, because of its two meanings—*life* and *save*—believed to have the power of *saving life*. And such was, with the heathen, ages anterior to the Christian era, the origin of baptism. This sacred ceremony was, therefore, typified in very remote times, for the enlightenment of all believers in the truth to be long after revealed. At least so must it be admitted by all the good Christians who have any faith in the doctrine of types.

We have already alluded to the radical identity in Gaelic of the words for *water* and *fish* (*uisge* and *iasg*), and to which I now beg to add the following from Higgins: "In the old Irish, *Ischa*, which is the Eastern name of Jesus, means a *fish*, and the Welsh V, is our single F; and F F is the Welsh F. Ischa with the digamma is F—ischa.

"In addition to what I have said in Book X., chapter iv., section 5, I have to observe, that Buddha was called, not only as we have seen elsewhere Fo or Po, but he was also called Dak or Dag Po—דג *dg*, which was literally the Fish Po, or Fish Buddha Pisces. See Littleton in voce Piscis. The Pope was not only chief of the shepherds, but he was chief of fishermen, a name which he gives himself, and on this account he carries a *poitrine*. On this account also, the followers of Jesus were fishermen. The name Dag Po was evidently Buddha in his eighth or ninth incarnation. The Buddhists, we must remember, claim to have the same number of incarnations as the Brahmins. It is very difficult to discover in what the difference between the two sects consists [5]."

[5] Anac. vol. i. p. 836. See note.

This learned authority does not mistake when he observes that *ischa* becomes with the digamma prefixed, equal to *fish ;* but he did not suspect that *ischa* is also with the digamma equal to *uisge*, which is the Gaelic of *water*, and Irish and Gaelic make, as it were, one and the same language. The identity of the two words is the less difficult to perceive when we remark that the *u* of *uisge* is equal to V, and which is proved by the word *whisky,* of which the *wh* represents the U of *uisge.* As to the digamma referred to on this occasion by Higgins, it does here but represent the aspirate *h.*

CHAPTER XXXIX.

WHY VISHNU IS REPRESENTED COMING OUT OF A FISH.
WHY WATER AND FATHER ARE SIGNIFIED ALIKE.

THIS view is further confirmed by *Vishnu*, who is the Indian Avatar just as Jesus is the Avatar of the Christians. And though Vishnu is represented as coming out of a fish, were it not for the aspirate—here replaced by *v*—he would no doubt be shown as rising out of water. It is scarcely necessary to observe that *vish*, the radical part of Vishnu, is equal not only to *fish*, but to *vash*, or the English verb *wash*, and the *was* of the German *wasser*, water.

There is something deserving of notice in the word *Avatar.* When we drop its initial vowel we obtain *vatar*, which cannot differ from *water*, nor from *vater,*

German of *father*. The identity of two such names as *water* and *father* can be easily explained. Water is, as we have seen, traceable to the idea life, and life to the sun; and *father*, as we shall see, means a *maker*, a well-known name of the sun. Hence though *water* and *father* have neither been called after the other; yet from both belonging to the same source, we can account for the identity of the words by which they are expressed, though such words might differ greatly in form from each other, if their roots had only been different.

CHAPTER XL.

ORIGIN OF THE TRINITY; AN ANCIENT TYPE.

Now, as the word *Avatar* means "the incarnation of the Deity in the Hindoo mythology;" and as this incarnation was the Son, we have thus another proof to add to those to be given farther on of the Father and the Son having been named alike. And this was another beautiful type of what was revealed long after by St. John. But the type does not stop here. In *vater* and *pater* we have the same word, and the radical part of each is *vat* and *pat;* and as the *a* of these two forms must have with different people obtained the nasal sound, it follows that *vat* is equal to *vant*, and *pat* to *pant;* and neither of these can differ from *rent* or *wind*. And wind or breath is, as every one knows, the meaning of *spirit*. And the Holy Spirit, or Spiritus Sanctus, or

Saint Esprit, is the Holy Ghost, ghost being here the same as *gust*, wind. We have thus in the same word *Father*, *Son* and *Spirit*, that is, three in one; so that when man believed in the Word as in God, he could not do less than regard these three persons as making, while being three, only one person. But why was not this doctrine composed of more than three persons? It must have arisen from the identity of two such words as *three* and *true*. Hence, the Saxon of three is *treo*, and this cannot differ from *treow*, which in the same language means *true*. The French say still, *trois fois bon*, by which they mean *très bon;* and *très* is the Latin of *three;* and *très bon* is rendered into English by *very good;* and *very* is the Latin *verus*, true. The French *vrai* is still the same word.

CHAPTER XLI.

ETYMOLOGY OF *ΙΧΘΥΣ*.

It was, no doubt, from *three* and *true* having been thus signified by the same word, that this hitherto mysterious dogma was not made to consist of more than three persons. The pious Christian, he who has the least faith in the truth of Divine symbols, must, from his being well aware that the Trinity can be traced back to the remotest times, receive its having been first known to the heathen as a genuine type of his own blessed doctrine. Farther on I shall be again obliged to refer to this subject, and so confirm still more all I have now said of it.

I have forgotten to analyze ἰχθύς. Its two first letters compose its root; and as they are, from being equal to οιχ, and consequently to αχ, and as this cannot differ from *ak*, nor *ak* from *aqu*, we see that its root is the same as that of *aqua*. And its θ or *th* having a vowel understood before it, ἰχθύς must be equal to *akithos* or a form of the same value, such as *akathos* or *akethas*. And as the common ending *os* is here as an article fallen behind its noun, such a word as *akith* must have long preceded ἀχθύς, and have then meant *water one*, or fish; *ith* having in this case the power of a pronoun, such as *is*, or *id* in Latin, and as *it* in English.

CHAPTER XLII.

CAT AND DOG.

THE etymology of these words leads to several others hitherto unknown.

"The word *cat*," writes M. Max Müller, "the German *katze*, is supposed to be an imitation of the sound made by a cat spitting. But if the spitting were expressed by the sibilant, that sibilant does not exist in the Latin *catus*, nor in *cat* or *kitten*, nor in the German *kater*. The Sanskrit *márjára*, cat, might seem to imitate the purring of the cat; but it is derived from the root *mry*, to clean, *márjára* meaning the *animal that always cleans itself*[a]."

[a] Vol. i. p. 407.

In my humble opinion a cat was never named from its habit of always cleaning itself, but from its being an animal remarkable for its address in *cat*ching or *tak*ing its prey; and I am further of opinion that such too is the primary signification of the word *dog*. And as all such ideas as *cat*ching, *tak*ing, *touch*ing, *tick*ling *hold*ing, *feel*ing, &c., must have been called after the hand, it follows that both *cat* and *dog* are indebted for their names—but indirectly—to this member. Hence according to the grammarian Servius, *catus* or *cattus* meant a *dog* as well as a *cat*. And *catellus*, which is radically the same word, means a *little dog;* and *catella* means not only a *little female dog*, but also a *little chain*. But why a chain? Because a chain is that which holds, and it has for this reason been called after the hand. Hence the resemblance between the French words *chaine* and *chienne*, and radically between *catena* and *cat*, and between *chain* and *canis*. In such a word as *touch*, we see a form equal to *touk*, that is *took*, the preterite of *take*, of which the root *tak* gives, when read from right to left, *kat*, which is equal to *cat*. And if we want to prove that this is no forced etymology, we need only remark that as *tickling* is *touching*, this idea is expressed in French by *chat*ouiller, of which the radical part means *cat*. But how are we to account for *felis*, a cat? by regarding its radical part *fel* as equal to *feel*, which idea must have been called after the hand, and this is confirmed by *felan*, the Saxon of *feel*, of which the root is *fel*. But there is no resemblance, I may be told, between *felis* and *canis*, nor between either of these and *manus*. To which we may reply that the same word does with time take several different forms, as is shown by one sign in an alphabet appearing as some twenty-four or twenty-six very different ones. Be it also observed that we have now no language as it was at its birth, that every one of them, even the most ancient, appears to be only a compound of several others no longer in existence. Thus I have no doubt but *feel* or *fel*, or some such form, must have once been a word for the *hand*, and have belonged to some dialect, in all probability long since forgotten. All we can now expect is to find a sufficient number of proofs for removing all doubt respecting the reality of our conclusions. In *gale* (Greek of *cat*) we see the same root we saw in the English word *glove*, that is, *gal;* so that we need only make its *l* take its form of *n*, and we obtain *gan*, root of *gant* (French of glove), and which is the same as *hant* or *hand*, as we have seen. And if we drop the n (the nasal sound) of *gant*, we obtain *gat*, which is the root of *gatto*, the Italian of *cat*. And read as in Hebrew, *gat* gives *tag*, that is, *dag* or *dog*. The intelligent reader c annot here help observing that in *gat* we have a form equal to the English verb *get*, which means to *obtain*, to *procure*, and this idea also must have been named after the hand. It was anciently written *gat*.

We may regard the genitive of *kuōn* (*konos*) as the original of *canis*, and say that *hund* in Saxon and *hound* in English may be referred to the same source. I learn from Dr. Schuster's German dictionary that *hindan* (an old German verb) means to *seize;* and as this word is equal to *hund* (Saxon and German of hound) it confirms the truth of my etymology; namely, that the dog was, as well as the cat, called after the idea of *cat*ching. As to *hand*, which bears the same form in Saxon, German, and English, no one can doubt of its being the same as *hund*. But how does Dr. Schuster account for its origin? He derives it from the old verb *hindan* (to *take*, to *seize*). This is the common mistake of all etymologists, arising from their ignorance of the origin of language. The hand could not have been named after *hindan;* it was *hindan* that must have been called after the hand; for if we allow *hindan* to be the original, and ask after what this idea was called, no one will be able to tell us without referring it to *hand.* Hand is therefore the original of *hindan,* and not *hindan* the original of hand. Dr. Johnson makes a similar mistake in his etymology of *hunt,* of which he writes : " Hunt, *v.a.* huntian, Sax. from *hund,* a dog." It must be admitted that in *hunt* and *hund* we have the same word ; yet neither of these two ideas received its name from the other, but they were both called after the idea of taking ; and as every such idea has been signified by a word meaning the *hand,* this accounts for the identity (in form) of *hunt* and *hund.*

The following from M. Littré will serve to prove beyond all doubt that to *hunt* has for its primitive signification *taking* or *seizing,* as we have just shown : " On trouve dans Du Cange, *captator,* chasseur, *captare,* chasser, *captatio,* chasse." As *captare* is equal to *capere* (to seize), this affords additional proof that such too is the meaning of to *hunt,* and consequently of *hund* or *hound.* In Latin *captor* means not only he who seizes or takes, as it does in English, but *hunter* also ; and that its root *cap* is equal to a form which must have once named the *hand,* we see on comparing it with the *cap* of the Latin *capo* (a castrated cock); and this must have meant *cut,* which idea was, as we have seen, called after that of *dividing,* primarily of making two parts of a thing, and which took its name from the hand, as already shown. And as *capo* in Latin means not only a *capon*, but an *eunuch* also, this is further proof that *cap* is equal to *cut*. We may therefore consider the *cap* of *capo* or *capon* as but a different form of the *coup* of *couper*, and this *coup* as but a different form of the *cout* of *couteau*, and *cout* as but a different form of *cut* in English. But we should bear in mind that neither the *cat* nor the *dog* was ever named after to *cut*, but after to *capture*, the identity in the form of the names of two such ideas as cutting and capturing arising from their being traceable to the same source, and not from either of them having been called after the other.

Now as by adhering to our principles, the origin of the words of a language of which a person may be said to know little or nothing, may be often traced to their primitive sources far more correctly than even by an educated native; we may perhaps be allowed to take the liberty of noticing the Sanskrit word for *cat*, which M. Max Müller informs us is *márjara*, and that its meaning is "the animal that always cleans itself." When we take *marj* as the radical part of this word, and remark that j had anciently the sound of i as it still has in German, but probably of long *i* as it seems to be composed of double *i ;* we bring it equal to *mari* or *marē*, the latter of which has the same meaning in Greek as *cheir*, that is, *hand*. And the Greek language is, say the learned, of the same family of languages as the Sanskrit. In this case the word in Sanskrit meaning *cat* may mean to *seize* or to *catch*, which ideas have received their names from the hand. It is for M. Max Müller, or some other learned Sanskrit scholar, to tell us if there be any such word. I, who know nothing of Sanskrit, can go no farther. But with respect to the word which in this tongue

U

means to *clean,* that is, *mrij;* and which M. Max Muller
supposes or rather believes, for he does not express a
doubt, to be the real meaning of *cat;* I beg to observe
that every such word is, according to my principles,
traceable to some other word meaning the *sun* or the
heavens, or one which is thence derived.   Thus I regard
clean and *clear* as the same word; and I believe *clear* to
be equal to *calor* (*heat*), though not from its having
been called after this idea, but from its having the
same origin.   That is to say, it belongs to the class of
words that signify the *sun, heavens, light, brightness,* &c.
Now does the Sanskrit word signifying, according to M.
Max Müller, to *clean,* that is, *mrij,* resemble any word
having this meaning ?   I cannot say if there be such a
word in Sanskrit, but I find two or three of them in
Greek, such as *mairō,* which means to *shine,* and consequently to be *clear* and *clean;* and *maira,* which means
the *shiner;* and to which may be added *maritē, live coals,*
and *mario,* to *have a fever;* all of which, though of different acceptations, are of the same class, and have the
same origin.   Another word which, in primary signification, is still the same, is *puretos* (the *burning or heat
of a fever*), and of which the root *pur* (*five*) is equal to
purus in Latin and to *pure* in English; and to be *pure*
is to be *clean* and *clear.*   Hence *purus* is explained not
only by *pure,* but by *limpid* also.   The French word
pourpre (*purple*) belongs to the same class, and is but a
different form of *propre, clean,* because it means what is
bright, clear, and *shining.*   Even the English word *fair,*
as in *fair* hair, *fair* complexion, is still the same word;
that is, radically; because meaning what is *light* or
clear.

   Now the Sanskrit word *mrij* (to *clean*) being traceable

to the same class of words to which *clear* and *clean* do also belong, I am strongly inclined to believe that M. Max Müller has made a great mistake in supposing that *mârjâra*, a *cat*, and the *mrij*, to *clean*, are radically the same word; their difference in meaning being as considerable as that which we perceive between the verbs to *capture* and to *clean*.

The latter etymologies must, as well as all the others by which they have been preceded, suggest many pertinent questions which I may not be able to answer, though it may be in the power of others to do so, and still by the application of my own principles. All I lay claim to is to have pointed out to others the way they should go, if they would further explore this hitherto unknown land upon which I have myself but barely entered, though having, however, gone sufficiently far into it to justify the pretensions I entertain as its first discoverer.

To give an instance of one of these pertinent questions I might be required to answer, it will be sufficient to mention the noun *chase*, in which I might be asked to show a form equal to any of the words significant of *taking*, which is the meaning I have assigned to names for *hand, hound, dog,* and *cat.* And if I were to admit that I could not perceive how the noun *chase* could be shown to be but a different form of word signifying the ideas here mentioned, some one else might find it very easy. Thus he might say, that according to one of my rules every vowel is susceptible of a nasal sound, and that *chas*, root of *chase*, is therefore equal to *chans*; that is, as two consonants have a right to a vowel between them, *chanis*, which as *ch* is reducible to C (witness *chat* in French, and *cat* in English), cannot differ from *canis*,

Latin of *dog,* and which I have already fully accounted for.

Some one else might say that he saw in the *chas* of *chase,* the word *cat* itself, and confirm thus his etymology. There is only one letter in the alphabet, and though this one letter takes some twenty-four different forms, yet some of these forms often interchange with others, and *s* and *t* do so very frequently; witness *besser* and *wasser* in German being *better* and *water* in English; and *glossa* and *thalassa* in Greek being also in this tongue *glotta* and *thalatta;* hence there can be no difference between the *chas* of *chase* and *chat.* And when we give, according to our rule, the nasal sound to the *a* of *chat,* we obtain *chant;* which, as the *c* of *ch,* may be dropped, brings *chant* equal to *hant,* that is, *hand, hound,* &c.

And if I be asked to give an instance justifying the liberty here taken of dropping the *h* of *ch,* as done to bring *chat* equal to *cat,* and now dropping the *c* in order to bring *chant* equal to *hant, hand,* &c., and if I were to answer that an instance of no such liberty occurred to me; might not some one else find one, and adduce the French word *chez* as a proof of what he advanced; for this word is known to be equal to the *cas* of *casa, house,* its h being dropped. But if we drop the c, this *cas* will become *has,* which cannot differ from *hus* (Saxon of *house*) any more than *farther* can differ from *further.*

And if I be asked to account for the *chase* in *purchase* as I have accounted for the noun *chase* in the sense of *hunt,* I may be greatly puzzled to do so; but some one more capable of applying my principles than I am myself may find this very easy. Such a one may say that as a thing purchased is a thing taken, the *chase* of purchase can be traced as easily to the hand for its origin as cat and dog have been. Thus he may say that in the French of purchase, which is *achat*, we have the word *cat* itself, its initial *a* having the power of *ad* in Latin, of *at* in English, and of *à* in French; so that the entire word may be explained by *purchased*, or as the French would have it, *pourchassé*, there being such an infinitive in this tongue (though we hear it no longer) as *pourchasser*. If purchase were to be rendered literally into English, it might be said to mean a *to-take;* that is, a thing *to take,* or *a taking.* And as *chase* has been shown to be equal to *chate,* that is, *chat,* and as this is the same as *cat,* and *cat* the same as *cut,* and *cut* the same as the *coup* of *couper,* it follows that *chat* cannot differ from the *chap* of *chap*man, which means a buyer. The *cheap* of *cheapen* is still the same word, as its Saxon form *ceapan* means simply to *buy;* Johnson shows it to have had this meaning in English also.

Now as it may be very properly observed that we cannot bring *chap* equal to *chat* without bringing also the *cheap* of *cheapen* equal to *cheat,* I may be asked if this word, which implies *deception,* should be also considered as meaning to *take.* In order to return a satisfactory answer to this apparent objection and difficulty, we should remember what has been already made self-evident, namely, that not only to *take* but to *cut* was named after the hand; and there is a word in English precisely equal to *cut,* which is *cute,* now generally replaced by *acute;* and that the idea of *cheating* must have been called after *cutting,* or, which is the same thing, after *acuteness,* can be thus proved beyond all doubt: what *cuts* is *sharp,* and a *sharper* is a *cheat.* And further be it observed that *catus* in Latin means not only, as has been shown, either a *cat* or a *dog,* but also

acute, sharp, or *subtle,* its root *cat* being equal to
the *cut* of *acutus,* past participle of *acuo* to *cut.* And
still further be it observed that *cute* is synonymous
with both keen and cunning, and that as *keen* means
what is *sharp,* so must cunning, of which the root *cun*
is but a different form of *keen.* It therefore appears
from both *keen* and *cun* being equal to *can,* and *cute* to
the *cat* of *catus,* that in *cute, keen,* or *cunning,* we have
words equal, when radically considered, to *catus* and
canis; this arising not from the cat or the dog having
received its name from the idea of *cutting* or *cunning,*
but from the idea of *taking* or *catching,* which, like that
of *cutting,* was called after the hand; whence the radical
identity of their names.

There appears to be no word of which the primary
signification has been hitherto less known than that of
cat. Several French philologists derive it from *catus,*
meaning *acute, sharp,* or *subtle.* This mistake arose
from its not having been known after what the ideas
of taking, catching, and cutting have been named. It
is radically the same word in a great many languages.
Court de Gébelin says : " Ce mot est 1° de tous les
dialectes Celtes, Irlandais, Gallois, Basque, et s'y prononce *cat.* 2° de tous les] dialectes Teutons, Ang.,
Flam., Allem. 3° Il est Latin, Grec, Finlandais, Turc,
Arménien, Ital., Esp., &c., même Heb. חתול, *hatul.* Il
tient au Latin *catus,* rusé, prudent [7]."

M. Littré avoids the mistake of deriving *chat* from
catus, meaning *acute, sharp,* or *subtle* ; but attributes
its origin to *catus* or *cattus,* in the sense of *cat.* He
does not, however, tell us what was the first meaning
given to *catus* or *cattus.* But this cannot, in any way,

[7] Dict. Etymologique de la Langue Française.

take from the merit of so eminent a lexicographer:
without our principles, it were not possible for him or
any one else to trace such an idea to its real source.

The following is all he says of its etymology: " Wallon, *chet;* Bourguig. *chai;* Picard, *cu. co.;* Provenç.
c a t ;Catal. *gat;* Espagn. et Portug. *gato;* Ital. *gatto;*
du Latin *catus* ou *cattus,* qui ne se trouve que dans des
auteurs relativement récents, Palladius, Isidore, et qui
était un mot du vulgaire. Il appartient au Celtique et
à l'Allemand: Irl. *cat;* Kymri, *kath;* Angl. Sax. *cat;*
ancien Scandin. *kottr;* Allem. mod. *katze.* D'après
Isidore, *cattus* vient de *cattare,* voir, et cet animal est dit
ainsi parce qu'il voit, guette; *catar,* regarder, est dans
le Provençal et dans l'ancien Français, *chatar.* Mais on
ne sait à quoi se rattachent ni *cattus* ni *catar;* la tardive
apparition qu'ils font dans le Latin porte à croire qu'ils
sont d'origine Celtico-germanique. Il y a dans l'Arabe
quittoun, chat mâle, mais Freitag doute que ce mot ap-
partienne à l'Arabe."

I perceive I have omitted, in noticing the ideas named
after the hand, to give a very plain proof of a word signifying *seizing* or *taking* having been thence derived. This
is shown by *prehendere* in Latin, of which the radical
part *prehend* is clearly for *perhand,* that is, *by hand;* so
that the French verb *comprendre* may be explained by to
seize, prendre being its root; and this is confirmed by
the Italian of *comprendre* being *capire,* as this cannot
differ from *capere* in Latin, meaning to *seize, cap* being
the root of each word, and not differing from *cat* any more
than the *coup* of *couper* can differ from the *cout* of *couteau.*

This etymology, which is very easy, will lead to one
much less so; namely, *præda* (a prey), of which the
radical part, *præd* is, from its *æ* receiving the nasal sound,

equal to *prænd*; and this, like the *prehend* of *prendere*, means also *by hand*; so that *præd* means *what is taken or seized.* Hence *prædo*, a *robber,* means simply *one who takes*, but in a bad sense; and *prædor*, to *rob*, being radically the same word, may be explained by to *seize* or *take*, and still in a bad sense.

The following mistake made by Dr. Johnson in his etymology of *cheat,* is another striking proof of the advantage to be derived from the discovery of principles by the application of which the real origin of words may, for the future, be made known to all who feel desirous of obtaining such information : " Cheat, *n. s.* some think abbreviated from *escheat,* because many fraudulent measures being taken by the lords of manours in procuring escheats, *cheat,* the abridgment, was brought to convey a bad meaning."

We should also notice what he says of the verb to cheat : " Of uncertain derivation ; probably from *acheter,* Fr. to *purchase* ; alluding to the tricks used in making bargains : see the noun."

It is true that in *cheat* and *acheter* there is radically, as we have shown, the same word, but in meaning they are widely different ; *cheat* being deducible from *cut* to *cute, acute* ; that is, *sharp,* whence *sharper,* a *cheat* ; and *acheter* having simply, as we have also shown, the meaning of to *take.* But no one ever saw more clearly than this great man the sense in which words are generally used. Thus, in defining the verb to *cheat,* he says, " It is used commonly of low *cunning.*" Still very true ; but he little suspected that in the *cun* of *cunning* we have a different form of *keen,* which means *sharp* ; so that a sharper might, did custom allow it, be called a *keener.* I recommend the word to all the lovers and professors of slang. I doubt if they have in their language one more expressive. Dr. Johnson, had he been acquainted with our rule, that one vowel may be replaced not only by any other vowel but by a combination of vowels, could not have failed to perceive in the *u* of the *cun* of *cunning* the *ee* of *keen ;* and this would have also enabled him to discover that the literal meaning of *knife* is a *keener*, a *cutter ;* but the knowledge of another rule, namely, that two consonants may have one or two vowels understood between them, would still be necessary in order to show how a knife has such a meaning. Thus this word with *ee* inserted between its *k* and *n,* becomes *keenife,* by which its radical meaning of *keen* is brought to light, whilst it is concealed by these two letters being left out. Now if we insert a single vowel, the first of the five, for instance, we discover something else, *kanife,* that is, *canif,* French of penknife; by which we see that *pen* does not, as in English, form a part of this word, and that its only meaning is *knife.* The *can* of *can*if is also but a different form of *keen.*

Now as the edge, and consequently the *sharp* part of a knife, is expressed in French by *fil* (a thread), I am inclined to believe that the literal meaning of the word *filou* (a *thief*) is a *sharper*, and that such also is our word *filcher,* which Entick defines thus : " a thief, rogue, cheat." I cannot help recommending this etymology of mine to M. Littré for the second edition of his noble dictionary. He gives several etymologies and conjectures from the learned respecting the origin of *filou,* but all of them are very unsatisfactory, as he himself admits, and Dr. Johnson is equally puzzled and candid in his attempts to account for *filcher.* Respecting this word, one of the meanings assigned to it by old Entick, as we have seen, is *cheat*, which I have shown to be equal to *cut*, and *cut* to have the meaning of *sharp*, root of *sharper;* so that from a filcher meaning a *cheat*, and from a cheat meaning a *sharper*, it follows, if *filou* and *filcher* be, as they apparently are, radically the same, that the first meaning ever attached to the word *filou* must have been that of *sharper*.

On referring to M. Littré's many definitions of the word *fil* (*thread*), and in which he never alludes to *filou*, he assigns to it not only the meaning of *sharp* (le tranchant d' un instrument coupant), but also the meanings of *keen, cunning,* and *cheating,* as the following will serve to show : " avoir le fil, être fin, rusé. Je connais ce fil-là, je connais cette ruse, cette tromperie. C'est un fil de commissaire, c'est une ruse qui a la prétention d'être très-adroite. Il a le fil d'un commissaire, il est très adroit."

Thus I have, I feel convinced, discovered for the French the original meaning of *filou*. I should observe that among the conjectures of philologists about the probable original of *filou*, M. Littré quotes the English words *file, fellow,* and *filch,* and the Greek words, *phēlētēs* and *philētēs, robber,* and *pheloō, to deceive.* He considers all these, however, as mere conjectures; and he concludes by observing that *filou* may be "un terme populaire ou d'argot venu directement de *filer."* But this is still nothing more than conjecture, proof is wanting : even if all these words were admitted to be radically the same as *filou*, we should be as far off as ever from its primitive meaning. We should never consider the mere circumstance of a word of one language being exactly the same, or nearly the same, as its equivalent in another language, as an etymology deserving of notice, if we cannot show how the meaning attached to either of them was at first obtained. What am I the wiser for knowing that *cheat* in English is *ceatt* in Saxon, if I know not after what idea *cheat* or *ceatt* was first called? Yet dictionaries of great pretensions are, in general, full of such etymologies. The English word *file*, suggested as the original of *filou*, seems to be a great mistake; and for this reason; namely, that had there never been such an instrument as a *file*, we should still have the word *filou*. Yet as a file is a thing of which the use is to *cut* and *sharpen*, and as a *filou* is a *sharper*, the two words may be said to have the same radical meaning; but which meaning would have been given to *filou*, had there never been a file. We may hence conclude, that when two words agree in both form and meaning, this should not be taken as a proof that either of them was named with reference to the other. *Feliculus*, which in Latin means a *little cat*, is also suggested among M. Littré's quotations as probably the original of *filou*; and we do admit that a word for *cat* may be also a word for *filou*. But why so? Because a *cat* was called after the idea of *taking*, and a *filou* or *sharper* after the idea of *sharpness*, and both these ideas (*taking* and *sharpness*) can, as we have seen, be traced to the hand, and it is only to this circumstance we should attribute their similarity in form whenever they *happen* to be expressed alike, or nearly so.

We may here end our notice of the words *cat* and *dog*; during which we have been so fortunate as to make, through the application of our principles, several other important etymologies. M. Max Müller should not have gone to the Sanskrit verb to *clean* in search of the original sense of cat. As the animal so named is very clever at *cat*ching its prey, M. Max Müller should have confined his views to the English verb to *cat*ch, in which we see the noun *cat* itself.　But this would be too simple and natural; learned philologists greatly prefer what is outlandish to what they find at home.　But if rats, mice, and poor little birds could speak, they would, I have no doubt, assure M. Max Müller with tears in their eyes, that however addicted the cat may be to licking, it is not less so, they are sorry to say, to *catching*, and that, for this reason, it was very properly called a *cat*, that is a *catcher*.

CHAPTER XLIII.

ESPIÈGLE.

EVERY philologist should endeavour to think for himself, and not believe as implicitly as he generally does in old etymologies; especially in those which have been long supposed to give the primary meanings of words. The etymology of the well-known French noun *espiègle* is, as it is given by Ménage, thought to be faultless, and hence it is copied by De Roquefort, M. Max Müller, even by M. Littré, and, of course, by every one else who has taken notice of it.　The origin of this word has, however, been entirely unknown to them all, as I am now going to show.　The account given of it by Ménage is as follows :—

" Un Allemand du pays de Saxe, nommé Till Ulespiègle, qui vivait vers 1480, était un homme célèbre en petites fourberies ingénieuses. Sa vie ayant été composée en allemand, on a appelé de son nom un fourbe ingénieux. Ce mot a passé ensuite en France, dans la même signification, cette vie ayant été traduite et imprimée avec ce titre : Histoire joyeuse et récréative de Till Ulespiègle, le quel par aucunes fallaces ne se laissa surprendre ni tromper." Quoted by M. Littré, under the word *espiègle*.

"Espiègle, enfant vif, malin, subtil, éveillé. De l'allemand *eulen-spiegel*, miroir des hiboux, des songes creux, composé de *eule*, hibou, et de *spiegel*, miroir[8]."

M. Max Müller's origin of *espiègle* is still more precise and positive: "The Latin *speculum, looking-glass,* became *specchio* in Italian; and the same word, though in a roundabout way, came into French as the adjective *espiègle, waggish.* The origin of this French word is curious [more curious than you imagine, my dear sir]. There exists in German a famous cycle of stories, mostly tricks played by a half-historical, half-mythical character of the name of Eulenspiegel, or Owl-glass. These stories were translated into French, and the hero was known at first by the name of Ulespiègle, which name contracted afterwards into Espiègle, became a general name for every wag[9]."

Nor does M. Littré entertain the least doubt respecting the reality of this derivation of *espiègle*. Thus alluding to the advantage of the historical account given of the words in his Dictionary, he dwells particularly on *espiègle* in the following terms : "Il est encore un autre service que l'historique rend à l'étymologie, c'est de lui signaler les cas où un mot s'établit par une circon-

---

[8] De Roquefort, Dictionnaire Etymologique.

[9] Lectures on the Science of Language, vol. i. p. 292.

stance fortuite. Dans l'ignorance de cette circonstance, on s'égare à mille lieues, cherchant à interpréter par la décomposition ou par la ressemblance un mot qui, d'origine, ne tient ni par la forme ni par le sens à aucun élément de la langue. Si l'on ne savait que espiègle vient d'un recueil allemand de facéties intitulé Eulen-spiegel (le miroir de la chouette) où n'irait-on pas en cherchant à ce mot une étymologie plausible[1]?"

Now as M. Littré informs us in the body of his Dictionary, that *spiek* is, in Wallon, for *espiègle*; and as Wallon is nothing more than very old French, he thus tells us how in his own language espiègle was first written. But *spiek* is precisely equal to *spieg*, and *spieg* to the *espieg* of *espiègle*; and as g and y frequently interchange, it follows that *spieg* is equal to *spiey*, and *espieg* to *espiey*; that is, *spy* and *espy*. And *spy* and *espy* are each for *espier* (now *épier*) in French; and the primary sense of each of these words is to *look*, but conventionally, to *look keenly*, to *discover*. And this meaning corresponds with Dr. Johnson's definition of *espy*, his words being: "To discover a thing intended to be hid." If there be not now in German such a verb as *spiegen*, it must have once been in this language, or a form of equal value. And we may say that *spähen* is this word, for its earlier form must have been *spoihen*, of which the radical part is *spoih*, and this is equal to both *spy* and *espy*. And the meaning given of *spähen* is "to *observe attentively*, to *discover*," which is precisely equal to Dr. Johnson's definition of *espy*, as just shown. The following from M. Littré, given under *épier*, is still the same: "Observer attentivement, essayer de découvrir, de pénétrer."

[1] Preface, p. 34.

And how well these meanings of the verb to *spy* or
espy suit the character given of Till Ulespiègle in the
passage we have quoted from Ménage : " Lequel par
aucunes fallaces ne se laissa surprendre ni tromper ;"
that is to say, he *spied* so well and so closely that he
was never duped, never taken in by any kind of
trickery.

An *espiègle* is therefore a spy, but conventionally a
facetious one ; and it is for this reason but a different
acceptation of *espion*, both words being radically the
same. And that the primary sense is spying, and that
spying is nothing more than looking, but conventionally
with a keen eye, appears self-evident. And that there
can be no real difference between spying and looking,
save conventionally, M. Littré himself must admit, on
reading his own words, in the body of his Dictionary, at
the end of his etymology of *espiègle* : " On remarquera
que l'Allemand *spiegel*, miroir, est le Latin *speculum*, d'où
le Provençal *espeth* ; Espagn. *espejo* ; Ital. *specchio* ;" for
these words, in which it is easy to perceive other forms
of *spy* and *espy* are rendered into English not as they
might be, by *spy*-glass, but *looking*-glass ; by which it
is shown that to *spy* means to *look*, but in a different
way, though, when radically considered, there can be no
difference whatever between to spy and to look.

I do therefore conclude that it is a great mistake to
suppose that *espiègle*, or a word of similar form and
import, was first introduced into France after the
manner philologists have hitherto so positively asserted.
Frenchmen have been always too keen, humorous, and
witty, to have remained until late in the fifteenth century
without such a character as is expressed by the word
espiègle. In all times there must have been hundreds of

such characters in France, and consequently a common name by which they were all well known. Your German is a much more serious character than your lively Frenchman, and it were consequently far more reasonable to suppose that such a word as *espiègle* first travelled from France to Germany than that it first travelled from Germany to France. But this opinion is of minor consideration. The main object of this inquiry has been to prove—and it has been proved—that *espiègle* is but a different acceptation of *espion*, and that its verbal form is *espier* (*épier*) in French, and *espy* in English ; and that its eldest known equivalent is, according to M. Littré, *spiek*, that is, in Wallon, which is very old French. *Espiègle* cannot, therefore, owe its first appearance in France to the history of the life and adventures of a German character named Eulenspiegel. It is a word probably as old as either *spy* or *espion*, or it may, for aught any one knows, be a great deal older.

Let us now endeavour to account for the origin of the root of *espiègle*. As the primary sense of this word is that of *spying*, it is easy to conceive that such an idea must have been first signified by a word naming the *eye,* this being the organ by means of which the act of spying, seeing, or looking, is effected. If we now regard *iegle* as the radical part, but not the root, of *espiègle*, we know that such a word cannot, according to the principles of our discovery, differ from *iogle*, nor *iogle*, when its first vowel is dropped, from *ogle*, which, as an English verb, means *to eye,* but conventionally *to eye* in a certain way, that is, sideways. But *ogle* being only the radical part of *espiègle*, we have to find its root, and this can be no other than *og;* so that the *le* with which *ogle* ends must be an article fallen behind its noun. There was, therefore, a time when *ogle* was *le og*, and when its meaning was *the eye*. But this article *le* appears to have been previously *el*, the German of looking-glass being spieg*el* and not spieg*le*. But when we allow the words *le og* or *el og* to coalesce, we shall obtain *leog* or *elog*, the latter being, when its *e* is dropped, equal to *log*. Now, the word for *eye* in Dutch being *oog*, we see that neither *leog* nor *log* can differ from *loog*; and as g takes often the form of k, what is *loog* but *look?* When we do therefore analyze *look* (*el ook*), we discover that it literally means *the eye*. Hence, to *look* at any thing is simply to *eye* it.

By the latter etymology we are led to perceive that *ogle* is the same as *okle*, and consequently as *ocle*, in which it is easy to discover a different form of the *ocul* of *oculus*, Latin of *eye*. In *ogle, look,* and the *ocul* of *oculus*, we have therefore but three different forms of the same word; and this may be also said of the root of each of these forms, that is, of *og, ook,* and *oc*. There was therefore a time when *oculus* was only *oc;* but when was that? Really I cannot say; but there is one thing of which I am very certain—it was not yesterday !

If we be now asked after what in nature the idea *eye* was called, I answer after *light*, and *light* having been called after the *sun*, it follows that the two objects, *eye* and *sun*, may, while language was yet in its infancy, have had the same name, with some slight difference for the sake of distinction; and which difference could be obtained by allowing different consonants to be heard on sounding the O. Hence in the picturesque language of low life, a man's eyes are not unfrequently styled his day-lights. A similar figure of speech is used in France by persons of the same rank. Thus when one Frenchman of the lower orders tells another that he will blind him

x

of an eye, one of his favourite locutions is, " qu'il va lui boucher un quinquet ;" that is, extinguish one of his lamps. Another proof that the *eye* has been named after light is this, that when a man is blind he is said to live in darkness, so that he who has the use of his eyes may be said to live in light.

Though a word serving to designate the eye may end with a guttural sound, as we have seen by *og*, *ok*, and *oc*, it might as well end with one of a very different kind. Thus we see by the *op* of *ops*, a word in Greek meaning the *eye*, that it ends with a labial ; and we see by the *eid* of *eidō*, of the same language, that the word for the eye ends now with a dental, for it is evident since *eidō* means to see, that this idea must, as well as spying and looking, have been called after the eye. And that a word for eye might have no consonant after it, is shown by the English verb to *see*, of which the root is *ee*, and it is so expressed in the language of Scotland. Dr. Johnson's definition of *to see* is therefore very correct, his words being "to perceive by the eye." But how is the *s* of *see* to be accounted for ? By remarking that as every initial vowel may take the aspirate h, *ee* (eye) must have once been *hee*, and that then by the aspirate having been replaced, as it often is, by *s*, *see* was obtained. It is in the same way we should account for the *v* of the *vid* of the Latin *video*, to see ; for this *vid* may be said not to differ from the *eid* of its Greek equivalent *eidō*, but by its initial vowel having taken the aspirate, and by this aspirate having been then not replaced by *s* but by *v*, by which it is also often represented.

These latter observations remind me that I should now account for the non-radical part of *espiègle ;* that is, for *esp*, *eigle* being, as we have seen, its radical part, though not its root, which is *eig*, as we have also seen. We know that there are several consonants that take an *s* before them, and that *p*, as we saw farther back, is one of those consonants, *pike* having in this way become *spike*. And *spike* might as well have been *espike*, which arises from an initial *s* being sounded as if it were written *es*, and such is the exact pronunciation of its name. This explanation will suffice for the presence of the *e* in the *esp* of *espiègle*, so that we have now only the *p* to account for; and this we do in the same way we have accounted for the *s* of *see*, and the *v* of *video*; that is to say, it has grown out of the aspirate, but probably indirectly; for the first change for the aspirate may have been *f* or *v*, each of which is often replaced by *p*. Now there being no difference between the *piègle* of *espiègle* and *viègle*, any more than there is between *April* in English and *Avril* in French, we may be sure that the root of this word, that is, *eig*, must have often been *vieg*, and as *g* is the same as *y*, *vieg* cannot differ from *voy*; that is, from the root of *voir*, of which the *i* must have been often *y*. In *vieg* we see also by the dropping of its *e*, the *vig* of *vigil* and *vigilant*, which idea must be traced to the *eye* as its primary source. In *ieg* we further see not only *eag*, which is the Saxon of *eye*, but since *g* and *y* are equal to each other, the word *eye* itself; for the root of the latter is *ey*, which, from its being the same as *eg*, is but different form of *eag*. Nor does the latter, though Saxon, differ in the least from the French *voy*, the ancient root of *voyr*, now *voir*. And this is confirmed by *eag*, when this word becomes by means of the aspirate *veag*; for *veag* cannot, as its *e* may be dropped, differ from *vag*, which is the same as *voy*, the latter having *i* understood with its *o*, so that it may be fairly represented by *voiy*, and consequently by both *voig* and *vag*, the latter being obtained by *o* and *i* coalescing and making *a*.

Another idea called after the eye, is *wink*, since to wink is to make use of the eye in a certain way. And as we may, when it suits, drop the nasal sound, *wink* cannot differ from *wik*, nor *wik* from *woik*, nor *woik* from *wak*, which is the root of *wake*, that is, *awake*, an idea that must, like *wink*, be also traced to the eye, as can be easily admitted. And by this etymology we confirm the one given above, showing that the *vig* of *vigil* and *vigilant* should be also considered as being a word for the eye; for the Latin of to *wake* is *evigilo*, of which the root is also *vig*, the *e* with which *evigilo* begins being no more of its root than the *a* of *awake* is a part of the root of *wake*. This etymology of awake is also confirmed by its root *wak* having already come out under its form of *wag* in several of the etymologies just given. And all this is still more powerfully confirmed by the important fact, namely, that *wag* happens to be the English of *espiègle*, as every French and English dictionary testifies. M. Max Müller little thought when telling his English readers, as we have seen in the passage quoted from him, that *espiègle* means a *wag*, he was then giving the real etymology of this word of which the origin has been hitherto so utterly unknown.

Now, on reading over my etymology of *espiègle* in order to correct mistakes and supply observations that should not be omitted, I have not, I perceive, accounted for the *us* of *oculus*. But it is nothing more than an additional article fallen behind *ocul*. *Oculus* must have therefore once been *os* or *us ocul*, and have then meant *the eye*, when by transposition *os* or *us ocul* became *oculus*. This word has, therefore, two articles attached to its root *oc*.

We have seen how the *ee* of *see* is in Scotch a word for the eye, and that it does not, like the *og* of *ogle*, nor the *oc* of *oculus*, end with a guttural sound, though this might very well be. Hence, when we do make it so end, that is, write *seeg* or *seec* instead of *see*, we discover the etymology of *seek*, and which is confirmed by this word meaning to *look* for; that is, to *see* for. Hence to *seek* any thing is to *see* for it; literally, to *eye* for it; just as in to *look* for any thing we have, also *il ook*, the eye. But as the *eek* of *seek* is precisely equal to the *ook* of *look*, why have we not, it may be asked, *sook* instead of *seek?* Simply because double *o* took the form of double *e*, just as the double *o* of *blood* became the double *e* of *bleed*. But this implies, I shall be told, that there must have been such a word as *sook*, or a form very like it; and there has, no doubt, been such a word, and which is made evident by the past time of *seek* being *sought;* for the *soug* of this word can no more differ from *soog* than the French word *troupe* can differ from *troop* in English; and *soog* is the same as *sook*. As to the *ht* of *sought*, it is nothing less than a corruption of *ed*, so that *sought* is for *sooked;* and, for the same reason, when the *oo* of *sook* is replaced by *ee*, *seek* in its past time should be *seeked*. And this analysis is confirmed by the logical language of children, who often use *seeked* for *sought*.

I have said that the eye has been called after light; and is not this confirmed by the word *sight*, which cannot differ from *light*, the *s* and the *l* with which both these words (*sight* and *light*) begin, not belonging to the root of either; for the former (the *s*) does but represent the aspirate *h*, and the latter (the *l*) is the remains of such an article as *il* or *el*. Hence when deprived of these two adjuncts (*s* and *l*), both sight and light are reduced each to *ight*, of which the root is *ig*, and as one vowel may represent not only any other vowel but any combination of vowels, *ig* can differ neither from the *og* of *ogle*, nor from *oog*, the Dutch of *eye*. According to this reasoning *sight* might as well have been written *sought*, by which the etymology of the former is confirmed, since the latter has, under its form *seek*, been traced, as just shown, to the eye.

But how, it may be asked, can sight and sought (two different parts of speech) be equal to each other? From a past participle having at the time been used as a noun. *Vu* is in French the past participle of *voir;* but it cannot differ from *vue*, which means *sight*. In English it is the participle present that is often used as a noun. Witness *the eating and drinking;* which in French would be now *le manger et le boire;* that is, the infinitive instead of the past participle. All this tends to prove that a verb is nothing more than a noun used verbally, and which I shall have occasion to prove farther on.

We should also show how it happens that *wag*, as the English of *espiègle*, and not differing, when radically considered, from a word for the eye, is, when a verb, significant of motion. Thus to wag the head, means to move it, but, conventionally, from side to side. But though these two words, the noun *wag* and the verb to *wag* are written and pronounced alike, yet they are otherwise no way related, though having the same root. The cause of their identity in form can be thus accounted for: the root of the verb to *wag*, that is, *ag*, is the root of the Latin *ago*, to act; and as this idea implies motion, it is, for this reason, to be traced to the sun, this object having been revered as the author of existence, and consequently of life and motion. And as we have already shown how *espiègle* has been called after the act of spying, and how this idea has been called after the eye, and the eye after light, and light after the sun, we thus prove the noun *wag*, which cannot differ from *eig* (root of *espiègle*), to be traceable to the same source (the sun) as the *ag* of *ago*, to act, and consequently to move; this root *ag* having, by the change of the aspirate *h* (which its vowel must have taken) for v, become *vag*, and then by the frequent interchange of v and w, *wag*.

But as we have already shown *wag* to be equal to the *wak* of *wake* and *awake*, and as *watching* and *watchfulness* are signified by such words, may we not suspect that here too the idea was named after the eye? And that so it was can be thus proved—But we should first observe that the *t* in *watch* is superfluous, just as it is in *satchel*, which ought to be written *sachel;* that is *sackel*, or *little sack*. The *t* has not been here inserted but that *ch* might be sounded *satch*, just as it is in *church*. Hence the German of the verb to watch is *wachen*. *Wach* is therefore the root of *watch;* and this must have been once only *ach*, the *w* having, as in *wake*, grown out of the aspirate, which must have once preceded the *a* of this root, *ach*. And such a form as *ach* is equal to *oich, och* or *oc;* by which we come upon the *oc* of *oculus*, and so discover that *wach* (not *watch*) is but another word for the *eye*. And if·any reader should doubt the equality of c and *ch*, that doubt must be removed when he observes that our word *rock* is rendered into French both by *roc* and *roche*. Another instance of the kind is afforded by *calling* and *challenge;* for when one friend has a mind to murder, after an honourable way, some other friend, it may be said with equal propriety that he has *called* him out, or that he has *challenged* him.   Hence a *challenge* is literally a *calling*, the word *out* being understood.

And these observations suggest others, of which we may notice one or two.   Thus we have traced the noun wag to the *eye*, the *eye* to *light*, and *light* to the *sun*; and the verb to *wag* has, as just shown, been traced to the same source; but *bag*—which can no more differ from *wag*, whether the latter be used as a noun or a verb, than Bill, the familiar of William, can differ from Will—cannot, I may be told, be traced to the sun either directly or indirectly.   It is, however, a mistake to think so.   A bag is something that contains, that holds; and this idea has been called after the hand, and the hand after the idea of making, and making, as already shown, after the supposed maker of all things, namely, the sun.   Thus a *bag* and the *sun* have been named alike, though neither has been called after the other.

Another observation suggested by our account of *espiègle*, is the following: We have seen how in the root of *vigil* and *vigilant*, that is, in *vig*, we have, when its *v* (grown out of the aspirate *h*) is dropped, a word for the eye; but how are we, when the v of the French word *veiller* (to watch) is dropped, to find in its root *eil* a word for the eye? for we should remark that in the Latin *vigilo* and the French *veiller* we have but two different forms of one word, so that if a word meaning the eye is in either of these forms, so ought it to be in the other.   And so it is.   Thus *œil* (the French of eye) becomes with *v* (the equivalent of the aspirate *h*) *vœil*, and this cannot differ from the *veil* of *veiller*, which must have been once written *œiller*, and have then had the literal meaning of to *eye*. The French academy should therefore write *vœiller* and not *veiller;* that is, when *v* (the representative of the aspirate *h*) is allowed to remain.

And if we want an instance of *œ* being equal to a single *e*, we have it in the Latin *œconomia*, of which *œ* becomes *e* in *economy* and the French *économie*.

So much for the etymology of *espiègle*, and the several other words to which it has drawn my attention.

Since this etymology of *espiègle* has been written, I have consulted several learned authorities, in order to see if they knew any thing of the origin of the idea *vigilance*, to which I have had occasion, as shown above, to refer several times, and have found that it must have been called after the eye. But every one else, as far as I have seen, traces this idea to bodily strength, which I cannot help considering a very great mistake. Thus the Latin *vigil*, which implies *watchfulness*, the *being awake*, is derived by Noel, Quicherat, and Daveluy from *vigeo*, verbal form of *vigor*, *strength*. The French *vigile* and *veiller* are traced by De Roquefort to the same source. And M. Anatolé's learned work contains an instance of the same mistake, since opposite the Latin *vigor*, I find not only such French words as *vigueur* and *vigoureux*, but also " *veille* (*vïgilia*) *veiller*, &c.; *éveiller*, *eveil; réveiller, réveil; surveiller, surveillance*, &c.; mots savants: *vigiles, vigilant*[2]." These mistakes could have never been made, had it been known that the v does here but represent the aspirate, which sign is *never*, as I have already observed, to be regarded as belonging to the radical part of any word. The French word *veille* is therefore reducible to *eille*, and *eille* is equal to *oille*, and *oille* to

[2] Manuel pour l'Etude des Racines Grecques et Latines, p. 420.

oelle, in which it is easy to perceive *œil*, the French of eye. Hence the verb *veiller*, to watch, must have first been *œiler*, and have then had the same meaning as the English verb to *eye* has at present. There can have been no greater mistake than to derive such a word as *vigilance* from one expressive of bodily strength. And *vigilance* is the primary sense of *wag* or *espiègle*, which character must have obtained his name from the keen and sly humour of his eye. As the number of M. Littré's dictionary containing the letter v has not yet appeared, we cannot say from what source he will derive the idea *vigilance*. When I traced *oculus* to *oc*, I was not aware that M. Littré had done so too ; but not through the application of principles such as I am developing, but from its being radically the same in three other languages, as the following passage serves to show : " Oculus est une forme diminutive d'un radical *oc*, qui se trouve dans le Lithuanien *akis*, le Russe *oko*, et le Sanscrit *aksha*, œil." M. Littré has here, unknown to himself, confirmed the truth of the system by which I am guided in the analyzing of words.

CHAPTER XLIV.

HOMO, ADAM, EVE, ETC.

ANOTHER very old etymology, not to be relied upon, is that of *homo*, or man. Every Latin dictionary and schoolmaster will assure you that *homo* is to be derived from *humus*, moist earth, of which man is said to have been made. But without daring to call in question this origin of the human race, I must make so bold as to assert that there is in meaning no more relationship between *homo* and *humus,* than there is between either of these words and figs or fiddle-sticks; and which I can prove, by giving the real etymology of both *homo* and *man.* But let us first hear what Messieurs Littré and Max Müller have to say on this subject. The former high authority expresses himself as follows, in his etymology of *homme,* first submitting to his readers the different forms of this word in several languages and dialects :—

" Berry, *houme ;* Provenç. *hom, home, om;* Cat. *home ;* Espagn. *hombre ;* Portug. *homem ;* Ital. *uomo ;* du Lat. *hominem.* Dans l'ancien français, au nominatif *hom* ou, moins correctement, *homs,* au régime *home ;* au pluriel nominatif, *li home,* régime *les homes.* C'est du nominatif singulier *hom* que dérive notre indéfini *l'on, on.* Pals-grave, p. 7, au xvie siècle, dit qu'on prononce homme, c'est-à-dire, *hon-m.* Sur l'origine de *homo* il n'y a que des conjectures : Bopp indique le Sanscrit *bhuman,* créa-ture, de *bhu,* être, mais on aurait en Latin *fumon ;* d'autres indiquent *humus,* la terre, *homo* signifiant dans cette hypothèse le terrestre."

M. Max Müller's account is as follows :—

" And how did those early thinkers and framers of language distinguish between man and the other animals? What general idea did they connect with the first conception of themselves? The Latin word *homo,* the French *l'homme,* which has been reduced to *on* in *on dit,* is derived from the same root which we have in *humus, humilis,* humble. *Homo,* therefore, would express the idea of a being made of the dust of the earth[1]."

[1] Lect. vol. i. p. 425.

At the end of this account, M. Max Müller refers to Kuhn[4], who is, I suppose, of his own opinion.

M. Littré does not mistake when he says: "Sur l'origine de *homo* il n'y a que des conjectures." As to its being derived from *humus*, he does not seem to believe it as very likely, since he calls this opinion an hypothesis. And so far he is right. But M. Max Müller thinks otherwise. According to him the pronoun *on* is a reduced form of *homme*, and is derived from *humus*, the soil, and "*homo* would, therefore, express the idea of a being made of the dust of the earth."

The first mistake made both by M. Littré and M. Max Müller in their endeavours to discover the origin of *homo*, is to say that *on*, as in *on dit* (one says), is but a reduced form of *homme*. This is so far from being correct, that when *on* appears as *om*—to which it is precisely equal—it is the *original* of *homme*, and even of the *hom* of *homo*. But which form is the elder of the two— *om* or *on*? The two words are of very ancient date, both having been well known names of the sun. Buddha, who is now allowed to have been adored as the sun, was also called OM, as the following serves to show: "Thou art the Lord of all things, the Deity who overcomest the sins of the Cali Yug, the guardian of the universe, the emblem of mercy towards those who serve thee—OM: the possessor of all things in vital form. Thou ART BRAHMA, VISHNU, AND MAHESA: thou art the Lord of the universe: thou art the proper form of all things, movable and immovable, the possessor of the whole, and thus I adore thee. Reverence be unto thee, the bestower of salvation. . . . I adore thee, who art celebrated by a thousand names, and under various forms, in

[4] Zeitschrift, i. s. 152, 355.

the shape of Buddha, the God of mercy. Be propitious, O most high God[5]."

On is also a name of the *sun*, and, as shown farther back, it is translated into Greek by *Hēlios.*

Now from both *om* and *on* being each a name of the sun; and from our knowing as we do, that this name means *one*, and that the word *one* is constantly used, and with great propriety, in the sense of *man*, in English, German, and French; it is hence natural to suppose that such too must have been the primary sense of *homo*, since its root *om* has, from its being a synonym of *on*, been shown to have this meaning. Hence if we say " every *one* is of John's opinion," our meaning is that every *man* is of John's opinion. The *man sagt* of the Germans is therefore the *on dit* of the French; that is, *one* says or *man* says. The following serves also to show that *homme*, which every one admits to be but a different form of *homo*, is the same as *on* : " *On* stands for *homme*, as it does in the very politest French to this day, *on dit* for *homme dit;* or, as anciently, *Preudon* for *Preud-homme*, as may be seen on the tomb of one of the high constables of France[6]."

Now from these two words *om* and *on* having once been names of the sun, and from *on* being used in the sense of *one*, and *one* in the sense of *man*, and from *one* being also the meaning of the name of the sun, it follows that *om* must, both from its being a synonym of *on* and a name of the sun, be also a word for *one*, and that such too must be the primary sense of *homo*, since *om* is its root.

---

[5] Moore's Pantheon. Quoted by Higgins, Anacalypsis, vol. i. p. 157.

[6] Cleland's Attempt to revive Celtic Literature, p. 122; and Anaca-lypsis, vol. i. p. 716.

But it will, no doubt, be remarked that *homo* has in Latin another meaning very different from that of *man*, as in *homodoxia*, for instance, where it is significant of sameness or equality; this word (*homodoxia*) signifying *same opinion.* Now, what are we to infer from *homo* meaning both *man* and *same?* Nothing more than this, that *same* must, like *homo* or *man*, mean also *one;* and if *same* can be shown to have this meaning, our origin of *homo* will be doubly confirmed. Let us now see if there be, as to form, any relationship between the words *homo* and *same.*

As the sign *s* before a vowel does frequently but represent the aspirate *h*, as is shown by the *s* of *septem* being for the *h* of *hepta;* it follows that the *sam* of *same* is equal to *ham;* and as the elder form of *a* is *oi*, and as the *i* of *a* or *oi* may be dropped, it follows that *ham* cannot differ from the *hom* of *homo.* This is confirmed by the Greek of *same* which is *homos*, and in which we see the *hom* of *homo.* We have, therefore, in *same, homo,* and *homos,* but one word, when these three forms are radically considered. Let us now see if the word *same* is ever used in the sense of *one. It is all the same,* does not differ in the least in meaning from *it is all one.* And in the locution *it is all one and the same,* we have —in order to give it more force—a repetition of the same idea, just as we have in *self-same.* And if *same* be here, as it certainly is, but a repetition of *self*, this proves it to be equal to *one;* since, as we shall see, such is the meaning of *self.* And Dr. Johnson, in one of his explanations of the word *one,* tells us that it means " the same thing," and quotes as an instance the following from Shakspeare:—

> " I answered not again,
> But that's all *one.*"

It is thus made evident that homo, whether used in the sense of *man* or *same*, is literally for *one*.

This etymology of *same* has induced me to see how M. Littré accounts for the origin of the corresponding word in French. M. Max Müller has paid particular attention to this word, which is *même*. M. Littré begins by giving its different forms in several languages and dialects, thus: "Bourguig. *moeme, moime;* Berry, *meime, metesane;* Espag. *mismo;* Portug. *mesmo;* Ital. *medesimo.* Le Provençal a *meteis, mezeis,* qui représente le Latin *metipse;* l'ancien Français *meisme,* le Provençal *medesme,* l'Italien *medesimo,* representent *metipsissimus,* superlatif de *metipse.* Dans le poëme de Boëce, un des plus anciens textes provençaux, on trouve *smetessma* qui est le Latin *semetipsissima.* On a voulu tirer *même* de *maxime,* attendu que *sanctus Maximus* a fait *saint Mesme,* et *sanctus Maximinus, saint Mesmin;* mais c'est une erreur dans laquelle on est tombé pour n'avoir pas tenu compte de l'ancienne forme; le mot primitif n'est pas *mesme,* mais *meisme,* qui ne peut être ramené à *Maxime,* sans parler des autres formes romaines qui ne comportent pas non plus cette étymologie."

Here we have many different forms of the same word, but we are not told how these forms were obtained, or what any of them did at first mean. With the exception of one or two, their first letter is an *m*, and some of them have a *d* or a *t* in the middle. But how is this *m* or *d* or *t* to be accounted for? And why should one of them begin with an S, and another have for its middle letter a *z?* No one can tell, not even M. Littré. Let us now see what we, who have the advantage of our principles, can do. But as M. Max Müller has paid particular attention to this word *même,* and as he fondly imagines that he has gone to the very bottom of it, let us first transcribe his account, and so kill, if we can with a safe conscience do so, these two learned and blessed birds with the same stone, as the observations applying to either will apply to the other. But I should ask their pardon for speaking of them thus familiarly. I am well aware that gentlemen holding their high place in public opinion should never be referred to but in very choice and respectful terms. I cannot, however, so much regret the liberty I have here taken, since in the common-place English locution I have thought fit to use, I can perceive another plain proof that the word *same* must have been first taken in the sense of *one ;* for to "kill two birds with the *same* stone," does evidently mean to kill them with *one* stone, or if you will with *one* and the *same* stone.

The following is M. Max Müller's account of *méme :*—

" How then can French *méme* be derived from Latin *ipse ?* By a process which is strictly genealogical, and which furnishes us with a safer pedigree than that of the Montmorencys or any other noble family. In Old French *méme* is spelt *meïsme,* which comes very near to Spanish *mismo* and Portuguese *mesmo.* The corresponding term in Provençal is *medesme,* which throws light on the Italian *medesimo.* Instead of *medesme,* Old Provençal supplies *smetessme.* In order to connect this with Latin *ipse,* we have only to consider that *ipse* passes through Old Provençal *eps* into Provençal *eis,* Italian *esso,* Spanish *ese,* and that the Old Spanish *esora* represents *ipsa hora,* as French *encore* represents *hanc horam.* If *es* is *ipse, essme* would be *ipsissimum,* Provençal *medesme, metipsissimum,* and Old Provençal *smetessme, semetipsissimum* [7]."

<hr>

[7] Lect. vol. ii. Second Series, p. 258

Whenever the philologist undertakes to trace one word to another, he should begin by giving us the etymology of the one which he believes to be the original. According to the passage just quoted, M. Max Müller assures us that *méme* in French can be traced (genealogically) to the Latin *ipse*. But we are not told how *ipse* obtained its present form, or after what idea it was first named. My conviction is that had there never been such a word as *ipse* we should have *méme*, and spelt even as it is at present. In order to make all this very evident, it will, I perceive, be first necessary to show whence *ipse* is derived, for the origin of this word is as much unknown as any other word ever yet spoken.

The roots of *ipse, ipsa, ipsum*, are *e, a, um*, and each of these roots means *one*, and it may, while retaining the same sense, have had, at different times and places, other forms than these. This is made evident by *ipse* and *ipsum* having also been *ipsus* and *ipsud*.

Nor should we consider the three letters (*ips*) preceding the *e* of *ipse*, as having been here first used for the purpose of heightening the sense; for, as we have shown, a word signifying *one* may, conventionally, signify also *same*, which is the real meaning of *ipse*. Then how have the three letters *ips* of *ipse* been obtained? In the following manner : The root *e* of *ipse* must have taken the aspirate *h*, and so have become *he*, and then by this aspirate *h* having been replaced, as it has often been, by the digamma or *f*, *he* must have become *fe* or *phe*; and as φ is equal to *f* or *ph*, *he* must have then become *phe*, or as it would be in Greek, φε. And as there is in this language a euphonic tendency to sound an S before φ, just as there is to sound it before *p* in, perhaps, all languages ; it follows that φε must have often become σφέ, which happens to be the Greek of *ipse*, and is in the Doric dialect written Ψέ, that is, *pse*. But why should this be? Because, as Donnegan testifies, Ψ is, in some rare instances, put in place of φ. Now from the great tendency there is to sound a vowel before an initial consonant, the p of *pse* became ip, and hence *pse* became *ipse*. But granting what cannot be denied, that the φ of σφέ is for the π or p of Ψε (*pse*), how are we to account for the i of *ipse*, since this word must, from *sp* being equal to σφ, be the same as *spe*, which, with i put before it, will not give *ipse* but *ispe?* This is accounted for when we remark that the two signs composing Ψ, that is, *ps*, do sometimes change places, so that *ps* becomes *sp*. Hence Donnegan observes as follows: " In the Attic dialect, Ψ is often resolved into its elementary letters, but reversed as to places ; thus σπάλιον (*spalion*) for Ψάλιον (*psalion*), σπέλιον (*spelion*) ψέλλιον (*psellion*) ἀσπίνθιον (*aspinthion*) ἀψίνθιον (*apsinthion*)."

We thus see that had not the root of *ipse*, that is, e, been aspirated, we should have now only *e, a, um,* or forms of equal value, instead of *ipse, ipsa, ipsum*. Hence some Greek words, of which the initial vowel did not take the aspirate *h*, are not preceded by Ψ (*ps*) whilst from some persons having aspirated the initial vowel of the same words, they begin with Ψ, *ps*, witness ψάμμος (*psammos*), ψάμαθος (*psamathos*), and ἄμμος, ἄμαθος (*ammos, amathos*). Donnegan, from not knowing the cause of the same words having and not having the sign Ψ before their initial vowel, says, " Ψ seems in certain words to have been added or omitted." He was not aware that this arose from some persons having aspirated the initial vowel of such words, and others not having done so.

From this etymology of *ipse*, it is obvious that its *ips* makes no part whatever of its root; and that this combination is, when considered by itself, wholly void of meaning. But when, from the constant interchange of *s* and *t*, the *pse* of *ipse* became *pte*, an inseparable particle was obtained, which, like *self* in *self*-same, strengthens the word it belongs to.

Noel's account of *pte*, though he knew nothing of its origin, is therefore very correct as to its use and meaning, when he allows us to understand that it is the same as both ψέ and σφέ, each of which is the Greek of *ipse*. His words are: " Pte (Dorien, ψέ, pour σφέ.) Addition syllabique, qui n'a aucun sens par elle-même, mais qui augmente la force du mot, *suopte pondere*, par leur propre poids."

So much for the origin of *ipse*, of which the first form must have been *e*, and the first meaning have been simply *one*, and if I could suppose—which I cannot—that its *ps* has been obtained otherwise than has been just shown, and that its equivalent *pt* or *pte* acts here under its form of *ps*, we might say that *ipse* means literally the *very one*, *absolutely one*, or *the one* par excellence; that is, emphatically *one*.

Let me now endeavour to trace *même* to its real source. I shall, perhaps, be more easily understood, if I begin with its Italian form *medesimo*. This word is, when analyzed, equal to *im-ed-es-imo;* which should be thus explained : *im* cannot differ from *un* any more than the *im* of *im*politus in Latin, and of *im*poli in French, can differ from the *un* of the corresponding word in English, that is, from *un*polite. But why should an *i* be joined to the initial *m* of *medesimo?* Because, as I have already often shown, initial consonants may, when the sense requires it, be preceded by vowels. The *ed*, which follows the *im* of *im-ed-es-imo* is for *et*, and consequently means *and*, just as the *un*, by which it is preceded, means *one*. We have thus obtained in *im* and *ed* two significant words (*one, and*). Let us now explain *es* and *imo*. The former cannot differ from *is*, the Latin pronoun; and as this word cannot differ in meaning from *one*, and as this is also the meaning of both a definite and indefinite article, it may be explained by either *this, that,* or *the,* according to the sense required. As to the last of these words (*imo*), it is, from *im* being, as just shown, the same as *un*, equal to *uno;* so that the four words contained in the single one, *medesimo,* mean literally *one and the one;* which is the verbatim translation of the Latin locution *unus et id-em,* that is, word for word, *one and the one;* but which is always understood to be for *one and the same.* This analysis is a very convincing proof that the *em* of *idem* is for *same,* which confirms what is shown farther back; namely, that the idea of sameness may be signified by a word meaning *one.* It is therefore obvious that the *e, a, um* of *ipse, ipsa, ipsum,* do each mean *one;* and that they might stand for *same* also, that is, without the three letters *ips* by which they are preceded, is equally obvious.

Here, too, by this analysis of *med-issimo,* we see confirmed our etymology of *homo,* both when it means *man* and *same;* for as its root is *om,* and as it did not become *hom* but by the o having received the aspirate; and as this aspirate (*h*) became *s*, whence *som,* and consequently from the o being entitled to i, and from o and i making *a*, this *som* became *sam,* which is the radical part of *same,* and but a different form of the *hom* of *homos,* which also means *same.*

The Greek ἅμα, which is, on account of the aspirate, equal to *hama*, and consequently to *sama*, means also *same*, conventionally *same* time, on which account it serves as an adverb. It is therefore easy to perceive that in ὁμο and ἅμα (equal to *homos* and *hama*) there is but one word, and that the radical part of each (*hom* and *ham*) is but a different form of the *sam* of *same*, and also of the *hom* of *homo*, whether the latter means either *man* or *same*.

But if the aspirate *h* of *homo* or *hama* was not replaced by *s* but by *f*, which is the more frequent change, we should then have, instead of *som* and *sam*, *fom* and *fam;* in the latter of which we see the *fœm* of *fœmina*, Latin of *woman*, and which was, says De Roquefort, pronounced *hœmina* by the ancient Romans. This observation coming, as it does, from a writer who knew not the primary sense of either *homo* or *fœmina*, is an invaluable proof of the truth of the latter etymologies. We now see that the *ina* of *fœmina* is for *una;* so that this Latin of woman, is equal to *homana*, which will become, if we give it a masculine form, *homunus*. There is therefore no more difference in meaning between *homo* and *fœmina* than there is between *unus* and *una;* the *o* of the former representing the masculine gender and the *ina* of the latter representing the feminine.

And when we now remark that the root of both *homo* and *femina* is the same as *om*, and that the aspirate *h* is as equal to *v* or *w* as it is to *f*, we see that *hom* may be fairly represented by *vom* or *wom*, in the latter of which we see the *wom* of *woman*, and also the *wom* of *womb;* the latter idea having been called after woman, and which is very rational, and as easily conceived as it is rational. But etymologists have made strange mistakes in their endeavours to find the origin of these ideas *woman* and *womb*. But before I advance a proof in support of this statement I wish to show that the aspirate *h* may, as just stated, be represented by the *w* of *woman*. The Greek of *wine* will serve for this purpose. It is written οἶνος; that is, when the soft breathing is changed for the rough one, *hoinos*, of which the root *hoin* cannot differ from either *voin* or *woin*; that is, when the o is dropped, *vin* and *win*, which are as equal to each other as *vent* in French is to *wind* in English, the *v* and *w* being thus often used indifferently. It is scarcely necessary to observe that *win* is for *wine*, such being its form in Saxon, and which cannot differ from *wein* in German; and, since e is the same as o, *wein* is the same as *woin*. We thus obtain, when the w representing the aspirate is left out, the *oin* of οἶνος. It is hence made evident that *h* may be replaced by *w* as well as by *f* or *v*, and that the *hom* of *homo* or the *fœm* of *fœmina* are precisely equal to the *wom* of *woman*.

The origin of *woman* is, according to my Webster, " enlarged and revised," "a compound of *womb* and *man*." I need scarcely assure the reader that this is a very gross mistake. And it has not, it would seem, been corrected by the latest etymologists, who, according to M. Littré, derive *femina* from the *fœ* of the Latin *fœtus* or *fetus*, and *mina*, in the sense of pap or the female breast. His words are: "D'après les derniers étymologystes, d'un radical *fœ*, qui se trouve dans *fœtus*, fecundus, et de mina, Grec μένη, suffixe participial, de sorte que fœmina, participe du moyen, signifierait, celle qui nourrit, allaite." See article *femme*.

We may now notice *womb*. We have already said that *womb* is to be derived from the *wom* of *woman*, and we are now going to prove it. The signs *m* and *b* being both formed by the meeting of the lips, there are many words in which they are found together, and where only one of them seems to be needed. This arises, no doubt, from some persons on closing the sound of a vowel by a compression of the lips, allowing the *m* to be heard, and others the *b*; and from others still allowing the two sounds to join and make as it were only one, this being caused by the same organ of articulation serving on the occasion. Hence, *womb* might be reduced to *wom* or to *wob*, and in Danish it is written *vom*. But *wob* appears to have no meaning. It is, however, very significant, as we may perceive on giving to its o its i understood, for we shall then obtain *woib*, which every German will at once admit to be the same as *weib*, in English, *wife*. When we now give to the *m* of *wom* the *b* which might attend it, we shall have instead of *wom, womb*; that is, when the *m* is dropped, *wob*, and consequently *woib* and *weib*. It is therefore evident that in *woman, womb, weib* and *wife*, we have radically but one word; and to which we may add their Latin and French equivalents, *femina* and *femme*. Indeed, the first representative in German of *femme* is, in Dr. Schuster's excellent dictionary, *weib*. Hence it is that *femme* means in French both *woman* and *wife*.

But how are we to connect *uterus* (Latin of womb) with any word signifying *womb?* I shall have occasion to show by and by, when I come to the analysis of father and mother, how two such words, which are so dissimilar in form, can be traced to the same source. But even here this apparent difficulty may—though not thoroughly —be explained. The origin of no word can be more concealed from the Latin scholar than *uterus*. The Greek

and French of this word (μήτρα and *matrice)* offer no
obstacle whatever, as every one can perceive that they
are but other forms of μήτηρ, *mater* and *mother*. But
uterus appears widely different from any of these forms,
and yet I can assure the reader that it is, when radically
considered, the same word. Quicherat, in his Latin and
French Dictionary (22, second edition), which is allowed
by all the colleges in France to be the best extant, suggests ὕδερος (*dropsy*) as the original of *uteros*, but he
wisely appends to this word a note of interrogation,
which he uses for indicating doubt. And so well he
may, for the two ideas are no way related. Yet words
signifying *water* may also signify *mother,* and for which
we shall see the cause in the proper place.

Now as *uterus* is, when we aspirate its initial vowel,
equal to *huterus,* and as this aspirate may, as shown
above, be changed for *w,* and as this sign in Sanskrit
becomes *m* in Latin, as we have already several times
shown; it follows that *huterus* cannot differ from *muterus,*
in the radical part of which, that is, in *muter,* it is easy
to perceive the German *mutter,* the Latin *mater,* and the
English *mother,* not to mention the corresponding word
in several other languages, which need not be quoted.
But how are we to account for *uterus* not having been
now *muterus* or *materus?* By supposing that the more
ancient form of *mater* must have been *ater* or *uter,* and
that from some persons not having aspirated the initial
vowel, with them *ater* or *uter* remained, whilst from
others having aspirated this vowel, and from the aspirate
having been changed for w, and w for m, both *muter*
and *mater* were produced.

Let us now return to *mcdesimo.* We have by the
analysis given of this word shown its literal meaning

to be *one and the same,* and that *unus et idem* in Latin
has exactly the same meaning. According to M. Littré,
meisme is, in French, the primitive form of *même,* and
M. Max Müller alludes also to this word as being the
same as *même* in old French; but how *meisme* has obtained this form, or what its literal meaning may be, we
are not told. But when we only drop the *d* of *medesimo,* we at once perceive that it cannot differ from this
very ancient form of *même;* so that this *meisme* has also,
when the *d* left out, is supplied, the literal meaning of
" one and the same."

All the other forms of *même* and *medesimo,* as given
both by M. Littré and M. Max Müller, may be now
very easily explained by the intelligent reader. If it
should be asked why there is no *d* in the Provençal form
mezeis given by M. Littré, the answer must be that z
having the sound of *dz,* the z was regarded as representing the *d,* and that it was for this reason used instead
of either *d* or *t.* And if it should be asked why there
is an s in the form *smetessma,* the cause of it is, that
there is a great tendency to sound this sign before
several initial consonants. Hence Donnegan says: "The
letter s is often placed euphonically before words beginning with consonants, especially *m* and *t;*" and of
which he gives several instances.

But how can M. Max Müller show any connexion or
derivation between *esso* in Italian or *ese* in Spanish, and
même in French? It is as if we were to assert that the
English pronoun *this* is derived from *same* or *same* from
this, when speaking emphatically, we say, "*this same*
man," instead of "*this man.*" It is true that *this* means,
when analyzed, *the one,* just as *idem* does in Latin, for
it is for *the-as,* or *the-ace;* yet notwithstanding this

similarity in meaning, *même* cannot be derived from either *esso* or *ese*, nor *esso* or *ese* from *même*.

But Max Müller makes a far more serious mistake when he here says that the French word " *encore* represents the Latin *hanc horam."* But this is a very old etymology, and a very bad one; and I am sorry to perceive that M. Littré has in his Dictionary, under the article *encore,* traced this word to the same source. But such mistakes are, when philologists have no fixed principles to guide them, always inevitable. There is not the least relationship in meaning—and very little in form—between *hanc horam* and *encore,* the former of which means *this hour,* whilst the latter means *twice,* of which the Latin equivalent *bis* is used in all French theatres, when a repetition is called for, whilst it is *encore* prevails in England. I am now going to show how both *bis* and *encore* should be analyzed, and their primary meanings be discovered. I have, I think, already analyzed B, and have found it to be composed of I and O, the latter sign having taken a form resembling the figure 3, in which we have also the parts composing S; so that B is equal to IS, and as *is* cannot differ from *ois, as,* or *eis,* and from each of these forms meaning *one,* such too must be the meaning of the sign B; and as the *is* following the B in *bis* has still the same meaning, the entire word is equal to *is, is,* or, if you will, to *as, as;* that is, *one one,* or *two ones.* Such, too, is the literal meaning of *twice* in English, for it is for *twa as,* contracted to *twice.* We should observe that as the word *as* is the French of *ace,* we may say that *twice* is same as *twa ace.*

Now for *encore,* or rather *encor,* which is its elder and more correct form; but a still more ancient one than either of these is *oncor,* and which is also given by M.

Littré; we may say that this word is composed of these three words—*on-ac-or*, that is, *one and one;* and this means *two ones,* just as *bis*—its equivalent in Latin—does. But does *or*, I shall be asked, mean *one ?* It does, and for this reason, that r is often used as another form of s. Witness, in Latin, *arbor* and *honor*, being also written *arbos* and *honos;* and in French *sur* and *sus* are allowed to be one and the same, la-des*sus* being for *sur* cela. Hence two of the old forms of *dessus* are, according to M. Littré, *desseure* and *dessur*. He gives also under *dessus, sus* and *sur* as the same word. Donnegan also observes that s at the end of words is, in Greek, often used for r, which could not be if both signs were not once regarded as but different forms of the same letter. Hence from the *r* of *oncor* being equal to s, the analyzed form of this word (*on, ac, or*) cannot differ from *on, ac, os ;* and from *os* being the same as *ois*, it is consequently the same as *as*, o and i being, as I have often shown, the signs composing *a*. I may also say that from *r* being also used for *n* (witness *bar* and *ben*, of which each means *son* in Hebrew), the *or* of *on-ac-or* cannot differ from *on;* so that this analysis is not more equal to *on, ac, os* than it is to *on, ac, on*.

When we now remark that the primary sense of so very common a word as *encore* has until now remained undiscovered, this should be taken as another very strong proof of the value of the principles by which this discovery has been made; and which proof must appear still stronger when we observe how very remote from truth is the hitherto supposed origin of this word.

Such words as *idem, encore, bis, dis, duo,* and *two* serve to show that the idea *two* has been signified in various ways; but we may expect to find it, when

analyzed, having literally the meaning of *one, one.*
Hence, as the Latin *bis* is, as just shown, equal to *IS, is,*
even so is its Greek equivalent *id—is;* that is, *dis,* or
one, one. The knowledge thus acquired shows how such
words as *duo* and *two* must be analyzed. The *uo* of *duo*
should be regarded as *ou,* and in other languages, as *ov*
or *ow,* and from the interchange of *w* and *m,* as *om,* and
consequently as *on, an, en, ein,* or *ain.* And as we have
thus made the O of *duo* precede its *u,* so should we make
the O of *two* precede its *w,* by which means we shall
obtain the same forms obtained under *duo.* But though
the literal meaning of every word signifying *two* is *one,
one,* we should observe that this literal meaning is also
equal to *the one,* as is shown by *idem,* which is literally
not only *one one,* but also *the one,* the first word of the
two having precisely the meaning of the definite article.
And when any two such words had this meaning, they
must have often signified the *sun* or some remarkable
person, *One* being then a well-known name of the sun.
Hence, such a word as *idem* must, as it is equal to *idom,*
when it appeared thus, *id-om,* have had, from its then
signifying *the sun,* as strong a meaning as we now give
to the two words *the Lord.* And how fully the truth
of this statement is confirmed by our merely observing
that when *id* and *om* coalesce, making *idom,* and the i
is dropped, *dom* alone remains, and which is the root of
Dominus, the Lord. But *id om,* I shall be told, might
as well mean *the man,* since *om,* as already shown, is the
root of *homo,* and this I am obliged to admit; but in
such a case the *id om* would mean some very particular
or great man. Let us therefore put *idom* in the form it
must have often had, and see what we shall obtain. We
know from what we have already stated perhaps a

hundred times, that when i is alone it has O understood, and that O and i when joined make *a*, which brings *id* equal to *ad*. And as O has, according to the same rule, i understood, the O of *om* is in the same way brought equal to *a*, so that the two words *id* and *om* cannot differ in the least from *Adam*. And such is the primary signification of this wonderful name, and such its only true etymology. Hence, from *om* meaning *one* and from *one* being the first of numbers, this accounts for Adam having been called the first man; so that his name means not only *the man*—the man *par excellence*—but the *first man*. Hence, in Turkey and other eastern countries, Adam is not a proper name, but the common name for man.

But as in English *ad* cannot differ from *add*, and as to *add* means to *unite* or to *join*, and as *un* is the root of *unite*, and of which the *oin* of *join* is still the same word; it follows since *one* is the first of numbers, that *ad-am* may have also the literal meaning of *first-man*, which confirms still more our etymology of this name. And to all this we add the following, as affording still further proof: "In, Sanskrit Al Chod is God, as it is in English," and in a note is the following: "When the Buddhists address the Supreme Being, or Buddha, they use the word AD, which means the First[s]." Now as *g* and *ch* are each guttural, we see there can be no difference between God and Chod, and as *g* and *ch* must have each grown out of the aspirate—for *h* does frequently represent *ch*—we see that the root of both these names is *od*, and this is like *ad* equal to *odd*, which, from its meaning *singular* (compare *odd* man and *singular* man) means also *one*, and consequently *first;* and which is still further

[s] Anacalypsis, vol. i. p. 199.

proved by *od* being equal to *oid*—i being understood
with O—and *O* and *i*, making, when joined, AD. But in
Hebrew also Adam is, according to Parkhurst, an appellative, or common noun. Thus in the only edition (1778)
of his Dictionary in my possession, he translates the
Hebrew (p. 5) of this word simply by *man*, and page
115, to which the reader is referred, it is thus explained :
" As a noun with a formative א *a*, אדם *adm, man*, the
appellative name of *the human nature*, because created in
the *likeness* of God (Gen. v. 1, 2). The most usual
derivation of this word, I am aware, is from אדמה *adme*,
vegetable earth, or mould, because man was formed of
the dust of the ground (Gen. ii. 7). But the judicious
reader cannot help seeing that Gen. v. 1, 2, speaks much
more plainly for the derivation I have given than Gen.
ii. 7 for the other. Compare Cor. xv. 45, 47 with 2 Cor.
iv. 4; Col. i. 15. אדם *adm* is also the proper name of
the *first man, Adam*[9]." Thus, according to Parkhurst,
Adam is both a common and a proper name. But
judging from what he says of it, it is evident that he
knew nothing whatever of its origin, not a particle more
than any one else. There is, however, in Hebrew a
synonym of Adam, since, according to his own showing,
it means *one*. This word is *ais*, feminine *ase*, and it is
thus explained in his Lexicon : " A being, or thing, subsisting or existing. This word has no relation to *kind*
or *species*; though, according to its different genders, it
has to *sex*, but is applied to almost any distinct being or
thing; as, for instance, to *man* (Gen. ii. 23, 24)[1]."

It is easy to perceive, from this definition of *ais*, that
it means not only *man*, as here shown, but *one* or any
one; and this confirms our etymology of both *homo* and

[9] Lex. Hebrew, p. 115.   [1] Lex., p. 251.

Adam. It is further confirmed by De Roquefort's etymology of the French *as:* "*As* vient du Grec *heis, ais, as,* un, dont les Latins ont fait *as, assis.*" And as the French *as,* and its English form *ace,* are each rendered into Latin by *unio,* which means *one,* this affords still further confirmation that both *homo* and *Adam* have each the meaning of *one.*

The French suffix *ois* (now *ais*) has also the meaning of *one* or *man.* Thus *François, Anglois,* is literally for French *one,* English *one;* that is, French*man,* English*man.*

This reminds me that I ought to give the etymology of our word *man,* which I was about to forget. As its initial consonant has a vowel understood before it, *man* is equal to *im-an;* and as we have already shown *im* to be equal to *un,* and as this word has the meaning of both a definite and indefinite article, namely, *one;* and as the *an* of man has also the meaning of *one;* it follows that *man* may be explained *a one,* or *the one.* Hence when we bear in mind that *a* is for *oi,* we discover that *man* is equal to *moin,* that is, *moine,* which is the French of *monk;* and every one knows that the person so designated has obtained his name from his living *single.* And when we drop the *i* of *moin,* we get *mon,* and *man* and *mon* are in Saxon equal to each other. This *mon* is also the radical part of the Greek *monos,* which means not only *alone,* but *one also.* The Greek pronoun *tis* should be analyzed in the same way as we have analyzed man; for it is equal to *it-is,* and consequently to *it-as* or *it ois;* and it should be explained *a one* or *the one;* that is to say, it is but another word for *one* when radically considered. And Greek scholars allow that *tis* has this meaning of *one,* or *any one,* though they know nothing of its origin.

· We see from the analysis of the Greek *tis* (it-is) that
its root *is* means not only *one*, but the verb *to be* also.
The cause of it is this : the idea of *unity* was called after
the sun, and the sun was anciently revered as the author
of *existence*, or of *being*.   And according to Parkhurst,
the word שׁיַ *is* " seems to have [in Hebrew] rather the
nature of a noun than a verb, taking after it several of
the same suffixes as nouns."   And alluding again to this
word in the same page (251), he says, "As a noun with a
formative א *a*, אִישׁ *ais*, feminine אִשָּׁה *ase*, dropping the
i, [it means] a *being*, or *thing, subsisting* or *existing*."

But how are we to account for *man* having, in
Saxon, not only the meaning it has in English, but
also, according to Bosworth, " sin, wickedness, crime "?
Your would-be philosopher will assert that it is because
man is born in sin, and that he is, for this reason, prone
to all kinds of wickedness and crime; but I, who am no
philosopher—not even a would-be one—(I ought to be
ashamed to acknowledge it), think very differently of
man—a little bit more charitably.   Let us now analyze
man just as we did only awhile ago when it was shown
to have a good meaning.   A vowel being due before
initial consonants *man* is equal to *im-an*, and from *im*
being the same as *un*—witness the *im* of the French
*im*poli and the *un* of the English *un*polite—it follows
that *im-an* cannot differ from *un-an*.   Let us now call
to mind what we have already seen, namely, that *an*
means *one*, and that *one* means *man;* according to which
analysis *un-an* means *no-man*, though it might as well
mean *a man* or *the man*, that is, if *un* were taken as an
affirmative and not as a negative.   But when the word
man has in Saxon the meaning, according to Bosworth,
of " sin, wickedness, and crime," we must consider the

un of *un-an*, as meaning *bad;* and that it takes this meaning in such words as *un*clean, *un*fortunate, and *un*healthy, becomes evident by their French forms *mal*propre, *mal*heureux, *mal*sain. But how is the word *mal* itself to be analyzed? Just as we have analyzed *man;* it is equal to *im-al*, that is, *un-al*, for as *al* and *el* were once well-known names of the *sun*, then adored as God, and as the idea *good* is, as shown farther back, to be traced to the same source, it follows that *un-al* (the analyzed form of *mal*) means literally *no-God*, *no-good;* that is, *ungodly*, *bad*, and consequently what is *sinful*, *wicked*, or *criminal*.

By thus knowing that a word meaning *one* may serve as a negative, we can easily discover what has been hitherto unknown, namely, the original of such negatives as *mis* and *dis*. *Mis* when analyzed becomes *im-is*, that is, *un-is;* which, from *is* being equal to *ois*, and *ois* to *us* (compare *croix* and *crux*), becomes *unus*, and *unus* is the Latin of *un*, so that *mis*trust is literally *un-trust*, that is, *no-trust*. We must, however, admit that *unus* might as well have meant *two* as *one*, for its parts, *un* and *us*, have each the meaning of *one;* but as its first part, *un*, serves only as an article to the second part (*us*), *unus* has obtained the meaning of *the one* or *a one*, and consequently not of *two*.

How easy it is now to discover the original of the synonym of *mis*, namely, *dis*, *mis*trust and *dis*trust having the same meaning! *Dis* when analyzed becomes *id-is*, and like *unus* it might mean *one, one;* but *id* serves only as an article; so that from *is* being for *ois*, and *ois* for *as*, the meaning of *id-is* must be *the one* or *a one*. That it might, however, as well as *mis*, stand for *two* is confirmed by the fact that *dis* has in Greek the

z

same meaning *bis* has in Latin. Hence *mis, dis,* and *bis*
make only one word. When *me* and *de* are used in the
sense of *mis* and *dis,* they should be regarded as their
contracted forms.

The etymology of the negative *mis* suggests that of
the verb to *meet,* hitherto unknown. The *m* of *meet*
being equal to *im,* and *im* being equal to *un,* it follows
that *meet* is equal to *u-neet,* that is, to *unite,* according
to which analysis a meeting would mean a uniting.

I have still an observation to make—a rather startling
one—respecting the analysis, given farther back, of
Adam. We have shown this name to mean *the one,* but
literally *one one,* or *two.*

Now if the author of Genesis conceived the name
Adam to mean *two*—as it really does, even as much so
as it means *the one*—he might be led to believe that the
first man was created double. And if this name *Adam*
meant, like *homo, woman* as well as man, might he not be
induced to suppose that Adam was of both sexes? But
why should it be thought that it does mean *woman?*
Because the *am* of Adam implies *existence,* and it is a
name which the great Author of all existence has given
to Himself, as we are told in the Bible; and so does the
word *Eve* or *woman* mean *existence,* for it cannot differ
from הוא *eva,* which Parkhurst says, " denotes permanent
existence, or *subsistence* [2]." And the first meaning which he
gives it when it is used as a verb is, *to be* [3]. But this verb
is in Hebrew written also הוה *eve,* as Parkhurst admits,
when referring still to הוא *eva.* He states as follows:
" In Chaldee it is the same as the Hebrew היה *to be* [4]."

And Parkhurst still under הוא *eva,* continues thus :
" As a noun, one of the divine names, He who hath per-

---

[2] Lex., p. 125.   [3] P. 126.   [4] Ibid.

manent existence, who exists eminently[8]." We thus see that the name *Eve* under the form *eva*, is also, like the *am* of Adam, a name of the Deity.

We saw also awhile ago that the Hebrew ‏יש‏ *is* with a formative ‏א‏ *a*, making ‏איש‏ *ais*, means, according to Parkhurst (p. 251), *man* (Gen. ii. 23), and that its feminine is ‏אשה‏ *ase*. But these two Hebrew words *ais* and *ase* are one and the same, with a shade of difference for the sake of distinction, and each of them is the verb *is*, which has the same meaning in both Hebrew and English. Now as I find in my little French and Hebrew Dictionary by M. René Bedel, that the word *femme* is rendered into Hebrew by ‏אשה‏ *ase*, it is thus shown that in Hebrew as in Latin the same word means both *man* and *woman*. Hence if the author of Genesis understood the name *Adam* to mean not only *one one*, or *double one*, but also *man* and *woman*, it is reasonable to suppose that he might believe the first man to have been created double and of both sexes. And if we need further proof that the same word may in Hebrew signify both sexes, Parkhurst supplies this proof, as is shown by the following, still under ‏הוא‏ *eva*. "And most generally ‏הוא‏ *eva* is used as the pronoun, third person singular of the common gender, he, she, it (though usually masculine). See Gen. ii. 11; iii. 15; iv. 20. For its use as a feminine, see Gen. iii. 12; xx. 2, 12; Lev. xiii."

The above etymologies may account for the following : "So God created man in his own image, in the image of God created he him ; male and female created he them." Gen. i. 27.

How is this passage to be understood? If it means any thing, it is that the man and the woman were created

[8] Deut. xxxii. 39. Ps. cii. 28.

at the same time. The words *male* and *female* make this self-evident; and which is further confirmed by the pronoun *them*, with which the verse ends, being in the plural number.

The Lord is even represented as speaking not to one person but to two, for He orders *them* to be fruitful and to multiply, and to replenish the earth and to subdue it. Yet in the next chapter, verse 18, the Lord is made to say, " It is not good that the man should be alone; I will make him an help meet for him." And three verses farther on the Lord is represented as causing " a deep sleep to fall upon Adam," and as making the woman out of one of his ribs, and then presenting her " unto the man," verse 22.

Now as the first woman cannot have been created twice, that is, at the same time with the man, and afterwards out of one of the man's ribs ; it is evident that this account of the creation of the first man and woman is not free from error. But can the author of Genesis have made such a mistake as the one here referred to ? Every astronomer and geologist in the world will assure you that the author of Genesis, whoever he was, has made many very serious mistakes. It is even difficult to conceive that the mistake in question can have been made by the same person, the two accounts of the creation of the woman being so very contradictory as to shock every one not wholly stultified by his religious fears and prejudices. But it is, for our purpose, enough to know that Moses is allowed by all learned men to have made at least some, if not many mistakes ; for this being granted, we can suppose he was likely to believe on perceiving the word *Adam* to mean not only *the one*, but *one one*, or *two*, and also *man* and *woman*, that the person so called obtained such a name because of his having been made double and of both sexes. But as the name *Adam* does not appear in Genesis under the form of *Ad-am* or *Ad-om*, that is, in two parts, we are led to suppose that this belief respecting the origin of the first man and woman must have long preceded the time when Moses is said to have flourished; unless, however, we allow him to have been a great philologist, and so, by his knowledge, to have analyzed the word *Adam* and discovered its primary sense, on seeing it under one of its earliest forms.

Am I likely to be censured for thus daring to insinuate that Moses has been led into the error of deducing out of the word *Adam* his account of the origin of the first man and woman? Of course I am. I may be told that such mistakes as physical science can demonstrate may be noticed, but that whatever does not come within the reach of such science must never be questioned, however contrary to reason it may appear. M. Max Müller says that Moses has been rightly stripped of his scientific knowledge[6], but he never presumes to hint that he can be stripped of any thing lying beyond the range of this science, however violently it may come in collision with reason, and all our best notions of the Godhead, truth, and religion.

But as it is an undoubted fact that Moses has, in the opinion of men eminent for their piety and scientific knowledge, committed several mistakes in his account of the creation; he may, because liable to err, have committed others, but such as reason and common sense only—and not the principles of any known science—can

---

[6] " The author of the Mosaic Records, though rightly stripped before the tribunal of Physical Science of his claims as an inspired writer, may at least claim the modest title of a quiet observer."—*Lect. Science of Language,* vol. i. p. 377.

attempt to refute. And such a mistake I take to be the two different accounts given by Moses of the creation of the first woman. And from reasoning thus I am strongly induced to believe, as the most plausible solution I can find, that it was from the word *Adam* signifying, under one of its earliest analyzed forms, not only *one* (whence the idea *first*) but also *double one*, as well as male and female, Moses wrote as he has done of the first man and woman. I forgot to mention, that in Sanskrit the word *Adam*, or *Adim*, is allowed to mean *first*, which is one of the meanings I have shown this word to have.

But I now find, on referring to Parkhurst, that I have omitted to state several other circumstances confirmatory of the truth of my etymology of this most important name. Thus under דמה *dme*, he says, " With a radical, but mutable or omissible ה *e*,"—by which Parkhurst shows that דם *dm* may be regarded as the root, since ה *e* may, though radical, be omitted. This *dm* cannot differ from *id-em*, vowels being understood before consonants ; and as *idem* means the *same*, it must also mean *one*, as we have seen, and consequently *even*, as we must admit on remarking that *uni* is not only the French of *even*, but that its root *un* (also the root of *unus*) cannot differ from *vn*, *v* being the same as *u*; and *vn*, with vowels supplied, is the word *even*. Let us now, while bearing this in mind, read what Parkhurst says of דמה *dme*. These are his words : " The general idea of this difficult and extensive root seems to be *equable, even, level, uniform*, æquare, exæquare, conformare" (page 114).

These are but other words for *sameness* and *identity*, or *one*, which is the radical meaning, as we have proved, of *homo, Adam*, and *man*. Farther down on the same page this Hebrew root is also explained : " A *similitude*, a *likeness.*" And this ought to be, for such ideas as *similitude* and *likeness* cannot differ from *sameness* in meaning, except conventionally. But I forgot to remark that the first meaning given to this root when it is used verbally, is " to make equable ;" and so it may signify to make *like*, and consequently *in the image of*.

Still under the same root, but on the next page (115), Parkhurst gives אדם *adm,* and explains it not only as a noun common, meaning *man*, but also as the proper name of the first man, Adam. And the next word under this noun proper is אדמה *adme,* and which is thus explained : " vegetable earth, or mould. It has, I suppose, been so called on account of its *evenness,* when compared with other kinds of earth."

Let us now call to mind, that when first analyzing the name *Adam,* it was shown to be equal to *Adom,* and that when the A of this word was dropped, we obtained the *dom* of *Dominus,* Latin of the Lord. The name Adam has, therefore, with other meanings, the following: the *Lord, first man, likeness,* and *earth ;* which meanings were sufficient to suggest the belief that *Adam* was the name of the *first man,* and that the *Lord* made him in his own *likeness* out of the *mould* or *dust* of the *earth.*

Several of the meanings above discovered by the use of principles hitherto unknown were long ago admitted by learned men, who saw not the consequence of their admissions. Thus their dictionaries told them that in Sanskrit *Adam* means *first,* and that in Hebrew it means not only *man,* but—then serving as a proper name—*the first man,* and even *earth.* But it did not occur to them that those meanings might have suggested the belief that *Adam* was the *first man,* and was made of *earth.* From their not knowing how to analyze the word *man,* they little suspected that it simply means *the one*, even as it does in German at the present hour. But, from their knowing that it must, in common with every other word, have a meaning of some kind or other, and on perceiving that it is very like a Sanskrit word which means to *think*, they have been led to assert—even without expressing a doubt—that man was named after this idea. Thus M. Max Müller says, "*Man* in Sanskrit means to *measure*; from which, you remember, we had the name of *moon*. *Man*, a derivative root, means to *think*. From this we have the Sanskrit *manu*, originally the *thinker*, then *man*. In the later Sanskrit we find derivations, such as *manuva*, *manusha*, *manushya*, all expressing *man* or *son of man*. In Gothic we find both *man* and *mannisks*, the modern German *mann* and *mensch*.[7]" And in his "Chips from a German Workshop," M. Max Müller says: "Man means the *thinker*, and the first manifestation of thought is speech[8]." M. Max Müller says also, "The moon, the golden hand on the dark dial of heaven [how very poetical!] was called by them [the sailor and the farmer] the Measurer—the measurer of time; for time was measured by nights, and moons, and winters, long before it was reckoned by days, and suns, and years[9]."

It is easy to perceive that *month* is for *moon-the*, that is, *the moon;* so that here the *moon* does clearly serve to show a certain space of time: the word *moon* has, however, never meant the *measurer*, nor when used verbally to *measure*. The moon is to the night what the sun is to the day, and it may, for this reason, be called the sun of the night. And it was, it would seem, so regarded in the beginning; for as words naming the sun mean *one*,

[7] Lect., vol. i. p. 425.　　[8] Preface, p. x.　　[9] Lect., v. i. p. 6.

as we have already often shown, so do those serving to name the moon express the same idea. In *Hēlios, sol,* and *sun,* the radical meaning of each of these words is *one.* This is made very plain by *sol,* root of *solus;* yet the *hēl* of *hēlios* is the same word; that is, it means *solus* or *one.* And as the *s* of *sun* has grown out of the aspirate *h,* this word has also the meaning of *one,* for its root is *un.* The Greek of moon is *selēnē,* and its root *sel* cannot differ from *sol,* nor from the *hēl* of *hēlios;* and what can show more clearly that the moon means *one,* just as the sun does, than its masculine and feminine forms *lunus* and *luna;* for the *l* of each of these words being the remains of an article, *unus* and *una* remain. *Lune* in French must be therefore for *l'une,* literally, *the one.* And the English word *moon* has still the same meaning, for it is reducible to *mon,* as is shown by *month,* and *mon* is the radical part of *monos,* which means both *one* and *alone.*

But if the moon meant the *measurer* or, verbally, to *measure,* after what, I should like to know, was the moon itself called? I shall be told that it was called after *Lucina,* or *lucere,* to *shine.* But this is a mistake. It is taking the derivative for the original. Neither the sun nor the moon can have been called after light, or to shine; but it was such ideas as *light* and to *shine* must have been called after the sun and the moon.

M. Max Müller does therefore mistake when he says (page 12), "No one doubts that Luna was simply a name of the moon [very true]; but so was likewise *Lucina* [also very true]; both derived from *lucere,* to *shine;*" but this is not so very true; for it is, I say, taking the derivative for the original.

But if to measure was not called after the moon, after what was it called? After such an instrument as a hand, a foot, or an arm, or a rod, the rod itself having marked upon it the number of hands or feet, or the length of the arm. This observation leads us to discover the origin of the English word *yard;* for when we regard its *y* as but a representative of the aspirate *h*, *ard* should be considered as its elder form; and *ard* cannot, when its *a* falls behind *r*, differ from *rad*, nor *rad* from *rod*. I find in some English dictionaries a curious confirmation of the truth of this etymology. Thus *verge*, which is the French of *rod*, has another meaning in this language, which I need not give; and I learn that *yard* has the same meaning in English. Hence the primary sense of the word in question is *rod*, and not *yard*. The Latin of rod (*virga*) has still the same meaning. I am even inclined to take the *meas* of *measure*, as equal to *pes*, Latin of *foot;* for it is equal to the *met* of the Greek *metron*, which means *measure;* and as the Greek preposition *meta* (with) is written also *peda*, so might the *met* of *metron* be written *ped*. And that *ped* is equal to the *pod* of *podos* (genitive of *pous*, Greek of foot) is shown by the *ped* of *pedē*, which, in this language means a *fetter*, an idea which was, I am sure, called after the foot, just as handcuff was called after the hand. The ablative of the Latin *pes*, that is, *pede*, is also letter for letter the Greek *pedē*, a *fetter*. I do therefore conclude this etymology by declaring that I believe *measure*, *metron*, *metre*, *mete*, *pes*, *pede* or *pedē*, and our words *fetter* and *foot*, to be all radically one and the same word.

We have now seen enough to feel convinced that the moon does not mean the *measurer* or to *measure;* but does *man*, a root derived, according to M. Max Müller, from the same source, mean to *think?* By no means.

It is not conceivable that while language was yet in its infancy, and the whole world in a very rude state, an idea so very refined and farfetched, could have been entertained by any one. M. Max Müller will find in the *man sagt* of his own language, in the *on dit* of the French, and the *one says* of the English, the only and real primitive meaning of *man*, namely, *one*, and which is clearly shown by our analysis of *homo*.

But M. Max Müller is not the only one who has thought that *man* was named after the idea expressed by the verb to *think;* Godfrey Higgins published the same opinion long before him, as the following passage, which ·I transcribe from his Anacalypsis [1], serves to show: "In the Hindoo mythology we meet with a very important personage, called MENU. He is allowed to be identical with Buddha, and with the sun, and to be surnamed Son of the Self-existent, or, in other words, Son of God. The word *Menu* signifies *mind* or *understanding*, and is closely connected with the idea of wisdom. It is, in short, but another epithet for Buddha. This root is closely allied to the root מנר *mnr;* whence comes the Minerva of the Greeks [2], and the English word *man*, and the Latin words MENS *mind*, *memini*, *to remember*, and the Sanskrit *man* or *men*, to *think*."

But this is a mistake—I mean as to the origin of the name *man*—and it is proved to be a mistake by Godfrey Higgins himself, since some hundred pages farther on (716) in the same volume, we are told that the French *on* stands for *homme*, the name of the high constable of France, *preudon*, being for *preudhomme*. I cannot account for this contradiction but by supposing that the passage just quoted, showing *man* to have been named

---

[1] Vol. i. p. 234.　　　[2] See Purkhurst, in voce מנר *mnr.*

after the verb to *think*, must have been in print some considerable time before he acquired the more correct opinion respecting the origin of the idea *man;* for *homme* does not stand for a different one.

In the second of the two passages above quoted from M. Max Müller we are told that *man* means not only the *thinker*, but that "the first manifestation of thought is speech."

This is also M. Renan's opinion, as we have already shown; this writer's apparent conviction being that as soon as man began to think he began to speak. But what is there in this opinion to recommend it? Nothing more than that it appears to be every one's impression, from the boy at school to the full grown professor of many languages. It is, however, very erroneous, very shallow, and, above all, very meagre, for it leads to nothing; not having even the merit of one of those rich blunders which, though destitute of common sense, may have something in them like imagination, and, from their very oddity, like originality also. But how very easily such an opinion can be confuted! Thus, how does the man born deaf, without the least defect in the formation of his mouth, manifest his thoughts? Certainly not by speech, but by signs; and so would all men have ever continued to do, even from the creation of the first man and woman down to the present hour, if they had not the power of giving to their mouth a circular form while calling attention, by the noise they then made, to the object (the sun) they were representing at the time. And such was, I say, the beginning of human speech; it grew out of a single sign; signs and not words having been the first and most natural means used over all the world for the manifestation of thought.

If I were not apprehensive of being led into other inquiries, a great deal more might be said of Adam and Eve, still serving to lead to the suspicion that a large portion of their history has been suggested by the meanings of their names. But one or two particular circumstances may be slightly noticed. We have seen how the name *Adam* is significant of *sameness*, which corresponds with its being equal to the Latin *idem*. But the name *Eve* has also this meaning; for as the *em* of *idem* is for *same*, the entire word meaning *the same;* and as the *m* of this *em* is equal to *w*, as we have often shown, and as *em* is consequently equal to *ew*, and as *ew* is reducible to *ev*, we thus obtain the root of *Eva* or *Eve*. And that *em* is allowed to have this meaning of sameness is proved by the following : " An *eme*-Christian, or *even*-Christian, is a fellow Christian, an *equal* Christian [3]." We should not omit to observe that the *ew* here noticed cannot differ from *ewe* (the female sheep); and that when we make the *w* of this word take its form of *ll*, just as it does in Scotch—*aw* being used in this language for *all*—we shall obtain *elle*, the French of *she*, which would make it appear that the word meaning *Eve* means *she* also. But if Adam and Eve have the same meaning, Eve, I shall be told, might as well mean *he*. And so it does, since in a passage we have already quoted from Parkhurst, *Eva* is there said to be of the common gender, and to be for *he*, *the*, or *it*. I learn that the pronoun *Iva*, which cannot differ from *Eva*, means in Sanskrit *she* [4].

I learn also from Godfrey Higgins[5] that *Adima* means not only the *first man*, but even the *first woman*. And the learned Pasor makes a statement to the same effect :

---

[3] Richardson's Dictionary.   [4] Asiat. Res., vol. v. p. 247.
[5] Anacalypsis, vol. ii. p. 175.

"῎Αδαμ, nomen Hebræorum proprium nostri parentis. Est etiam appellativum, et valet idem quod homo, tribui-turque non solum viro sed etiam fœminæ." Lexicon.

I was forgetting to observe, that in the passage quoted from Parkhurst under דמה *dme*, one of the meanings he gives of this root is *even (evening)*, which is in English written also *eve*. And as Parkhurst tells us that the ה *e* of this root may be omitted, it follows that its דמ *dm* is precisely equal to the Latin *idem*, vowels being under-stood before the *d* and the *m*. And as *idem* is the same as *Adam*, so is it the same as *Eve*, and hence the expla-nation of *even* given of דמה *dme* appears to be very correct; but not more so than the *eme* in *eme*-Christian, meaning, as just shown by Richardson, *even*-Christian.

If we now examine ἀνήρ and ἄνθρωπος, we shall be obliged to admit that neither of them differs, as to its primary sense, from *homo, adam,* or *man*. The ending ηρ of ἀνήρ appears, in perhaps all languages, under various forms, such as *ar, er, ir, or, ur, our, eur,* &c. And as the *an* which precedes the ηρ of ἀνήρ has still the same meaning, that of *one*, *anēr* is, literally, for *one-one*, that is, *the one*, there being no difference in meaning between *one* and the article *the*, as we have already shown.

But *anthrōpos* differs so considerably in form from *anēr*, that all the philologists who have noticed this word have been led to give it quite another origin. It is, however, the same as *anēr*. But the Greeks have often, for the sake of euphony, inserted a letter where a people less addicted to make alterations in words for the sake of sound could not think of doing so. Thus the long e (η) in *anēr* being equal to *ee* (εε), and this not suiting their delicate ears, they have on some occasions inserted a *d*, and thus made *anēr* become *ander*. Thus instead of *anēr*-

agatheō, they have written *andr-agatheō*, which is for *ander-agatheō*. Now this *ander* must have been once preceded by an article, such as OS, and so have been OS *ander*, meaning *the man;* and OS *ander*, must, by transposition, have become *anderos*, but from the e of this word having been dropped, the O was lengthened; that is, instead of ἀνδέρος they wrote ἀνδρώος, which is equal to *androos*, and this they have lengthened by the insertion of a *p* to *androopos*, the *p* having necessitated the usual ending (ος) of Greek nouns of the second declension.

Another proof that the Greeks must have had a strong tendency to insert a *d* in *anēr* is shown by the genitive of this word being not only *anēros*, but *andros* also; and that *andros* must have once been *os ander*, and so have served as a nominative, I have not the least doubt.

It is scarcely necessary to observe, that from *d* and *th* having exactly the same power, there can be no difference between *andrōpos* and *anthrōpos*, any more than there is between *D*eus and *Th*eos; or than there is between *bad* in German, and *bath* in English; or than there is between our two words *burden* and *burthen;* or between the two Greek words *anderon* and *antheron*, each having the same meaning, that of a *bank* or *mound*.

According to this etymology of *ânthrōpos*, it is but a different form of its original *anēr*, and it has consequently the same meaning, that of ONE.

I was forgetting to notice the Latin *vir*, but, judging from what we have just seen of the corresponding word in other languages, it is easy to conceive that its most original meaning must have been also that of *one*. When we regard its *v* as having grown out of the aspirate, and as consequently being no part of its root, *ir* alone remains, and as this is equal to *oir*, so is it to *ar, er, our, eir, or, eur,* and many others. And every such ending will be found to mean *one,* or *any thing.* Hence *baker* is *one* who bakes; *butcher, one* who butchers; *printer, one* who prints; and a *snuffers* is *a thing* that snuffs, or, when applied to a man, *one* who snuffs. And as the v of *vir* may be replaced by several other signs, such as b, f, w, or m, it follows that *vir* might also appear under such forms as *bir, bar, fir, far, wir, war, mar,* with a great many others equal to all and each of these. This serves to show that the *ēr* of *anēr,* and the *vr* of *vir* are as one and the same word.

CHAPTER XLV.

FATHER, MOTHER, GENITOR, AUTHOR, AND ACTOR.

WE are now about to enter upon an inquiry relating to the origin of names which are, perhaps, of all others, the most known, though nothing appears to be less so than the ideas after which they were first called. These names are such household words as *father, mother, genitor, author,* and *actor;* after which—but in the next chapter—I intend to show the primary sense (equally unknown) of several other familiar names, such as *daughter* and *son,* with many other etymologies.

M. Max Müller in his " Chips from a German Work-shop[6]," says, "The principles that must guide the student of the science of language are now *firmly established.*"

There can be no truth in this bold statement, for, if it were true, two such men as Messrs. Max Müller and

[6] Preface, p. xix.

Littré would know the primary signification—in no matter what language—of so common-place a word as father; but they now know no more after what this idea was first called than they did when only seven years old.

M. Max Müller's definition of *father* is as follows : " Father is derived from a root *pa*, which means not to *beget*, but to *protect*, to *nourish* [7]."

M. Littré assigns also to *father* the meaning of to *nourish*, but seems to prefer that of *master*, as the following serves to show : " Les uns le tirent du radical *pa*, *nourrir*, les autres du Sanscrit, *pati*, maître ; ce qui est plus en rapport avec l'idée que l'antiquité s'est faite de *pitri*, πατήρ, paterfamilias."

I learn from M. Max Müller, that in Sanskrit *father* is *pitar*, which, as *i* is for *oi*, and *oi* for *a*, brings *pitar* equal to *patar*, and *patar* is but a different form of *pater*. Let us now apply our principles. The *p* of *pater* being for the aspirate, it must be left out, as no radical part of *pater;* the *at* which follows the *p* of *pater* is therefore the root of this word. But what does it mean? Under its present form I can perceive no meaning that will apply to *pater;* but knowing, as I do, that *a* is for *oi*, I see that *at* (root of *pater*) is equal to *oit*, and, as according to my principles, one combination of vowels is equal to any other, it follows that *oit* cannot differ, save conventionally, from *ait*, which is the root of the Greek *aitios*, an *author*. Now this is a meaning that will apply to *pater*, for every child knows that his father is the author of his existence. But this is only telling me that *father* and *author* have the same meaning, but it does not give me what I want to know—the primary signification of either word. When we prefix to the English word

---

[7] " Chips from a German Workshop," vol. ii. p. 22.

author an *f*, as a substitute of the aspirate *h*, to which its initial vowel is entitled, *author* will become *fauthor*, in which it is easy to perceive *father;* but this only confirms what has been already shown, namely, that *father* and *author* are synonyms. If we take the French of *author*, that is, *auteur*, and give to its initial vowel the *f* in *fauthor*, we shall obtain *fauteur*, which has no meaning that can apply to father. But let us take the original of author, namely, its Latin form *auctor*, and prefix the representative of the aspirate, that is, *f*, and we shall get *fauctor* for *auctor*. And what is *fauctor* but *factor*, and a *factor* is a *maker*, for a vowel being due between its *c* and *t*, it is literally *facitor*, *facit* (he makes), being the third person singular of *facere*, to make.

And such must be the primary signification of *father* in all the languages ever spoken. When men first expressed their ideas by words, they must have regarded the father of a child as its maker, than which nothing can be more easily conceived. But there are other proofs of the truth of this etymology. What is the Greek of *maker?* It is *poiēt*, of which the radical part *poiēt* becomes in Latin the *poet* of *poeta*, in which we have an instance of one combination of vowels being equal to any other, since here the *oiē* of *poiēt* is the *oe* of *poet*. But if *poet* were to be written *poit*, it would be still the same word. And what is *poit* when its *o* and *i* meet, composing *a*, but the *pat* of *pater?*

We see, therefore, in *father* and *poet* the same word, though neither idea was called after the other; their identity arises from each word having *maker* for its original meaning. The Latin *fiber*, which means a *beaver*, is also widely different in signification from both *father* and *poet;* but as it means, as shown farther back, a *maker* or *worker*, it is, primarily considered, still the same word, its *i* being for *oi* or *a*, and its *b* being equal to *th*, as we may see by comparing *uber*, in Latin, with its Greek equivalent ou*th*ar.

Now as *maker* was one of the well-known names of the *sun*, it follows that *sun* and *father* were in the beginning expressed alike; not because a *father* was called after the *sun*, but because his name means a *maker*, an idea called after the *hand*.

How now are we to trace *pater* or *father* to a name of the sun? By remarking that its root *at* or *ath* cannot differ from *ad*, and we saw farther back that when the Buddhists invoked their God—who was the sun—they used this word *Ad*. Nor can it differ from *od* which is the root of *God*, and God was also a name of the sun (then written *Gad*), as we have seen it admitted in the passage quoted from Isaiah by Dr. Jamieson. And when the *a* of *ad* received the nasal sound, it became *and*; that is, when here the initial consonant is aspirated, *hand*, of which the primary signification was *maker*, also one of the names of the sun. In short, every word of one syllable must have been, or it may at least have been, a name of the *sun*.

What difference can we now find between O, the first name of the sun, and *Ad?* In meaning there is none, and their difference in form is to be thus accounted for: from the I having been so often attached to the O, to show that the O then meant *one* and not the *sun*, it was thought, after the original use of the I was forgotten, that the two signs should never stand apart from each other; and hence OI was used instead of O, and served as a name of the sun just as the O had previously done. But when the O and I coalesced and became *a*, and then when the teeth were allowed to meet at the close of this sound, the name *Ad* was obtained. But with some people the O and I never coalesced, and this accounts for EI and IE, which are other forms of OI and IO, having named both the true God and the sun, as we have already shown from Parkhurst.

Now *at* being the root of *mater* just as it is of *pater*, we are allowed to infer that the mother was, as well as the father, regarded as the author of her child's existence.

What then is the difference in meaning between *pater* and *mater?* There is none; they have each the same meaning—that of *maker;* and it was only by the *m* having been used for *p*, that the mother's name could be distinguished from the father's. In Greek the interchange of *p* and *m* occurs frequently. Thus, Donnegan observes: " In the Æolian dialect, as also in the Laconian, *m* and *p* are often interchanged; thus *oppa* for *omma, peda* for *meta*," &c. The word *mother* may have therefore with some people been used for *father*, and have been taken for a noun masculine. And this has happened, as to sex, as we shall see.

Before confirming any further these etymologies, let us notice *genitor*, and afterwards return to *father* and *mother*. The Greek form of *genitor* is *genetēr*, which, when we drop the nasal sound, becomes *geeter*, that is, *getter*, which means both one who *gets* and *begets*. This idea must, like that of father, have been named after the hand. And as the French word *gant* (a glove) was named from the hand, it follows that the *g* of the former word is the *h* of the latter, and as this aspirate (*h*) is frequently changed for *f*, the *get* of *getter* cannot differ from *fet*, that is, *fat*, radical part of *father*, and which is equal to the *pat* of *pater*. As *get* is but a different form of *got*, and as *got* is the same as *God*, we

·thus see how *genitor* can, like *pater*, be shown to be radically the same as a name of the sun. And as the feminine of *genitor* is *genitrix ;* that is, when written in full, *genitorix ;* we see that both words are alike, the ending *ix* of the latter only serving to distinguish the feminine from the masculine, just as the *m* of *mater* serves to distinguish this word from *pater.*

We have already stated M. Max Müller's assertion that *pa* does not mean to *beget*, but to *protect*, to *nourish;* after which he continues thus :—

"·The father as *genitor*, was called in Sanskrit *ganitár*, but as protector and supporter of his offspring he was called *pitár.* Hence, in the Veda these two names are used together, in order to express the full idea of father. Thus the poet says (I. 164. 38) :—

> Dyaús me pitâ ganita.
> Jo(vi)s mei pater genitor.
> Ζεὺς ἐμοῦ πατήρ.

"In a similar manner *mâtar, mother,* is joined with *ganitri, genitrix* (Rev. iii. 48, 2), which shows that the word *mâtar* must soon have lost its etymological meaning, and have become an expression of respect and endearment. Among the earliest Aryans *mâtar* had the meaning of *maker,* from *ma,* to *fashion ;* and in this sense, and with the same accent as the Greek μήτηρ, *mâtar,* not yet determined by a feminine affix, is used in the Veda as a masculine. Thus we read, for instance (Rev. viii. 41, 4):—

> ' Sáh mà'ta pûrvyam padom.'

' He, Varuna (Uranos) is the maker of the old place.'

"Now, it should be observed that *mâtar* as well as *pitar* is but one out of many names by which the idea of *father* and *mother* might have been expressed. Even if we confined ourselves to the root *pa,* and took the granting of support to his offspring as the most characteristic attribute of father, many words might have been, and actually were, formed, all equally fit to become, so to say, the proper names of *father*. In Sanskrit *protector* can be expressed not only by *pa*, followed by the derivative suffix *tar*, but by *pá-la, pá-laka, pa-yú*, all meaning *protector*. The fact, that out of many possible forms one only has been admitted into all the Aryan dictionaries, shows that there must have been something like a traditional usage in language, long before the separation of the Aryan family took place[8]."

And this single circumstance, that *father* is expressed in all the Aryan dictionaries by the same word, and not by any of the many words signifying *protector*, serves to show that *pitar*, which cannot differ from *pater*, any more than *pater* can from *father*, does not mean a *protector* in the sense of *father*, but, as I have shown, a maker. I wonder M. Max Müller did not take advantage of his being well aware that *mâtar*, which is the same as *mater*, had not only the meaning of *maker*, but was also used as a masculine. This might have convinced him that *pitar* or *pater* had the same meaning, and that the two words were consequently one and the same.

But that father and mother may be expressed by the same word is shown by Donnegan under *phuō*, who refers to Aristophanes as employing *phusas* in this double sense.

When showing how the *pa* of *pater* is reducible to *oi*, a name of the sun, I forgot to observe, that when only its *o* is dropped, we have in the *pi* which remains, a name of the Deity, for it is the radical part of *pius* (*pious*), which means *godly;* and this idea must have

---

[8] "Chips from a German Workshop," vol. ii. pp. 22—24.

been named after God. Hence, Godfrey Higgins, as the reader may recollect, when remarking that the definite article happens to be the name of the Deity in several languages, mentions, among the rest, the Coptic article *Pi*, as having these two meanings. Hence the people that first used the adjective *pious*, must have had *Pi* as the name of their God, and so must this word have been a name of the *sun* also, which was, with all men, the first object of Divine worship.

Though I have already shown *author* to be, when its initial vowel is aspirated, equal to *fauthor*, that is, *father;* and though I have also shown that its Latin equivalent *auctor* is, and still by means of the aspirate before its initial vowel, equal to *factor*, literally *facit-or ;* I wish to draw the reader's attention to this important word *author* once more. And why so? For the sole purpose of showing to philologists how much they stand in need of the principles by which I am guided, when tracing words to their earliest meanings. Now what is, according to M. Littré, the original meaning? It is *augere* and *ojas, ojas* being a Sanskrit word which, he tells us, means *force*, that is, *strength.*

Now, if M. Littré knew that initial vowels may or may not be aspirated, he would have seen that *author,* which happens to be one of the forms he gives for *auteur,* cannot differ from *fauthor,* and this he would see at a glance cannot differ from *father.* And still by applying the same rule, he would see that *auctor,* the Latin of *author,* was equal to *fauctor,* which, by applying the rule, that a single vowel is equal to a combination of vowels, cannot differ from *factor,* and a *factor* is like a *father* and an *author,* a *maker ;* and this he would confirm by applying the rule which says, that two consonants have often a vowel understood between them ; as this rule would bring *factor* equal to *facit-or*, which is literally a *maker*, as *facit* (he makes) serves to show. But as the aspirate or any of its substitutes may, when found necessary, be removed from initial vowels, it follows that the *factor* of *facit-or*, is the same as *actor* when its *f* is dropped. And is not an *actor* one who *acts*, one who, like a *father* or an *author*, does something? And what he does is an *act*, and he is its *author*, its *doer*, its *maker*.

Now, if I stood in need of some very respectable authority to support what I do here so positively advance, namely, that an *author* is an *actor*, I have just found this very respectable authority. And who is it, the reader asks, because wishing to know if he can equal M. Littré? To which I answer, that my authority is, in all respects, as great a man as M. Littré; and he is so for this simple reason, that my authority is M. Littré himself. Thus the third on the list of the several different forms and synonyms of the word *author* given in his dictionary, is the word *actor* itself, just as it is written in Latin. Yet in the face of this overwhelming proof given by himself against himself, his derivation of *auteur* is " Italian *autore*, de *l'auctorem*, *augere*, *accroitre*, radical Sanskrit, *ojas*, *force*." But what relationship can M. Littré find between the idea expressed by *author*, and one signifying either *increase* or *strength?* However a man might *increase*, or however *strong* he might be, neither of these attributes would imply that he was, in any sense of the word, an *author*. But why does M. Littré make such mistakes, and with which his fine dictionary abounds? Because he does not know any more than his correspondent, M. Max Müller, or any one else, how man first acquired the use of speech, and how, from the knowledge thence derived, he learned to express his ideas.

CHAPTER XLVI.

DISCOVERY OF THE PRIMARY SIGNIFICATION OF DAUGHTER AND SON, WITH SEVERAL OTHER ETYMOLOGIES.

THE first meaning attached to the word *daughter* has been long since as completely forgotten as that of *father, genitor, author,* and *actor.* For the present I wish to notice this word under one of these forms: *duhitar* in Sanskrit; *dauthar,* in Gothic; *daughter,* in English; *tochter,* in German; and *thugatēr* in Greek. In these we have but so many variations of the same word, so that to account for any one of them is to account for them all. Let us now hear what M. Max Müller has to say of not only the Greek of *daughter,* but also of *father* and *mother,* of which, as we have already fully explained and shown, this very learned gentleman knew not the earliest meanings. These are his words: "What should we know of the original meaning of πατήρ, μήτηρ, and θυγάτηρ, if we were reduced to the knowledge of one language like Greek? But as soon as we trace these words to Sanskrit, their primary power was clearly indicated. O. Müller was one of the first to see and acknowledge that classical philology must surrender all etymological research to comparative philology, and that the origin of Greek words cannot be settled by a mere reference to Greek[9]."

This happens to be a great mistake, as I am now

[9] "Chips from a German Workshop," vol. ii. p. 74.

going to prove. But first it may be necessary to show what is, according to M. Max Müller's conviction, the original meaning of *daughter*. "It is," he says, "a name identically the same in all the dialects, except Latin, and yet Sanskrit alone could have preserved a consciousness of its appellative power. *Duhitar*, as Professor Lassen was the first to show, is derived from *duh*, a root which in Sanskrit means to *milk*. It is perhaps connected with the Latin *dūco*, and the transition of meaning would be the same as between *trahere*, to *draw*, and *traire*, to *milk*. Now the name of *milkmaid*, given to the daughter of the house, opens before our eyes a little idyll of the poetical and pastoral life of the early Aryans. One of the few things by which the daughter, before she was married, might make herself useful, in a Nomadic household, was the milking of the cattle, and it discloses a kind of delicacy and humour, even in the rudest state of society, if we imagine a father calling his daughter his little milkmaid, rather than *suta*, his *begotten*, or *filia*, the *suckling*. This meaning, however, must have been forgotten long before the Aryans separated. *Duhitar* was then no longer a nickname, but it had become a technical term, or, so to say, the proper name of *daughter*[1]."

We thus see that M. Max Müller is supported in his etymology of *duhitar*, Sanskrit of *daughter*, by his countrymen, O. Müller and Professor Lassen. He allows us to understand that it is only by referring to Sanskrit, and not by any means to Greek, that the original meaning of this word can be discovered. Let us now see how far this is true, by beginning with his own language and finishing with Greek.

[1] "Chips from a German Workshop," vol. ii. pp. 25, 26.

The *toch*, or radical part of *tochter*, cannot differ from *tok*, *ch* and *k* being a very common interchange, as we see by comparing *speech* and *breach* with *speak* and *break*. Now the tok thus obtained, and which cannot differ from the *toch* of *tochter*, is the radical part of *tokos* in Greek, and which takes these other two forms, *tekos* and *teknon*. And what do they mean? The two first mean a *child* or any thing *begotten*, and the last is thus explained by Donnegan: "A child, son, or *daughter*." And for the verbal form of these three words, I am referred to *tekō*, an assumed form of *tiktō*, which means to *beget*. Now had the word *tiktō* been written *tuktō* or *thugtō*, to both of which forms it is precisely equal, no German would have ever imagined that it was absolutely necessary for discovering the meaning of *daughter*, to go to a language so very little known as Sanskrit—even among the learned themselves. And still less would they have imagined that such a word must in the beginning have meant a *milkmaid*, for it signifies only one *begotten*, male or female, and its meaning alludes no more to the milking of cows than it does to the knitting of stockings or to the carding of wool. But this mistake has suggested the fragment of a nice little idyll; and I am sure that every young poet and poetess will regret that M. Max Müller's etymology of *daughter* or *duhitar*, is not true. That idea of calling a newborn infant a milkmaid is so very fanciful, and also so delicately humorous, as M. Max Müller allows us, I think, to understand.

But we should be always on our guard against fanciful ideas when tracing words to their original sources. I could myself, perhaps, give M. Max Müller stronger proof than he himself has given, that a *daughter* means a *milkmaid.* Thus the *thug* of *thugatēr* cannot differ from *dug,* any more than burthen can from burden; and a *dug* is the teat of a cow; so that a female baby might very well—according to this absurd notion—be called a *dugger* or *duggist,* from being obliged while milking a cow, to handle its dugs. And though this etymology would be very faulty, yet, in my humble opinion, M. Max Müller's is not less so.

But why do I not allow myself, in my etymologies, to be led astray by fanciful notions? Because I have been so led too many times already, so that I am now doubly on my guard against every etymology bearing in the slightest degree the appearance of fancy. And then I have the advantage of certain fixed principles unknown to my predecessors, by which I am constantly checked and kept within rational limits whenever on the verge of going wrong.

It is thus shown that *duitar* or *thugatēr,* which words are, in M. Max Müller's opinion, identically the same, means a *daughter* and nothing more. But after what was a daughter called? After her parents; that is, after her father and mother, which, as already shown, have each the single meaning of *maker,* an idea called after the hand, that member with which things are made. But was not such a word as *tokos,* for instance, called after *tekō,* the elder form of *tiktō,* to *beget?* I should say so if I could suppose that verbs were first invented, and nouns afterwards; but my conviction is that man must have first given names to things, and that he then used those names verbally. Hence, the *tek* of *tekō,* or the *tik* of *tiktō* must have been once a name meaning either *father* or *mother,* or both. But how is this to be proved? By first asking if there can be any difference between the radical parts of the Greek *thugatĕr* (θυγάτηρ) and its Sanskrit *duitar;* that is, between *thug* and *duh?* To which the answer must be, There can be no difference whatever. And if the *g* of *thug,* and the *h* of *duh* were replaced by any other two consonants, these radical parts would be still precisely equal to each other. When we therefore leave out the *g* and the *h* of *thug* and *duh,* we shall have in what remains, that is, in *thu* and *du,* the roots of *thugatĕr* and *duitar;* and these roots are as equal to each other as the *th* of *burthen* is to the *d* of *burden;* and the *th* of the one and the *d* of the other might be replaced by any two signs in the alphabet without causing (except conventionally) the least difference in meaning. Thus I learn from M. Max Müller[2] that the Sanskrit word *su* means to *beget;* but the *phu* of the Greek φύω means also to *beget;* and neither *su* nor *phu* can differ from the roots *thu* and *du* of *thugatĕr* and *duitar,* which shows that these two words for *daughter* have merely the meaning of the *begotten;* but they are conventionally feminine. And as one of these roots, namely, *phu,* does not differ from the *pu* of the Latin *puer,* we see that either of them—for they are equal to each other—might as well mean a *son* as a *daughter,* the idea expressed by the word *begotten* being the only sense in which they must have been first taken, whether male or female.

Why now do these several roots, if they be all one and the same, begin with different consonants, and compound signs, such as *th* and *ph?* Because these consonants and compound signs, have, I feel convinced, grown out of the aspirate *h.* Thus such a root as *thu* must have once been *u,* then *hu,* after which the most

---

[2] "Chips from a German Workshop," vol. ii. p. 30.

probable change was by means of the digamma; whence *fu* or *phu*, then *thu*, and at later periods, *tu, du,* and *su.* Every one knows that there is, perhaps, no interchange in Greek more frequent than *t* and *s*; and that *d* and *s* do also interchange is shown by such words as βάδος and ὀσδή being the same as βάσος and ὀσμή.

But how are we to account for several of the roots just noticed being personal pronouns? Witness *su* and *tu* in Greek and Latin; *thu* in Saxon; *du* in German, Swedish and Danish; all of which being represented in English by *thou.* The identity here referred to is explained by what was shown farther back; namely, that such pronouns as *I, thou, he, she,* and *it,* in English, as well as their corresponding forms in all languages, do not differ from one another save conventionally, and that each of them means a *being,* literally an *existence,* and nothing more; and for this reason, all such words do not differ in meaning from the verb *to be.*

I learn from M. Max Müller[3] that a Sanskrit word for son is *putra;* of which the radical part, *putr,* cannot differ from *patr* any more than *further* can from *farther;* and *patr* is, when the vowel here due between *t* and *r* is supplied, the same as *pater,* and this is but another form of *pitar,* Sanskrit of *father.* But where is the necessity for this analysis of a Sanskrit word for son? It is but to confirm still more what has, perhaps, been already sufficiently proved—that a son obtained the same name as his father from his having been called after him. M. Max Müller, when referring to this Sanskrit word for son, says, that it "is of doubtful origin, probably of considerable antiquity, as it is shared by the Celtic branch (Bret. *paotre, boy; paotrez, girl*); the Latin *puer*

---

[3] "Chips from a German Workshop," vol. ii. p. 30.

is supposed to be derived from the same root." To this statement M. Max Müller might have added, if he knew it, that the Sanskrit of *father* (*pitar*) is also derived from the same root, and that it does not differ from *putra* (Sanskrit of *son*), nor even from *paotrez*, a *girl*, save conventionally.

In one of the roots above noticed, namely, in the *phu* of the Greek φύω, to *beget*, we see a form nowise different from *pha*, *pa*, or *fa*; that is, from the *pa* of *pater* (πατήρ), in both Greek and Latin, and the *fa* of *father*. And when φύω takes its substantive form, it becomes *phutor* (φύτορ), and it is then thus explained by Donnegan: "one who engenders or produces; a generator; a *father*." We thus see that the *phu* of *phuō* might as well mean a *son* as a *father*, since it cannot differ from the *pu* of *puer*, Latin of *son*. And another proof of this is afforded by *geneter* (γενετήρ); which is allowed to be the same as *genetes* (γενέτης), and the meaning of the latter is, according to Donnegan and every one else, "a *father*—a *son*." And against this fact—that the parent and the child have had in the beginning the same name—there should be no contending; for it is admitted by men who had no knowledge of the principles of the twofold discovery to which I lay claim. But even facts, I shall be told, are seldom sufficient to convince such persons as have for a long period of their lives imbibed false notions respecting no matter what belief, whether religious or scientific. And that the same word must, as we have seen, mean *father* as well as *mother*, is also admitted by Donnegan, who, under φύω, gives φύσας, on the authority of Aristophanes, as meaning "a *father*, also a *mother*, both parents included."

How easily all this can be understood when we admit

what every one can conceive, namely, that the words *father* and *mother* have each the meaning of *maker*, and that the names of their children have, because called after their parents, been made to signify what is *made*.

But there is still, besides *putra*, another word in Sanskrit for *son*, namely, *sûnu*, which M. Max Müller derives from *su* to *beget;* and this is no mistake. But there is a root of this root, and which is *u*. How then are we to account for the *s ?* By making it represent, as usual in such cases, the aspirate *h*. The now obsolete form of υἱός (*a-son*) namely, υἵς, is, therefore, very correct; for as its aspirate may be represented by *s* or by the digamma (ϝ), its root is equal to both *su* and *fu*, in the latter of which we have the φυ of φύω; and as the representative of the aspirate *h* is never to be regarded as belonging to the root of a word, it follows that φύω is for ὕω. But as φύω when reduced to ὕω means to *wet* or to *make wet*, and is radically the same as ὕδωρ, *water*, we want to know why a word meaning to *beget* should be equal, when radically considered, to one significant of water. I have already had occasion to show, even several times, that water has, like bread, been called after that which it serves to support, namely, *life;* and as to *beget* means to *give life*, we thus account for two words so opposite in meaning as to *beget* and to *wet* being, when closely examined, exactly alike. And as the υω of σύω is still equal to the υω of φύω, to *beget*, and to ὕω to *wet*, it cannot be regarded as a different word, though it means to *shake*. But as to shake implies motion, and consequently life or existence, we can thus account for such an idea having been expressed not differently from either φύω or ὕω. Now, though philologists were to find out, as they probably might, the radical identity of φύω, ὕω, and σύω, they could not, however, without the help of those principles which have grown out of the discovery of man's first word, ever account for three ideas so dissimilar having been signified by the same word. I am here reminded of what we saw farther back, namely, that *vater* is the German of *father*, and the Danish of *water;* nor can *vater* differ from *father* or *pater*. If we now return to the Sanskrit *su* (to *beget*), we perceive, on giving the nasal sound to its *u*, that it is the same as sun, and consequently as son, which is confirmed by M. Max Müller, who admits that *sunu* is the Sanskrit of *son*, and that in the Gothic and Lithuanian languages it is written *sunus*. But this authority mistakes when he asserts, as he does, that *su* was a verb when the original of *sunu;* for as a son was called after his father, *su* must have first served as a noun, and afterwards as a verb. And *su* did not then differ in meaning from the *pa* of *pater*, nor from the φυ of φύτορ, noticed above, and shown to have for one of its meanings that of *father*.

When we now observe that the *a* of *pa* and the *u* of the φυ of φύω are not only equal to each other, but, as we have often seen, to *oi* also, we discover that the *pu* of *puer* is the same as *poi;* and this is confirmed by the Greek *poir* (πώῐρ), which is allowed to be its original. And this affords further proof that a son was called after his father. And as the *poi* of the Greek πώῐρ, cannot, from the common interchange of *b* and *p*, differ from *boi*, we thus discover our word *boy*. But in the Greek *poir* we see something else. When its *o* and *i* coalesce, making *a*, it is *par*, that is, *bar*, and this is the Hebrew of *son* or *boy*. *Par* is also the radical part of *pario* to *beget*, and of *parens* or *parent*. Nor can either *bar* or *par* differ from the Hebrew *bra*, which means to *create, make,* or *form.* Let us also observe that as *boi* is equal to *ba*, so is *ba*, when read from right to left, the same as *ab*, Hebrew of *father;* and in which, as well as in *am*, Hebrew of *mother*, we see both *pa* and *ma*, that is, *papa* and *mamma.*

When we now call to mind that *parent* means a *maker*, because named from the hand, it is reasonable to suppose, since its radical part *par* has, with its other meanings, that of *by*, that this idea also is to be traced to the hand. Hence, when we say, " cela a été fait *par* moi," the literal meaning is, " that has been done *hand me ;*" that is, the *hand belonging to me* did it. And when *by* implies proximity, as in *sit by me*, the meaning is *sit at the hand to me;* that is, at the hand belonging to me. This too is confirmed by *près* being the radical part of *present;* since to be *present* is to be at *hand.* And to *present* a thing to any one is to *hand* it to him. Hence, the Latin of the noun *present*, that is, *munus*, cannot differ from *manus.* But if *present* means being *at hand, absent,* I may be told, should mean being *from hand.* And no doubt the idea of *absence* might be so expressed very well ; but it happens to be signified by the preposition *from* and the verb *to be.* Thus *absum urbe* is, literally, *I am from town.*

By thus tracing words to their primary source, we account for those equal as to form having sometimes very different meanings. Thus *by*, when implying proximity, cannot, as a vowel may come between b and y, differ from *boy.* But as the idea *boy* was, as we have seen, named after *father*, and as *father*, as we have also seen, means a *maker*, and that such too is the meaning of *hand*, we cannot be at a loss to know why *by* and *boy* are equal to each other in form though so different in meaning; for if *boy* can, because called after *father*, that is, *maker*, be traced to the idea *hand*, even so can *by* be traced to the same source; for if I say, " My friend stood *by*," it is as if I were to say, " My friend stood *present;*" that is, stood at *hand*.

The elder form of *boy*, that is, *boi*, suggests another etymology. When the *o* and *i* of this word coalesce, producing *a*, *boi* becomes *ba*, in which we see the *ba* of both *baby* and *babe;* so that each of these words seems to be a diminutive of *boy*, and to have first been *boi-y* or *boy-ee*, when it must have meant a very little child of either sex. There are many words of which the sense is lessened by the addition of *y*. Thus watery is less than water, just as milky is less than milk. But, judging by the sound, we should say that *y*, when signifying a diminutive, must have first been *ee*, which, as it represents the sound given to I in at least many languages, and as this letter means *one*, and is consequently the least of numbers, it would seem for this reason, as well as for its very slender sound, to have been adopted for the purpose of signifying a diminutive. Hence it is that in French an *iōta* (which is the name of the Greek I) means the least conceivable portion of any thing.

According to this etymology of *baby*, it must have first been *boi-ee;* its *ee* being for *i*, and *i* for one (I), the least of numbers. But how are we to account for the second *b* of *baby?* By aspirating the *ee*, and by then changing the aspirate for any one of its substitutes that will make sense of *ee*. Thus when we write *ba-fee* for *ba-hee*, we get no sense; nor do we when we change *f* for *v;* but when, instead of *v* we try *w*, we get a very significant word, namely, *wee*. Hence, a *wee boy* means in English a *very little boy*. And when we now make W take its form of B, as we do when instead of the name Will we use Bill, we shall have *bee* instead of *wee*, and consequently *ba-bee* instead of *ba-ee*. This etymology is confirmed by the German *bube*, which is evidently the same word, though meaning a *boy* and not a *babe* or a *baby*.

Bébé in French is still the same word; and in order to conceive how this can be, it will be only necessary to bear in mind what has been shown above; namely, that *boi* is equal to *poi*, and *poi* to the *pu* of the Latin *puer;* for as *e* is equal to *o*, and as *o* has *i* understood, there can be no difference between the *ba* of *baby* and the first *bé* of the French *bébé*. But how are we to account for the second *bé* of *bébé?* By recollecting what has been also shown above; namely, that it must have come from a word meaning *one*, and from one being the least of numbers, that *bé* must have been made to serve as a diminutive. Hence, the German *wenig*, which is significant of *littleness*, becomes, when its *w* (here, as above, a substitute for the aspirate) is dropped, *enig*, of which the root *en* is for *ein*, and *ein* is the German of *one*. English philologists derive *wee* from *wenig*, and these words are, it is true, radically the same; but we are not told what their primary signification may be: there is no hint given that in the beginning either word stood for *one*.

M. Littré derives the Greek *iōta* from the Phœnician *iod*, which is also for I; but this *iod* is to be found both in French and English. Thus when we drop the *i* of *iod* we get *od*, now written *odd*, and an *odd* person is a *singular* person; that is, he is *one* person out of many, so that unity is still implied. And as the *iod* here mentioned is the *iot* of *iota*, we thus see that *od* is the same as *ot*, and that this form of *iod* or of *iot* must mean also *one*, and consequently signify *littleness.* Hence, *ballot* is the diminutive of *ball.* But this ending (*ot*) takes in English the form *et*, its *o* having been changed for *e;* witness *river* and *rivulet, tabour* and *tabouret, flower* and *floweret*, with many others. This ending is also very common in French; witness *histoire* and *histoirette, fille* and *fillette, soufflet* and *soufflette*, &c. Now as the idea *one* may be signified in several ways, it follows that the English *et* and the French *ette* might have been represented differently; witness only *eaglet* in English being *eaglon* in French, and *tabouret* being also *tamborine :* the *ine* of the latter being for *one*, or for a form of equal value, such as the German *ein*, or *un* or *une* in French. And when any of those endings serve to signify the feminine gender, the meaning of diminutiveness is still implied, the female of all animals having been ever considered less than the male.

In Saxon the words for *son* and *daughter* call for a few more observations. In this language the verb *magan* means *to be able ;* that is, *to have power, to have might.* And as its radical part *mag* is also the radical part of the Latin *magnus*, we see that the latter idea—that of *greatness*—has been also expressed by a word meaning *power* or *might.* But these two inflections of *magan*, namely, *mag* and *miht*, bear no resemblance, I may be told, to *sunu*, which is the Saxon of *son.* But let me consult Bosworth, and see if I can find any forms resembling *mac* or *mag.* I do. Witness *maga* (of which the radical part is *mag*), having for two of its meanings *son* and *powerful ;* that is, *son* and *mighty.* Two other names for *son* in this language is *maeg* and *maega*,

which is radically the same as *mac* in Irish and Gaelic.
And that the sun was with this people revered as God,
is sufficiently proved by our Sunday, to which we now
assign the meaning of the Lord's day.

Let us now see if any of those words meaning a *son*
may also mean a *daughter*. The first I find is *mæge*,
which is explained a *kinswoman*, a *daughter*. Nor can
this *mæge* differ from *mæg*, which is the present tense
of *might*, as we have seen; so that, as the *mag* of
magan means both *son* and *powerful*, or *mighty*, even
so does the word for *daughter*. Another word for
daughter is *mægth* (that is, *the mæg*), and of which the
three first meanings given by Bosworth are these : " a
maid, virgin, daughter." And another of its meanings
is *power;* that is, *might.*

And what do I now perceive in this word *power,* so
often given with words for son and daughter? It is
nothing but another form of the old Greek word *põir,* a
son. But why should this be? Because a son·has,
from having been called after his father (a maker),
obtained a name equal to one of the titles of the sun,
which is also that of *artificer* or *maker*[4]. And this
circumstance of the same words meaning not only *son*
and *daughter* but *power,* also were sufficient to prove
their identity ; I mean the identity in meaning of *son*
and *daughter.*

But as both son and daughter have each the meaning
of *maker,* from having been called after their parents;
and as the idea of making is to be traced to the hand,
and from the hand to the sun, whence this idea named
maker first came, it follows that what we call *power*
should be also a word for the *hand,* as well as for *son* and

[4] See Anacalypsis, p. 587.

daughter, and consequently for the supposed maker of all nature—the *sun*. And the word power has these different meanings, as I am now going to show; and by doing so, I shall be obliged to make two or three rather important etymologies, and such as no philologist has hitherto suspected. As the *o* of power has *i* (as usual) understood, and as *o* and *i* make *a*, it follows that the *pow* of power is equal to *paw*, and a paw is a hand, the hand of the leg, conventionally the foot of a beast, and its hand also. We are therefore to regard the *w* of paw as *tt*, and this accounts for the French form *patte*, anciently written *pate*. As *pat*, radical part of *pate* or *patte*, is equal to *pot*, the *i* of the *a* being dropped, we thus obtain the *pot* of *potentia*, and so discover that the *pow* of *power* and the *pot* of *potentia* make but one word. And that the *t* of these forms might as well be *d* is shown by *potere*, the Italian of *power*, being also *podere*. It is even shown by the French *pouvoir* being also *puissance*, that both *t* and *d* might be replaced by *s*, and which is further confirmed by the Latin *posse*, *to have power, to be able*.

In the Saxon of *foot*, that is, *fot*, we have, from the equality of *p* and *f*, still the same word. And as *paw* or *patte* is in Flemish *poot*, this, for the same reason, cannot differ from *foot*. Now, from the foot being, I say, the hand of the leg, it is consequently but another word for *hand*, and it may, for this reason, be significant of *might* or *power*. Hence, the *pod* of *podos*, genitive of *pous*, Greek of *foot*, is the *pod* of the Italian *podere*, *power*. Nor can this *pous* differ from *pais* (παῖς), which, in Greek means both a *son* and a *daughter*. And when we compare the genitives of the two words (witness *podos* and *paidos*), the resemblance becomes more apparent.

And as anciently the *r* was changed for *s* at the end of Greek words, *pais* (παῖς), a *son* or *daughter*, may be regarded as equal to *pōir* (πώϊρ), which has in this language the same meaning. Nor let us forget that *pōir* (πώϊρ) is the same as power, for this will serve to show that *pais* (παῖς) cannot differ from the *puis* of *puissance*, which has also in French the meaning of *power*.

I need scarcely observe that in the *pot* of *potentia* and the *pat* of *patte* (*paw*) we have the *pat* of *pater*, and the *fath* of *father;* because all this is, according to our principles, self-evident, as every one must perceive[b].

There is another word for daughter in Saxon besides those we have seen. I am surprised that M. Max Müller did not class it with those which are identically the same as *duhitar* in Sanskrit. This Saxon word for daughter is *dohtor*, which, as *d* is equal to *t*, and *h* to *ch*, cannot differ from the German *techtor*. Now, as *daughter* in English is but a different form of all those to which I refer, let us see if it can be shown to have the meaning of power, like its other Saxon representatives. In its radical part *daught* we need only change its *a* for *o*, and we get *dought;* and this is the radical part of *doughty*, which, when in use, meant *powerful,* as every one knows. And this is confirmed by the Saxon of *doughty*, that is, *dohtig*, of which the radical part *doh* is also the radical part of *dohtor;* that is, as *h* is equal to *ch*, *dochtor.* But this, I shall be told, is the same as *doctor*, and that

---

[b] As the *pat* of *pater* means, when a verb, to strike gently, and as the hand or the fingers are for so doing employed, this affords additional proof that such a word is traceable to the source to which we have shown it to belong. If we read *pat* from right to left, the meaning will be still the same—that of striking gently with the hand or the fingers.

the primitive meaning of such a word is the *learned* or *wise one;* whence *doctus*, in Latin. And so it ought to be, for all these words are at last traceable to a title of the sun, and this object, from being thought to have been the author of all things, was called the wise one, and which is the meaning, according to the learned, assigned to the name of Buddha; who was, it is now allowed, once worshipped as the sun. But how is such a word as the *dought* of *doughty* to be traced to a word meaning the *hand?* By remarking that its *ou* cannot differ from *oi*, and that *dought* is consequently equal to *doight*, in which it is not difficult to perceive *doigt* (French of finger), and the *digit* of its Latin form *digitus*. And a finger has been called after the hand, and both words have for this reason been used indifferently.

But how does it happen, I may be asked, that the sun, which is the same in both Saxon and English, and nowise different from son, as is shown by its form in other languages, is so very unlike the word *hand?* In order to discover the cause, we should remember that its very earliest form was *O*, and then *oi;* and that from *O* having received the nasal sound, it became both *on* and *om*, and each of these has been a well-known name of the sun, as shown farther back. Now how did *on* become son? By its having first taken the aspirate *h*, and then by this aspirate having been replaced by *s*, which, as already shown, has often happened. But before the aspirate was changed for *s*, *on* must have been *hon*, which is the radical part of the Saxon *hond*, written also *hand*, as in English. Hence, as *son* has grown out of *hon*, it follows that the latter is the elder of the two.

Let us now confirm this account of the origin of son,

by noticing *sol.* This word must have first been *ol*, and then *hol*, and then, by the aspirate becoming *s, sol.* This *ol* is also equal to both *al* and *el*, which were, as Parkhurst testifies, names not only of the true God, but also of the sun ; and when such a form as *el* took the aspirate it became *hel*, which is the radical part of *hēlios*, Greek of *sun;* and when the aspirate of *hēl* was changed for *s, hēl* became *sel*, which is the radical part of *selēnē*, Greek of *moon;* so that *hēlios* and *selēnē* are, we may say, the same word, since they do not differ from each other but by their endings. Hence we may suppose, with tolerable safety, that *selēnē* has been named after *hēlios.*

But the aspirate has been also often replaced by *b*, so that *Al* or *El* has become *Bal* or *Bel*, and even *Bol*, which are well-known names of the sun. Now, when *on* was *hon*, as shown above, it became *bon*, on its aspirate being replaced by *b*, and this idea was called after God, and God also was a name of the sun, as we have seen.

CHAPTER XLVII.

ETYMOLOGY OF BROTHER AND SISTER, ETC.

HAVING said so much about father and mother, son and daughter, may I not attempt the explanation of brother and sister? In Sanskrit the words for *brother* and *sister* are, according to M. Max Müller, *bhrátar* and *svasar.* And of these two words he says, " The original meaning of *bhrátar* seems to me to have been he who *carries* or *assists;* of *svasar,* she who *pleases* or *consoles—svasti* meaning in Sanskrit, *joy* or *happiness*[6]."

When endeavouring to discover the original of a word, we should begin by looking out for its earliest form, which, unless it be a word composed of several others, is generally its root; and this, when found, should be considered as having the meaning of the whole word. If we take *bhrat* as the radical part of *bhrátar,* we see at a glance that it means *boy* or *son.* And is not a brother a son? And if this be granted, it follows that it must have the same meaning as the one given to father, after which son has been called, as we have shown. But according to M. Max Müller, it may signify one who *carries* or *assists.* And if it has the meaning of *son,* it may also mean *carrying* or *assisting,* for these ideas are traceable to the hand, and the hand is not only a maker—whence the meaning of both *father* and *son*—but it is also that which *carries* or *assists,* as well as that which *takes* and *gives,* not to mention a great many other different meanings, as we have seen. Hence if we find two words in a language very like each other in form, we are not to suppose that either of them was derived from the other. When we come to such a conclusion, the agreement in sense between every two such words must be very close. It seems more reasonable to suppose that a *brother* (who is really a son) should be called a *son,* than one who *carries* or *assists.* We have taken the *bhrat* of *bhrátar* as its radical part, and as meaning as much as the whole word; and that this was no mis-

[6] " Chips from a German Workshop," vol. ii. p. 25.

take is shown by the Slavonic language, in which *brother*
or *bhrátar* is, without an additional suffix, expressed
by this word *brat* itself; that is, according to M. Max
Müller, who shows that it is so written in some seven
or eight different languages.

Parkhurst, in his Hebrew Lexicon, suggests that a
son (*bar*) may be the old English word *bern* or *barn* (also
a *son*), and that such too may be the word *brat;* the very
word which means a *brother* in the Slavonic language,
and is radically the same in some seven or eight other
languages.

But if *brother* or *bhrátar* means a *son*, it follows—
since a son was called after his father, and since the
earliest form we have of the latter was *fa*, or, which is
the same thing, *pa*—that the earliest form of *brother* or
bhrátar must be also equal to *fa* or *pa*, and this would
reduce the word *bor*, *bhrátar*, or *brother*, to *ba*, which is
equal to *pa* or *fa*. But this reduction may be made still
less, and for this reason: I perceive that words beginning with *b, f, v, p, m,* or *s*, are generally indebted for
these signs to the aspirate *h*, which, when it does not
itself remain, is generally replaced by one of them.
Now supposing that the *b* of the reduced form of *brother*
or *bhrátar*—that is *ba*—is only a representative of *h;* it
follows that *ba* must have once been *ha*, and have then
meant as much as the entire word, *brother* or *bhrátar*,
does at present. And this analysis is so likely to be correct, that *ha* (but read from right to left) is the Hebrew
of *brother*. I do not mean to say that our word *brother*,
or any other of its seven or eight different forms, is derived from the Hebrew *ha* or *ah;* but what I do mean
is this, that, notwithstanding their difference in form,
they are radically the same.

M. Renan alludes somewhere in his work on the Origin of Language (but I cannot now find the place), to the wide difference in form between the Hebrew of *brother* (*ah*) and I think *bhrat* or *frat*. But he does not attempt to account for the origin of either word. And this accords with his system of language, if that which is no system may be so called.

As to the ending of the word *brother*, or any of its other forms, it is to be accounted for just as we have accounted for the ending of the Greek *thugatēr;* that is, we are to consider it as a compound pronominal article fallen behind its noun.

Let us now endeavour to trace *svasar* (Sanskrit of *sister*) to its original meaning. M. Max Müller supposes it to mean " she who *pleases* or *consoles—svasti* meaning, in Sanskrit, *joy* or *happiness.*" Neither the *s* nor the *v* of *svasar* should be regarded as belonging to the root of this word. It must have first been *asar*, when the *v* was obtained from the *a* by which it is followed having been aspirated, and the aspirate having been replaced by the *v*, as it often is. The *v* in Sanskrit is, it would seem, the same as *w;* and hence it is that, like this sign, it is here preceded by *s*, there being a euphonic tendency to sound *s* before *w*. In the *svas* of *svasar*, Sanskrit of *sister*, and the *sweos* of its Saxon form *sweoster*, and the *schwes* of the German *schwester*, we have—but slightly different in form—the same radical part of each of the three words; and such too is the *sor* of *soror* in Latin, the French word *sœur*, and to which we may add the *sis* of *sister*, not to mention the *sor* of *sorella*, or *sur* of *suora* in Italian. Here every word for sister, with the exception of the French *sœur*, has a pronominal article fallen behind it, the precise meaning of which is shown by the *ella* of the Italian sor*ella*, from which none of the other endings can differ in meaning though they do in form ; and every one knows the meaning of *ella*. When we do, therefore, remove these endings, and also the prefixes (all of which have grown out of the aspirate), we shall have, in what remains, the root of each word. Thus in the Sanskrit sva*sar*, we shall have *as;* in the Saxon swe*oster*, *os ; es* in the German schw*ester; or* in the Latin sor*or; œur* in the French s*œur ; is* in sis*ter*, and *or* and *uor* in the Italian sor*ella* and su*ora*.

When we now recollect that every vowel, or combination of vowels, preceding a consonant, constitutes a root, and that all the roots of a language are, like all its letters, equal to one another, and that the sole difference in meaning between them is but conventional ; it follows that the Hebrew word *ah,* which is a root, and means *brother,* cannot differ from any of the roots of the words meaning *sister*. According to Parkhurst, this word *ah* means, when written *aht* or *ahut*, a *sister*, from which we may infer that the *t* or *ut* with which it ends is for indicating the sex. This authority does not therefore mistake when he makes the two words for *brother* and *sister* have the same root[7].

Let us now see how sister is expressed in Saxon. It is by *mage ;* and this word is equal to *maga*, which is in this language one of the words for *son,* as we have already shown ; so that the literal meaning of *mage*, or *sister*, is a *female son ;* in other words, a *daughter*. But what is the Saxon of brother? It is *brothor, bruthor,* or *brether,* according to Bosworth ; so that its radical part *bro, bru,* or *bre,* is also the same as *bar* in Hebrew, that

[7] Lex., p. 8.

is, *son ;* and also the same as *bern* and *barn* in Old English, as well as *brat,* which is *brother* in Slavonic. And here be it observed that as the Hebrew *bar* (a son) cannot differ from the Hebrew *bra* to *make* or *create;* neither can the *mag* of *maga,* a *son,* nor the *mag* of *mage,* a *sister,* differ from the *mac* of *macian,* to *make* or *create,* in Saxon. Another word in this language, which is precisely equal to those meaning son and sister is *mæge,* and this word means *daughter. Mægth* is another form of it, differing only by the article (*th* or *the* at the end), and the three first meanings given of it by Bosworth are these:. " A maid, virgin, daughter."

But the ideas *brother* and *sister* are not signified in all languages alike. In Greek the words for *brother* and *sister* are ἀδελφὸς and ἀδελφὴ, and their literal meaning is, *same womb,* a being a construction of ἁμα (*same*), and *delphos* being for *delphus, womb.* In Gaelic I find a word for brother, which serves to prove that the primary signification of this idea is, as I have shown, that of *son.* The word is *macsamhuil,* which has the literal meaning of *son-likeness, mac* being for *son* and *samhuil* for *likeness.* In *mac,* which is the Irish of *son,* it is easy to perceive the root of the Saxon *macian,* to *make,* as it is also of the German *machen.* We still see in this *mac* the root of the name of the Deity, referred to thus by Bryant: " Macrai was a contraction for Macar-Ai, or the place of Macar, a title of the Deity[3]."

Is it not now easier to conceive that men must, while language was yet in its infancy, have named brother and sister after son and daughter than after the fanciful ideas suggested by M. Max Müller, according to whom the word *brother* is supposed to mean " one who *carries*

[3] Analysis of Ancient Mythology, i. 67.

or *assists,*" and the word *sister* to be for "she who *pleases* or *consoles.*"

I learn from M. Max Müller that *ma* in Sanskrit means to *fashion* or *make.* This I knew before, but not from an acquaintance with Sanskrit, of which I happen to be wholly ignorant; but from my own principles, which must in time to come serve the philologist more than a knowledge of fifty languages. But how could I learn, the reader may ask, by the use of my discovery or its principles, that such a word as *ma* means, when primarily considered, to *make?* I learned it in the same way as I learned the primary signification of *pater,* to which the reader may refer, if my etymology of the word be already forgotten. It is also easy to perceive that in *pater* and *mater* we have the same word, the difference between them in sex being only conventional; and which M. Max Müller confirms when he admits that the Sanskrit of *mother* is sometimes *masculine.*

It is further easy to perceive that as the *a* of *ma* is entitled to the nasal sound, this word cannot differ from the *man* of *manus,* nor from the *ma* of *mare* in Greek, which is also as well as *cheir,* a word for the *hand.*

But I shall be here most likely reminded that the English word *mare,* the female of the horse and now meaning *mother,* is the Latin of *sea;* but this can be very easily accounted for. We have shown the sea to have been called after water, and water after life, and life after its supposed *creator* or *maker,* the *sun.* Hence from a word for the *sea* being thus traced up to the sun it is equal to a word for *maker.* We should further observe, that as the Sanskrit *w* is often represented in Latin by *m, wari* being *mare,* there can be no difference between *mater* and *water,* though a mother was not called after water.

Now as a son has been named after his father, how does it happen that *bar,* Hebrew of *son,* has an *r* in it, and that *ab* (*father*) has none? We should observe that the *b* of *bar* does here but represent the aspirate *h,* which, from its not being a radical part of this word, should be left out, so that *ar* alone remains; and as *ar* is, like *ab,* a *root,* we should regard it as but a different form of *ab,* and as having, in all probability, often served as a name for *father.* The *par* of *pario* and *parens,* and which is equal to *bar,* confirms this opinion, its root being also *ar,* and its *p* being a representative of the aspirate *h.* And in *bra* and *pra* we have still the same word. While now bearing in mind that father and son have had the same name, because the son was called after his father, and that the father was like the sun, called a *maker;* we can easily account for the following from Higgins: " Pra in the Baly or Bali, the sacred language of Judia or Odiaa, the capital of the kingdom of Sion, signifies the *sun* and *the great living God* [9]; that is, the *creator* or *former,* giver of forms. From this has come *Pra ju-pati,* or the Lord of mankind, which means *father, ja, creator* [1]. This *Pra* is evidently the Hebrew word ברא *bra,* to *create* or *form,* of the first verse of Genesis. It is singular that Parkhurst gives the verb ברא *bra* to *create,* but no noun for Creator. But though it may be lost now, it cannot be doubted that the verb must have had its correspondent noun. I have before observed that this word PR or BR is said by Whiter always to mean Creator [2]." But here, with respect to *bra,* Higgins mistakes; the noun for ברא *bra* is not lost; it is the same as באר *bar,* Hebrew of *son,* of which the *a* has fallen behind

---

[9] La Loubère, pp. 6, 7.   [1] Asiat. Res., vol. viii. p. 255.
[2] Aua., vol. i. p. 431.

its *r;* and we are assured that it was by His Son or the Word that God made the world.

We have thus discovered an important type ; and it becomes more evident when we observe that באר *bar,* which means the *son,* is the radical part of דבר *dbr,* that is, *debar,* which means the *Word*[3]. Hence, in very remote times the heathen was told, through language, that the Son was the Word, and that he was also the Creator, And as the *b* in Hebrew is, as well as in Greek and other languages, often changed for *m,* it follows that the *bar* of *debar* cannot, when read from right to left, differ from *ram,* and this is confirmed by אמר *amr,* in which we have the same three letters, and it means not only a *word,* but a *lamb* also[4]. Hence it is that the Son is frequently called the Lamb of God, *Agnus Dei.* In אמר *amr* it is also easy to perceive, when we read as above, ῥῆμα, the Greek of word, for this form becomes, when its *ē* is dropped, *rhma.* In *debar* when its non-radical part, that is, *de,* falls behind, *bar,* it is equally easy to discover our *bard;* and as *b* is a common form of *w,* bard is the same as *ward,* that is, *word.* But though a *bard* is one who deals in words, we are not to suppose that his name is to be thence derived. As *bra,* to *create,* is the same as *bar,* which is the radical part of *bard,* we are obliged to admit that the name of the person so called does not differ in meaning from that of poet, of which the Greek form ποιητής signifies a *maker,* a *creator,* an *author,* &c. We have also this meaning in *mar,* which from the identity of *m* and *b* (compare מריא *mria, fat,* with בריא *bria,* which has the same meaning[5]) cannot differ from *bar,* the *son;* and the *ma* of *mar*

---

[3] Parkhurst, Lex., p. 104.   [4] Ibid., p. 22.
[5] Saunders, Heb. Lex., p. 52.

signifies in Sanskrit to *make* or *create*, and is allowed to be the root in this language of the word meaning *mother*. Hence, the same term may signify *father, son,* and *mother*. This can be easily accounted for when we observe that father and mother have the same meaning, that of maker, and that the son has been called after his parents. This can be still more easily conceived by comparing such words as *creator* and *creature,* which are clearly one and the same word, the slight difference between them in form being only for the sake of distinction. And it ought to be so, since the creature was made by the Creator.

But if the sun was the creator, his name in English, Gothic, Saxon, German, Danish, and many other languages over the world, which are all radically the same word, bears, I may be told, no resemblance in form to either *bar, bra,* or *creator*. But it should be remembered that all roots, however they may differ in appearance, are, like the letters of an alphabet, equal to one another. Hence there is no difference, except conventionally, between the *un* and *on* (which are the roots of the word for sun in the languages just mentioned), and any other root, such as *ab, ac, ad,* &c. The cause of so many names of the sun ending with *n,* or, which amounts to the same, with *m,* arises from the tendency with many people to give the nasal sound to vowels. Hence, the first name of the sun, that is, O. became *on, un, an, am, om, um,* &c. Thus, according to Bryant, "*son, san,* and *zan* have the same signification," and are names of the sun. As to the *s* and *z* of these words they do but replace the aspirate, so that *on* and *an* are the roots, and nowise different from the *un* of *sun*. Another well-known name of the sun was *aun;* and which is thus confirmed by the following : " *On* or *Aun* was the Egyptian title of the sun, whence the city of *On* was expressed by the Greeks *Heliopolis*[6]." How these names of the sun may vary while being still radically the same as *on* or *un*, we see by their being also written "*Ain* and *Aven*[7]."

Another very different form of these names, in which we see the nasal sound preserved, is *Ham;* that is, *am* with the aspirate. " Ham was," says Bryant, " esteemed the Zeus of Greece, and Jupiter of Latium. From Egypt his name and worship were brought into Greece, as indeed were the names of almost all the deities there worshipped. He being the Apollo of the East, was worshipped as the sun, and was also called Sham and Shem." Here the *am* and *em* of Sham and Shem, are the roots of these words, and the *sh* by which they are preceded does but represent the aspirate *h*. Hence, such persons as did not aspirate the initial vowel of each of these words must have used *am* and *em* as names of the sun. The sun is signified in Hebrew, not only by Al or El (which was also the name of the true God), but by שמש *sms* also; we thus see that this Hebrew name is the Sham and Shem made here to represent the word Ham. Bryant, referring again to Ham, continues thus : " His posterity esteemed themselves of the solar race. The chief oracle in the first ages was that of Ham, who was worshipped as the sun, and styled El and Or ; hence these oracles are in consequence called Amphi, Omphi, Alphi, Elphi, Orphi, Urphi." Here the first syllable of each of these words represents the name

---

[6] Anacalypis, vol. i. p. 110.

[7] See Holwell's Extract from Bryant's Analysis of Ancient Mythology, p. 175.

Ham; yet how widely they differ in form from this name Ham! As to the second syllable, *phi*, it is the φη of φημί, which signifies a *saying* or an *oracle*; so that the literal meaning of *Omphi*, and its other forms, is the oracle of Ham.

Referring once more to Ham, Bryant says, " He was the Hermes of the Egyptians, and his oracle was called Omphi, and when particularly spoken of as *the oracle*, it was expressed P'Omphi, and P'Ompi. The worship of Ham or the sun, as it was the most ancient, so it was the most universal of any in the world. It was at first the prevailing religion of Greece, and was propagated over all the sea coast of Europe; from whence it extended itself into the inland provinces. It was established in Gaul and Britain; and was the original religion of this island, which the Druids in after times adopted. That it went high in the north is evident from Ausonius, who takes notice of its existing in his time[8]. Ham was also the same as Petor and Osiris[9]."

We have just seen that two of the roots representing Ham as the sun, are *or* and *el*; of which the first cannot differ from *oir*, nor *oir* from *ar* (*oi* making *a*); and when we now give to *ar* the aspirate *h*, it will become *har*, whence *bar*, because *b* represents the aspirate. And that the *r* of *bar* is here equal to *n*, we can have no doubt when we observe that *bar*, Hebrew of son, is also written *ben*, as every one knows. And the *en* of *ben* cannot differ from *an*, *on*, *un*, and all such forms, which were once so many names of the sun. Nor can *bar* differ from *car* any more than *bear* can, when radically considered, differ from *carry*, or the French verb *charier*.

---

[8] Ode 4—10. [9] Holwell, p. 209.

And as *bar* becomes *bra* (Hebrew of to *create*) so is *car* equal to *cra*, which is the same as the *crea* of creator.

It is worthy of remark that the *har* just noticed as equal to *bar*, the *son*, is, saving the aspirate, the root of *haris;* and referring to this word, Higgins says, "*Heres* signifies the sun, but in Arabic the meaning of the radical word is to *preserve,* and *haris* is said to mean *guardian, preserver.* Hara-Hara is a name of Maha-Deva, which is Great God. *Heri* means *saviour.* When people are in great distress they call on Maha-Deva by the name of Hara-Hara[1]."

I had occasion farther back to show that one of the many titles of the sun was the Saviour. Farther on, referring again to *Haris*, Higgins says, "*Kreshen* is one of the thousand names of God in the Hindostanee dialect. *Creas, Creama, Cheres, Creeshna, Cur, Cores,* and κῦρος all mean the *sun.*" Drummond says: "חרש *hrs* may be sounded *choras, chros, chrus.* This word signifies *faber, artifex, machinator.*" And, according to Volney, "Artificer was an epithet belonging to the sun[2]."

All these names are very suggestive. Every intelligent reader must now perceive at a glance that the *Har* of *Haris* cannot differ from *bar*, the *son;* and that *Har* means the *sun*, and also *saviour,* and so was the sun, as learned men admit, known to the ancients by the title of *saviour.* It is also very easy to perceive in such a form of *Haris* as *Chrus*, the *Chris* of *Christos,* and even *crux.* And Christ, the Saviour, suffered on the cross. According to Bochart, "The Chaldean name of the sun is חרש *hrs, Chris,* hinc et Persis sol dicitur Κῦρος, teste Plutarcho[3]."

All this is, I say, very suggestive, and must be ex-

[1] Anacalypsis, vol. i. p. 313.　　[2] Ibid., vol. i. p. 587.　　[3] Ibid.

tremely gratifying to him whose faith in the doctrine of
types is wavering and wants additional proof. In one of
the names just given, we have seen also that of the Indian
god *Kreshen* [4], who, from his having been born of a virgin
and crucified for the salvation of a sinful world, must be
received as another very startling type, and the more so
as he is allowed by the learned to have long preceded the
Christian era.

But neither this Indian god, nor Mercury, nor Bacchus, nor Buddha, nor Hercules, though they are all
allowed by many good Christians to be genuine types
of their Saviour, can surpass, in this respect, the types
so often here afforded by a knowledge of the origin of
language. The India God Creeshna or Christna is, it
must be allowed, a very close type, even as to his name.
And that Buddha is not to be despised as such, the following may serve to show :—

" Jayadeva describes Buddha as bathing in blood or
sacrificing his life, to wash away the offences of mankind,
and thereby to make them partakers of the kingdom of
heaven. On this the author of the Cambridge key [5]
says, ' Can a Christian doubt that this Buddha was the
type of the Saviour of the world [6] ?' "

And that the adherents of this doctrine are firm in
their belief, and that they cannot conceive why others
should not be equally so, the two passages which I am
now going to transcribe from that most zealous and orthodox Christian, Dr. Parkhurst, will, I have no doubt, fully
confirm. Hercules is now the type, who, though he is
said to have been the son of Jupiter, if he flourished in
our degenerate days, would, from his rather equivocal

---

[4] It is spelt also *Christna* and *Creeshna.* See Anac., vol. i. p. 585.

[5] Vol. i. p. 118.   [6] Anacalypsis, vol. i. p. 309.

conduct on some occasions, receive no higher praise than such as we are now accustomed to allow to a brigand chief. But Parkhurst first refers to him thus: "Hercules, by whom, as we learn from the Orphic hymn, was anciently meant the *sun,* or rather the solar light, was commonly represented in a human form, clothed with a *lion's* skin; the human form, as usual, intimating the expected Saviour." As a high authority favourable to his opinion, Parkhurst refers the reader, in a note, to Spearman's Letters on the Septuagint, p. 88. His second notice of Hercules is as follows: "It is well known that by Hercules in the physical mythology of the heathen was meant the sun or solar light, and his twelve famous labours have been referred to the sun's passing through the twelve zodiacal signs; and this perhaps not without some foundation. But the labours of Hercules seem to have had a still higher view, and to have been originally designed as emblematic memorials of what the real *Son of God,* and *Saviour of the World* was to do and suffer for our sakes: Νόσων θελκτήρια πάντα κομιζωνί. *Bringing a cure for all our ills;* as the Orphic hymn speaks of Hercules. But on this subject see more in Mr. Spearman's excellent Letters on the LXX., p. 88. To what that learned writer has observed I beg to add a curious passage from Mr. Spence's Polymetis [7]. Besides Hercules strangling the *two serpents* sent to destroy him in his cradle, ' What,' says he, ' is more extraordinary than this, is that there are exploits supposed to have been performed by him, even *before* Alcmena *brought him into the world.'* To which he [Spence] adds in a note, ' This is perhaps one of the most *mysterious* points in all the mythology of the ancients. Though Hercules was born not long before

7 Dial. ix. p. 116.

the Trojan war, they make him assist the gods in con-
quering the rebel giants[8]; and some of them talk of an
oracle or tradition in heaven that the gods could never
conquer them without the assistance of a MAN[9].' " Thus
Mr. Spence. Parkhurst continues thus: " And can any
man seriously believe that so excellent a scholar as he
was could not easily have accounted for what he represents as being so *very mysterious?* Will not 1 Pet. i.
20, compared with Hag. ii. 7, clear the whole difficulty;
only recollecting that Hercules might be the name of
several *mere men,* as well as a title of the future Saviour?
And did not the *truth* here glare so strongly in our
author's eyes, that he was afraid to trust his reader with
it in the text, and so put it into a note for fear it should
spoil his jests at page 125 ? "

I regret not to have Spence's work by me, that I might
see at page 125 what these jests were, but it is evident
that Parkhurst did not approve of them, and he further
confirms his belief that Hercules was a genuine type of
his Saviour by referring, as he does, in support of his
opinion, to passages in Scripture itself[1].

That many very learned, pious, and sound orthodox
Christians do therefore believe in the doctrine of types
cannot be any longer doubted. And when these symbols
are conveyed through language, as they seem to be, why
should they not be received with as much confidence as
when they are indicated through the Life and Adventures
of a Hercules, or any other heathen divinity?

Another very startling type suggested by language
now occurs to me. I have already told the reader more

[8] Virgil, Æn., viii. lin. 298.
[9] Apollodorus, Bibl., lib. i., and Macrobius, Lat., lib. i. cap. 20.
[1] See his Lexicon, p. 302 and 469.

than once that in the beginning the son was called after
the father; whence it happened that the same word signified both the parent and the child.   But it does not
occur to me that I have given so striking and important
an instance of it as the one to which I now beg to draw
the reader's most serious attention.   I learn from M. Max
Müller's " Chips from a German Workshop [2]," that in
Sanskrit *su* means to *beget*, and that *sunú* is in the same
language the word for *son*.   By this we see since the *u*
of *su*, to *beget*, is entitled to the nasal sound, that this
word cannot differ from *sun*, which is the radical part of
sunu (a son), so that the same word means the *begetter*
and the *begotten*, the latter having been called after the
former, which accounts for both ideas having the same
name.   Let us now observe that a begetter is a father,
and that the primary signification of father is, as we have
seen, a maker, which was a name of the sun, as it is still
of our Creator, of whom the sun was a type.   But the
root of every such word as *sun* and *son* is *un* and *on*, and
this root means *one*, just as *sol* (whence *solus*) does.   The
creator has been thus typified by language; that is to
say, a simple word has told the whole world that there
is but *one* God, and that HE has *one* Son.   How was it
to be known in the beginning that there is only one
God, and this too at a time when there was no divine
revelation communicated to the heathen?   It was, however, then well known, not to the multitude, it is true,
but to all the great minds to whose superior wisdom the
rest of mankind has been ever since so largely indebted.
Hence Higgins justly observes, " Socrates, Pythagoras,
Plato, Zoroaster or Zeradust, &c., acknowledged *one*
supreme God, the Lord and First Cause of all [3]."

[2] Vol. ii. p. 30.   [3] Anacalypsis, vol. i. p. 43.

But how could they have acquired this knowledge if not through language? The sun was their type. And it was also the sun first told the whole world that the Creator had an only Son, this being clearly typified by the meaning of the word *sun* itself in all languages, which must have been that of both *one* and *son*. But ages after the creation of language, and when men began to express themselves poetically, they may have given other names, and consequently other meanings to the name of the sun; but it could not have been so in the beginning when our glorious orb was signified by a single sign (the O), and then by whatever consonant sound happened at a later period to follow and join with this its earliest name. There are several names in Hebrew for the sun, of which one is, it would seem, *sur*. Thus Higgins says, "The word for the sun is in Hebrew *sur*, in Chaldee *Tur*[4]."

When the sun obtained this name, it must have been signified by *ur*, but previously by O, then by *oi*, whence *u*, and then *ur*; when from the *u* of *ur* having been aspirated, and from the aspirate having been replaced by *s*, *sur* was obtained. But when the *u* of *sur* received its consonant sound, and this word became *svr*, and when *svr* with vowels supplied took the form of *savar*, that is, *saver*, it was then easy to perceive in modern languages one of the ancient meanings of the name of the sun, that of a *saviour*, a meaning the learned allow it to have had, though why it had this meaning they could not divine.

In *Surya*, which is, according to Higgins[5], a name of the solar divinity of India, we see also *Sur*, this ancient name of the sun. We have it likewise in *Surē*; and

---

[4] Anacalypsis, vol. i. p. 607.   [5] Ibid., vol. i. p. 136.

Maurice says, " Persæ Σύρη Deum vocant[6]." By this we see that the same word means *sun, Saviour,* and *God.*

CHAPTER XLVIII.

SAVITAR.

THESE etymologies suggest another very important one, and though it is a Sanskrit word, men who are supposed to be very learned in this language seem to know nothing of two meanings which I, who am ignorant of Sanskrit, can prove this word to have. I allude to *savitar,* which, according to M. Max Müller[7], is as well as *Surya* (just noticed) one of the names of the sun. Now as the *i* of *savitar* has *o* understood, and as *o* and *i* compose *a,* it follows that *savitar* is for *savatar,* which, from its *s* being omitted, because only replacing the aspirate, becomes *avatar,* and this Sanskrit word, which is not to be found in Johnson, is thus explained by Webster: " The incarnation of the Deity in the *Hindoo Mythology.*" But the real original meaning is, we now see, not the incarnation of the Deity, but the incarnation of the sun. When this belief first began to prevail, the sun must have been then revered as God. Now as *savitar* has not been shown to mean *saviour,* neither has it been shown to mean *avatar.* On consulting M. Max Müller's index under *savitar,* I am told

---

. [6] Ant. Ind., vol. ii. p. 203.   [7] Lect., vol. ii. p. 379.

it is called, as a Vedic name of the sun, the *Golden-handed;* but for its meaning I am referred to page 411, vol. ii., where the only meaning given of the word *savitar* is this: " The *sun*." Why *savitar* was called the *Golden-handed*, I shall endeavour to show presently. Let us now consult M. Littré. His etymology of *avatar* is thus given : " Sanscrit *avatara*, de *ava*, qui est le ἀπό des Grecs et le *ab* des Latins, et de *tri*, passer, dont le radical *tr* ou *tar* se trouve dans beaucoup de mots des autres langues Aryennes."

According to this etymology, *avatar* is composed of two significant words; of *ava*, which from its representing ἀπό in Greek and *ab* in Latin, means *from;* and *tri*, which, we are told, means to *pass*. As to what M. Littré says about *tr* or *tar* being the radical part of *tri* (to pass), and that it is to be found in many words of other Aryan languages, this is not to add a third meaning of any kind to the two meanings, *from* and *pass*, already given. Now, if this distinguished philologist were to write on a thousand little bits of pasteboard as many words picked out of a dictionary with his eyes shut, and if then, on having shaken them up well in his hat, he were to draw out the two first he chanced to lay his fingers on, these two would, in all probability, comprise as reasonable an etymology of *avatar* as the one he has here given us in this fine dictionary of his. In short, this etymology has not so much as the mere shadow of common sense; it lies thousands of miles away from the truth; it is meagreness personified, not having even the merit of a rich blunder, such as I have myself often made while feeling my way.

With respect to *savitar* having the meaning of *Golden-handed*, M. Max Müller says, " It was a very natural idea for people who watched the golden beams of the sun playing as it were with the foliage of the trees, to speak of these outstretched rays as hands or arms. Thus we see that in the Veda, *savitar*, one of the names of the sun, is called *golden-handed*[8]."

But it seems to me that this metaphor can receive an explanation very different from all those it may have hitherto obtained. Have I not already told the reader "many a time and oft," that the sun had anciently, because then revered as God, received the name of *maker*, and that the hand also was called a *maker*. And what follows? Why, that while language was yet in its infancy, these two very different ideas, *sun* and *hand*, must have been signified by the same word, with some very slight difference in sound for the sake of distinction. And at a time when the WORD was revered as God, and when every thing it signified was respected and believed as so much sacred truth, this circumstance that the same word meant both sun and hand could not fail to suggest the erroneous belief that the sun had a *hand*. But why was it thought to be a golden hand? It was not because gold was called after the sun, but because it was called after its *bright* colour, and this colour took its name from the sun; so that sun and gold must, without either having been called after the other, have had at first the same name, with, perhaps, scarcely a sign of distinction to prevent their being confounded.

It must have, therefore, been from these three words, *sun*, *hand*, and *gold*, having been once found to be very much alike, if they were not then completely so, that men were, out of their reverence for the WORD, first led to

[8] Lect., vol. ii. p. 377.

believe that the sun had really a *hand,* and that this *hand* was of *gold.*

Every lover of poetry is well aware that the epithet *golden* is frequently applied to the sun. Hence Parkhurst justly observes that "the poets abound with passages comparing the *solar orb* or *light* to *gold;*" and of which he quotes many instances[*]. Hence he gives זהב *zeb* as meaning not only *gold,* but also *clear, bright* and *resplendent.* But what have we in the Hebrew *zeb ?* A form precisely equal to the *sav* of *savitar,* the *sun.* We therefore see that *zeb* is the same as *zev,* and we know that *zev* cannot differ from *zav,* any more than *elder* can differ from the *alder* of *alderman ;* so that *zev* is exactly equal to *zav.* And if we now write *zavitar* instead of *savitar,* will not every one say—even persons so ignorant of the permutation of letters as not to know that *s* and *z* do constantly interchange—that in *zavitar* and *savitar* we have evidently the same word.

Now the *sav* of *savitar,* and the *zab* of *zabitar* are radical parts of these words; their roots are *av* and *ab ;* the *s* and *z* of each word being substitutes for the aspirate *h,* which is *never* to be regarded as belonging to the radical part of any word whatever. Now as the root *av* is the same as *ab,* and as *ab* is the Hebrew of *father,* and as father means a *maker* (as we have seen), and as the sun was once called a *maker,* and as the hand has still the same meaning, it is thus made evident that *ab* might serve to signify both *sun* and *hand,* and that it may have often done so. But has it ever done so ? Not that I know; perhaps it never has. And why so ? Because all roots are as one and the same word, and never differ in meaning from one another except conventionally. There

[*] See Lex., p. 140.

is, therefore, no difference between two such roots as *ab* and *ad*, so that either of these two roots may have been often used for the other.   Under *adad* Parkhurst says, " The sun, whom the Assyrians called *Adad*, that is, says my author, *One* (perhaps from the Chaldee חד, *hd one,* by reduplication חדחד, *hdhd, one alone, eminently one*), is by them sometimes figured as a man, riding upon a lion, surrounded with rays[1]."   And in Higgins I find the following : " We have found God called *Ad* in India and in Western Syria[2]."

Now every name of the true God was anciently a name of the sun, and this is confirmed by the following, taken also from Higgins : " In Sanskrit *Al Chod* is *God,* as it is in English."   And to this he adds the following note : " Al-Choder is the Syriac and Rajpoot *OD,* only aspirated, and with the Arabic emphatic article *AL.* When the Buddhists address the Supreme Being, or Buddha, they use the word *AD,* which means the *first*[3]." And why does *Ad* mean the *first?* Because it means *one*, and because *one* is the *first* of numbers ; and *one* is also a name of the sun.   Hence *sol* is the English word *sole*, and the Latin *solus.*

The *ad* here noticed is, we say, precisely equal to *ab* (Hebrew of *father*) ; and as *ad* was the name of the *sun*, so might *ab* have also been ; and as יד *id* is the Hebrew of *hand*, and as this word cannot differ (save conventionally) from *ad*, any more than *bid* and *bade* in English can differ from each other, it is thus shown that such a word as *ib* might also have meant the *hand*.   But *ib*, I shall be told, does mean the *hand*, for it is equal to *ab*, and *ab* is the root of *habere*, which might from the

---

[1] Parkhurst, Lex., p. 302.   [2] Anac., vol. ii. p. 181.
[3] Anac., vol. i. p. 198.

dropping of the aspirate, have been *abere*, as is shown by *avere* in Italian, and *avoir* in French ; and every such idea as having or holding must be traced to the hand for its original source. *Ib* is even to be found in the sense of *have*, as is made evident by *exhibere* being for *exhabere*, and of which, from the preposition *ex* being now significant of height, the primary sense must be *holding up;* the ideas *have* and *hold* being each traceable to the hand.

An additional proof that *ad* and *ab* are equal to each other is shown by the permutation of their consonants *d* and *b* (compare *udder* and *uber*, *verb* and *word*, *beard* and *barbe*, &c.) since, for the same reason, these two words themselves may interchange. The conclusion to which we may, therefore, safely come is this, that though *sun* and *hand* have each the meaning of *maker*, yet, from the roots of a language being equal to one another, and from their being, for this simple reason, as liable to interchange, as the letters of which they are composed, it follows, that the *sun* may be signified by one root, and the *hand* by another. But though this will give different forms to the words for *sun* and *hand*, it will not cause the hand to have a meaning different from that of *maker;* but when the sun takes one of its other meanings, as that of *shining*, or *brightness*, for instance, the hand cannot then, since it is not, like the eye, a luminous object, be said to express such an idea, or any other, when relating to the sun, than that of *maker*.

We have thus shown why the sun (*savitar*) was styled the *golden-handed*, and we can in the same way account for some other myths relating to this divinity; but M. Max Müller appears convinced that he has accounted for them all—I mean those under *savitar*. Hence he says, "All these myths and legends which we have hitherto

examined are clear enough; they are like fossils of the
most recent period, and their similarity with living
species is not to be mistaken [4]."

M. Max Müller does, however, mistake, and so do the
Brahmans themselves mistake in their explanations of their
own myths.   Let us now read the following from M.
Max Müller : " But to return to the golden-handed sun.
He was not only turned into a lesson, but he also grew
into a respectable myth.   Whether people failed to see
the natural meaning of the golden-handed sun, or whether
they would not see it, certain it is that the early theological treatises of the Brahmans tell of the sun as having
cut his hand at a sacrifice, and the priests having replaced
it by an artificial hand made of gold   Nay, in later
times, the sun under the name of *savitar*, becomes himself a *priest*, and a legend is told how at a sacrifice he *cut*
off his hand, and how the other priests made a golden
hand for him [5]."

Having already accounted for *savitar* and his golden
hand, all we have now to find out is to tell why this
golden hand of his was *cut off*, and why he became one
of his own priests ; and, thanks to the knowledge acquired
through our discovery of the origin of language, both
these circumstances can be very easily explained.   Thus,
I have already shown that all such ideas as are expressed
by the words *cutting* or *striking* are to be traced to the
hand as their primitive source.   Hence no matter how
widely a word meaning to *cut* or *cut off*, may differ in
form from one for the hand, it is not the less evident that
the idea expressed by the verb to *cut* must have been
called after the hand.   Now the English *cut* has not so
much as one letter in common with *hand*, and yet in *cut*

[4] Lectures, vol. ii. p. 379.   [5] Lectures, vol. ii. p. 378.

and *hand* we have the same word. Thus by comparing the Latin *cornu* with its Saxon and English equivalent *horn*, we see that *c* may represent *h*, and that *cut* is there-fore equal to *hut;* and as every vowel may or may not take the nasal sound, it follows that *hut* cannot differ from *hunt*, nor *hunt* from *hant*, nor *hant* from *hand*. By again comparing *horn* and *cornu* we perceive that *c* is here for the aspirate *h ;* and as this sign is *never* to be reckoned as any radical part of a word, it follows that its substitute, the *c* in *cut*, may be left out, by which *cut* is reduced to *ut;* and this is the same as *at*, and consequently as *ad* and *ed*, in which, as shown above, we have the Hebrew words for both *sun* and *hand*.

Another very plain instance of *hand* and to *cut off* being expressed alike is afforded by the Greek words *cheir* and *keir*, for as *ch* and *k* are equal to each other[a], we may say that these two words are letter for letter one and the same; yet *cheir* (χείρ) means the *hand*, and *keir* (κείρ) means to *cut off*, being the radical part of κείρω, which has this meaning. But *cheir* or *keir*, I shall be told, bears no resemblance in form to *savitar;* but Chrisna, the Indian Saviour, was, like *savitar*, an avatar, that is, an incarnation of the *sun ;* and *chr* is the radical part of his name, and so is it of *cheir* (χείρ), the *hand*. Savitar and Chrishna are, therefore, two names of the same person, so that what is told of the one will apply to the other.

And as Chrishna is, like Buddha, Hercules, and other heathen divinities, allowed by many learned Christians to be a genuine type of their Saviour, so is his name, whether we spell it Chrishna, Chreshna, or Christna—for it takes these and several other forms—radically the

[a] See Donnegan, under *k* and *x*.

same as *Christos*, but of which the elder form was *Chrēstos*
(χρηστός). And this word, like *agathos* (ἀγαθός), means
good, an idea named after God; and Christ is represented
as God. And there is besides *cheir* and *keirō*, another
idea named after the hand, which is radically the same
as both *Christos* and *Chrestos*; this word is χρώστω, which
means to *touch, feel, handle,* &c. Nor is the word for
gold wanting, as is shown by χρυσός, of which the radical
part *Chrus* cannot differ from the *Chris* of *Christos*, nor
from the *Chrish* of Crishna.

We should still observe that the roots of all such
words as *Christos, Chrishna, Chrusos,* and *Chrōstos* are *ir*,
ur, and *or;* for as the *ch* is here for the aspirate, it should
not be counted, and what follows the *r* of these words is
to be regarded only as the usual ending of nouns and
adjectives in Greek. As a proof that such a word as
cheir (χείρ), the *hand,* and which is radically the same as
Christos, Chrishna, &c., can be reduced to *ir*, we need
only mention *hir* in Latin, which, as every one knows, is
for the Greek *cheir;* for when we drop, as we may do,
the aspirate of this word *hir, ir* alone will remain. And
as the *i* of *hir* is for the *ei* of *cheir*, so may it be for any
other vowel combination, since all vowels and their combinations are equal to one another. Hence the *ir* of *hir*
is as equal to *aur* as it is to *eir*, and as *eir* becomes by
the addition of the aspirate, *cheir*, so may the *aur* of
aurum (Latin of *gold*) become *chaur*. And that the *aur*
of *aurum* may take the aspirate is proved not only by our
rule (often confirmed) that every initial vowel may or
may not be aspirated, but also by the fact itself, since
hauron (αὔρον), a word of rare occurrence, and which
means *gold*, takes the aspirate *h*, though *aurum*, of which
it is but another form, has no such sign. Now as the

chru of *chrusos* (this other word for *gold*) becomes, when the *u* returns to its place, *chur*, and as *h* is the same as *ch*, we see that the *haur* of αὗρον is equal to *chaur*, and *chaur* cannot differ from *chur;* that is, from the *chru* of *chrusos*, the more usual word for gold. We have thus shown that in *chrusos, aurum,* and *hauron* we have radically but one and the same word.

We have, therefore, accounted for the myth which says that Savitar's hand was cut off at a sacrifice, and replaced by a golden one. We have seen how it arose from the same word which named *Savitar* or *Chrishna,* having meant *sun, hand, gold,* and *cut off.* But the myth adds that *Savitar* or the *sun* became a priest; that is, one of his own priests; in other words, a priest of the sun. This part of the myth is very easily accounted for. Savitar's priests were of course called after himself, and this must have led to his name and that of a priest being alike[7]. It was after this manner that from the son having been called after the father they both obtained the same name, which was the origin of that admirable type by which men were first told that the father and the son are one and the same person. It is clear that this word *Crisean* is still but another way of writing *Chrishna.*

Another curious myth relating to savitar is mentioned by M. Max Müller; but neither he, nor that great philologist, Grimm, whom he quotes, has been able to trace it to its real source, as I shall have occasion to prove presently. But let me first enable every reader, by what I am now going to show him, to discover by himself, and that too very easily, the origin of this myth.

---

[7] Since this was written I have met with the following: " The Bramanick Kreeshna, an incarnation of the Deity, is the Irish Criscau, *holy, pure,* whence *Crisean,* a priest."—*Anacalypsis,* vol. i. p. 586.

The following analysis of the English word *gold* will suffice to prepare him for the task.

Every one must admit that the initial consonants of the Latin *hesternus*, the German *gestern*, and the *yester* of *yesterday*, are precisely equal to one another, by which we see, since these three words have the same meaning, that the aspirate *h* may be represented by both *g* and *y*. Now as *gestern* is equal to the *hestern* of *hesternus*, it follows that *gold* is equal to *hold*, and *hold* is, from the interchange of *l* and *n*, equal to *hond*, and *hond* to *hand*. Hence, any word meaning *gold* may also mean the *hand*, though neither of these ideas can have been called after the other. Then why are they expressed alike? The reader must, by this time, know very well why. He must know that it arises from the hand having—because of the constant use we make of it—been called a maker, after our once supposed maker, the sun. Then was gold called after the sun? No: but after the colour of the sun, which is that of a bright yellow. To find the word for the sun in *gold*, we need only observe that *hold*, which is but another form of it, does not differ from *held*, save conventionally, and the radical part of this word is *hel*, which is not only the *hel* of the Greek *hêlios* (the *sun*), but when the aspirate is dropped—thus reducing it to *el*—it serves in Hebrew to name not only the sun, but the true God. *Hel* had also in other parts of the world the same two meanings; thus I find in Parkhurst the following: "Damascius, in the Life of Isidorus, tells us that the Phœnicians and Syrians call Cronus or Saturn "Ηλ, Hel; and Servius, speaking of Belus the Phœnician, affirms, "All in those parts (about Phœnicia) worship the sun, who in their language is called

Hel;" and again he says, "God is called *Hal* in the Punic or Carthaginian tongue[8]."

Hence in *El*, *Al*, *Hel*, and *Hal*, there is but one word under these several forms, and the first use ever made of these forms was to name the sun; but as men became more enlightened, the same words were made to designate the true God, the sun having only served as a type of the belief not yet revealed. And what could have been, for this purpose, more suitable than that the grandest object in nature should serve as a type of our Maker.

But where is the word signifying to *cut?* We have it in *held*, which cannot differ from *geld* any more—as shown above—than the *hester* of *hesternus* can differ from the German *gestern*, *g* being here, as it often is on other occasions, a substitute for the aspirate *h*. Though *geld* means now to *cut* in a particular way, it must have once meant to *cut* in any way. But how can this be known? From its being the same as *held*, and *held* the same as *hand*, after which the idea expressed by to *cut* must have been first named.

Another proof that the word signifying *gold* may also mean to *cut* now occurs to me. This is shown by *gladius*, the Latin of *sword;* for *glad*, its radical part, must have first been *gald*, and *gald* cannot differ from either *gold* or *geld*. Hence the κοπ of κόπις, Greek of *sword*, is the same as the κοπ of κόπτω, to *cut*. This etymology leads to another. Though the *glad* of *gladius* is equal in form to the *glad* of *gladness*, yet the latter idea was never called after a *sword;* but from *l* interchanging with *u*, *glad*, which is the same as *gold*, cannot differ from the *gaud* of *gaudium*, Latin of *gladness;* from which we may infer, since gold is remarkable for its

[8] Lex., p. 12.

brightness of colour, that to be glad is to be *bright*. Hence to be *dark* or *gloomy* is the reverse of being *glad*, just as it is the reverse of *brightness*. To look bright is therefore to look joyful.

But as there can be no difference between the forms of two such words as *gaudium* and *gladium*, nor between either of these and *gladius*, and as this shows the ideas expressed by *joy* and *sword* to be signified alike, why, we may ask, should this happen? It arises from the *gaud* of *gaudium* being one of the many names of the *sun ;* and from the hand being, as we have often shown, traceable to the same source; and from the idea *cut*, after which that of *sword* has been called, having been signified, as we have also seen, by a word for the *hand*. Hence, though *gaudium* and *gladius* are, in form, equal to each other, they are not at all so in meaning. God, a name of the sun, is the same as *gaud;* just as the *jov* of *jovial*, another word expressive of *gladness*, is the same as Jove, and Jove was the sun.

But as the *hester* of *hesternus* is not only equal to the *gester* of German *gestern*, but to the *yester* of *yesterday* also, it follows that *hel*, a name of the *sun*, must, from this equality of *h* and *y*, be equal to *yel*, which is the radical part of *yellow;* and *gold* has, from its brightness, been called after the colour named from the sun. We may, therefore, consider the Ξ of Ξανθός as equal to Z or Σ, and so write this word Zανθός, in the *Zan* of which we have a name of the sun, or Zεύς, that is, Jupiter. In Ξάν we have even, as Donnegan observes, the Æolian and Attic form of σύν, and as this word means *with*, and as its primary signification is *one* or *union*, as I shall have occasion to show presently; it is, therefore, in both form and meaning, precisely equal to our word *sun*.

How now are we to find in the Latin *flavus* (*yellow*) a name of the sun? We are to observe that its radical part *fla* must have first been *fal*, and *flavus* have been *falvus*, now written *fulvus;* and the latter word serves to prove that *flavus* is equal to *falvus*, since its present form (*fulvus*) means also *yellow*. Hence in Ennius *fulvum aes* means *gold*, but literally *yellow* copper. The *fla* of *flavus* being thus the same as *fal*, we know, from the constant interchange of *f* and *h*, that *fal* is the same as *hal*, in which we have the radical part of *halios*, this being the Doric of *Hēlios*, the *sun*. We have also just seen, in a passage quoted from Parkhurst, that *Hal* was the name of *God* "in the Punic or Carthaginian tongue," but it must have first named the sun. This etymology becomes more evident, when we observe that another form of both *flavus* and *fulvus* is *helvus*, which means a *pale red ;* so that it is, like its other forms, traceable to the name of the sun, its radical part *hel* and that of *hēlios* being exactly alike.

By these investigations we are led to discover the original signification of the English word *fallow*, both when it signifies ploughed ground and a certain kind of deer; the two ideas having been each named from a colour somewhat between red and yellow. It seems that all colours with a shade of light in them are but different forms and acceptations of one another, and that they are, for this reason, to be traced to the same source —the name of the sun. Thus, in Italian, *giallo* is explained both *yellow* and *pale*, which are very different colours. And though the usual word for *pale* in this language is *pallido*, it is, however, also explained by *sbiadato ;* but *sbiadato* is, I find, rendered into French by *bleu clair;* that is, a *light blue*.

I was forgetting to observe, that another variation of

flavus, fulvus and *helvus* is *gilvus*, which means a *carnation*, or *flesh-colour*, or still that of a *brick half-burned;* which is, I believe, about the same colour as is signified in English by the word *fallow.* We have also in the *gil* of *gilvus* a word for *gold*, since it is the radical part of the verb to *gild*, which means to overlay with gold. Nor should I fail to observe, that in Saxon *geldan* means to *gild;* yet, in its radical part, we see the word *geld*, noticed above, and meaning to *cut.*

M. Littré gives, under *jaune*, several forms of this word, such as *gene, jane, gane, galbinus*, &c., but nothing indicating that the name of such an idea is to be traced to that of the sun. Gébelin, though he is very seldom right in his conjectures, has, in the present instance, been more fortunate: " Jaune couleur semblable à celle de l'or, du soleil; Ital., GHIALLO; All. GHEL (*sic*), de l'Orien. HEL, *soleil*[9]." But could Gébelin have ever supposed that *flavus* and *hel* are radically the same word? We may safely assume that he could not.

The reader must be now sufficiently prepared to account for the origin of the myth, which both Grimm and M. Max Müller have failed to explain. The latter gentleman, it will be remembered, has expressed himself fully satisfied that he discovered why the sun was believed to have had a golden hand, and he seems to think his explanation very natural and very easy; but referring to what follows, he says, " But if we dig somewhat deeper, the similarity is less palpable, though it may be traced by careful research. If the German god *Tyr*, whom Grimm identifies with the Sanskrit Sun-god[1], is spoken of as *one-handed*, it is because the name of the

[9] Dictionnaire de la Langue Française.
[1] Deutsche Mythologie, xlvii. p. 187.

golden-handed sun had led to the conception of the sun
with one artificial hand; and afterwards, by a strict logical
conclusion, to a sun with but one hand. Each nation
invented its own story, how *Savitar*, or *Tyr*, came to lose
their hands; and while the priests of India imagined
that *Savitar* hurt his hand at a sacrifice, the sportsmen
of the north told how *Tyr* placed his hand, as a pledge,
into the mouth of the wolf, and thus losing it, with an
Indian legend of *Surya*, or *Savitar*, the *sun*, laying hold
of a sacrificial animal and losing his hand by its bite.
This explanation is possible, but it wants confirmation,
particularly as the one-handed German god has been
accounted for in some other way[2]."

The intelligent reader must perceive that M. Max
Müller mistakes, when he so confidently asserts that it
was the myth of the golden-handed sun suggested what
is told of the German god *Tyr*, who, it appears, was also
said to have only one hand. But as *Tyr* lost his hand
from its having been bitten off by a wolf, we are led to
suppose that had the Indian god never been heard of, the
myth of the German god would have been just as it has
been found. But why so? Because all languages, from
their having emanated from the same source, lead to the
same results, this arising from the human mind being
also the same over the whole world. It must be admitted
that *Tyr*, a name of the sun, is but a different form of
sur, which has the same meaning; this being as evident
as that *glotta* and *glossa* are in Greek the same word, and
that so are the German *besser*, and its English form *better*.
And *sur* is the radical part of *Surya*, which is allowed to
be the same as *Savitar*, the *sun*, and *Savitar*, as I have discovered and shown, is the same as *Avatar*. But where is

[2] Lect., vol. ii. p. 379.

the wolf? The wolf is not difficult to find, as I am now going to show.

The reader will please to recollect I had occasion to show farther back, that *sav*, the radical part of *savitar* (the *sun*), could not differ from *Zeb*, which, according to Parkhurst, means both *gold, splendour*, or *brightness*, and that every such idea was to be traced to that great object which is the source of light and splendour. I had also, then, occasion to show that *zeb* cannot differ from *zab*, and that if *savitar* was written *zavitar*, every one would take these two words to be one and the same. Now the Hebrew of wolf is, according to Parkhurst, *zab*, which cannot differ from *zav*, any more than the *hab* of *habere* can differ from its English equivalent *have*. If a speaker were, therefore, to pronounce *zabitar* at only a very short distance from some twenty persons, ten of them at least, if not more, would think they had heard *savitar*, so much do these two words resemble each other in both sound and form.

We now see why the god Tyr and the wolf have, in the same story, been brought together; it must have arisen from the name of the sun and that of the wolf having been designated by the same word. But why do I consider *Tyr*, some one may ask, as if it were written *Tur*? It is because *y* is the same as *u*, as almost every one knows. There is, therefore, no difference between the words. And that *Tur* is the same as *sur*, a plainer proof than the one I have already shown now occurs to me, and which I give on the authority of Higgins, who says, "The word for the Sun is in Hebrew Sur, in Chaldee *Tur*[3]." We have, therefore, made it self-evident that *Tyr* is *Tur*, and that *Tur* is *sur*.

[3] Anacalypsis, vol. i. p. 607,

But why should the wolf have a name not different from that of the sun? The cause of it is this: The wolf has been named from its swiftness of foot, which implies motion, and this idea has been called after life, and life has been called after the sun, the once revered author of existence. Hence Parkhurst says: " זאב *zab* denotes not only *a wolf*, but also *impetuosity*, to *hasten*, move with *swiftness*, festinavit in incessu." This authority shows also how the different names of the wolf do each imply rapidity of motion, in support of which he quotes several ancient authors [4].

We now see why the wolf was sacred to Apollo, or the sun; it arose from this animal's name and that of the sun having been expressed by the same word. But, as I have already shown, every two such words might be very different in form though *never so in meaning*; it follows that an animal called after its lively motion might not be made sacred to the sun. But why should not every two words found to be alike in meaning, be also alike in form? I have already told why; it is because the roots of a language are all equal to one another; and as they do, for this reason, interchange, and as they are not alike in form, they appear as so many different words, though like the letters of an alphabet, which also differ in form, they are all as one and the same word.

Let us now return to the form *Tur*, which is precisely equal to the sun-god Tyr, and ask how it happens, since *Tur* cannot differ from the *taur* of ταῦρος, or of *taurus* (a *bull*), that it was not this animal deprived Tyr of his hand? There are two answers to this question. The first is, that the bull does not, like the wolf, attack with his

---

[4] See his Lexicon, p. 137.

mouth but with his horns; and the second is this, that in Old German the word for bull had probably, as it has still, a root very different in form, though not in meaning, from that of *Tyr.* The root of this word is *yr*, that is, *ur*, and that of the German *bulle*, and its English equivalent bull, is *ul*. And as this root cannot differ from either *El* or *Al*, of which each is a well-known name of the sun, the bull became, thanks to his name, sacred to the sun. But why should the bull obtain a name not different from that of the sun? Because he is among his own what the sun is in heaven; that is to say, he is the *monos*, the *high* one, the chief, the *monarch* of the tribe of animals to which he belongs. Hence, the bull has, all over the world, been often worshipped as a god.

But why was the wolf made to *bite* off Tyr's hand, that is, the hand of the sun? We have already fully accounted for the sun having had his hand *cut* off; and what difference can there be between to cut off and to bite off? We know that the idea to *cut* or *cut off* must be traced to the hand, as I have clearly proved; so that if we find to *bite* or *bite off* expressed by the same word, it will necessarily follow that the act of biting should be also traced directly or indirectly to the hand. Now, the Greek verb δάκνω means to *bite;* but its radical part *dak* cannot differ from the δέκ of *deka*, which means *ten,* another word for the hand, as is shown by the *ten* of *tenere* in Latin, and *tenir* in French, of which each means to *hold,* and consequently to have in hand.

A plainer instance still, that the idea *bite* means *cut,* and must, for this reason, have been called after the hand, is afforded by these two Greek words δέκηρ and δέκερ; of which the first (*deker*) means a *beggar,* that is, one who holds out his hands; whilst the second (*deker*) means a *biter;* that is, one who *cuts.* But if to bite has been called after the teeth, what shall I say? If so, the teeth must have been called cutters, so that to *bite* will still mean to *cut.* And that the same word might mean both *ten* and *tooth* is shown by comparing *ten* and the *den* of *dens* or *dent.* But a still plainer instance of this is the Saxon *teotha* and *toth;* for the radical part of *teotha* is *teoth,* and which, as the *e* of this word may be dropped, cannot differ from *toth;* and *teotha* means *tythe,* now, but incorrectly, written *tithe;* and by this word, the idea *ten* is signified. As to *toth,* it is the Saxon of *tooth.* Hence, with at least some people, a tooth meant a *cutter,* and did not, for this reason, differ from a word for the hand, to which source the idea to *cut* must be traced. But, as shown farther back, to cut was also called after the mouth.

From thus knowing all we do of the hand, we can account for many apparent anomalies which have until now appeared wholly inexplicable. Why, for instance, does ברא *bra* mean in Hebrew not only to *create,* but also to *cut*[5]? Every reader of these pages can now tell why, though without the knowledge thus obtained it were not possible. But a child acquainted with these principles can, after a moment's reflection, declare with certainty that it must be ascribed to the circumstance of the two ideas *creating* and *cutting* being traceable to the hand as their original source.

But the present Hebrew word for the hand, which is יד *id,* bears no resemblance, I shall be told, to ברא *bra;* but we should observe that *id* is a single root, and that it cannot differ in meaning from any other root, except conventionally. Now, ברא *bra,* to

[5] See Sanders' Heb. Dict., p. 80.

create, must have first been באר *bar*, that is, before the
a fell behind the *r;* and then it meant the *son*, and
it is, when under this form, also the radical part of
debar, which in the same language means the *Word*.
And the Son was, we are told, the Word, and it was,
we are also assured, by His Son or the Word that the
Lord *created* all things. Another excellent type. But
as the *b* in *bar* represents the aspirate *h*, an earlier form
of this word must have been *ar*, and which cannot differ
from either *ad* or *id*, the latter being the Hebrew of
hand, and the former, as shown above, being a name of
the *sun*, the supposed creator or maker, and to which
source the hand must be traced for its original. But as
the Hebrew word ארה *are* means to *gather, pluck*, or *crop*[6],
an idea called after the hand, and as *ar* is the root of
this word, it must have once been used for יד *id*. But
as in English *hard by* is for *hand by*, that is, *at hand*,
and as *ar* is the root of *hard*, we see that even in our
own language *ar* must have been once used for *hand*.
We have still the same root in χείρ and μάρη, the *eir* of
the one being equal to the *ar* of the other; so that in
Greek also, as well as in Hebrew and English, *eir* or *ar*
must have once meant *hand*. A root very different in
form from both *id* and *ar* is *os*, which must have been
also a word in Hebrew for the hand, since the verb עשה
ose means to *make*, and as our Maker is our Creator, this
verb may be regarded as a synonym of ברא *bra*, to *create*,
which must have been called after the hand. A further
proof that this Hebrew verb must have been named from
the hand is עשר *osr*, since this word means *ten*,
an idea, as we have seen, called after the hand.
Hence it is that this word means also *many;*

6 See Parkhurst, Lex., p. 32.

and why so? Because this idea also has been called after the hand, as we had occasion to show farther back.

I may now return to the sun-god Tyr, out of whose name the latter etymologies have grown. All that is said of him in the passage quoted from M. Max Müller has been sufficiently accounted for with the exception of his name, signifying to *bite off*, of which something remains to be said. *Tyr* is but a different form of *tur*, and *tur* but a different form of *sur*, one of the names of the *sun*. And as *ur* is the root of *sur*, and as its *s* is for the aspirate *h*, and as this sign is frequently represented by *ch*, we see that *sur* cannot differ from *cheir*, Greek of *hand*, after which the idea to *cut off* has been called, as we see by comparing χείρ and κείρω, as already shown. And the idea to *bite* is the same as to *cut*, both ideas being traceable to the hand. Hence, if wolves were accustomed to use knives instead of their teeth, we should hear of the wolf having cut off Tyr's hand; for, that his name under its form *sur* might mean to *cut off* as well as to *bite off*, another very clear proof now occurs to me: *sur* must, from the identity of *u* and *v* have been often written *svr*, which is not only equal to *saver* and *saviour*, as we have shown, but to *sever* also; and this verb means to *cut*.

We may here end our notice of *savitar, surya*, and *tyr*, all allowed to have been names of the *sun*. Now, what have I discovered during this inquiry? That *savitar* means *saviour* and *avatar;* that this name has also, when analyzed, the several meanings of *hand, gold*, and *cut*, which led to the belief that *Savitar* was *golden-handed;* that his hand was cut off, and that it was replaced by one of *gold*. I have also accounted for the origin of the

E C

belief that Tyr's hand was bitten off by a wolf, and that this myth arose from the same word signifying *sun, wolf,* and *bite* or *cut.*

And because knowing nothing of Sanskrit, to which the myths above noticed chiefly belong, I have been obliged, during this inquiry, to apply the principles of my discovery to other languages, being well aware that as all words have sprung from the same single source, they must, when rightly and closely examined, be found to have, with very few exceptions, similar meanings. And if words have not led, with all people, to their having the same myths, this should be ascribed to all men not being equally credulous or superstitious. A single wise man may, just as well as a clever impostor or wild fanatic, have often so far influenced the minds of a whole country as to have induced its inhabitants to think differently from those of several other countries. But the same myths have been discovered in different parts of the world, though between the natives of such parts no connexion has ever existed. And to what should this be attributed? Not to accident, certainly, but to the fact that as all languages are radically the same, they have, on many occasions, led to similar results.

CHAPTER XLIX.

A FEW IMPORTANT ETYMOLOGIES AND TYPES.

LET me now turn to some account what I have just shown while proving the identity of the three names of the sun—*tyr, tur,* and *sur.* The root of these names is *ur,* and it can no more differ from *ar* than *further* can from *farther;* and which is confirmed by the *ur* of *urere,* to *burn,* being the *ar* of *ardere,* which has the same meaning.

When we now observe that the aspirate *h,* which must have often preceded both *ur* and *ar,* was changed for its common substitute *b,* these two words, *bur* and *bar,* must have been obtained. In *bur* we see the radical part of *burn,* and in *bar* the radical part of *barn;* and these two words, though they express very different ideas, can be each traced to a name of the *sun.* Thus *bur* cannot, from the identity of *b* and *f,* differ from *fur,* nor *fur* from the German *feuer,* nor *feuer* from its English equivalent *fire,* and every one can conceive this element to have been called after the sun, which was anciently worshipped as the god of fire. How different from *fire* is the idea expressed by the word *barn!* This idea can, however, be as easily traced to the sun as fire. A barn was named after what it is made to hold, namely, corn; and from corn being a principal support of life, it took its name

E c 2

from life, and life from the once supposed author of life,
the sun ; so that *barn* and *sun*, though neither idea was
called after the other, are as one and the same word. As
bar (whence the Latin *far*) is the Hebrew of *corn*, it
confirms the etymology of *barn*, which has been named
after corn.   I have already shown that *bar* is the Hebrew
of *son*, and that it cannot differ from *bra*, which in the
same language means to *create*, nor from the radical part
of de*bar*, which is the Hebrew of the Word ; and I also
then called the reader's attention to what the Christian
is taught to believe, namely, that it was by His Son or
the Word the Creator made the world; and all this, I
thought, should be regarded as an excellent type, and to
which I have now something more to add.

As *B* and *M* interchange, and of which I have already
quoted several instances, there can be no more difference
between *Bar* and *Mar* than there is between the Hebrew
words *Bria* and *Mria*, which, as shown above, have the
same meaning—that of *fat*.   Now *Mar* is the radical part
of *Maria*, or *Mary*, who was the mother of *Bar*, that is, of
the *son*.   But as she was a virgin, how, I may be asked,
could they who first made words have called a *mother*
a *virgin?*   The answer should be, that in the beginning
there was no difference in meaning between *virgin* and
girl; and as every such offspring was called after her
supposed *maker*, the consequence was, that the maker and
the object *made* were signified alike.   At present the
difference in form between the words *begetter* and *begotten*
is very slight, but at first it must have been a great deal
less so ; so that the child was named as the parent, that
is, the one *made* as the *maker*.   Hence in the *mad* of
madre, and which cannot differ from the *mat* of *mater*, or
the *moth* of *mother*, we have the past participle of *make*.

How happily all this is confirmed by *made* and *maid*, the slight difference in form between these words being only conventional, and a maid is a virgin ; but its first meaning must have been a *made*, that is, one *made*, having been then named after *maker*, that is, after *mother*. This knowledge leads to the discovery of the primary signification of the German words *magd* and *mädchen*, which, it is easy to perceive, are but other forms of *maid*—their poetical representative—and not different from the *macht* of g*emacht* (*made*), participle of *machen*. What will the German school think of this etymology, coming, as it does, from one who knows nothing of their language ? They will admit, for the Germans in general reason well, that the discovery which has led to this etymology, as well as to so many others hitherto unknown, cannot but be true ; and that it must, in spite of all opposition, be one day received and made use of, in exposing to the general view the many long-concealed myths and mysteries of language.

The reader will please to recollect I was showing, when interrupted by the latter digression, the identity of the names signifying mother, Mary, virgin, and son, but I forgot at the time to observe that *Bar* (the *son*) is also written *Ben*, occasioned by the interchange of *r* and *n* ; but this is no proof that the *Mar* of *Maria* is not still the same word, since this name was often written *mania*, the cause still being the interchange of *r* and *n*[7].

But the idea *virgin* does not appear to have been expressed by all people in the same way, as I am now going to show, by the etymology of *virgo* in Latin, and παρθένος in Greek, the origin of both these words appearing to be now unknown. The *vir* of *virgo* is the Latin

[7] See Anacalypsis, vol. i. p. 308, 309.

of *man*, but its *go* has here no visible meaning; I am, therefore, obliged to have recourse to the principles by which I am generally guided. By giving to the *o* of *go* its nasal sound, this ending becomes *gon*, which is also without meaning. Let us, therefore, apply another of our rules: *o* has always *i* understood, which, when supplied, makes *gon* become *goin;* that is, when *oi* takes its form *u* (compare *croix* and *crux*), *gun;* and this is the radical part of the Greek *gunē*, a *female*, a *woman*. We have thus obtained two significant words, one meaning *man*, and one meaning *woman*. But is not this a strange way of signifying *virgin?* It would seem so; but when we turn to account our tymology of *homo*, we shall find it very natural. We have shown *homo* to mean *one*, and nothing more. Now *vir*, of which the primary signification has, like that of *homo*, been also unknown, means also *one*, and nothing more. Let us only observe, that the *v* of *vir* is here for the aspirate, which is never to be counted, so that *ir* is the real word for *man*, and this *ir* takes a great many other different forms, such as *ar, er, or, air, our, eur*, &c., and these are roots, and—like other roots—they have each, when primarily considered, the meaning of *one;* for their other meanings, however numerous they may be, are only conventionally different from one another. According to this explanation, *virgo* (*virgunē*) must be for these two words, *one* and *female*, that is, the *female one*. But this meaning, I shall be told, would apply to a married woman as well as to a virgin. This is very true, and *virgo* has been so used. Thus Virgil, referring to Pasiphaé, who was then the mother of several children, says :—

At *Virgo* infelix tu nunc in montibus erras.

· Now when *virgo* was first made to signify a *married woman*, the primary signification of *vir*, that of *one*, could not have been lost. That the *go* of *virgo* is, as I have shown, equal to the *gun* of *gunĕ* is made evident by the genitive of *virgo* being *virginis*, of which the part *gin* cannot differ from the *gun* of *gunĕ*, for its *i* having *o* understood, *gin* is for *goin*, and there must have been a time when *virgo* was *virgoin*, and as *virgoin* is equal to *virgun*, its genitive must have therefore been *virgoinis*, and also *virgunis*, whence *virginis*. But when *virgo* was *virgoin*, many persons must have left out the nasal sound, and so have reduced *virgoin* to *virgoi*, which, by the dropping of the *i*, became *virgo*.

What is now the primary meaning of *gunĕ*? It is seen when we drop its *g*, which is here but a representative of the aspirate; for the *unĕ* which remains is for *una*, feminine of *unus*; so that *gunĕ* has, like *homo* and *vir*, the meaning of *one*, the different acceptations of all such words being only conventional.

I have now a very convincing proof of the truth of my etymology of *virgo*. The Saxon word *mæden* has not only the meaning of *virgin* or *maid*, but also that of *female*; thus Bosworth renders *mæden cild* into English by a "*female child*," and *mæden mann* is explained by the same learned authority a *virgin*, though it means literally a *female man*, which can only be accounted for by giving to *man* its real original meaning, that of *one*. It is thus made self-evident that I have now discovered what has not been hitherto known, the real meaning of these three important words, *homo*, *vir*, and *virgo*. And to what may I ascribe such a discovery? To the knowledge of man's first word, and the principles thence derived. Without this knowledge neither could I nor could any one else tell why such a word as *virgo* means both a *virgin* and a *mother*, and still less could they tell why a word meaning *man* (*vir*) should be its radical part.

Let us now notice the Greek of *virgin, parthenos* (παρ-θένος), of which the etymology is also unknown. As α is equal to *oi*, the *par* of *parthenos* does not differ from *pōir* (πώιρ), which is an old word in Greek, meaning *boy* or *youth*, and is the supposed original of the Latin *puer*. The etymology of *virgo* should lead to the suspicion that *thenos* (this other part of *parthenos*) must have the meaning of *female*, and that the entire word has literally the meaning of "*female young one;*" in other words, a *young female*. But there is no such word in Greek as *thenos*, and it is therefore necessary to make this word take some other form of equal value. To obtain such a form we need only observe that *n* and *l* do often interchange; thus πνεύμων is written also πλεύμων, and βέλτιον is written βέντιον; by which it is made evident that *thenos* cannot differ from *thelos*, nor *thelos* from *thelus* (θῆλυς), which means *female*. *Parthenos*, a *virgin*, has therefore that meaning which the etymology of *virgo* has led us to suppose it should have.

Nor can the *par* of this word differ from the Hebrew *bar*, a *son;* and as *bar* is the radical part of the Hebrew *debar*, a word, so is *par* the radical part of *parole* in French. But I shall, no doubt, be reminded that as the son was called after the father, *par* should, if these deductions can be relied on, have also the meaning of *father;* and it has this meaning, since it is the radical part of *parens* and *parent*. Another proof that the *par* of *parthenos* is the same as the Greek *pōir* (πώιρ) can be obtained by our observing that in the *par* of *parere* (to *beget*) we have this *par;* and that this word does not, when used as a verb, mean the *begetter*, but the *begotten*, is shown by the Hebrew word יֶלֶד *ild*, which, when a noun, is thus explained by Parkhurst, "a son, a child, a young man, a lad," but when a verb, the same authority explains it thus : "To procreate or breed young, to beget or bear [8]."

As this word *ild* differs, in form, considerably from *bar*, which has the same meaning, we should observe that its root is *il*, which is equal to both *oil* and *al*, and as all the roots of a language are as one and the same word, there can be no difference, except conventionally, between *al* and *ar*, and *ar* is the root of *bar*, of which the *b* does but represent the aspirate *h*. By taking the same liberty with *al* it will become *bal*, and as *al* is, in Hebrew, one of the names of the *sun*, even so is *bal*. This serves to show that *ild* and *bar* make radically the same word. In *ild* it is also easy to perceive our word *child*; the difference in the appearance of the two words is to be ascribed to the aspirate *h* having been attached to the *i* of *ild*, and then, from this aspirate having been represented, as it frequently is, by *ch*. This etymology is confirmed by the Saxon of *child* being *cild*, which cannot differ from *child* any more than *cat* can differ from its French equivalent *chat*, which shows that *ch* can be reduced to *c*; and that both *c* and *ch* have come from the aspirate *h* is equally evident. We have, therefore, in the Hebrew *ild*, and the Saxon *cild*, and *child* in English, but one and the same word.

In the Hebrew *ild* it is easy to perceive something else not undeserving of notice. It is, as shown above, not different from the form *ald*, its *i* being for *oi* and *oi* for *a*; and when the *a* of *ald* falls behind the consonant by

[8] Lex., p. 233.

which it is followed, as vowels frequently do, *ald* will become *lad*, which is, as we have seen, one of the meanings given by Parkhurst to *ild*. However, the words *child* and *lad* may be, therefore, made to differ from each other in meaning, that difference can be only conventional; and the identity of these two words serves to confirm still more our etymology of *parthenos*. Thus, according to Bosworth, *mœden cild* means "a female child." But since *child* and *lad* must have been once the same word, it follows that *mœden cild* might as well be explained *a female lad*, which is, according to our etymology, the meaning of *parthenos*.

There are still two other words in Greek for *virgin* and *boy*, namely, κόρη and κόρος, of which the different endings show the different genders. And the radical part of each of these words, that is, *kor*, is but a different form of χείρ, the *hand*, which, from its signifying the idea *maker*, proves still further that both virgin and boy were, in the beginning, named after their parents (father and mother), since each of these words means also *maker*.

It is now easy to account for the difference between *cheir* (χειρ) and such a form as *pōir* (πώιρ), for as *ch* does but represent the aspirate, it may be dropped and be replaced by any other representative of this sign; and as *b* and *p* are very common substitutes for the aspirate *h*, it follows that *cheir* may be replaced by *beir* or *peir*, neither of which can differ from *boir* or *poir*, and both of these, by the coalescing of *o* and *i*, become *bar* and *par*. And as we have often shown *b* to be replaced by *m*, we see that *bar* is equal to *mar*, which is therefore but another form of *cheir*, and it may for this reason mean *hand*. Nor does this etymology need proof, since *marē* (μάρη) is, as well as *cheir* (χείρ), a word for the *hand*. And, as

Maria does not differ, as shown above, from *mania*, it follows that the *mar* here noticed as another form of *cheir* cannot differ from the *man* of *manus*, Latin of *hand*. Hence, though there is not a letter in common between *cheir* and the *man* of *manus*, they make, however, but one and the same word.

From thus knowing that *bar* is equal to a word for the hand, such as *cheir*, and the *man* of *manus*, we discover in English the primary signification—hitherto unknown—of this word *bar*, whether we use it as a noun or as a verb. When a noun, it means, say all dictionaries, a *hind*erance; and when a verb, they say it means to *hind*er. But in the *hind* of *hind*erance, as well as in the *hind* of *hind*er, we have the word *hand* itself; for the *i* of *hind* having *o* understood, and as *o* and *i* make, as I have often shown, the letter *a*, it follows that *hind* is the same as *hand*. *Hind*erance should be therefore written *hand*erance, and *hind*er should be *hand*er. But might not *hind*er, I may be asked, be written also *hend*er? Most certainly it might; and it is so written, for as *h* is constantly replaced by *f*, *fend*er is the same as *hend*er; and a *fend*er is, says Webster, "a utensil employed to *hind*er coals of fire from falling forward to the floor."

And as *par* is the same as *bar* (witness *pōir*, Greek of the Hebrew *bar*, a *son*), we can, therefore, account for its being the radical part of *parer* in French, and *parar* in Spanish; for these verbs mean to *defend*, to *parry*, and they are therefore, like *bar*, to be traced to the hand. But *parer*, in French, I shall be told, means also to *beautify*; and so it ought, since to beautify is to make *hand*some, which is an additional proof that *par* is still a word for the *hand*. In short, every word signifying to *form*, or to *make*, must, in no matter what language, have first been a word for the hand.   Hence the Hebrew *bra*, to *create*, and which must have once been *bar*, and have then meant not only *create*, but also both *son* and *word*, as already shown, cannot differ from the Greek *cheir* (*hand*), and, radically considered, *creator* is still the same word, and so is *creature*, that is, the *maker*, and that which he has made ; in other words, the *father* and the *son*.   And this, too, is a genuine type, and it was made known in language to the heathen, previously to its having been divinely revealed by St. John : " Holy Father, keep through Thine own name those whom Thou hast given Me, that they may be *one* as *we* are *one*," chap. xvii. ver. 11.   " I and My Father are *one*," chap. x. ver. 30.   " And the glory which Thou gavest Me I have given them ; that they may be *one*, even as *we* are *one*."

CHAPTER L.

LORD.

To the well-known English lord, M. Max Müller refers thus : " Lord would be nothing but an empty title in English, unless we could discover its original form and meaning in the Anglo-Saxon *hláf-ord*, meaning the *source of bread*, from *hálf*, a *loaf*, and *ord*, *place*[9]."

Now how would any one of my readers, having the least confidence in my principles, analyze the word *lord*,

[9] Lectures, vol. i. p. 125.

if he had never seen this Saxon derivation of it? He would analyze it just as I have analyzed the word *look ;* which, he may recollect, is for *il-ook;* that is, the *eye, oog* (which is equal to *ook,* being the word for *eye* in Dutch); and he would therefore say that *lord* must have once been *il-ord,* and that from the *o* of *ord* having *i* understood, and from *o* and *i* making *a, ord* is the same as *ard,* and consequently, from the identity of *r* and *l,* as *ald* or *alt,* root of *altus, high ;* so that the literal meaning of *lord* would, according to this analysis, be the *high,* that is, the *high one.* Now, on opening my Gaelic dictionary, and looking out for *ard* (which is written also *airde*) in this language, I find the following English words as explanations of it : " High, lofty, mighty, great, noble, eminent, excellent;" and when used as a noun, it is explained, " A height, an eminence, a hill, a high land, an upland, heaven." Now *ord,* which is but a different form of *ard,* is thus explained in Saxon by Bosworth : " A beginning, origin, author; a point, an edge, sword, the front of an army, battle array." And in derivatives, adds the same authority, it denotes " first, original," &c. We thus see that the primary sense is still the same, whether we write this word *ard* or *ord;* so that we may define lord—that is, *il ord*—the *high one,* the *great one,* the *chief one,* the *mighty one,* or even the *heavenly one.* And these are meanings that correspond far better with our idea of lord than " the *source of bread,*" which is given by M. Max Müller, and does not differ from the meaning he tells us he has received from the "Rev. Dr. Bosworth, Professor of Anglo-Saxon at Oxford," and which is as follows: " loaf or bread origin, cause or author of bread, or support." These explanations of *lord* are also supported by Grimm, and of course by all other philologists.

But how, I shall be asked, am I to account for the *hláf* of *hláford*, which is so evidently the word *loaf*? I have two explanations to give of this word. I have no doubt that *hláf* means *loaf*, but not in *hláford*. It should be observed that in Saxon the sign *l* is often aspirated, as every one must admit on looking over those words in Bosworth that begin with *hl*; witness *hlid* and *hlist*, which are in English *lid* and *list*, the aspirate having been dropped. But this aspirate may follow the *l* as well as precede it, as we see by such words as *half, calf, self,* &c., the aspirate being now, as it often is, represented by *f*. When we now assume that *hláf* is not in *hláford* for *loaf*, this word must be considered as equal to *hlf*, which will be giving to the *l* two aspirates, one before and one behind; and granting this, it follows that lord must have been once written *hlford*, and that then, from the tendency there is to insert a vowel between two consonants, *hlford* became *hláford*. But such persons—and they were many—as did not aspirate the *l* in *hlford*, must have both written and pronounced this word as if it were only *lord*.

Let us now show the primary signification of *loaf*, and so confirm the above etymology. In *loaf* and *life* we have the same word, and the former must have been named after the latter, because from its having in Saxon the meaning of *bread*, it serves to support life. Hence *living* and *livelihood* have each the meaning of *food;* and *live*, which is the root of both these words, cannot, any more than *life*, differ from *loaf*. In Saxon the word for *life* is *lif*, and *lif* is the root of *lifen*, which Bosworth explains *livelihood*, and bids you see *leofen*, to which he assigns the meaning of food, and its root *leof*, is, as well as *hláf*, our word *loaf*. This custom of calling certain kinds of food after life obtains also in French, witness only *la vie* (*food*) and *les vivres* and *la viande.*

Now it being made thus evident that in *life* and *loaf* we have the same word, and that this may be said even of *lif* and *hláf* in Saxon, what proof have we that *hláford* means the *author, source,* or *origin* of bread, any more than the *author, source,* or *origin* of life? Indeed, the latter meaning is far more probable than the former. But I accept neither. Lord is, I am sure, a very ancient word, and that it did not become *hláford,* but from the great tendency once prevailing with some of the Saxons to aspirate the *l.* And the circumstance of this sign not being aspirated in *lif, lifen,* or *leofen,* may serve to show that its aspiration did not prevail with all.

And that the aspirate may be found after the *l* as well as before it, the etymology of the Saxon and English word *self* (hitherto unknown) will serve to show. I am well aware that *self* is nearly the same word in several languages; but as we do not learn from any of these languages after what it was man first expressed such an idea, we may well say that its etymology or primary sense has been hitherto unknown. As the *f* in *self* does but represent the aspirate *h,* or some sign that replaces this aspirate, such as *b, p,* or *v,* it must be dropped as not belonging either to the root or radical part of this word. Now, *sel* (the remaining part of *self*) may be also reduced to *el;* that is, by assuming that its *s* has replaced the aspirate *h,* and that *sel* must have been *hel* before it became, by the change of *h* for *s, sel.* But what is the meaning of *el?* As it appears also under the form of *al,* and as both these words do each mean *the,* and as they have been also well-known names of the sun, and as the primary sense of the emphatic article *the* is *one,* and as this is also one of the first meanings of the name of the sun, it follows that it may be assumed that *one* is also the meaning of *self*. But before we try how far this meaning will apply, let us see if there be an exact agreement between the reduced forms of *self* just noticed. As to *sel*, it cannot, from the common interchange of *e* and *o*, differ from *sol*, nor *sol* from *solus*, which from its meaning *alone*. must have for the meaning of its root, *one*. In *sel* we have also the *hel* of *hēlios*, Greek of *sol*. As to *al* and *el*, in which we have earlier forms of *hēlios* and *sol*, they have been already explained.

Let us now see if any word of which the radical sense is *one*—such as *alone, only*, or *solely*—can be used instead of *self*. If we say, "That book was written by himself," our meaning is, "That book was written by him *alone*, or by him *only*, or by him *solely*." But if we say, "That book was written by *myself*," and do then put *alone* instead of *self*, we shall have, "That book was written by *my alone*," which cannot be said. But when we make *me* take the place of *my*, we shall have, "That book was written by *me alone;*" by which we see that *my* is for *me*, and that *myself* is really for *me-self*, and which is made evident by *himself*, which is not *his-self*. It is also made evident by *moi-même* in French, which cannot be written *mon-même* any more than *lui-même* can be represented by *son-même*.

We have thus discovered the real etymology of *self* (hitherto unknown), and have shown that it is radically the same as *solus*, and that it may be rendered into English by *alone, only*, or *solely*.

This etymology of *self* suggests others; but they must be left unnoticed, as they, too, might lead me on farther.

But with respect to *lord*, or its Saxon form *hláford*,

I beg to ask this plain question: How does it happen that none of the great German or Saxon philologists could perceive that in such a Saxon word as *lif* (*life*) we have but a different form of *loaf?* It arose from their not being aware that a single vowel is equal to a combination of vowels, and that when two or more words agree in sense, and do not differ otherwise than by this difference in their vowels, they should be regarded as making only one and the same word. And if those philologists had hitherto known that *o*, when not attending its *i*, is always then to be considered as understood, they would have perceived that the Saxon *lif* (*life*) is equal to *loif*, and *loif*, by the dropping of its *i* to *lŏf*, which, when its *o* is lengthened, does not differ in sound from *loaf.* The *lif* of *lifen* (*food*, or *livelihood*) is to be accounted for in the same way, and which is confirmed by the *leof* of its synonym *leofen*.

There is still an observation which I forgot to make when analyzing *lord.* I should have remarked that its radical part *ord* is not only, as we have seen, equal to the *all* of *altus* (*high*), but also to *old*, and that in this respect it agrees with the Latin *senior* (*lord*), which implies *age*, and is radically the same as *senex*, *old*. And there is still something else to be observed. As we have found the *ord* of *lord* to be equal to *ard*, it follows that the entire word cannot differ from *lard*, the grease or fat of swine; from which it would appear that this idea has been also named after height; and this is confirmed by the German word *gross*, of which the form is equal to *grease* in English, and to *graisse* and *gras* in French; yet this German word *gross*, which is still the same in form as *gross* in English, is rendered into French by *grand*, and is used, like this word, in the sense of both *great* and *tall.*

It would therefore seem that the ideas expressed by such words as *great, tall,* and *big,* were once signified alike, with some slight difference for the sake of distinction, and which might be obtained by assigning to these words different places with respect to their nouns, as we see by *grand,* in French, which, when placed before its noun, means *great,* but *tall* when placed after it. It would, therefore, seem that the fat of an animal has been regarded as the *biggest, most bulky,* or *highest* part of its flesh, and that this will account for two ideas so different from each other as *lord* and *lard* having the same name.

In the *tall* of *tallow* we have a very plain instance of the fat of an animal being significant of *height.* And the *tall* of this word is but a different form of the *alt* of *altus.* It must have first been *it-al,* and then have meant the *sun,* after which *tallness* was called. And when *it* and *al* coalesced *tal* was obtained, but when the article *it* fell behind its noun *al* both words became *alit,* which, by the dropping of the *i,* made the *alt* of *altus.*

By the knowledge thus obtained we are led to discover that, since *lard* in French is *bacon* in English, the root of the latter, that is, *bac,* is but a different form of *big,* just as *big* is but a different form of *pig.* And this is confirmed by the Greek and Latin of *pig* being *sus,* which is as a prefix significant of height in both Latin and French. When the word *cochon* is applied to a man, as it frequently is in France, it means, says De Roquefort, " un homme *très gros* et *très gras;* " and as a *big* man is in English what we do also understand by *un homme gros et gras,* we may, therefore, conclude that a *pig* was first named from its being a bulky and fat animal; and as this idea is well expressed in Latin by *pinguis,* and as every vowel may take or lose a nasal sound, it follows that the *ping* of *pinguis*, which is its radical part, does not differ from *pig*. And that *pig* might also, like *sus*, signify *height*, is shown by our remarking that it is but a different form of *pic*, which means in French a *high* mountain, and is the same as *peak* in English, and *peac* in Saxon; by which we see that the same word, under slightly different forms, may signify not only *big*, *fat*, or *bulky*, but also *high* or *tall*.

I thought, on closing the last sentence, I had done with all my observations on the word *lord*, but there is yet one more which I cannot help making. We have seen from Bosworth that, besides several other meanings traceable to the same source, it serves to signify "a *point*, an *edge*, or a *sword*." This arises from such an idea as a *point* meaning the *top* or *highest part* of whatever it refers to. Hence it is that the *pic* just noticed cannot, from the tendency there is to sound *s* before *p*, differ from the *spic* of *spiculum*, a *lance*, any more than *pike* can differ from *spike*. The knowledge thus acquired leads us to the etymology of *sword*, hitherto unknown. In Saxon, *sword* is expressed not only by *ord*, as just stated, but also as it is in English; and in German, Dutch, Danish, and Swedish, it is almost the same word. But to know this is not to know in what way *sword* came by its present form, and after what idea it was first called. But knowing, as we now do, that its radical part must be *ord*, since it was once so designated in Saxon, as we find it admitted by Bosworth, we have only to discover how its *sw* was obtained. The *o* of *ord* must, as vowels frequently do, have taken the aspirate *h*, and this sign must have been replaced by *f* or the digamma, and the digamma by *w*, which is also a very common change, and then, from the euphonic tendency there is to sound *s* before *w*, witness *wan* becoming *swan*, and *wet* becoming *sweat, ord* must have become *sword.*

As I shall have more to say farther on of ideas very similar in meaning to *sword,* this word needs not, for the present, be submitted to further inquiry.

We have thus seen how, by applying our principles, *lord* is the original of *hlaford,* and that Grimm, Dr. Bosworth, and Professor Max Müller do all three mistake, when they suppose this word to mean the *source of bread,* or the *place of bread ;* and that the cause of their mistake must be ascribed to their not having, in the first instance, considered the h as only an aspirate, and then the f as another aspirate, there being in Saxon a tendency to aspirate the $l,$ and to have the sign of the aspiration either before or after it.   And as two consonants may have a vowel inserted between them, this accounts for the a in *hlaf.* We do, therefore, conclude that the three signs, $h,$ $a,$ and f are not in any way radically related to the word *hlaford,* which, as all persons cannot have aspirated its $l,$ must have once been *lord,* or have had a form of equal value, such as *lard, laird, loord,* &c.

END OF VOL. I.

GILBERT AND RIVINGTON, PRINTERS, 52, ST. JOHN'S SQUARE, LONDON.

www.ingramcontent.com/pod-product-compliance
Lightning Source LLC
Chambersburg PA
CBHW052346110726
47901CB00005B/1373